The Sapphire Flute

Book One
The Wolfchild Saga

For Janann,

Always follow your heart!

The Sapphire Flute

Book One
The Wolfchild Saga

by

Karen E. Hoover

Valor Publishing Group, LLC

This is a work of fiction, and the views expressed herein are the sole responsibility of the author. Likewise, characters, places, and incidents are the product of the author's imagination, and any resemblance to actual persons, living or dead, or actual events or locales, is entirely coincidental.

The Sapphire Flute

Published by Valor Publishing Group, LLC
P.O. Box 2516
Orem, Utah 84059-2516

Cover art copyright © 2010 by Cash Case

Cover design copyright © 2010 by Valor Publishing Group, LLC

Valor Publishing, Valor Publishing Group, and the Valor Sword & Shield are all registered trademarks of Valor Publishing Group, LLC

ISBN: 978-1-935546-07-8

Printed in the United States of America
Year of first printing: 2010

To my biggest cheerleader and greatest fan,
the woman who told me I could do anything
if I wanted it badly enough
and was with me from the first word until the last.

I only wish she were here to cross the finish line with me.

I love you, Mom.

Earlene Gillespie
9/6/1931 - 8/6/2008

Acknowledgments

It's hard to know exactly who to thank when the first words of this story were written over seventeen years ago. For all those who helped in the early years, you know who you are, and I thank you—for the feedback, the late-night brainstorming sessions, and the encouragement when everything felt like drivel. This book would not have become what it did without those beginnings, and for that, I thank you.

There are a few people in particular who deserve some individual thanks, though, and this is the place to do it. First, Darla Isackson, for telling me that the only way I wouldn't get published was if I quit writing, and who encouraged, pushed, and pulled me forward at times to keep me moving ahead. Thank you for sharing your wisdom and for believing I could do it.

Second, my dear friend Shari Bird, who spent many a morning walking with me pounding out the details of my stories and believed in me when I forgot to believe in myself. She's got to be the best butt-kicker in this world. Thank you, Shari, for your love and encouragement, and for loving my stories almost as much as I do.

For Tristi Pinkston, editor and friend extraordinaire, who saw the potential in me and helped me on my journey to publication long before she became my official editor, and for Candace Salima, who always encouraged me, and when Valor Publishing Group opened its doors, invited me in and gave my book a home. I'd also like to add thanks to BJ Rowley and Muriel Sluyter for all their hard work on the book, and Cash Case for the AMAZING cover.

For all the friends and critique groups who've seen the rounds of this story, I thank you.

I'd be nowhere without my family, and wish to thank them for their patience, tolerance, and encouragement, despite simple dinners of fruit, toast, and cheese, and the many, many days and nights I've spent up the canyons writing, or buried in the basement. Gary, thank you for encouraging me to follow my dreams and helping make it real. Austin and Robert, thanks for being the amazing kids you are and for understanding this crazy need I have to throw words on a page.

And most especially I'd like to thank my Heavenly Father—for without His gifts and guidance, I would be nothing.

Prologue

Jarin smoothed the final rope of stone decorating the altar. The orange magic of Bendanatu flowed through him in a circle of energy that allowed him to mold the cold stone with his hands. There was no dust to blow away, no chisel marks to scar the perfection of the glossy black surface. The heat of his hand alone sculpted the pictures and polished them as smooth as onyx until they reflected the candlelight by which he worked. He sat back on his heels and inspected his creation.

The flat panels on the top and sides depicted the seven Guardians of Rasann creating the world, each holding a keystone that rooted magic to the land. C'Tan had been adamant that the altar remain untainted by color, leaving only the dark of the onyx she brought him.

If he'd had his way, the altar would burst with color, from the sapphire of Klii'kunn's flute to the deep amethyst of Hwalan's hand-held eye. Jarin sighed with a small ache of regret, but still he was pleased. The interwoven vines running along the upper edge had turned out particularly well, roping in and out in endless knots that were the best he'd ever done, but then, there was reason for that. This was not just any commission he'd taken. This was for his sister, C'Tan—or Celena Tan, as she'd been called as a child.

He rubbed his hand over the top one last time, his fingers catching slightly on the raised image of S'Kotos holding a heart-shaped gem. Why C'Tan had wanted The Destroyer on the altar's top, he didn't understand. She'd given him some kind of convoluted explanation, but it had made no sense.

Jarin shook his head and stood. He separated the fine chains hanging about his neck and placed a finger on the stone that hung at his throat. It warmed at his touch, suddenly alive and listening, prepared to transmit every word he spoke into his sister's waiting ear. No matter how often he used the stone, it always amazed him that he could speak to C'Tan as if she stood before him, whether she was in the kitchen or riding her dragons in a neighboring county. He could hardly wait to share his news. The altar was *done!* Nearly a year of work, and it was complete.

The spell activated instantly, catching C'Tan mid-sentence as she spoke.

". . . don't want any excuses. The master requires the child's soul in order to negate the prophecy."

Jarin froze in shock, holding himself completely still as he listened to the unfolding conversation, expecting any moment for C'Tan to laugh at the joke she was playing at his expense.

"Yes, I have a rather full understanding of that, Mistress," Kardon, C'Tan's servant, said, "but I am not sure you are aware that she is not the only child of the prophecy. The keystones must *each* be held by a balanced one in order for Him to be sealed. She will be drawn to the stones, so why not use her to find them? Why waste this resource when it is so close?" His voice gave Jarin the chills, as it always did. It was as cold as a midwinter freeze and just as dead. "She is only one link in the chain."

"Yes, but she is a link within our grasp here and now, and the Master wants her sealed. Besides, have you forgotten she is the link to them all? She is The Chosen One! The Binder! Distasteful as it may be, she must be soulbound to that stone." Her voice was different than Jarin remembered, full of bitter anger and razor scorn.

12

"I have no qualms binding the babe to the stone, Mistress. I only question your motives in following S'Kotos' directions."

There was a slap that made Jarin wince.

"Never question my loyalty to the Master," she said, her voice low and menacing. "Now go and collect Shandae before I decide to offer *you* on that altar."

Jarin's heart froze again at his daughter's name, the cogs finally turning into place in his brain. Shandae, his little baby girl, was the child of prophecy? *She* would bind The Destroyer? Of course he knew the legends. He'd grown up hearing them, playing the parts as a child, but he'd never really believed them—until now.

Jarin yanked the chain from his neck, sickened with panic and fear, and flung the stone at the altar. Instead of bouncing off the slick surface, it stuck to the image of The Destroyer as if it were made of tar instead of stone. Chills raced up the back of his neck, and he did the only thing he could.

He ran.

By the time he reached the main hall, he'd shifted into the form he inherited from his father. Hair sprouted across his body, his nose lengthened, his back curved, and in an instant Jarin had gone from man to wolf, his clothes merging with the snow-white fur. Only the pendant his father had given him years before still thumped against his breastbone. Its magic never had allowed him to hide it with his clothes.

Once across the drawbridge, his paws dug at the soggy earth, kicking up clods that spattered his hindquarters, littering the grass behind him as he raced toward home. If he'd been in man form, he would have been cursing, shaking his head at his blindness and stupidity, but he wasn't. Tonight he was wolf, snarling through the grass, praying he was not too late to save his child from the betrayal of C'Tan. His own sister was willing to steal the life of his child. His hackles rose at the thought.

He wasn't even three hills from the castle when he knew time had run out. The riders were being sent. Jarin's sharpened wolf senses could hear C'Tan scream at her guard. "After him! Bring him back alive, or I'll have your hearts!" The horses tore across the drawbridge, hooves tharumping, chain mail clinking as they raced away from the castle.

Fool! he thought. He should have taken the stone with him— that would have given him more time to escape. But what was done was done. Time was the one thing he needed, and he'd thrown it away with the communication stone. Obviously C'Tan had found it already. Jarin glanced over his shoulder at the loud "hyah!" echoing across the hills. They were nearing the top of the first hill now. The captain of his sister's guard whipped his horse down the other side. Jarin guessed he had a five, maybe ten-minute lead on the guard.

It wasn't enough!

He howled, putting on a burst of speed that took him up a grassy slope, past the ghostly forest of whispering aspen, through the flower-filled meadow, and up a final hill. His muscles bunched as he labored up the steep slope, breath coming hard until at last he reached the crest and paused. For only a moment he took in the glowing magelight Brina had left burning and allowed himself to feel the ache of loss.

His sister was gone, to be replaced by an enemy who only looked like her. What had happened? Jarin shook it off before he loped down the hill, a low growl coming unbidden to his throat. It wasn't the first time his sister had hurt him, but he'd never expected her betrayal.

The light of home pulled him on, guiding him as a lighthouse for a storm-tossed ship—warm, yellow, and safe. But tonight the light was a beacon for his pursuers as well as for him, and he did not want the evil ones to be guided so easily. With a single whisper of thought, the light went out, and Jarin sat panting in the darkness, his haunches chilling on the damp ground as he took time to change into human form once more. He couldn't surprise Brina with that bit of himself—not tonight. He'd never quite known how to tell her about his other form, and now he chafed at the delay.

14

His body shifted, like clay molded by an unseen hand. The hunched wolf stretched and straightened until he stood erect, with only a few pops to settle his spine. The thick hair withdrew to a single mop of black, and Jarin shrugged his clothing back into place.

He stepped through the thick wooden door, shutting it firmly behind him, then placed a hand on each side of the doorframe. The stones he had embedded in the wood months before began to hum under his touch, and in seconds he had activated the protection spell. The air shimmered around him, and the magic settled into the wood with a whoosh. That would hold C'Tan's guards for a bit, maybe long enough to save his family.

"Brina, I need you!" he called to his wife, racing to their bedroom at the back of the house. Pulling out bags from the trunk at the foot of their bed, he stuffed them with whatever clothing lay nearby.

"What are you doing home? I thought you were going to be helping your sister late tonight. I've got dinner on the stove if you're hungry," she answered, stepping from the kitchen and wiping her hands on her apron.

Jarin wasted neither words nor time. "We've got to go, Brina. Get Shandae and meet me at the stables."

"Whatever for? Jarin, you're scaring me. What's going on?"

"C'Tan . . ." he choked. He dropped his head, but forced himself to hold his composure. "C'Tan has betrayed us. We must leave."

"C'Tan? Betray us? But she's your sister!"

He stopped what he was doing long enough to meet his wife's eyes. "My sister no longer," he said, gritting his teeth. "We've got to leave."

Brina hesitated only a second longer, then left the room, returning quickly with little Shandae.

Jarin took her in his arms and glanced at the sleeping one-year-old, so peaceful in sleep and spirited when awake, so much like the both of them in the best ways. He brushed a lock of dark hair away from the child's face. He laid the babe gently on the bed and pulled the emotion inside. Not now. He couldn't deal with it now.

"Grab whatever food you can."

"All right, Jarin, but why? What's going on?" Brina ran to the kitchen and frantically stuffed a satchel, fruit hitting the floor in her frenzy. Jarin watched her through the open doorway for only a moment before he returned to his packing.

"C'Tan has turned to S'Kotos, and she wants Shandae," Jarin said over his shoulder.

He glanced across the room at her silence and watched as her eyes turned from the warmth of mid-day to an icy winter gale. She nodded sharply to her husband as if afraid to speak.

And then time ran out. The sound of horses thundered down the hill, slipping and squealing in the wet grass, the guards cursing as they tumbled.

"Leave, Brina!" Jarin said, gathering up the bags and the sleeping child.

"What do you mean, *leave?* You're coming with us!"

"I'll be right behind you," he tried to reassure her, but his heart felt the lie. "I'm going to send the horses up to the hilltop. Anything else you need, take it now," he said, tying off one of the bags and laying it at Brina's feet. He took his small family into his arms and began to pull the power to him that would save them, but he suddenly realized there was one thing he had left to do.

He slipped his pendant from beneath his shirt, the final gift his father had given him. It would no longer do Jarin any good, but it *might* save the life of his child.

Jarin whispered to the carved silver wolf as he tied the necklace around his daughter's neck. Fear made his hands shake, desperation made his eyes tear, but the chant never faltered.

"Keep her safe. Hide her from the magic eye," he begged of the amulet.

The enemy was at the door. He could feel C'Tan breaking through his spells one by one.

It was almost too late, but he would save his family, no matter the cost to himself. Shandae *must* live. He brushed away the baby's hair and placed his palm gently on the side of Brina's face. She blinked rapidly for a moment, then set her jaw. He wrapped his arms tightly around them both and let the breath of power roar to life, a cyclone of magic circling tightly around his family.

"I love you," he whispered. Then he let go.

"No!" Brina screamed, reaching for him, but it was too late. Her hand passed through his arm as her body was instantly transported to the hill overlooking their home.

His attention immediately switched to the horses corralled on the far side of the valley. *"Monster, Bluebell. Go to the woods and wait for Brina. Keep her safe."* The horses sent a questioning thought but immediately agreed, and Jarin felt them race toward the fence and soar over in a single leap.

Within seconds, his thoughts were back with his wife.

"Go home to your sister, Brina. Kalandra surely has forgiven you by now, but if you cannot do the same for her, go to Ezeker in Karsholm. At the very least, seek out the Bendanatu. What family I've got, you can find through them. Be safe, love. Now go," he whispered through the line that still connected them. He sent a final swell of love before letting go, her angry, pleading cries cut off like a knife. He only hoped he'd have the chance to make it right.

Cold spread from toe to top and he shivered, trying to shake away the winter of body and soul that settled over him. Death awaited him tonight. He could feel the icy breath of the specter watching from the darkness. Deep in his bones, a voice whispered that his time had come.

Jarin gathered more of the breath of power. He pulled it to himself until he nearly glowed with it—enough to burn himself out if not released soon. It was no different than an archer putting arrow to string, or a swordsman going into fighting stance. He was prepared to use magic to defend himself and only hoped it wouldn't be necessary. He had one chance to do this and do it right, and could only pray it would work.

The barrage on his shields reached a crescendo, and he knew he could hold them no longer. Rather than damage himself fighting a lost cause, he pulled all the power of his shields into himself, closed his eyes, and waited.

There was a moment of breathless silence, and then the door exploded inward in a shower of splinters. Jarin didn't even duck. He knew who would be on the other side when the dust settled.

C'Tan.

Jarin didn't say a word. He watched as the air cleared and his sister stepped through the doorway, her red satin robes glittering in the magelight that still bounded about the room from the broken protection spell, her pale yellow hair standing up with the static of it. She paid it no mind. Instead her eyes sought his immediately, the rage in them as visible as the magelight.

"We seem to have a problem," she said, her voice full of ice.

"Not of my causing. Why don't you come in, and we can discuss it."

"I think not." She smiled, though it never reached her eyes. "You have something that belongs to me."

"She was never yours to take, Celena." Jarin leaned against the wall, arms across his chest, trying to hide with casual arrogance the fearful power he'd pulled to himself, waiting for the right moment to be released.

"Don't call me that," she snarled. "Give me the child."

"No."

The time was close now. The suppressed power burned. Jarin hugged himself tighter to keep from shaking as C'Tan left her guard at the doorway, pushed past him, and tore through the house. She howled in frustration and rage, moving from room to room and finally circling back to him. Her hands glowed with a blue flame that engulfed them, but did not burn.

"Where are they?" she hissed from between clenched teeth.

"Gone, Celena Tan. You will *not* have my child." His eyes flashed fire. C'Tan began to laugh.

"You're a fool, Jarin. I've got S'Kotos and all his agents at my beck and call. You might be able to fool me for a time, but you can *never* escape The Destroyer. S'Kotos wants the child every bit as much as I do, though for different reasons. We'll find her. It's a shame you won't be around to see it."

"What happened to you?" His voice shook with anger and the power that burned within, but at least the fear was gone.

C'Tan stopped laughing, and Jarin saw a flash—small as it was—as some humanity returned to her eyes, haunted and pained. *That* was the girl he'd known, the child he'd loved—but the ice returned and she shrugged.

"Life happened. Enough said. I don't want to do this, Jarin. Give me the child and you can live. You can always have more children. You *must* give me *this* child."

That was too much. Even with all he'd heard from her, he could not take the callous dismissal of his only daughter any longer. Jarin let the power surface and simmer just below his skin.

"I'll *not* let you use my child for evil. You're insane."

"Don't call me that!" she screeched. Her eyes narrowed in anger, and the blue flame around her hands burst once again to life. She drew back her arm as if to throw the ball of fire, but paused. Her eyes focused on the cyclone of sparkling energy in which he'd immersed himself.

She cursed and hurled the flame at him as she raced for the doorway, but it was too late. Jarin relaxed his hold on the power, and it roared to life like a tornado, twisting outward quickly. Stones littered the yard as the walls bowed, the beams high above sagging with the sudden loss. Chaos reigned as his home began toppling about him. Jarin's ears ached with the blast, but he was not done. He reached out one hand and a great rope of flame shot toward his sister, lassoing and holding her in place as the house collapsed around them. The flames never touched Jarin—he was used to his gift. There was nothing that could hurt him here. Relief flooded through him as C'Tan tried to run for the door. She wasn't going anywhere. The lasso tightened around her as she struggled, her hair and clothing catching fire as she fought and screamed in his grip.

There was a great crack directly above. Jarin looked up to see the squared wood he'd cut and formed with his own hands, the largest piece of the house, fall directly toward him. He lunged out of the way, throwing himself to the left, but the wood ricocheted off another fallen beam and followed him. On his knees, there was nothing more Jarin could do. The wood caught him across the chest, and he had but a moment of regret before he was pinned by the tree-sized beam. It crushed the breath from his lungs. What small margin of control he had over the whirlwind was lost.

He'd burned himself out, and now C'Tan's flames were going to finish the job.

The fire burst around him, and Jarin was able to turn his head just enough to see that he was not the only one caught in the conflagration. C'Tan lay pinned beneath a pile of rubble, half in and half out of the doorway. Her hair was burned almost completely away, her skin a reddened mass of flesh. Perhaps the blast was enough after all, enough to destroy the enemy he'd once called *sister*.

Jarin choked with the heat and smoke as darkness glazed his vision.

At that moment he knew. Death had come to claim him.

Brina screamed when the house crumbled. She stepped out of the treeline and looked down the hill at the ruins of her home, then sank to the earth. She clutched Shandae as sobs racked her body. Ash and smoke carried up to her, and she choked with the smell of blackened earth and burning flesh, but still she did not leave. She watched as C'Tan's guard pulled her from the burning rubble and raced her back to the castle. She watched as even the stone burned and melted in the heat. At the top of the hill, she fell to her knees and wept as her entire life went up in smoke.

The horses snorted and stamped. Shandae awoke once or twice, but went back to sleep quickly with her mother's constant rocking. Brina was unsure if she rocked to comfort herself or the sleeping child.

Jarin was gone. The link that had always grounded her—the bond between them—had snapped the instant Jarin had been taken by death. She'd felt a flash of crushing weight, the sear of flame, an ache of relief and regret as he'd slipped from this life into the next.

As the black of night turned to the misty gray of morning, Brina picked her way down the slope to inspect the ashes of her home, unable to leave until she saw proof that Jarin was truly dead. She knew she was going against Jarin's dying wish, but she couldn't help herself. She had to know.

She got as close as she could, but the heat of the charred remains and the baking stones would not let her get close enough to know for sure.

There was no way Jarin could have survived the blaze, but she couldn't give up hope, despite the severance of their bond. She couldn't live without him. Jarin had saved her from her murderous father, had taken her from Kalandra's scorn and Tomas's disbelieving taunts. They'd never believed the horror she'd witnessed. Only Jarin had given her a way out of her past, a place to forget.

Brina screamed at the sky.

"Why?"

She fell to her knees, pleading with the heavens for an answer.

"Why?" she whispered as the tears fell unchecked.

As she knelt before the ruins of her home, staring into the embers of the fire that had destroyed her life, she remembered Jarin's final words, one line in particular standing out:

"Go to Ezeker in Karsholm . . ."

Brina couldn't go to her sister, as Jarin had suggested. She couldn't afford to take the chance that her father would find her there. And she knew nothing of the Bendanatu and had no desire to start now.

No, the safest place was with few people, a place where no one knew her so she could forget her old life and start anew. She and Shandae had to hide, from her family as well as C'Tan. She had to be dead to all of them. C'Tan knew how to find her otherwise.

And so she took a new name, one she'd avoided for most of her life, for it was full of ache and loss. It belonged to her battered and dead mother and her long-gone sister who had died at her father's hand; a name that reflected their pain and the agony of betrayal and was now etched in her very soul. What other name could there be, now that deadness pierced her heart and soul?

"Marda," she whispered.

But what of the child? What name would reflect her loss, yet keep her anonymous to C'Tan?

Brina, now Marda, stared into the glowing coals for an answer. They blinked and wavered back at her, and she suddenly knew. A bitter smile crept across her face as she stared at her baby, so much like her father, and brushed away a lock of dark hair as he'd done not so long ago.

"Ember," she called the sleeping child. "Ember Shandae. For the glowing coals our lives have become."

Marda nodded once and dashed away the tears that had plagued her the night long. She could afford them no more. She turned her back on the stone and coals. Straightening her shoulders, she left her home and heart behind.

Chapter One

Kayla cradled her flute in the crook of her arm and curtsied to the politely clapping nobles. Her stomach jumped as she waited for her final and favorite song to begin. She glanced upward, gauging the morning light. She wanted to finish her performance just as the sun crested over the outdoor theater. The applause died quickly, and still she waited for the expectant stillness to come over the room before she nodded to the orchestra behind her. She had more to accomplish with this final song than just entertainment for nobility or a welcome to the king. Oh yes, there was *much* more at stake.

The strings whispered a soft tremolo, the short strokes vibrating with sharp intensity that would carry her through the visions she needed to play. She lost herself in the sound as it began to build, the lower strings entering, the brass adding its muted blow, and Kayla closed her eyes to better see the picture within her mind, the image of home searing her eyelids in vivid detail.

And then she began to play.

Soft, so soft it seemed only a breath of sound, the flute came alive with her kiss. The instrument became her voice, expressing the poetry she felt in her soul, passing on the memories she held there.

Her audience lived her thoughts without ever realizing what she had done, never knowing the doors she had opened between them. Even she didn't know how she did it, but this once she took a chance on their ignorance and dared to try. She had to. It was the only way she could complete the path she'd set for herself ten years before.

The sight of a hawk greeting the morning sun spun out with her breath, carrying the crowd on a journey with her above the towers of Darthmoor to weave amongst the snapping piñons, past the strong walls of her home. As she played, the quiet room drew her more deeply into the music until the audience faded away. The music was a place all its own. The hawk called again through her flute, and the strength of Darthmoor answered in the brass. Back and forth, the call, the answer, until the hawk flew away and the horn and drum sang a song of pride and strength that came from the very stone of the keep itself.

The song was simple, easily played, the images familiar to all in attendance. There was neither man nor woman there who had not stood on Darthmoor's walls, witnessing the rising and setting of the sun, the majesty of the mountains that guarded them, so the pictures were no surprise to the audience, causing no suspicion as she tampered with their thoughts. Her heart raced, and she could not help the light sweat that broke out on her brow, but her hands held calm and unwavering as she pulled the assembly into the height of her dream.

Selfish.

She knew she was being selfish in this performance, too focused on impressing the right people to play it with passion, but she had grown so tired of the insults, the dismissals as if she were below the people of Darthmoor, unworthy of even their glance. Now she held more than their glance.

Much more.

She had their adulation. She could see it in their eyes, in the way they held themselves so perfectly still, bound by her power. They were lost in her music, unknowingly caught in her spell, and she

only prayed it would be enough to free her fa⸱
chains. *Not selfish*, she told herself. *This is for ⸱*
this for Mother, she whispered in her mind. Hardening ⸱⸱
poured herself into the final phrases of music. The image ⸱⸱
setting and moon rising came, and all of Darthmoor lay still in the
silence of night. Her final note faded away to nothing. It was done.
All that remained was to see the reaction.

Kayla lowered her head, still holding the flute to her lips,
reluctant to let the moment pass when she was so at one with the
music. There was not a stir—not a rustle, not a single breath as the
audience sat transfixed for several long seconds—and then the room
seemed to breathe a collective sigh before it erupted around her.
She'd done it! There was no way they could keep her family exiled
after that performance. People surged to their feet and clapped
madly, whistling and howling their praise. Even King Rojan beamed
as he stood and applauded.

Kayla took a deep breath, the tension leaving her shoulders.
She actually let a smile creep through for a moment as she curtsied
time and again.

The audience quieted as the curtains descended, the
conversational buzz already beginning, but she ignored it. There was
nothing more that could be done, and she felt confident her plan
had succeeded.

Kayla gathered her rosewood case from the back of the stage
and fell to cleaning and taking apart her instrument, smiling to
the first violinist and mouthing a thank-you for his good work.
He beamed back at her and bowed. She latched the case and
wound her way down the stairs to mingle with the crowd she had
just finished entertaining. Before stepping into the grand hall,
Kayla checked her hair to be sure her ears were covered. It
wouldn't do to remind them of her half-evahn heritage when she'd
just gained their approval.

The Duke and Duchess Domanta waited for her at the bottom
of the stairs. Kayla was disappointed their son Brant was not with
them. He'd promised he would come.

"Congratulations, Kayla. That was an *amazing* performance," the duke said, taking her hand and pressing it to his lips. "I have never heard *Darthmoor's Honor* played with quite such fervency. Not since Rajanya himself played it. Masterful."

"Why, thank you, sir." Kayla looked at him from beneath her eyelashes, bowing over his hand. "Praise for such a humble player is vastly appreciated."

The duke laughed. "Despite growing into quite an attractive young lady, you have not changed one bit from the little sprite who used to hide in my stables and steal away my son."

"Hush, sir!" Kayla mockingly reprimanded the man she loved and earnestly hoped someday to call Father. "You'll ruin the reputation I am working so hard to gain, and how *then* could I earn your favor?"

He roared a great belly laugh that rang across the room, then patted her cheek and met her fiery eyes with twinkles of his own.

"You needn't worry of *me* ruining your well-earned reputation, my dear. Right now you could talk the king into presenting you a duchy of your own."

Her heart raced. The duke was hitting a little too close to home.

He gave her shoulders a squeeze and spoke low, compassion and laughter lacing his voice. "I'm not sure how the nobles will accept a titled outsider, especially one of mixed parentage. Darthmoor will never be the same again, that's for sure, but personally? I think it would be great fun." He gave her shoulder another squeeze and released her, smiling. "It's about time the pompous wake up and let go of their prejudice toward the evahn, don't you think—even if it is only in letting a half-evahn into their elite circle."

Kayla's smile froze. The duke was much wiser than he appeared and had come right to the heart of the matter. She let it go because she knew he meant well, though she never appreciated mention of her half-human status.

A genuine smile crept across her face. This man reminded her once more of why she loved his son so very much. Brant and his father were two of a kind.

"Why don't you come by and see Brant later," the duke continued, winking. "I'm sure he'll want to congratulate you himself. He was very unhappy about having to miss your performance today, but that's the way of it when you run an estate. Sometimes things cannot wait."

Kayla's heart quickened a bit. Brant had been behind her completely since the day they had decided on a plan to restore her family honor. She laughed to remember it now. They'd only been seven and ready to take on the world, and now ten years later their dreams just *might* be ready to appear. "I'll be there, sir. You can count on it."

"Good. I'll let Brant know to expect you."

Brant's mother then spoke, and Kayla groaned inwardly. "I wasn't sure what to make of you at first, young Kayla, but you have done your family proud. Your performance was marvelous. All my boys were absolutely *enraptured* when you began *Darthmoor's Honor.*" A gangly young man with foppish hair and rouged cheeks walked up behind the duchess and took her arm at the elbow. "Oh, have you met Matios? His sonnets are simply *divine.* I'm sure the two of you have *much* in common."

The boy drew himself up proudly, and Kayla fought the urge to roll her eyes. It seemed there was a new "artistic genius" in residence at Dragonmeer each month, all of whom the duchess insisted on calling her "boys." Sometimes it was a musician, at other times an artist or poet, but so far as Kayla could tell, none of them had a single ounce of talent.

"I'm afraid I haven't had the pleasure," Kayla answered, taking his limp hand in her own.

He kissed her knuckles, a sloppy kiss that left her wanting to wipe her hand on the back of her dress. But that would be the quickest way to offend the duchess, and she had only just gained some slight measure of favor from Brant's mother. She'd always longed for the woman's approval, but the evahn prejudice was too well-rooted in the heart of her society. Kayla had learned long ago it was a hopeless battle. Until society changed, the woman would never like her.

27

"Kayla! Lady Kayla!" a young girl called from the middle of an approaching swarm. Saved from having to find something unobjectionable to say, Kayla excused herself from the duchess's snare and turned to face the gaggle of girls that surrounded her.

"Oh, you were sensational, lady. I wish *I* could play like that," the leader cooed. Kayla had to fight a smile with the girl's fawning. She couldn't have been more than twelve or thirteen.

"I'm so glad you liked it," Kayla said, bowing her head in acceptance. It was only polite, despite the girl's age.

"How'd you learn to play like that?"

"Lots of long hours and hard work, I'm afraid. And a good teacher never hurts." Kayla gave her staple answer, though it was not entirely true in her case. Besides, what she spoke was truth . . . it just wasn't *her* truth.

"Excuse me," called a voice from Kayla's left. Her heart stilled. It was a voice the entire kingdom knew. She turned slowly and curtsied to the tall, skinny man who looked more like a scarecrow than a living being.

"Chamberlain Pedran, to what do I owe this honor?"

Pedran cleared his throat. "His Majesty wishes to speak with you privately, Mistress Kayla. Would you please follow me?"

"Of course," she gushed, embarrassed at how heartfelt her response actually was. She could not afford to let anyone know just how much this meant to her.

"Excuse me, it was nice meeting you," Kayla called as she left the group of young girls who had so kindly saved her from Duchess Domanta. She wanted to like the woman, for Brant's sake, if nothing else, but it had never been an easy task.

Kayla turned and nearly stumbled as a huge hooded man stepped in front of her. He held a long box under his arm, much like the rosewood case she used for her flute. She stared into the cowl of his robe for just a moment, catching a flash of white teeth and shadowed curl across his cheek, though whether it was a scar, or hair, or something else, Kayla couldn't tell. The man nodded slowly to her, gave a slight bow, then faded into the crowd. Kayla shook herself.

She felt odd, but threw the feelings aside to scurry after Pedran out of the great hall and through the corridors of Dragonmeer. They wound upward quickly through the long ramps that led from level to level. Kayla had lost her breath by the time they reached the fifth floor, and Pedran wasn't even breathing hard, despite his advanced years.

Now Kayla's hands shook as they hadn't during her performance. She'd never met the king before, and her stomach was understandably jumpy as she approached the great double doors to his personal quarters.

"Wait here, please," Pedran ordered, though not unkindly.

Kayla nodded as he slipped inside and, she assumed, into the king's presence. She stood there only a minute at most before the chamberlain returned, the hooded man she'd nearly run into at his side. Pedran held the door open wide, and once again the stranger nodded toward her as if he knew her somehow. He reached up to pull the cowl forward, so she never caught sight of his face, but his hand was covered with blue tattoos that swirled in random patterns. It gave Kayla chills. She watched him turn to her right and stroll casually down the hall, his strength apparent in the roll of his shoulders and sureness of his step. Why was he meeting with the king? Such a strange man. She shivered and glanced toward Pedran, then back at the cowled figure, but he was gone. She jumped when the king's chamberlain spoke.

"The king will see you now, Mistress Kayla. This way, please." Pedran bowed slightly and lead the way through the door. For some odd reason, it surprised Kayla that such a large hinge hardly squeaked. Kayla completely forgot the stranger as she passed the doors to the king's hall.

The room was amazing.

Kayla couldn't take it all in at a glance and so found herself ogling about like a village girl. The ceiling of this one room was higher than her entire house, with sweeping, arched beams and windows. There were tremendous lengths of velvet at the glass, marble on the floors, and more gold in ornamentation than Kayla had seen anywhere. It was too much, almost offensive to her in the misuse of such needed funds. An entire family could live for a year on the gold from a single lamp, and there were *dozens* of them.

Without her noticing, Pedran had stopped before the king, and Kayla bumped into him. She reddened, stepped back, and bowed nervously.

"Pardons, Pedran, Majesty," she said, bowing again, more slow and deep the second time, examining the king from beneath her lowered lashes.

King Rojan was in his middle years. He was not a tall man, nor was he large, and though he did not seem to be powerful in appearance, the energy and strength of his position rolled off him in waves that were undeniable.

"It's all right, Kayla. It's a bit ostentatious for my taste, too." King Rojan gestured at the gaudy décor and smiled.

Pedran cleared his throat. "Your Majesty, I have not yet presented the girl to you. Etiquette, sir, is—"

"I know, Pedran, I know," he said, pinching the bridge of his nose. "Go ahead and present her so we may speak."

Pedran cleared his throat again, and Kayla could tell that he disapproved, but he straightened himself and continued as if he hadn't been interrupted. "Your Majesty, I present to you Kayla Kalandra Felandian, daughter of Countess Kalandra and Felandian of the evahn kingdom of Fashan."

"Welcome, Kayla." The king's voice was soft, but full of strength. "It is an honor to meet one of such great talent."

Kayla curtsied low before him. "Thank you, Your Majesty. I am honored that you think so."

The king chuckled and Kayla looked up, startled. "You know I'm right, Kayla. You couldn't play with such passion and confidence otherwise. I felt you . . . shall we say . . . *tinkering,* my dear. We need to talk."

The king turned to his chamberlain and dismissed him with a wave of his hand. "You can go, Pedran. Kayla and I have some matters to discuss."

Pedran seemed confused. "Sir?" The old man stepped forward and whispered loudly in the king's ear, though Kayla still heard every word. "I am always a part of your meetings. Have I done something to offend Your Highness?"

King Rojan shook his head with apparent patience and spoke softly. "No, Pedran. Kayla and I have some personal items to discuss, and I wish to do it alone. Take no offense, my friend."

Pedran nodded stiffly and bowed his way from the room, pulling the large doors shut behind him.

Kayla's heart hammered in her chest. He had *felt* her today? How was that possible? She would never have used her power if she'd thought she would be caught. She had only meant to right some injustices. If she had been nervous before, now she was close to terror as she stood shaking before her king.

She was not relieved by his next words.

"I have heard of that which you seek."

Kayla was still.

"You are a *bit* young for a duchy yet, but I don't think you'll have much longer to wait. You shall have your title in time."

Kayla's heart slowed. A title? She hadn't expected it so quickly, but would take any hope she could, even if it was only a carrot dangling before her at the moment. The king's word was law. If he said she would have her duchy, then she would have it, and she couldn't help the relief that washed over her.

"That is not the reason you were summoned, though, my child. I brought you here to present you with a gift . . . and a calling." The king moved his hands from his lap, and Kayla saw he held the box she'd seen earlier. He stroked its length with gentle, loving fingers.

"This belonged to my grandfather," he said as his fingers trailed down the polished surface of the box. "He gave it to me to keep safe until I found its new guardian, and I believe that should be you. Your playing today showed me not only your abilities, which are tremendous, but also your heart. And it is the latter that is most important."

31

King Rojan opened the box, and a faint blue glow shone from its depths. Her eyes widened.

"What do you feel?" he asked as he turned the box around for her to admire.

She sucked in a breath of awe. What *didn't* she feel would have been a better question. Kayla knew of this flute, as it was the dream of every flautist alive to possess it. It was made of sapphire, said to have been cut whole from mines that birthed the stones of power, and was supposed to have incredible power. Legend told of its ability to manipulate the elements and give the bearer protection with its bond. The flute tickled her senses in a way nothing had before, not even the visions the music brought. She felt warm, alive, multiple—as if there were more to her than just the self that stood before the king. She felt powerful and humble, weak and strong. There was no end to the contrasts she felt. She stared at the instrument and finally met the king's eyes with frustrated confusion, unable to mouth the things her heart spoke.

King Rojan smiled. "That's what I thought. You can feel it, can't you? You feel it the way you felt the music today." He leaned forward, intense and anxious.

Kayla could only nod.

He sat back, apparently satisfied.

"I have it on the best of authority that S'Kotos himself has been trying to get his hands on this instrument since it came into existence. It is not just a gift, but also a calling."

He beckoned her even closer and signaled for her to kneel before him, then took the flute in his hand and rested the mouthpiece on the crown of her head. It sent an electric shock through her. Whispers of music echoed through her entire being, and his next words seemed to have been spoken in the vastness of the concert hall and not the cloth-lined walls of his quarters.

"Kayla Kalandra Felandian, I hereby call thee to bear this flute in defense of Darthmoor. I name thee Guardian of the Crystal Flute and bearer of the sapphire power. I transfer the calling, I give the gift, I call you up to take this upon you. Guard it with thy life, thy heart, thy hearth, for in the end it will stand against S'Kotos in healing the world Rasann. Dost thou accept this calling?"

His voice echoed in her mind, and she knew she would forever remember every single word. "With all my heart," Kayla heard herself respond, awe in her voice.

"And wilt thou stand against S'Kotos and his evil minions throughout time?"

"I shall."

"Evahn folk live a long time, Kayla. It could be many years before you are called to give up the Sapphire Flute. Are you sure you wish to accept it?" He seemed to be straying from the formal speech, but it didn't matter. Kayla would do anything in her power to obtain that instrument. She could feel its soft tones calling to her as it lay upon her head, and her hands itched to hold it, her mouth longing to bring life to the sound.

"Your Majesty, I would die before letting it fall into the hands of The Destroyer. I shall guard the flute with my very soul."

King Rojan smiled. "Then claim thy calling, Kayla, for the flute was made for thee to possess."

Kayla lifted her hands slowly toward the glowing blue flute that sang her name, but as she reached, the king pulled it from her head and laid it back in the box. She nearly cried out when it left her head, her hands automatically reaching for it. The king took her wrist and met her eyes.

"One last thing, child, and this is the hardest to ask of you. The age of The Chosen One is upon us, and the time will come that he will call you up to stand with him against The Destroyer. Until The Chosen One claims you, you must not play the flute."

Kayla's heart fell. Not play it? It would be sheer torture! The most beautiful sound, the purest tones, would not be hers to play?

"Kayla, hear me." The king's voice pressed at her, and his hand squeezed her wrist to the point of pain. "You *must* listen. If you play this flute before it is time, you could destroy us all. Do not let S'Kotos find it because the allure was too great for you to resist. This is the flute of the Guardians. It can be heard by any who are tuned to it. So long as the flute does not sound, it will hide itself. You must guard yourself against The Destroyer and his minions, *especially* from C'Tan." Kayla shivered at the name of The Destroyer's most terrifying disciple. "She would claim the flute for herself and has been searching for decades. Do not take the chance and call down S'Kotos upon us! Guard it, hide it, keep it safe, but do not play it until the time is right. Do you understand?"

Kayla nodded. She would do anything to get the flute, even if it meant hiding its sound from other ears. Her eyes were drawn back to it hypnotically.

The king sighed. "Then its power is in your hands. I pray that you will keep us safe."

"Yes, Your Majesty." Kayla eagerly took the box and pressed it to her breast. "I will guard it with my life."

He smiled sadly. "I'm afraid that's what it will take, child."

Chapter Two

Ember sat on the roof of her stepfather's home, the rough shingles putting slivers in her backside. But at the moment she didn't care. She was too busy enjoying the privacy the roof provided and pondering the change her dreams had taken the night before.

There had never been a time she'd been without the dreams, at least not that she could remember—dreams all varied on the same theme—magic. Most nights Ember was in a group of some kind, other times she stood alone, but the one consistent thing in each of the dreams was the blonde woman who attacked and destroyed her with magic each and every time. No matter what resistence Ember used against the woman in her night-time visions, she always won and Ember was left dead.

But last night had been different. Ember had dreamed of a group of seven, each one glowing with a different color. Of them all, she recognized only her stepbrother Aldarin—and an unknown woman who had visited her in previous dreams.

Ember stood in the midst of the group, holding a staff topped with a crystal. Streams of light flowed from each of the other six into her staff. One of the men wore glowing armor and battled with a black dragon, while another of her group played a sapphire flute and battled a mage with sound. The blonde woman stepped back and stumbled against something, and was destroyed instantly, her eyes staring blindly. This was the first time anyone in her dreams had used magic against the woman—also, this was the first time Ember had survived.

There was a part of her that knew the dreams were more than common, something much bigger than herself. They seemed a prophetic vision.

The desire to learn magic had been with her from her earliest times. Her dreams now revealed what could be if she obtained her power. If this vision really did come true, if she ever did have to face this woman, she just might survive.

For some reason Ember glanced up right then, just in time to see Devil's Mount in the far distance explode and spit its depths into the sky.

She wasn't worried; not really. The spells Ezeker and his coven of magi had cast over Karsholm protected the village from the mountain's fiery breath. Still, she shivered as another blast exploded upward, adding to the ever-growing mass of gray ash blocking the sunrise. The sky darkened as she watched.

The upward thrust of mushroom cloud reached its pinnacle, and it began to fall earthward, small green sparkles dancing on its leading edge. Ember caught her breath, her heart racing with excitement and fear as the sky grew dark as midnight and the magelights flickered on, having been extinguished only a half hour before.

As the noise and concussion of the blast reached her, she clapped both hands over her ears, astounded at the volume even at that great distance from the mountain. She buried her head between her knees until the sound faded, leaving her ears ringing and sounds muffled. She shook her head and blinked as the magelights so recently burst to life, sputtered and died completely.

Ember stared in astonishment. That was not supposed to happen. Not once in her sixteen years had she ever seen the magelights extinguished in the dark. They were as dependable as the morning sun. She stared for a long time, sure that at any moment the lights would flicker back to life, but the orbs remained dark.

Instead, delicate flakes of ash began to settle around her, turning her brown hair into a mass of gray that set her to coughing. That was *definitely* not supposed to happen. No weather should penetrate the shields unless the magi allowed it. The domes over Karsholm held back everything that threatened the city—even rain, when it came in flood-like amounts. The ash falling around her told her the mage shields had dissolved. The smell was awful, much the way she imagined S'Kotos' Helar must smell; full of acrid smoke hinting of burning oil and rotten eggs. Still, she stared at the lamppost until white fluttering wings landed on its top. The white hawk that always seemed to be watching screeched and awoke her to the reality of the situation. He screamed again, then rose into the air and flew at her, as if shepherding her back to the house, green swirls trailing in his wake.

Ember's heart pounded in her chest, the fear finally taking over as she realized how little distance a day's journey truly was from a fire-spewing mountain. She scrambled up and over the cedar shingles, then dove through the window to her room. She slammed the window shut and latched it, little poofs of ash swirling around her, settling to the floor. The hawk fluttered to a landing just outside her window and cocked his head. His piercing eyes caught hers, a faint green glow coming from his shoulders.

Ember blinked, but the glow was gone by the time she opened her eyes. *Strange*, she thought.

She stared outside as the ash began to cover everything within sight. In a very short time the air was so thick with it, she could no longer see past the rooftop, let alone to the high road that marked Paeder's property.

"Great. Happy birthing day to me." She kicked the wall, only distantly feeling the pain in her big toe.

At that moment all she wanted to do was crawl back into bed and bury her head under her blankets. She had a feeling the eruption of Devil's Mount was going to create problems for her mother—problems she didn't want to deal with today. There was enough going on without her mother's overprotectiveness getting in the way.

Paeder's cough echoed up the stairs to her room. He usually woke up coughing, but not like this. Today her stepfather sounded as if his lungs were turning inside out. It had to be the ash. Ember doubly cursed the volcanic explosion.

The medicines worked less each time, and the sickness that rotted his lungs stole his life, until his mountainous strength faded to nothing more than a fragile shell of the man he'd once been. Ember had already lost one father—she really didn't want to lose another, and it didn't seem there was anything more Ezeker could do for him.

She threw herself off the bed and crept down the stairs, hoping for a moment to visit with the man who had been her father since before she could remember. Her mother's voice stopped her at the mid-landing.

"Get out of here! Get, get!" Marda yelled. Ember heard a flutter of wings and the window slam shut. She was sure the white hawk was in Paeder's room again. It seemed to like her stepfather, for some reason, and only Marda was bothered by it. The twins had crept close enough to pet the bird on several occasions, but never Ember, no matter how she longed to caress the silky feathers.

Glass clanked against spoon as Marda poured medicine for Paeder and tried to soothe his cough. Ember crouched down on the stairs and watched through the railing.

"Take it, Paeder," Marda pleaded.

"It isn't working," Paeder said. His breath came in strangled gasps that sounded painful. They probably were, though the man rarely complained.

"Now, now, it will help for a while. Take the medicine, Paeder," Ember's mother soothed, but there was no denying the steel in her voice. There was the slurp of medicine and a clank as the spoon was laid on the bedside and the deep hacking began to subside. Ezeker's magic increased the potency of the syrup, and though it would take effect quickly, it didn't last long anymore. None of them wanted to face the truth, though it was there staring at them in Paeder's hollowed eyes—he was dying.

"You're going to break her heart," Ember's stepfather finally croaked. That stole Ember's attention in a way nothing else could. Her breath caught and set her heart to racing in an angry pitter-pat. She froze on the stairs, her ears straining to hear more.

"Hush, now, husband. We all do what we must." Marda's voice caught. She picked up a fallen blanket and began to fold it. "I don't dare send her now. This eruption is not natural. There is ill afoot— I can feel it."

"You can't know that. You can't hide her forever, wife. She needs a chance to live." Ember's heart squeezed at the pleading she heard in his voice. There was never any doubt that Paeder loved her, whether they shared blood or not. He'd raised her. She was as much his child as the boys, and she knew it.

"I know she does, but . . . not yet. I can't let her go to those trials. I can't afford to take the chance," Marda said from just inside the door. Ember glared at her mother's head. She was going back on her promise again. Ember's stomach burned with disappointed anger.

"But you already promised her—" a cough cut Paeder off.

"I know, I know, but I just can't. She'll understand."

Paeder gave a sharp blast of laughter before coughing again. Marda gave him another spoonful of the syrup.

"This blasted ash. It does nothing but rush you to your grave. What a time for the shields to fail." The snarl in Marda's voice was obvious. "I'll send Ember to town for more medicine."

Paeder caught his breath enough to answer. "Don't do this to her. She deserves the chance to try. It's her *birthing day*, Marda. Don't ruin it for her," he begged.

"I have no choice. She will not go to the trials, and I will say no more on it."

Ember crouched in the middle of the stairs, despair battling with anger. Marda had *promised*. Promised! It wasn't fair.

Her mother chose that moment to exit Paeder's room and stopped briefly when she saw her daughter on the steps. She paused only a moment, then moved to the sink and began to scrub at the dishes.

"So I suppose you heard?" Marda asked, as if it was of no importance.

Ember scowled at her mother and made her way to the kitchen. She crossed her arms over her chest and leaned one hip against the counter. "Which part? The one where you send me to town running errands on my birthing day? Or where you tell Paeder I can't go to the mage trials?"

"Well, I'm glad to have that out of the way. I'm sorry, Ember, but you can't go." Marda didn't even have the decency to look at her.

"What do you *mean,* I can't go? I *have* to go! You've been finding some excuse or another for eight years, and this is my last chance."

Marda continued washing dishes. "Just what I said—you're not going," she answered, an edge creeping into her voice.

"But, Mum—"

"But *nothing,* Ember," Marda said as she threw the dishrag back in the water and turned to face her daughter. "What do you want me to do? Plug up Devil's Mount just so you can go to the trials? In case you haven't noticed, all the magic is out. *All* of it. There's no protection over Karsholm or the roads, no running water, no weather charms—nothing. It's all gone. How do you expect to get to Javak under these conditions?"

"We can take the boxcar," Ember said, referring to the wagon the family rarely used. "It would protect us."

"And what about the horses? What will protect them? How are they supposed to breathe in all of this?"

That stumped Ember. "I don't know, but Ezeker will come up with something. I have to do this, and so does Paeder. He's got to get some help at the Mage Council, and I'm still having the dreams. Ezeker said—"

"I know what Ezeker said," Marda interrupted and turned back to her dishes. "Paeder can't go out in this anymore than you can. It will kill him. And as for your dreams, well, we've had this conversation before. They're only dreams. They don't mean anything. I'm sorry, Ember. You're not going."

Ember couldn't drop it. This was her last chance. The next trials would be after her seventeenth birthing day, and by then, she would no longer qualify. "You let the twins go—why not me?"

"Your brothers are men." Marda shrugged. "Besides, I had no say in that decision, and you know it. That was for their *father* to decide."

As if Ember wasn't acutely aware she didn't have a father. That hurt almost as much as her mother's stubborn refusal. Ember lost her temper. "I can't believe you! It's *my* life, it should be *my* decision, not yours, and I want to go!" She couldn't help stomping her foot.

Marda remained silent, and Ember gave up talking to her. She wouldn't change her mother's mind, not in a million years, but there was no way she was going to miss the trials this year. She'd find a way. Somehow. Her dreams had shown her it was something she had to do if she hoped to survive. In the meantime, she had to get out of the house before she *really* lost her temper.

The door slammed as she stormed from the house. She was angered further when her mother called out as if nothing had happened between them. "Don't forget to pick up Paeder's medicine from Ezeker's!"

Ember pretended she couldn't hear as she pounded across the yard, the chickens scattering from her path to the high road, finding her way more by memory than sight. Between the ash and the tears that started the moment she slammed the door, she could hardly see a thing. She knew she was being rude, but at the moment she was too hurt, too angry, to care. She'd get the medicine, but not because of Marda. She'd get it for Paeder.

"It's not fair." She kicked at the ash that dragged at her feet. "It's my birthing day, and I should be able to have at least *one* thing I want. Can't she let up just this once? I only want to *try* to be a mage. It's not like they'd accept me anyway," she grumbled out loud, then sneezed.

41

From her earliest memories, the magi had fascinated her, and she'd become particularly attached to her uncle Ezeker. The things he did to help people were astounding, from concocting the medicines that kept people like Paeder alive, to the simple kindness of fixing imperfections like clubbed feet and cleft palates. Ember wanted to make something of her life as he had, not settle for being just a wife and mother like Marda. There was nothing *wrong* with her mother's life, she supposed, and it was something she wanted someday—but she just wanted *more.*

Ember rubbed at the pendant that never left her skin, tracing the familiar form of the emerald-eyed wolf's head. At times like this, it acted as a worry stone, helping to free her from the vice-like grip of anger.

"Ember!" A voice called from behind her. She spun, startled, having completely missed hearing the hoof beats through the ash.

"Aldarin? Is that you?" she hollered, recognizing her oldest stepbrother's voice through the curtain of gray. "What are you doing out in this stuff? Where's Ezeker?"

"He's at the Sipes'. Little Waeli smashed his hand pretty bad, and he's got quite a bit of repair work to do if the boy is going to use it again." A light cut through the darkness until Ember was finally able to make out her stepbrother through the ashfall. "What are you doing out in your nightgown?"

Ember only then realized she hadn't dressed. "I had a fight with Mum and forgot to change," she answered rather sheepishly.

Aldarin chuckled, but didn't pursue it. He pulled her up on the back of his horse. Ember wrapped her arms around his waist as he turned the horse to take her home. "What time would you like us to pick you up for the trials?"

"I can't go," Ember said, fighting the wave of anger and disappointment that washed over her.

"What do you mean, you can't go?"

"I asked Mum the same question not ten minutes ago."

Aldarin grunted. "What is wrong with that woman? She's been promising you for . . . how many years now? What are you going to do?"

"I don't know."

"Sure you do, Sis. You stay home and listen to Mum." Ember could hear Aldarin's grin.

She snorted. "Not likely."

"Meaning?"

"Meaning I'm going, whether she likes it or not. I'll walk there if I have to, but I am not going to miss these trials, not again. I can't afford to do so. I've at least got to try." Her thoughts turned to Paeder once more. If she could make it through the mage trials, she'd have a chance to help him. There had to be something magic could do that medicine could not.

"Good for you, Em. So, what's got her so worried this time?"

"I overheard her telling Paeder that she thinks the volcano isn't natural and I'd be in danger."

Aldarin was quiet for a long moment. "She could be right," he finally muttered, but continued without explaining. "So, do you want to come with us? We've got horses to spare, and with half the guard tagging along, Marda can't do much about it—though you might want to consider sneaking out, just to be on the safe side."

Ember laughed, knowing full well he was right. "Oh, yes. Most definitely."

"Good," he said and squeezed her hand. "Only, do you think you could get dressed first? I really don't think you'll make much of an impression in your dirty nightgown."

Ember slugged him in the shoulder, but continued to laugh as he carried her through the darkness toward home.

Chapter Three

Lady Kayla! My lady, wait. I must speak with you!"

Kayla looked over her shoulder and saw him—young, well-dressed, but bouncing up and down to get her attention. She grimaced. When would they ever let her be? She clutched the bag containing both flutes to her chest and pretended she couldn't hear the boy. He was probably one of Duchess Domanta's "lads," and Kayla couldn't take any more today. She was exhausted in every way possible. Sleep had been in short supply the night before, with her nerves as agitated as they'd been.

She picked up her pace, frantically searching for a cab to take her home. She knew she should turn and let the boy dote on her— that's what one did when one was trying to make an impression—but she was just too tired to do it. Spotting an empty coach, she scampered toward it with as much dignity as her dress would allow.

"Please, mistress, wait!" the young man begged from behind her. Why couldn't he just go away? All Kayla wanted to do was get home to tell her family of the king's gift and promise of a duchy.

"Are you free, sir?" she asked the elderly chauffeur.

"Yes, miss," he said, tipping his hat and giving her a lop-sided grin. "Where'd ye be goin'?"

"The Balania residence on Marlon and Weils," she answered and took his outstretched hand. But before she could pull herself up, a strong grip took her elbow.

"Lady Kayla, I been chasin' ye all the way from Dragonmeer."

Kayla groaned, though not out loud. It wouldn't make the right impression, and after all the years she'd put into creating her public face, she couldn't escape from it now—not when she was so close to getting what her family needed. Instead, she turned to the boy and put on a moderately polite expression.

"The duke," he panted. "He be wantin' ye to have this and said I was to wait for instructions." He handed her a folded piece of sweaty parchment, and Kayla opened it with distaste. The boy had the decency to redden as she shook the paper open, holding it by the barest of corners. She began to read:

My dearest Kayla,

I have spoken with King Rojan, and he has advised me of your new and upcoming status. Congratulations. My wife has been nagging at me to have a bit of a party for a while, and I think this would be the perfect excuse. Would you be willing to come to a ball in your honor this evening at Dragonmeer? I've sent Joyson with the coach and instructions to take you any place you wish between now and then. Bring your nicest gown. The ball will start at eight.

Duke Domanta

Kayla had lost her aversion to the paper after the first line, and by the time she had finished, she gripped it with joy. She pulled it to her chest, fighting herself to keep from jumping in the air with excitement, but she could not help the glow she felt in her eyes as she turned back to the boy she assumed was Joyson.

"Miss?" the elderly chap asked as she moved away, and she quickly returned, embarrassed that she had forgotten him in her excitement over the letter.

"I'm sorry, sir, I won't need your services after all, but thank you for your assistance."

"No problem, miss—perhaps another time."

She turned and took the boy's arm. "All right then, where's this coach of yours?" she asked. He pointed down the street to a magnificent carriage moving toward them. It was completely enclosed, with curtains at the window to keep out the dust. Kayla had never ridden in a carriage so fine, but she tried to contain herself. It wasn't seemly to act childish over such a simple thing. After all, she was seventeen, practically a woman.

The carriage driver stopped the matching horses before her, as Joyson led her to the door. He opened it and extended his hand to help her up.

"My lady, your carriage awaits," he said in a very gentlemanly manner, with no trace of country accent. Kayla grinned at his cliché use of language, beautiful as it was. She took his hand, stepped up, settled herself in the deep velvet cushions, and crossed her ankles.

"Where to, Lady Kayla?" the boy asked, leaning slightly into the carriage.

"Home, Joyson. The Balania residence on Marlon and Weils," she said for the second time that day. Joyson nodded at her and, shutting the door, hopped up on the side of the carriage.

"Marlon and Weils, driver," he called out, and immediately the coach began to move.

Kayla twitched the curtain aside and could see the boy standing beside her. Their eyes met, and he smiled.

"I was afraid I wasn't goin' to catch ye, miss," he said, reverting to his native accent.

"I must admit, I was hoping you wouldn't," Kayla found herself telling him. "I thought you were one of the duchess's artsy friends, and I just couldn't *stand* the thought of another conversation on the qualities of sound or the distinctive color of Darthmoor."

She grimaced and the boy laughed.

"One o' them folks? Nay, lady, I'm afraid I don't have an artsy bone in me body. I can build a decent cabinet, but couldn't tell ye pink from chartreuse." He flashed his dimples at her, not the least self-conscious.

"How long have you been in the duke's service, Joyson?"

"Not long, miss. Me mum's been working in the kitchens since I was a wee lad, but the duke wouldn't take me on until I'd got me learnin' first."

"And what exactly do you do?"

"A bit o' this and a bit o' that. Whatever the duke or Lord Brant need done. Mostly I run around fetchin' things for 'em."

"And what were you fetching today?" she asked, curious.

"You," he answered impishly.

Laughter welled up inside of her. The boy was a delight. No wonder the duke wanted to keep him with his family.

The carriage rolled to a stop shortly thereafter, and Joyson pulled the door open for her.

"Here we are, miss. I'll be waitin' here for ye when you're ready to leave."

Kayla nodded, suddenly too excited to talk and no longer tired. She was home, and there was so much to tell her family! She nearly ran up the walkway to her uncle's home where she and her mother had taken permanent residence. The front door opened before she got her hand on the latch. Uncle Tomas filled the entryway with his lean frame, his face anxious as he greeted her.

"Well?" he asked, all nerves as his hands clasped together so tightly his fingers were white.

Kayla schooled her expression and answered primly. Mother would never approve her answering with the exuberance she felt bursting inside her heart. "It would seem that our family's good name has been restored."

"Wonderful!" Tomas leaped forward and hugged her with relief.

"As I knew it would be," Lady Kalandra spoke, coming from behind her brother, her velvet voice laced with pride. Kayla's

48

mother took her hands into her own and pressed them to her forehead, imitating the evahn gesture of gratitude. Nothing more needed to be said.

"Tell us all about it," her uncle's lively tenor begged, drawing her into the sitting room. "Leave nothing out, dear; we've been waiting for this most of your life."

"The music was divine. Of course, when I first entered, and they saw who was to play, they were not happy. Even Lady Domanta looked down her nose at me." Kayla knew she was talking too fast, but she couldn't help it. The excitement had taken over.

"Lady Domanta has a prejudice against women who perform in public," her mother answered.

"Ah, well, that explains it then." Kayla nodded. "I think I changed her mind, though. She was one of the first to approach me with praises, right after the duke himself. She was also one of the first on her feet when I played *Darthmoor's Honor*. You should have seen it. Everyone was absolutely silent while I played and just about erupted out of their seats when I was done. The king was almost in tears! It was amazing!"

Lady Kalandra lost her decorum at that point. She clapped her hands together, threw back her head, and laughed. Kayla could not remember a time she had ever seen her mother laugh. It was pleasant and genuine, and Kayla found herself joining in.

"Oh, Kayla. What a joy you are to me," the lady said, wiping tears from her eyes. "What began as a game has become something you have fully earned. So, what title has the king bestowed upon you?"

Kayla's grin widened. "Well . . ." she said, drawing out the moment. "He said I was a little young for it still, but that I would soon become a duchess."

Tomas whooped and leaped from his chair to do a little dance around the room. Lady Kalandra laughed again at her younger brother's excitement.

"Tomas, do sit down. The neighbors will believe you've finally gone mad if you don't quiet yourself."

"I don't care, Sis! What news! Little Kayla, a duchess," he said, reaching out to ruffle his niece's hair.

She scowled at him and smoothed her blonde locks, pulling them down over her ears self-consciously. He knew how much she hated people to mess with her hair.

When Kayla turned back to her mother, Lady Kalandra was staring at the box the king had given her. One eyebrow quirked, and her head tilted in obvious curiosity."Kayla, what is that box you carry?"

"This?" Kayla held up the wooden box that held her pride. "This is another story." Her voice went very quiet, full of reverence, as she sat upon a footstool and leaned forward to tell about the rest of her day. "After I finished my performance, Pedran approached me. The king wished to see me. Privately. Not even Pedran was privy to that meeting."

They stared at her, obviously shocked. Kayla understood the feeling. She continued, setting the narrow, wooden box on her lap. She caressed it lovingly as she spoke, imitating the king's movements of only a few hours before. "He spoke of my performance, of course, and told me I would be getting a duchy when I was just a little older. Then he gifted me this." As she spoke, she undid the clasps that held the box closed and opened it for her family to admire. Lady Kalandra gasped, her hand going to her mouth.

Tomas fell back in his seat and stared at Kayla as if she'd grown a second head. He whistled in awe. "Is that what I think it is?" he asked in hushed tones.

Kayla nodded. "It's the Sapphire Flute, and," she paused for effect, "the king has just made me its guardian."

Stunned silence met her announcement. Lady Kalandra's mouth was open with an "oh" of surprise.

Tomas spluttered. "But . . . bu—but why you?" he asked.

"Why not me?" Kayla responded, a little miffed, though she tried to calm herself. Did they have no confidence in her, after all she had done? "He said my playing had shown him my heart, and evidently he thinks I'm good enough to guard the flute with my very life. The words he said were amazing. I didn't know King Rojan could be that eloquent."

"They were probably not his words, Kayla," Tomas spoke, his eyes on the blue light of the flute. "Can you remember what it was he said?"

The words were burned in Kayla's heart and mind and were sealed there with the light of the flute itself. Of course she remembered. She repeated them, and Tomas nodded as she finished.

"It fits with what I've read. I was able to obtain a copy of one of the holy books of the Priests of Sha'im. They have one who is traditionally guardian over the Armor of Light, and the words with which they transfer guardianship are similar. It is a great honor you have been given, Kayla. Greater, I think, than you will ever really know. Guard it well, child."

"Believe me, I will."

Kayla's eyes took in the beauty of the softly glowing flute once more. She couldn't quite put words to the feeling that ached within her heart. It was part love, part possessiveness, and part awe. She closed her eyes for a moment, the after-image of the flute burned into the back of her eyelids. She took a deep breath and, having broken the flute's spell on her, closed the lid with a soft click.

"By the way," she said, being deliberately casual. "Duke Domanta invited me to his home this evening. He's having a ball in my honor. Would anyone care to join me?"

"In your honor? When did he decide that?" Lady Kalandra asked. Kayla knew that tone. Her mother was not happy.

"Just after he spoke to the king, I guess. He sent his boy after me to bring me home in their coach. Will you come?"

Kalandra and Tomas looked at each other and shook their heads. "We cannot. Your grandfather claims he is dying, though it's the fifth time this season, and he was miraculously healed every time we came at his call." Tomas rolled his eyes, and Lady Kalandra's lips tightened. "But you know how he is. If I don't go, I'll lose my inheritance entirely, and then where would we live?"

Kayla didn't trust herself to respond where her grandfather was concerned. He was the one who had begun all this nonsense and disinherited Lady Kalandra when Kayla was born.

Kayla's mother sighed. "I do so wish I could have heard you play. Perhaps you could play the Sapphire Flute for us now—give us a sample of your own brand of magic."

Kayla shook her head. "I can't. The king told me I must not play it, though it tears my heart."

"He gave you guardianship and then gave you limits? You, the greatest flautist in a century, and you cannot play this flute? That is wrong, Kayla. *You* have guardianship; it is *you* who must decide when the time is right."

Kayla was surprised at her mother's vehemence. "Mother, I cannot. Perhaps another time."

Lady Kalandra nodded stiffly and began gathering up her needlework. "I must prepare for our departure. Enjoy your party, Kayla. Don't be gone too late, and *please* don't get into any more trouble with that rascally son of the duke."

Kayla grinned. "Brant is harmless, Mother."

The lady snorted at that, but did not respond. She'd always had something against Brant—it was nothing new.

"Don't mind her sharpness," Tomas said, putting an arm around Kayla's shoulder as Lady Kalandra left. "She always dreads these confrontations with your grandfather. I think he calls her just to annoy her, but tonight we have much to tell that should set his heart aflame. I, for one, very much look forward to seeing the look on his face when we tell him that not only does his half-evahn granddaughter have all of Darthmoor wrapped around her finger, but she is now also guardian of the Sapphire Flute. He'll be gnashing his teeth for weeks. Keep it up, Kayla. Let all of Darthmoor know what the Balanias are made of." He patted her on the shoulder and left the room.

Kayla resented the last. She wasn't a Balania—she was a Felandian. The Balanias lost their claim on her when her mother had been disowned. So far as she knew, the only honor left in the

Balania name came from Uncle Tomas. He held ten times—a hundred times—the honor his father had. She would do nothing for Balania honor, but she would do it for her mother.

Lady Kalandra had lost nearly everything she valued—a mother and sister to death, another sister who had disappeared entirely, her home, her station in life—and still she held on to her dignity. Kayla could do nothing to change what her grandfather had done, but she *could* provide a new home for her mother, a place where she felt of worth. And the king had shown Kayla today that the time was soon. Very, very soon.

With that thought, she raced up the stairs to her room and tried to find a proper dress for the party.

Chapter Four

Aldarin dropped Ember off in front of the bathhouse. She waved her thanks to her stepbrother and tromped up the stairs, scratching at her bare arms. Her skin was so gray with ash, it seemed she'd been painted from head to toe with the stuff, and it itched. She could hardly wait to climb in the deep pool that was heated by the same vein of magma that fed Devil's Mount.

The white hawk was back again.

Ember stopped with her hand on the door and looked up at the bird perched above her. For once she was close enough to see his green eyes, bright as the emeralds in her wolf pendant. The bird cocked his head, examining her, and Ember was startled to realize no ash touched him. She blinked, and for just a moment the green glow was back over his shoulders. It was like the ghost image one sees after looking at the sun. *It must be from the eruption. Probably some gasses in the air making me delusional,* she thought as she rubbed at her eyes and tried to get her heart to slow.

It scared her that she was seeing things, whatever the reason. She got chills as she opened her eyes and saw the bird was still there, staring at her, and realized this being was not normal. It was something more—though what, she didn't know. The white hawk tilted his head once more, beat his wings, and launched into the sky, quickly disappearing in the darkness.

Ember went into the bathhouse and locked the door, grateful for once that her mother had set the bath up with candles rather than magelights. Otherwise, she'd be bathing in the dark. With relief she lit the candles, pulled off her now-filthy nightgown and tossed it in the hamper, then started to scrub.

Once clean, she pulled the cord that would sanitize the tub and watched the heated water swirl around her. Clean water fell from above, scalding her head almost to the point of pain, while the drain below her siphoned the liquid to who knew where. When no more gray dirtied the bath, she climbed out.

She was drying herself off when someone banged at the door.

"Just a minute," she said, toweling her hair dry. She wasn't sure how she was going to manage it, but she had to find a way to keep the ash out of her hair. It had taken much longer to wash, and she wasn't about to do it again the same day.

"*If only I had one of Ezeker's weather charms . . .*" she thought wistfully.

Those little things were amazing. It didn't matter what fell from the sky, the charm would surround her with an invisible dome that shucked it all aside, keeping her clean and dry. Well, nothing to be done about it. Wishes wouldn't bring a weather charm to her, and she had no power to stop the ash or create her own shield. She'd just have to settle for plain old farm-girl ingenuity and figure something out.

Once Ember was dry enough to climb into her spare clothes, it was only a matter of a minute before she was dressed and ready to go. She finally settled the dilemma of her hair by wrapping the damp towel around it and tucking the ends inside.

She looked around to make sure all was in order for the next person and, satisfied, opened the door, surprised to see Aldarin waiting for her. His gleaming uniform made her scowl.

"Aldarin, how do you stay so clean in this stuff?"

"I thought you'd *like* the clean look," he said, running his hands down the crisp lines of his shirt, "but if you prefer the ash, I guess I'll give this weather charm to Marda instead," he teased.

"Give me that, you big goof," she said, laughing and reaching for the amulet that hung from his hand. "I was just wishing for one of these. Maybe my luck is changing for the day." She settled it around her neck, layered over the wolf pendant, and thankfully unwound the towel from her hair. She blew out the candles and stepped from the bath house. Immediately, a small magelight around Aldarin's neck sprang to life and lit their way.

"Hey, how is it your magic is working when all of ours is out?"

Aldarin glanced at her and looked down at the blue light. "Ezeker respelled it before he sent me for you." He took Ember's elbow as they climbed the short hill toward the house. "Something in the blast blew out all the spells, but it doesn't prevent any new ones from being cast. Ezeker and pretty much everyone from the mage academy are running around respelling things as fast as they can." Ember headed for the front door, but Aldarin pulled her around the side of the house. "It will be days before they get it all done, especially with the strongest magi respelling the dome over Karsholm, but it will get done eventually."

"So what are you doing here, anyway?"

"Ezeker thought you could use a ride into Karsholm," Aldarin answered. "He would have sent me with Da's medicine, but he thought you could use the time away, and besides, he's got a birthing day gift for you and wanted to give it personally."

"Really? A present for me? He doesn't usually do that—hey! What's Monster doing here?" She rounded the corner to see not the gray palfrey Aldarin usually rode, but the midnight stallion her stepfather had raised and sold to the mage academy.

"He's mine now—a gift when Ezeker promoted me to *captain* of his Guard."

Ember squealed. "Captain? Really, you mean that?"

He nodded. "I only found out last night when they set up the roster for the mage trials. I've been promoted. The youngest captain in three hundred years, they say. Who knows—at this rate, I'll be a general by the time I'm thirty."

Ember laughed with delight. "Oh, what a birthing day present! You could not have given me a single thing better."

"Good," he said, helping her up onto the towering beast, "because I was too poor to get you anything this year. Sorry, Sis." Ember scooted back onto Monster's rump. Aldarin jumped up, then swung his leg wide over the stallion's neck and settled into place before nudging Monster forward.

"Yeah, right," she said, digging her fingers into the flesh just above his boney hips. "You always give me the best presents. Come on, Aldarin. What did you get me?"

Her brother tried to hold in his laughter, but squirmed when she found his one and only tickle spot and dug at it mercilessly. "Nothing, Sis. You haven't been good enough to get a present from me this year," he teased, laughing.

"Aldarin, don't be mean! Please?" she begged and stopped tickling him just long enough for him to pull his mail shirt down even farther.

"Nope, huh uh. I'm not saying a word, and you can't make me."

"I'll bet I can." Ember dug at his hips again, but found only chain mail. "Grrr. I thought you loved me," she pouted.

Aldarin changed the subject. "How is Da doing? I haven't had time to stop by for a while, and to be honest, it's just too hard seeing him. He was always so strong and healthy, and now . . ."

Aldarin didn't need to finish. Ember knew. She still lived with it, after all—smelling the sickness and hearing the deep hacking coughs night after night and seeing her stepfather waste away before her eyes. It was too much to bear.

Ember sighed. "He's alive, but I don't think he wants to be. It's only a matter of time before the lung sickness takes him. Mother fights it, but even she has had to admit that his days are numbered." She gave his arm a squeeze. "He misses you, Aldarin. I think the greatest joy you could give him would be to spend as much time with him as you can spare. I know he would never say it, but you are his greatest pride. You live the dreams he never could. Guard to one of the greatest magi of our time? How could a father not be proud of you?"

Aldarin shrugged. "I'll do what I can," he promised, urging Monster into an easy lope, eliminating any further conversation.

The trip was made quickly, and within a matter of minutes they had reached their destination. Ezeker's tower was lit up in full glory, blue and orange magelights beaming in strips that ran from street to rooftop. The sky was still dark as a moonless night, but Ezeker lit the whole area with his magic. A distinct line of ash circled around his tower as if a great, invisible dome covered his home and had swept it all aside—his oversized version of a weather charm that somehow still functioned. She knew she shouldn't be surprised. The weather charm she wore was active, after all, so why not his shields—but seeing magic still working on such a grand scale was amazing.

Ember threw her leg over the back of the stallion and slid down his side while Aldarin looped the reins through a ringed post just inside the gate. He led his sister across the courtyard.

It was odd to hear footsteps again instead of the swish-swish of ash against Monster's legs. The courtyard they crossed was small; only seven noisy steps before the thick wooden door stood beneath Aldarin's outstretched hand. He caressed the wood with his fingertips, and Ember was startled to see faint trails of green light sparkling in the tracks of sweat he left behind on the dusty door. She blinked, but the tracks faded when her eyes opened again. She shook herself. It had to be some strange effect caused by the gasses that had erupted from Devil's Mount. The smell *did* make her a bit lightheaded. Oddly, it was easier for Ember to believe she was hallucinating than the impossibility of magic coming from Aldarin.

The door clicked and swung slowly open.

"Wait for me, and I'll let him know we're here. He's probably upstairs packing, even though I told him not to," Aldarin said. Moving to the left and through an alcove, his heels clicked as he jogged up the stairs, chain mail chinking. Ember could follow his movement above her, his voice echoing as he called for the master. The sounds faded as he made his way to the upper levels, then silenced for a very long while.

Ember sat at the stone table with its mismatched wooden chairs and waited.

The main area was dark, the only light coming from Ezeker's green room where he grew herbs and medicines each year and raised his own tomatoes and cucumbers as well. Some years there was even melon, and Ember remembered many a New Year celebration that included Ezeker's bright red, out-of-season melon that was as ripe and warm as the middle of summer. She breathed in the smell of life that surrounded her and relished the fragrance. She closed her eyes, then immediately snapped them open again, heart pounding.

For just a moment she had seen something more—green swirls and surges and spikes as she had seen around Aldarin's hand on the door. With her eyes open she could see nothing, but when she closed them . . . there again, twirling in a ghostly dance that unnerved her. Was she going crazy? How could she be seeing things that weren't really there?

Now that she thought about it, she'd been seeing the green sparkles all morning, ever since the volcano exploded. She remembered the dancing light at the edge of the cloud and the swirling lines that hung in the hawk's wake. Could it really be as simple as volcanic gasses?

Ember was beginning to think not. Her heart pounded as she thought of the possibilities. Hadn't one of her grandparents gone insane? Hadn't they complained of seeing things nobody else saw? She had a vague memory of Paeder's father running full into the barn siding, chasing a huge butterfly no one else could see. He'd knocked out some teeth with that hit.

That had to be it. Ember gnawed at her thumbnail, knee bouncing up and down in agitation. She was going insane. The tears welled up, and she was so lost in her panic that she jumped when Ezeker's voice sounded from behind her.

"That's not a good sign." He sat down in the chair across from her and motioned toward her bouncing leg. "What's bothering you, child?" he asked, forcing her eyes to meet his.

Ember didn't dare say. She couldn't bear to think he might confirm she was going crazy. She battled within herself, and the tenderness in his eyes finally sent it pouring out.

"I'm seeing things, Uncle, and it scares me to death."

Ezeker was still. "What kind of things?"

"Green spikes and whorls and stuff. Aldarin put his fingers on the door, and I saw it then. And earlier this morning around the eruption. But figured I was hallucinating because of the gasses from the volcano. I saw it again in your green room. I've never seen anything like it. I'm going crazy, aren't I?" She was sure he would say yes, but instead he laughed.

"Oh, heavens no, child. I've been waiting for this to happen, and it's certainly taken its time about it."

Ember's heart stilled for a moment, then its beat returned to its usual pace. Her hand dropped from her mouth to slap the table. "You mean this is normal?"

"It is when you are coming into your power," he answered, smiling as he reached and placed a gnarled hand over hers. "Green is the color of life. It is perfectly natural for you to begin with this color. Others may appear later."

Ember didn't really hear him beyond his telling her she was coming into power. She really *could* be a mage? Not just in a dream, but in reality? Her heart pounded again, but it was no longer in fear.

"What you are seeing *is* life: the force, the energy, the power in all living things. This is good. This is *very* good. If you can see the power of life, you can tap into it and borrow from it. That is, in part, what I do when I heal things and help them grow."

"So, do you think I could help Paeder?" she blurted the desire of her heart.

Ezeker shook his head. "I'm afraid he is too far beyond your reach. He is beyond even my abilities. I have spoken with your

61

mother about taking him to the Mage Council at the trials. Perhaps the council can heal him when I alone cannot, but I fear she has waited too long."

"He's dying, then."

"Yes, child, he is." Ezeker brushed Ember's hair back from her face, then let his hand rest on her shoulder. "The medicine will ease his cough and help him sleep, but there is nothing more I can do. I only hope your mother will set aside her feelings for the magi and allow us to at least try."

"I'd talk to her, but you know how much good *that* would do," Ember said, only slightly bitter. She knew her mother well enough to understand that the quickest way to doom an idea was to talk to her about it.

"It will not always be thus, Ember." He squeezed her shoulder, then let go. "Now, if memory serves me right, and it usually does," his eyes twinkled at her, "you're due at a birthing day celebration." Ezeker stood and shuffled to one of the chairs on the far side of the table. There he took up a small, wooden box from the cushion and handed it to her. "Happy birthing day, child."

Ember's fingers trembled as she took the box in her hands. It was made of thin cherrywood, with the top nestled over the bottom. She gave the lid a slight shake, and it came free. She gasped, so stunned that she sat there absolutely dumbfounded, until Ezeker took the box from her, chuckling, and set it on the table. He moved behind her and pulled on the leather thong around her neck until her pendant lay upon his palm—the pendant her father had given her. Ezeker wrapped Ember's hand around the amulet.

"Hold this," he said, pulling the cord from the ring. He took a silver chain from the box and threaded it through the pendant, then pulled the ends up and around the back of her neck. He whispered a few words, and a slight surge of heat grazed her neck as the ends of the chain were merged together as one. Ember twisted the necklace around and could not find where it had been joined, so perfect was it.

62

"This chain is spellcast," he said. "It will not break, nor will it tear your skin, though it will do serious harm to anyone who tries to take it from you."

She glanced up at him, tears in her eyes. "I've never had a finer gift, Uncle. Thank you."

"Oh, we're not done yet, child." He gathered the other two items from the table and grinned at her. "Your father gave these to me for safekeeping long before he died. Somehow he knew he might not be here to do this himself. I was told to give them to you when I felt the time was right. Today is that day."

He held in his hands two of the most unique pieces of jewelry Ember had ever seen. They were a set of what most would call slave bracelets, matching in every detail. A wolf, twin to the one at her neck, sat upon a ring, with emerald eyes peering straight ahead. A single fine chain ran from the ring to a carved wolf head the size of a coin, and from there a short link joined ring and coin to a scrolled bracelet.

The bracelet also carried the wolf theme, but in representations of the phases of lupine life. Each part was beautiful, in and of itself, but all together they were magnificent.

Ezeker slipped the ring on her middle finger and bent the bracelet around her wrist, then joined the ends together with a single surge of light and heat. The piece was beautiful on her wrist, and knowing it came from her father was just . . . overwhelming.

The second bracelet and ring went on her left hand just as easily, and a few whispered words from Ezeker had them sealed in place. It amazed her. She kept expecting the metal to pinch, but wearing it was no different than a leather glove or a silk scarf, and it was even lighter than she imagined the latter to be.

Ember sat admiring her two new ornaments when the eyes of the wolves on both bracelets and her pendant began to glow with a brilliant light that nearly hurt her eyes.

She put her hand over her eyes, her heart racing. The light got brighter. She could see the green glow through her fingers and wanted to do nothing more than rip the bracelets off. The light sparkled across her skin like miniature lightning bolts.

She squealed and shook her arms, trying to fling the bracelets from her, but the action had no effect. Her heart beat so fast, it felt as if it would rip its way up her throat or explode any moment. Why would her father have given her a gift that would do her harm? No, he wouldn't.

Her skin began to itch as the light brightened. It terrified her. The entire day had her scared and doubting herself, and now this was happening—it had to be Uncle Ezzie's magic. "What are you doing, Uncle?"

Ezeker was silent.

She glanced up at him, her eyes narrowed against the piercing light. Her stomach dropped at the shock on his face.

"I'm not doing anything, child," he croaked.

Ember's skin prickled as she watched the light from the jewelry fade, but with the diminishing light came the sound of a coal popping from a fire, then a flash of green that faded quickly, but took the detail of the chain with it. What had been three dimensional before, so obvious to touch and eye, began to melt into her skin.

Ember was horrified. "Get it off, get it off!" she screamed, clawing at the bracelet. But there was nothing to grasp. It was a mere shadow of itself, fading quickly into her hands. She expected the chains to burn, but they didn't. She shook like a tree in the wind, but there was nothing to be done. All she could do was watch as the chains continued to merge with her skin, as if they were nothing more than lotion or soap to be absorbed.

The ring-bracelet sank just as the chains had—flattening until at last they appeared to be a tattooed decoration instead of removable jewelry. She touched one shaking fingertip to the gleaming eyes twinkling at her from the back of her hand, but it felt no different than her normal skin.

And then it started all over again as the necklace she wore—the one her mother had told her so often never to remove—flared to life. Bright emerald eyes flashed intensely as the necklace, too, faded from the silver pendant she'd worn, to a light silvery-gray tattoo with green eyes flashing from the bottom of her sternum.

Ezeker was as stunned as she. "Well, never in all my years . . ." he whispered.

Their eyes met and held. Ezeker's eyes shone with every bit as much fear as she knew was in her own.

Ember held up one hand. "Can this come off?" she asked, her voice shaking.

"I don't rightly know, child. It should. But then again, *that* should not have happened." Ezeker touched the middle of her inner wrist where the ends of the bracelet joined, and whispered a few words. Ember felt the surge of power and heat, but it dissipated into her skin with no change in look or feel.

The old man scratched his bald head. "I am certain your mother is going to be rather unhappy about this."

"No questioning that," Ember responded, still staring at the fading lines of silver. "She's going to hate it." Her face softened as she caressed the image of the wolf in her palm and traced the lines across the back of her hand. "But, you know what?"

"What?" he whispered, pale and shaken.

Ember grinned at him, suddenly happier than she had felt in a very long time. "It's worth it. She can't do a thing about it—and from my father, to boot," she whispered, awed. "I couldn't ask for a better birthing day gift. It's beautiful, don't you think?"

Ezeker just nodded his head and smiled.

Chapter Five

C'Tan stood in her bedroom, bare stone walls surrounding her. Only the luxury of a large feather bed with red silk sheets made it look at all like a place to sleep. The room was round and gleamed with shiny black stone, a lair she had created for herself out of a lone mountain jutting from the midst of a dead lake, a dwelling that was not and never had been a home. An unfamiliar sense of wistful longing sneaked into her heart. The last place she remembered as home was a little shack in western Nifan, a place with a mother who loved her and a brother she adored . . . but that was before, in her previous life, when she had been young and innocent and beautiful, before her brother had become another enemy eliminated by her hand.

"Jarin." She spoke his name aloud. Even after all these years, it was beyond her understanding how she could love and hate someone so much, like the love she'd held for her mother and the hate for her father burned into one.

Ever uncomfortable with the memories of her past, she waved her hand in a plucking motion and pulled a brass mirror from thin air. It appeared before her as if it stood upon a stand, and yet it hovered, unsupported and unmoving in the center of her room.

The mirror never lied, and each time she summoned it, the hate in her heart knifed a little deeper. For a moment she stood within the illusion of what she had once been—tall, beautiful, with a lush figure, hair the color of golden apples, and a face so beautiful, it was as if the Guardians had molded a masterpiece in her.

And then Jarin had created the monster behind the mask.

Her eyes narrowed as she let go of the magic that hid the truth from the world. The blonde brows and pale locks that flowed to her shoulders disappeared, and in their place was a reddened scar. Somehow in the inferno that claimed Jarin's life, S'Kotos had used fire to carve his mark upon her, the symbol for fire starting at the end of her chin and rippling upward to the crest of her head. It mattered not that he wasn't present during the battle. He was the Guardian and master of fire. It did his bidding and marked his servant as his own. She had truly been her master's creature since that moment.

There was something about destroying the person you loved most in the world that killed the heart. What was left of Celena Tan still ached for what had been, for the innocence she held before, and not the monster she had become. Her thoughts circled back to the same place they ended every morning of every day since that dreadful fire—back to the one person who could have ended her torment and freed her from S'Kotos—the child of her brother.

The Chosen One.

Her teeth ground in frustration. For fifteen years she had been searching for that child. For fifteen years she had failed. Without Shandae, she could never be free. Without Shandae, S'Kotos could not be destroyed, for it was *she* who must bring the keystones together and banish The Destroyer. Only with that act would C'Tan be free.

C'Tan could bear the sight of her scarred and fallen state no longer. She was hideous and it shredded her soul a bit more each day to witness it. She bent and gathered up the red robe, pulling the silk around her and belting it at the waist.

A light tap sounded at her door. She waved her hand at the mirror, sending it back to its home until she had need of it again.

She gathered illusion around her once more: the blonde locks, the slightly over-ripe figure, the perfect face. None saw her in her true state. None but the mirror saw her emaciation, her scarred body, and hairless features. Only she and S'Kotos knew the truth behind the mirror.

Armored in illusion once more, she gestured at the door, opening it to the man who had once been her master, but now served her unquestioningly. C'Tan turned her back on him and sat on the end of the bed, legs curved beneath her and a single arm supporting her body as she listened to Kardon's daily report. She interrupted him almost immediately, as she always did.

"Have you found her?"

His eyes hardened. His opinion of C'Tan's obsession with the wolfchild had been expressed often enough that C'Tan knew what the look meant. "Nay, mistress. Jarin has hidden her well. We can only wait until the power takes her and hope that the strength of her magic will overwhelm that which hides her from us."

"That is too long!" she spat. It was the same every day.

"Not so long now, mistress. Fifteen years have passed. Most children have reached their power by her age. Any day now, a year at most, we shall find her."

"You base a lot upon that hope, Kardon. I hope for your sake that you are right."

Kardon did not even blanch. The morning report continued, but C'Tan's mind was elsewhere. It wouldn't be long, and the child would be within her power.

"*Soon, now, and you will be mine, Shandae. Hear me and fear,*" she called into the echoes of her mind.

There was no answer. There never was.

Chapter Six

Kayla pulled the heavy wooden door shut behind her with a resounding boom, thrilled to have made such a bargain with the dressmaker. She had three hours before her ballgown would be finished—three hours to enjoy the city and dream of all the things she could purchase when she was settled in her duchy. She only wished Brant were there. Shopping was always so much more fun when he was around.

Kayla turned to the right and meandered down the street, glancing in the shop windows and fingering the wares of the street vendors. She turned right at the next intersection, heading for her favorite jeweler, when a familiar form stepped from the bootmaker's shop and nearly collided with her.

"Brant! What are you doing here?"

The duke's son smiled, took her hand, and bent over it in an extravagant bow. He finished with a gentle kiss to her knuckles, so much more pleasant than the kiss his mother's artsy friend had given her that morning. Her heart beat a little faster, and she had to remind herself to breathe when he pulled away. She laughed and threw her arms around him when he straightened, then gave him a kiss on the cheek.

"I'm here for you, silly. I stopped by your uncle's place to pick you up, and he said my father had already taken care of you. I figured you'd head this way first. I know you better than you think, my dear. Besides, my riding boots were in some desperate need of repair." His blue eyes sparkled as he kissed her cheek, his lips lingering just a little longer than was proper. Kayla tried not to blush, but the heat rose through her pale skin. Brant pretended not to notice. "I sent Joyson and Miash on a little errand for me. I didn't think you'd mind."

"Of course not," she said, placing her hand in the crook of his elbow. They strolled slowly toward the jewelry shop.

"So, what do you think of the ball?"

Kayla didn't know where to start, so she smiled up at him, her eyes aglow. Brant laughed.

"Why am I not surprised? And your uncle has approved of your staying the night?"

Kayla nodded. "Yes. Dragonmeer is a little too far outside of town to be trekking back home in the dark. It only makes sense that I would stay over. My uncle said he was sure you'd do the right thing by me, whatever that means."

"Well, he's certainly right there," Brant answered before pulling her into the jewelry shop. "Father thought if we're going to have a party, we might as well make it one for the history books. Besides, it's about time somebody did something good for you, especially after such a magnificent performance. There's only one catch," he said, eyes twinkling at her as he took her hand and led her through the store.

"What?" She was too giddy to be wary.

"You've got to play for us again," he said, his face completely serious.

"Of course."She tried to act casual, as if the request didn't bother her in the least. She had been asked to play for royalty on short notice before, but not at her own party. That thought was a little unnerving, and the butterflies started up like they hadn't that afternoon.

72

She tried to forget by distracting herself. Brant was always a great distraction.

They wound their way among the displays, pointing out certain favorites—diamond rings, sapphire broaches, and the one Kayla loved most, a gold bracelet with carved gemstone charms. It was horrendously expensive. All she could ever do was look and dream, and it wasn't the first time she'd stood transfixed over the case and looked at all the detailed carvings in the multi-colored stones. For some reason it represented everything Kayla's mother had given up for her.

"Beautiful, isn't it?" the storekeep asked, as he always did. Kayla only nodded, entranced by the stones.

Brant shook his head, grinning, and moved to the front counter to speak to the storekeep in low tones. Kayla couldn't hear what they said and didn't care, really. She determined, as she always did when she entered this shop, that when she got her title and had some money, she would come in here and buy this one thing for herself as a symbol of what she had accomplished. She only hoped it would still be here when she was finally able to afford it.

Brant wrapped his arms around her from behind and put his chin on her shoulder. "Hungry?" he asked.

"Starved, but I was saving my appetite for the banquet tonight." Kayla took his arm again and they strolled into the open air.

He stopped just outside the door and laughed. "If you're starved now, you'll be nothing but skin and bones by dinner. Father always eats late." Brant rolled his eyes. "Why don't you run around the corner and get a couple of sausage rolls to tide us over? I've got to pick up a package for Father, and then I'll meet you back here." He dug in his belt pouch for some coins and held them out to her.

"Sure." She took the coins and left with one final glance at the charm bracelet through the window.

The pie vendor was half-blind and missing his right leg from the knee down, but could do more by touch and smell than most people could with two good eyes. Even her uncle's cook couldn't make sausage rolls like old Mikal.

73

Mikal's sausage rolls were very different from those made by other bakers, which were just patties nestled between two halves of a bun. Mikal layered meat mix over apple dough, rolled it up like a log, and cooked it that way. It was amazing. The grease from the sausage softened the dough, and the apple, cheese, and onion in the sausage mix balanced the sweetness with savory. Kayla couldn't help herself—she bought two, ate one of hers on the spot, and bought another two for Brant.

She walked as she ate the final roll and was just wiping the grease from her mouth when Brant rounded the corner and caught her by the elbow.

"Where to now, Miss Kayla?" he asked, playing the gallant that he rarely was.

"I was thinking about a walk through the gardens." Kayla smiled up at him. She loved the brightness in his eyes and the strength of his chin. He had grown so handsome over the years.

"Marvelous idea," he responded, and they walked slowly arm in arm through the central courtyard, past the gaudy fountain, and into the portion of the royal gardens that was accessible to all Darthmoor.

As children, this had been a favorite spot for littles while parents were visiting or doing business. She had spent many an evening crouching in the rose bushes playing hide and seek or monster in the dark. No one had ever thought to look for her there, and for some reason she had never been stuck by a single thorn—probably her evahn blood put to some decent use. She missed those days, before she knew what she was and how it hurt her family to be different.

Outwardly, she didn't show much of her evahn heritage. Yes, she was on the slender side compared to most of the girls of Darthmoor, and she had received plenty of teasing for that. Her hair was light, the color of honey, and her eyes the palest crystalline blue. And though that was not unheard of, it was definitely uncommon. The only noticeable difference between her and the other girls was the distinctive point to her ears, though it was neither as large nor as full as a true evahn's. She kept her hair long and always styled over the tops of her ears so as not to remind the people of her dual nature. So far she had been mostly successful.

Brant and Kayla strolled through the rose gardens, the delicious scent perfuming each breath. A small group of instrumentalists sat in the middle of the garden and played. Kayla stopped, closed her eyes, and listened to the harmonies they created as they strummed and fiddled their way through an original piece. They were good—very good, in fact.

She stood in silence for quite a while until Brant interrupted her thoughts by clearing his throat. "I hear the king is going to grant you a duchy."

Kayla nodded, glancing at the small group before succumbing to Brant's gentle tug and moving on. "He said I was a little young still, but it sounds like he's made up his mind." She glanced back at the musicians one last time and sighed. "It's taken long enough. I've been working at this since I was seven years old and finally understood my mother's position."

Brant popped the last bite of sausage roll in his mouth and licked his fingers. "I know. I was there when you decided, remember?" He bumped her hip with his own.

Kayla elbowed him in the ribs. Just a gentle nudge, nothing her mother could consider improper. "Of course I remember. You were the one who gave me the idea." She hugged herself, remembering how young and naïve she had been. "I was never really sure I could do it. It still amazes me."

"I was sure." Brant stopped walking and met her eyes. "I knew if anybody could weasel a title out of the king, it would be you. I've never known anyone so lovably devious." His eyes sparkled with mischief.

"Hey! You're the devious one, not me. I'm just sweet little innocent Kayla the half-evahn, not much to worry about or bother with." She couldn't help the bitterness that crept back into her voice.

Brant took her chin in his hand and caressed her mouth with his thumb, raising her eyes to meet his own. Kalya's heart stopped beating for a second as their eyes met, almost electric, and Brant

75

leaned toward her until their noses almost touched. "There is a lot to bother with, Kayla, and I'm certainly paying attention." She started to object, but he silenced her with a kiss.

For a moment the world stopped turning, and the skies froze above her. Brant's air mingled with her own, and for the first time in her life, Kayla felt whole. Brant pulled away much too quickly, leaving her gasping as the world slowly began to spin again. Kayla couldn't speak. She just stared at him, not sure what to do or say next. Her mouth opened and shut several times.

Brant laughed. "Close your mouth, Kay. You look like a fish." She snapped it closed and glared at him, though there was no heat in it.

He chuckled and cradled her face in his hand. "Oh, Kayla. How long I've waited for that."

"Why?" she finally whispered.

"Why did I wait, or why did I kiss you?"

She grinned. "Both."

Brant laughed, but his twinkling eyes didn't mean he was not hearing her or taking things seriously. He took her in his arms and held her close, whispering his answer in her evahn ears, and for once it didn't bother her to have someone so close to them. She shivered at his breath.

"The answer is complicated, Kayla." Her name from his lips sent new shivers of joy coursing through her. "The biggest reason also seems the most unreasonable, and I'm almost afraid to mention it." He was quiet for a long moment, and Kayla was afraid he would say nothing more, but guarded, cautious, he spoke again. "You know my father loves you, much as he would his own child, but he has to look to the future and furthering the cause of Dragonmeer. He made it clear to me early in my life that he expected me to marry well, and, unfortunately, in this one thing I cannot afford to go against him. He would never approve our marriage if you held no title."

"Marry?" She pushed back a little so she could meet his eyes, though she still stood within his arms. She almost couldn't speak or swallow for the lump in her throat. Her heart pounded, and it seemed as if her stomach had climbed up to keep it company. "Who said anything about marriage?"

He cocked his head to one side. "Well, I thought you would want to marry me. Haven't we been the best of friends forever?"

"Well, yes, but you can't just assume these things, Brant. You have to woo me."

"Woo you?" He snickered. "Kay, it's me," he said and finally let her go. "I know you love me. Why do I need to go through all the silly nonsense of bringing flowers and singing love songs? Why not just do it?"

Kayla crossed her arms and stomped a foot, dignity be damned. "I *like* all that silly nonsense, Brant. It's customary, it's expected." She was trying very hard to hold her temper. Brant was being uncharacteristically dense. "And how do you know I love you? Have I ever told you? You need to *prove* these things, not jump to conclusions because we've always been *friends*."

"You may not have spoken your love, but your body has told me a thousand times as you casually brushed against me, and your damp palms as I've held your hand, and that kiss . . . you can't deny the love in that kiss, Kayla." Brant gently took her hands.

Kayla blushed, but pulled from his grasp. "That may be so, but it's not the same thing. You have to woo me." She shrugged. "Besides, I don't have my title yet. The king could still change his mind."

"He won't," Brant said, full of confidence. "Besides, I hear he made you guardian over something very special. He has to ennoble you after that."

"He does?" Kayla's eyebrow quirked in surprise.

Brant seemed puzzled by her ignorance. "Of course. These kinds of things just aren't granted to commoners."

The anger flooded back like a whirlwind. Kayla's raised brows collapsed over her eyes, her arms crossed again, and she jutted her chin. "So now I'm a commoner."

Brant's voice went up a notch as he expelled an exasperated huff. "That's *not* what I meant!" He took a deep breath and ran his hands through his dark hair. "Look, can we just start over? I wasn't trying to get you upset with me; I was trying to ask you to marry me."

Kayla's heart melted even though she wanted to be angry with him. He took her hands in his own again and looked at her shyly. This was new territory for both of them.

"I love you, Kayla. Please, be my wife?"

"But what about the wooing?" she asked, still disappointed that he wouldn't even *try* to win her over. This was not the way she had expected a proposal to go.

Brant shook his head and smiled at her, then got down on one knee and pulled a small wooden box from his pocket. "Will this do, my love?" he asked, holding the box up for her to take.

Kayla's hands shook as she reached and took it from him. The hinge creaked and snapped back as it opened. She gasped at what lay inside. Her eyes welled up with tears as she tore them away from the box to meet Brant's gaze, and then were immediately drawn back to his gift.

It was the charm bracelet.

Ruby, sapphire, diamond and pearl, jade and emerald, yellow citrine and moonstone sparkled like pieces of the stars. All the colors of the rainbow and beyond were reflected in the charms for which she had longed. She was afraid to speak or move for fear it would be a dream that would evaporate in her fingers.

"Kayla, I love you more than life itself. Please be my wife," Brant whispered as he got slowly to his feet, took the box from her, and fastened the bracelet about her wrist. Feeling its weight on her arm, hearing the soft tinkle and chink as the charms tickled one another, made it real. Kayla drew in a breath at last, released it slowly, and met Brant's soft eyes with tears in her own.

"Oh, yes, Brant. Oh, yes, yes, yes!" she answered and threw herself into his arms. Then she whispered, "Now that's what I call wooing."

The moment was exactly right. Perfect.

Chapter Seven

Lightning flared overhead, but all that fell from the skies was more ash and char. They kicked up from the shod hooves of Aldarin's midnight stallion and blew out in straight streams that curled away from the mount's cloth-covered nostrils. The world had turned a monotonous gray, and for once Ember prayed for a rainstorm to clear the skies and wash it away.

But that was not to be. Ezeker had told her the lightning was caused by the eruption, not an impending storm. Unfortunate, but there was nothing to be done. Even Ezeker could not control the weather, though he had been kind enough to let them keep the weather charms.

Ember sat behind Aldarin on the stallion, her arms around him. Not two minutes into their journey home, Aldarin unwrapped her arm from his waist and began to examine the bracelets embedded in her skin. He pressed the image of the wolf engraved on the back of her hand, then turned her arm over to examine the inside of her wrist. He turned it further to study the pinky side of her hand, and Ember's elbow twisted painfully.

"Uh, Aldarin, my arm doesn't bend that way," she said, grimacing.

"Sorry," he said, immediately releasing her. "It's just so fascinating. It's hard to believe these were real chains and cuffs only an hour ago. If I hadn't seen them in Ezeker's box, I'm not sure I would believe you. And who would have ever thought the pendant would do the same. They must be part of a set. Why else would they all react that way?" He rubbed his thumb over the back of her hand once more. "I wish I had been there to see it."

"You're the first one to see it after the fact—that's got to count for something." Ember rubbed at her wrist.

"Yeah, and one of the first to see your mother's face when she finds out, which counteracts the thrill of first sight. If it's not a curse, it sure seems like one."

Ember groaned. "Thanks for reminding me."

"What? I thought you didn't care what she thought."

"Well, that was before, when I was caught up in the excitement of it. Now I've got to face her, and she's going to be livid. You don't know her like I do. She's not your mum." Ember scrubbed her palms on her pants.

"She may not have birthed me, Ember, but she is every bit as much my mother as she is yours," Aldarin snapped, which was unlike him. "Quit feeling sorry for yourself. If you don't like the way she treats you, then say something about it." He sat stiffly in the saddle, as if to pull away from her. "You're old enough to make your own decisions, and too old to pout when Marda disapproves. I've certainly had my share of run-ins with her, so don't even go there."

Ember was a little taken aback. "When? I've never heard Mum say a single negative thing about you. You're perfect."

Aldarin laughed, a great belly laugh that had them both shaking on the horse, and Monster looking over his shoulder, snorting at them with disgust. "Oh, let's see. There was the time I tipped you into the pigsty when you were three, and the time I put burrs in Tiva's saddle blanket when he was learning to ride and, oh! The time she caught me kissing Melina Tidy, and—"

"What? You kissed Melina? Ewww!" Melina may have been beautiful, but she was the snottiest, most self-loving girl in Karsholm. She hated Ember with every bone in her body, and the feeling was mutual.

Aldarin chuckled. "Hey, I was twelve. What do you expect?" They rode in silence for a moment before he continued. "Most recently, there was my entering the guard. I still haven't heard the last of that."

"I never knew." Ember wrapped her arms around his waist once more. "I knew she nagged at me all the time, but I've never heard her say a thing to any of you boys. I just figured it was me she didn't like."

"Oh, she likes you. She loves you. She loves us all, which is why she nags us so much. She just wants us to be better, that's all. Think about it, Ember. When has she ever reprimanded you in front of anyone else? Besides Paeder, I mean?"

Ember thought. She really thought, long and hard, and could not come up with a single instance in her life when the boys had been around during her arguments with Mum. Either they had been out and about, or Marda had politely said, "Ember, let's go for a walk." It was only then that they'd had their little talks.

"Huh," Ember said, stumped and surprised. "Never, Aldarin. I don't remember a single time you guys were around."

"And there you have it. We've all been cornered by her 'little walks and long talks,' Sis, but she never tried to embarrass us, only guide us." Aldarin covered her hand with his own. "She's the only mother the twins and I remember, so don't go saying she's not my mum, okay?" Aldarin still sat stiffly, though he squeezed her hand as he said it.

Ember felt fully chastised and a little embarrassed. She'd never really thought of it that way. Paeder was the boys' father, and Marda was Ember's mother—that's just the way it was. It had never occurred to her that the boys might miss *their* mother every bit as much as she missed her own father, little as she knew about him. Maybe the boys were better sons than she was a daughter because she never really thought of Paeder as "Da." He was just Paeder, her mother's husband.

"Okay, Aldarin. I'm sorry. I hadn't realized, and I shouldn't have judged. It's just hard sometimes. I love my mum, but I never feel like anything is good enough for her, and I'm not the person she wants me to be."

"I think she's afraid, Ember. There seems to be an awful lot of fear tied up in her heart regarding you, especially where magic is concerned. I don't think she holds you down because she doesn't approve, I think it's because she doesn't want you to get hurt like . . ." Aldarin stopped, and Ember snatched at the conversation.

"Like what?" she prodded.

Aldarin shook his head and locked his jaw. She could see the muscles working, as though he had glued his teeth together to keep from talking. "Like . . . someone she knows," he finished, rather lamely.

"Who?" Ember prodded again.

"Just someone. I'm not supposed to talk about it. Besides, it's her business, and if she wanted you to know, then you would know, okay?"

"No, not okay. Aldarin, she never tells me anything, not about herself, nor my father, and especially not about who he was, or what he did, or anything about his family. I ask, and she clams up, so who else am I supposed to ask? And if I'm not supposed to know, how come you do?" Ember was a little hurt that her mother might have spoken to Aldarin about things she would not tell her own daughter.

"I overheard her talking to Ezeker a couple of weeks ago when she didn't know I was around. It's not like I was trying to eavesdrop, but sometimes when Ezeker doesn't want his guards to be obvious, he has us sit in the curtained alcove. That's how I knew he had spoken to her about the mage trials. Now, please don't ask me any more questions, or I'll be breaking her confidence, and Ezeker's trust in me. You don't want me to do that, do you?" He grinned at her over his shoulder, but his voice was serious and pleading. Ember knew it had always been hard for him to say no to her, and today was no exception.

She knew she shouldn't push, but there was something inside her that said, "Ask him. Ask now." How could she refuse her heart even though her head screamed at her to leave things alone?

"Aldarin, please. I don't know why, but—" she halted, not sure how to go on. "I need to know. It's the only way."

"Blast it, Ember! You don't know what you're asking! I can't!"

"I know you can't, Aldarin. I know it goes against everything that seems right and fair, but answer me truthfully. Isn't there a part of you that whispers I need to know? Mother will cradle me in cotton and try to protect me my entire life unless I know the truth. All her prejudice and rules are wrong. I don't know why, and she will not tell me! Please, brother."

Aldarin slumped forward in defeat and pulled Monster to a halt in the middle of the road. "Off," he barked.

"But—" she objected.

"I said off, Ember. I can't talk to you about this without seeing your face, and I won't do it on the back of a horse. Get off," he repeated, his voice angry, but determined.

Ember threw her leg over Monster's back and slid down, Aldarin shortly behind her, his long strides quick as he led Monster under the oak trees that lined the road. Monster nosed aside the small amount of ash that had sifted through the trees and set to eating what greenery he could find. Aldarin leaned against a tree, his eyes blazing at his sister.

"I'm not happy about this, I hope you know. It's not fair of you to use me this way. Not only is it unethical, but it could get me into a heap of trouble with both Marda and Ezeker. I could get demoted just because I can't say no to my sister—" He took a deep breath and rubbed his hand through his hair. "—because she's right." Resigned, he hung his head and gathered himself to speak.

Ember waited, too tense to do anything but stand still and straight.

"Ezeker has wanted Marda to tell you the truth from the very beginning, and has done everything he knows to persuade her, but she's too scared about what might happen to you if she does. I don't understand the entire situation, Ember. I only overheard one conversation, and not a lot of it makes sense to me, but I will tell you what I know." He looked down at his boots, then met her eyes.

"Your mother has not exactly lied to you, but . . . she has held back a lot of the truth. Here's the truth as *you* know it." He counted the facts on his fingers. "Your father was a stone sculptor. He died in a fire when you were a baby. You came to Karsholm because Ezeker was your only family. Those are the three big ones. All true. All lies." He stopped then and scrubbed his hand through his hair once more, seeming to work up his courage.

"Ezeker is *adopted* family. He trained your father in his chosen profession, but they do not share blood. Your father *did* die in a fire, but it was a fire caused by an evil woman named C'Tan, and I got the impression somehow that there was a connection between them, though I'm not sure what it was. And . . ." Aldarin took a deep breath now. "Your father was killed because . . . because he was a mage—and because he was protecting you. You are the one C'Tan was after, Ember, and I don't know the reason, but it's why your mother does everything she can to keep you from magic. She's afraid that with magic in your veins, you'll somehow draw C'Tan to you and be destroyed just like your father. She loves you more than anything, and it's tearing her up to have to lie to you like this, but it's the only way she thinks she can keep you safe. Ezeker feels differently and has told her time and again, but she won't listen."

Ember felt the blood drain from her face. Aldarin stopped and straightened, watching her with obvious alarm. She flushed with heat as fear washed over her so thick she thought she was going to vomit, and then anger so intense she could barely control the tremors that shook her from head to toe. It was the fear that won out in the end when she realized what had happened to her that very afternoon. Ezeker said the magic was awakening within her. The magic really did run through her veins. No wonder Ezeker was encouraging her to get to the mage trials. Without his saying a thing, she understood what his thoughts were on the situation—because they were a direct reflection of her own.

"Ezeker thinks training will prepare me for the confrontation with C'Tan, doesn't he? It's going to happen sooner or later—my dreams tell me that—and if I'm trained, my chances of survival will increase. Right now I'm powerless." She looked to Aldarin for confirmation.

His stunned eyes and slight nod were enough for her to know she was right.

The anger flashed bright again. "What's Mum trying to do, get me killed?"

Aldarin was at her side in an instant, gathering her in his arms. She wanted to fight it, but this was Aldarin. She could resist him no more than he could resist her. They were as close as blood—closer, maybe.

"No, no, Ember, just the opposite," he said, his voice smooth and earnest. "She feels that keeping you away from magic entirely will keep C'Tan from finding you . . . ever. Obviously she's not thinking straight. The power that wells up from inside of you is *not* something you can muffle and hide. It's a part of who you are, and can no more be changed than . . ." he glanced around, "than I could turn that oak tree into a mare for my stallion."

The laughter burst out of Ember before she could stop herself. Now was not the time to be laughing. She stopped quickly.

"Come on," Aldarin said, taking her hand. "Let's get home and see to a birthing day celebration."

"I don't feel much like celebrating right now, but I guess it would look kind of funny if I didn't show up to my own birthing day dinner, wouldn't it?"

"Are you kidding? You miss a party? Yeah, it would be noticed." Aldarin swung himself into the saddle. She scrambled up behind him, and in an instant, they were back on the road. Ember's thoughts scrambled about her head, one phrase echoing more loudly above the others.

"What's she trying to do, get me killed?"

It was a question that had no answer.

Home looked different after the things Ember had learned that day. Changed, somehow, though she knew, truly, that the change lay within herself.

Riding up to the gate, Ember spotted her seventeen-year-old stepbrothers galloping in the field east of the house. The twins had set at least a dozen magelights aflame over the field. They had also set up a shield similar to Ezeker's so the ash was shucked away from the house, barn, and field.

Tiva stood on the bare back of one of Ember's favorite mares, Diamond Girl, a spotted horse named for the half-diamond in the middle of her forehead. He braced himself with one foot on her shoulder and the other on her rump, his arms outstretched as Diamond Girl ran in large circles around the pasture.

"Giddy-up," his voice reached Ember across the field. "Faster, girl, faster!"

"You're gonna break your neck if you don't watch it, Tiva," Ren called, laughing. Ember saw him then, sitting astride another of the family favorites, Brownie, who was as sweet and obedient a mount as Ember had ever known. Typical of the boys—Tiva doing the outrageous thing and Ren sitting by, laughing.

For twins, they were about as similar as the sun and the moon. Tiva had blond hair, and lately he had taken to greasing it so it stood in spikes on his head. Ember couldn't understand why he'd bother, as the grease stunk like old cheese, but he thought it made him look handsome. Ren, on the other hand, had dark hair that lay softly over his forehead, enhancing the earth-brown eyes that seemed to see into her soul, unlike Tiva's crystal-blue eyes that were constantly laughing.

Aldarin and Ember trotted up to the gate and sat watching the twins for about ten seconds before Tiva noticed them.

"Em!" he yelled, waving wildly, still balanced on the back of the mare. He let Diamond Girl circle once more. When the horse got to the point closest to the gate, Tiva did a back flip off the mare, landing softly on his feet with outstretched arms and a cocky grin. He ran to the gate and opened it in time for Aldarin to dismount and lead Monster in, then shut the gate behind them while Ember slid off.

Ember turned around in time to be crushed in Tiva's rather smelly embrace. He pounded her on the back, nearly winding her with his enthusiastic backslapping. Ren rescued her, thankfully, before she suffocated.

"Let her go, twin. Can't you see you're killing her with your love?" Ren's eyes twinkled as he kicked his leg over Brownie's neck and jumped down. Tiva let go of Ember only long enough for Ren to wrap his arms around her and do nearly as sound a job of crushing her as Tiva had. He squeezed until her back cracked and she laughed, begging him to let go. Ren just chuckled, gave one last eye-popping squeeze, and set her on her feet. She promptly smacked them both on the arm.

"When did you get back? I thought you were in school until harvest festival," she asked while they stood rubbing their biceps and grinning.

"Yeah, we thought so too, but they let us out for the mage trials, seeing as how we have to help all the instructors and senior magi there," Tiva said, rolling his eyes. "I thought being a mage would be pretty cool and glamorous, but mostly it's just grunt work. We have learned a thing or two, but nothing really neat yet."

Ren started laughing. Tiva scowled at him.

"Except we learned to levitate, and Marda caught Tiva *literally* scaring the crap out of the cow with his practicing," Ren told her, dancing away from Tiva's reach as his twin took a swing at him. "It was pretty hilarious, seeing old Moomoo trying to run in the air and bucking about, but definitely not nice. Marda must have agreed because she chased Tiva out of the barn with a switch. She didn't catch him, though."

Tiva reddened. "Well, they *did* tell us to practice, didn't they?" he said, sulking and casting daggers with his eyes. Ember didn't like that look. It always led to trouble, and since Ren looked to be bursting with laughter, she decided to change the subject.

"I don't think they meant for you to practice with the cows, Tiva, but trust you to find levitating the livestock appropriate. So, what did you bring me for my birthing day?"

"Birthing day? It's your birthing day, Em? Gee, I'm sorry, I completely forgot," Tiva answered with his usual lack of seriousness. "What about you, Ren? Did you remember to get her something?"

"Of course I did. Don't tease her like that, Tiva. It's her special day, and sixteen is a pretty important one, don't you think?" Ren answered, putting a protective arm around Ember's shoulder. He didn't wait for Tiva to answer. "Of course, it's not like I have much money, being a poor apprentice mage and all, so I got you the best present I could afford. It was free. I found it in the rubbish heap and polished it up a bit. That should do just fine, eh?"

Ember answered by slugging him in the shoulder again, hard. But she grinned as she did it and raced him back to the house, the magelights following overhead.

"Don't forget to wash up, boys!" Marda's voice called from just inside the door. She poked her face around the corner and smiled as she saw Ember. "Happy birthing day, dear. I'm glad you made it back. I was afraid you'd miss your special dinner." Marda leaned out the door and tossed a rag toward her daughter. Ember snatched it out of the air. "Clean up and come sit down. Supper's about on the table." Marda withdrew her head, and Ember heard the clank of a few pot lids being set aside and the flow of water into the sink.

"I wonder what she'd do if we didn't wash up. Do you think she'd throw us out?" Tiva asked as he stuck his hands into the cold running water Ren had turned on for him.

"Nah," answered Ren. "If she'll put up with that stink in your hair for as long as she has, I imagine about the worst she'd do is make you go without your supper for a night or two. Might be good for you," he said, giving his twin a solid thump on the stomach that showed no sign of a bulge. Tiva nudged Ren with his hip, throwing him off balance. They both collided with Ember, nearly knocking

88

her backward into the horse's water trough. Ember glared at them, but it was all in play.

Ember let the boys go into the house ahead of her before she washed. Once her hands were toweled dry, she pulled down her sleeves to cover all but her fingertips. She was grateful the twins hadn't seen the tattoos that stained her hands and wrists, and especially hoped her mother wouldn't notice. If she had gloves, she would happily put them on, but her mother would be sure to notice so blatant an attempt to hide something. There was nothing else she could do without drawing attention, so she followed her brothers, and within a few short moments they were all seated around the large table. Even Paeder had come from his sickbed to join them. He looked weak and feeble, but his eyes shone when he saw Ember and beckoned to her.

He wrapped one arm around her waist and another around her shoulder and pulled her to him. "Happy birthing day, step-daughter," his hoarse voice whispered in her ear. He gave her a dry peck on the cheek. Ember patted his back and pulled away, thinking he was done, but Paeder took her wrist and slipped an envelope into her hand. She was afraid for a moment he'd seen the tattoo in her palm, but he didn't give it a second look. Surprised, she paused, questioning him with her eyes.

He waved a frail hand at her. "Later," he said, winking. "When you're alone."

She nodded and smiled at him, putting a hand on his shoulder before she sat down.

Dinner smelled delicious. Marda had made Ember's favorite meal—a spicy egg and green bean soup with onions to be eaten with flatbread and a dollop of sour cream, with apple pudding for dessert.

Ember ate slowly, trying to make everything last. She knew better than to ask for seconds. Marda's idea of femininity included small portions and no seconds. It never seemed fair, the way Marda held Ember down. Ember worked as hard as the boys did—it was only right that she get the same kinds of rewards.

"Is it gifting time yet?" Tiva asked Paeder, who looked to Marda for an answer. She gave a slight nod. The twins looked at each other and grinned, both of them squirming in their seats like five-year-olds. "Can we go first?" Tiva asked his father. Paeder answered nonverbally with his usual shrug.

"This is from both of us, Ember," Tiva said. "We made it ourselves, though I did most of the work."

Ren slugged him. "Don't listen to him, Ember. We split the work up half and half." He handed her a paper-wrapped package—very sloppily wrapped, she noticed, but wrapped nonetheless. The twins waited expectantly while she opened it.

The object was heavy and round, and Ember couldn't figure out what it might be, as it felt like nothing more than a stone. She untied the strings and pulled the paper away to find . . . a very unassuming piece of plain granite, about the size and shape of a large duck egg.

"Oh. A rock." She hadn't really believed Ren when he'd said he dug her gift out of the garbage. The disappointment hit her hard.

"Pull it apart," Tiva said, rolling his eyes.

Ember pulled slightly. The rock slid apart, two halves of a whole. She gasped, absolutely incredulous. The flat side was a rainbow of color in an inward spiraling pattern. It was not paint, but real crystal embedded in the rock, symbols etched over the surface.

"It's beautiful," she said, then paused. "But what is it?"

"We were hoping you'd ask," Ren answered. Tiva reached across the table and snagged the two pieces of paper the stone had been wrapped in. He unfolded them and set one half of the stone, spiral down, on top of a blank piece of paper in front of Ember, then placed the other page in front of himself. He pulled a blackstick from behind his ear and grinned as he wrote something down. Tiva then placed the second stone on his paper and whispered to it, as though it were a living thing. It lit up with rainbow light for a brief second and seemed to suck the writing from the paper itself. It gathered the black scribbles like a sponge taking in water, and then the stone in front of Ember lit up, and the words that Tiva had written spread themselves across her page. She gasped, and it was with a trembling hand that she moved the rock sitting before her to read the message:

Pretty neat, huh? Thought you would like these sending stones so we can keep in touch better. Hate to be an evahn giver, but we've got to take one back to school with us for it to work. Happy birthing day, Emmie. We love you.

Ember looked up and met her brothers' eyes with mist in her own. "I don't know what to say, guys. This is amazing. Thank you very much."

Tiva shrugged, embarrassed now that their gift was so well-received. "It's nothing, Sis. We've sort of been missing you, and this way we can talk even if we're not together."

Ember scooted back her chair, went over behind the twins and wrapped an arm around each of them. Then, avoiding Tiva's smelly hair, she gave them both a sound kiss on the cheek.

"I miss you too, and thanks. It's an incredible gift, and I'll keep it with me no matter where I go." Ember's thoughts flashed to her planned departure for the trials. She meant what she said, on multiple levels. The stones would ease her conscience a bit.

"Well, I don't know if I can top that," Aldarin said, reaching for his saddle bag, "but I saw this and thought you might like it, with winter coming on."

He pulled a bulky package from his bag and handed it to her. She unwrapped it and found several items of clothing—a new sable brown cloak with a hood, soft and light as silk with fur lining the hood and edges. There was also a pair of gloves, and socks made from the same light material.

"Those are all warm-spelled, Sis. You'll never get cold when you're wearing them," Aldarin said.

Ember threw her arms around him. He knew her better than anyone. Her biggest complaint of working in the winter had always been the cold. It was the most wonderful, practical gift he could have given her, and she told him so. Feminine, but not too much so. He grinned at the praise.

Marda spoke then, her deep brown eyes gleaming. "I left your gift on your bed. Go see it and come show us all, dear," she purred. Ember knew that tone. It said, "Don't fight me, sweetheart." Ember already had a pretty good idea she was going to hate her mother's gift, but she pushed herself away from the table and made her way up the stairs to her room.

Sure enough, laid out on the bed was the frilliest, most annoyingly gaudy pink dress Ember had ever seen. Did her mother not know her at all? Her brothers, who didn't share her blood, gave her gifts she could use and love, and her mother, the woman who birthed her, gave her this? She could hardly stand to look at the dress, let alone put it on. It wouldn't be so bad if it were blue instead of pink. She caressed the silky material, closed her eyes, and tried to imagine it blue—the deep, dark blue of her midnight pool, a silvery moon shining on its surface. The ache for acceptance, for love of herself as an individual, and especially as a daughter, tore through her heart, and Ember felt something begin to build. It was a hum, a slight vibration that started in the pit of her stomach and spread outward like Ezeker's cough medicine. She clung to the feeling and hugged the dress to her as if it represented everything lacking in her life.

Something itched in her hands—and then it burned. Ember cried out and dropped the dress to examine her hand for the blister she was sure to find . . . but there was nothing. Her hand looked perfectly normal, but for the faint glow winking at her from the wolf's eye. It faded quickly, and Ember looked down at the dress to see if there was a pin, or nettle, or firebug. Something had to cause the pain.

She gasped at what she saw.

The frilly pink dress that had existed only a few seconds before was gone, and in its place was the dress she had seen and wished for in her head, all the frills and lace missing. She reached down and picked it up, sure she was imagining things. But no—the dress before her was as real as the gift from her mother had been.

Ember's head started to swim, and she had to sit down. Blue silk in her hands, she collapsed in the middle of the floor and stared at the fabric, unbelieving.

"Ember, are you all right? I heard you cry out . . ." Marda's voice came from the doorway. Ember heard the hesitation in her step. She could nearly hear the beat of her heart as her mother caught sight of the dress. Marda's voice was cold and fearful when she spoke again. "That is not the dress I left on your bed. Where did it come from?"

"From my head, Mum. It came from my head," Ember responded, a little panicked and overwhelmed by the understanding of what had happened. "I saw it in my head, and then it was there," she continued, gesturing wildly.

Marda didn't move for several long seconds from the spot that seemed to have rooted her to the floor. She stepped forward slowly and took Ember's hand from the folds of the dress that lay in her lap. She paused, utterly still, staring for a long moment at the tattoos on Ember's wrists and hands before she pulled back the sleeve and examined the recently acquired wolves. Ember was suddenly very grateful for the high-collared shirt that hid the embedded pendant. Marda prodded at the dark chains on Ember's hands when the wolf's eye suddenly winked at her with a flash of emerald light. Marda jerked, but did not let go. She took Ember's chin in her other hand and pulled it up so that her daughter would meet her eyes as she crouched down beside her.

"Where," she asked in almost a whisper, fear and anger fighting in her voice, "did you get that?" She pointed with a sharp jab at the wolf on the back of Ember's hand.

Ember met her gaze without backing down. There was nothing to be done about it now. "From my da," she responded, and watched her mother nearly faint at the words.

Marda let go of Ember's chin as she sat down heavily on the floor. "What?" she whispered, gray as the ash that fell outside.

"I got it from Da . . . through Ezeker."

Ember proceeded to tell her mother the whole story. She could gauge her mother's emotions by the color of her skin, the set of her lips—and the more Ember spoke, the angrier Marda became. When she was finally done, Marda was furious.

"That meddling old man. I told him to mind his own affairs, and he just couldn't leave well enough alone, could he? He'll be hearing from me, you can be sure of that, and if I have anything to do with it, he'll be out of this town for good. He had no right—"

"He had every right, Mother," Ember interrupted. "He was following instructions left for him before you even came here. He was only doing what you didn't have the courage to do." She regretted the words before they left her mouth, but she couldn't bite them back.

"I beg your pardon?" Marda demanded, whispering in her anger. "Who do you think you are, child, to judge me so? You have no idea why I do the things I do—"

"Yes, I do, Mother," Ember interrupted again. "I know more than you think. I know why you don't want me to draw attention to myself, and I know why you want me to stay away from magic. I know my father was a mage, and I know he was killed by C'Tan because she was trying to get to me! Isn't that enough?"

Marda's grief crushed her a little more with each revelation, but instead of speaking, she drew herself up and became angrier. "Get it off, Ember. Take that chain off and throw it away. You have no understanding of the trouble to which this leads. Get rid of it. Now!" Her voice rose.

Ember stood and faced her mother, outwardly calm, but inwardly angry and very determined. "No," she responded, her arms folded over the midnight dress.

"What?" Marda hissed. Her eyes narrowed in anger.

"I said no, Mother. I can't. And even if I could, I wouldn't. You've given me nothing of my father's. Nothing! No memories, no stories, no old treasures or tokens. Nothing. This, *this*," she said, thrusting her hands out before her, "is the one and only thing I have had in my entire life that was mine from him alone. This, and a pendant that seems more like a slave chain than jewelry. You use it to control me by never allowing it to leave my skin. Enough, Mother. No more.

Ezeker has done nothing to harm me, and much more to help me than you have." Ember paused, then decided to reveal the last of it. "I am going to the mage trials."

"No!" Marda whispered, terror on her face. Ember was untouched by it. She knew what she had to do.

"Yes. If I am ever to survive this evil mage, C'Tan, I must do it with knowledge and training under my belt. Maybe I'm destined to die by her hand . . ." Marda choked at that phrase, but Ember continued relentlessly. "But maybe, just maybe, I can survive, if I know what I'm doing. It's the only chance I've got."

"You don't even know if what Ezeker says is true! How can you base a life-changing decision on the words of some old man?" Marda demanded, her eyes desperate.

"Ezeker didn't tell me, Mum."

Marda looked lost for a moment, as if the thought of anyone else knowing the truth boggled her. Ember almost took it back, almost told her the truth about Ezeker's hidden cove where Aldarin had listened in. Her heart ached, knowing how much she was hurting her mother, but it was something she had to do.

Marda didn't answer.

Ember sighed. "Mum, it's too late for me to turn back now." She laid the dress in her mother's hands as a reminder of the magic that was already manifesting itself in her daughter.

Marda took it with a sob and turned her back. Ember stood still, watching her for a long moment, unsure what to do next. It seemed the best thing was to give Marda some time. She'd get used to the idea eventually, whether she liked it or not.

Ember moved past, debating whether to rest her hand on her mother's back as she left, but she couldn't bring herself to do it. Instead, she paused long enough to say, "I love you, Mum. I'm sorry," before she walked down the staircase.

Her brothers and stepfather stared at her as she headed toward the front door. Obviously the argument had carried down the stairs. There was no point in waiting for Ezeker to pick her up in the morning. She'd go to him tonight.

The boys stood in silence, only Paeder smiling at her. They seemed to be in awe more than anything, amazed that she'd actually had the audacity to stand up to Marda.

"Good for you, sweatheart," Paeder whispered as she opened the door. She turned and gave him a half-smile. He winked at her, and she almost cried. Instead, she blinked hard and held it in, nodded once, and went through the front door, unsure if her mother would ever speak to her again.

Chapter Eight

The dress was more beautiful than Kayla could have imagined. It was lovely, with the bodice in deep blue velvet with silver laces and trim. The ensemble was amazingly simple and complex at the same time, and Kayla couldn't have asked for more.

She laid the dress and cape across her temporary bed at Dragonmeer, slippers and jewels beside them, and smoothed out the minute wrinkles that had appeared during the short coach trip to Brant's home.

She was about to begin unpacking her small trunk when there came a light tap at her door.

"Enter," she called.

A lithe blonde entered and curtsied with a huge grin spread across her face. "My name would be Sarali, miss. Master Brant wanted me to help ye with the bags and anything else ye might be needing. I'm yours for as long as ye'd be needing me."

Kayla was instantly grateful. "Wonderful. Sarali, is it?" she asked the small woman as she swooped about the room like a bird coming in to roost.

"Yes, Miss Kayla, Sarali it be, though I know me name doesn't fit me voice. Me husband changed it on our wedding day. Seemed the proper thing to do at the time," the girl prattled on. She didn't seem to be more than sixteen or seventeen by voice and figure, but her face showed a few lines etched there by time. Kayla upped her assessment by half. Perhaps twenty-five or thirty? It was hard to tell. Sarali seemed to be one of those ageless people who would look as good at fifty as they had at seventeen.

"So you're married?" Kayla sat on the bed, careful not to disturb the dress, and chatted with the girl as she worked.

"Yes, miss. I'd be married to the big lug of a chef."

"The man with the tattoos? From Ketahe?" Kayla asked, remembering her first sight of the man as their coach pulled into the stables. He had been in the back of the castle, his arms loaded with miscellaneous boxes that looked heavier than any normal man should be able to carry, but he was certainly *not* normal. The man was huge, and Kayla had been frightened by him at first. Though he seemed vaguely familiar, she knew she'd never met the man. He had seemed so fierce with all the tattoos, and she had heard many tales of the terrifying strength of the Ketahean people. They were known as warriors, not cooks, and she had never imagined one of them being married to a little sprite of a thing like her new chambermaid.

Sarali nodded with pride. "He be the one. The form behind the tattoos isn't much to look at, and he can't speak a word of common, but he's a great cook and a man full of passion." She shrugged. "A girl can get mighty swept up by his kind, if ye catch me meaning, lady." She grinned from ear to ear, not the least bit embarrassed, though Kayla could feel herself reddening at the girl's admission.

"Oh . . ." Kayla tried to regain her composure. "Thank you, Sarali. It is a pleasure to meet you. I'll be sure to let Brant know how wonderful you've been."

"Oh, he'd be knowing that already, miss. Sir Brant and I have an understanding, and he'd not have assigned me to ye if he weren't already a mite pleased with me work." And with that she turned and flounced down the stairs, leaving Kayla breathless in her wake.

Kayla sat in her room for a long minute before she pulled out the final two items from the beaded satchel she'd carried all day long. The first was the flute she'd played for the nobles that morning, and the second was the Sapphire Flute. She ran her hands across the polished wood, and it seemed that she could almost feel the flute calling to her from inside its case. It hummed and throbbed in her heart and mind, calling like a siren to free it from its prison. She was mesmerized, entranced by the feelings that lured her, taunted her to open the case. Should she? Did she dare?

She was saved by the sound of another knock at the door. She snapped her eyes toward the entry with mixed feelings of relief and reluctance, and stood only long enough to shove the case beneath her mattress.

"Enter," she called for the second time that evening. The door opened slowly, and Brant stuck his head in.

"Everything okay in there? Did Sarali get you settled?"

"She certainly did. She's wonderful, Brant. However did you know I needed her?"

"I'm not completely uncivil, you know. I *am* the son of a duke, and I know how you ladies work. Especially you, Miss Kayla," he answered, face splitting in a mischievous smile.

Kayla got up from her perch on the bed and opened the door. "Get in here, you big cream puff," she demanded, pulling at his arm.

"I can't go in there, Kay. It wouldn't look decent," he answered, fully serious for a change.

"And when has that ever stopped you?" she shot back. His reluctance faded only a little, and she yanked him inside and shut the door behind him. Brant looked about like a cornered rat, and Kayla started to laugh.

"I'm not going to attack you in my bedroom just because you proposed to me, silly. We've slept side by side many times in total innocence. Do you really think I would take a chance of ruining things now?"

He looked a bit chagrined at that point, but was still a little wary. She decided it would be best to change the subject. She moved to the side of her bed and dug beneath the feather mattress, finding the hard lump in no time at all.

"Here. I know you want to see this."

Kayla flipped the latches of the long wooden case and lifted the lid. The Sapphire Flute lay within, almost welcoming her with its light. She lifted it tenderly, as if it were a newborn babe. Brant feasted on the flute with eyes of wonder and reached out one tentative hand to touch the shining blue form.

"Is it . . . ?" he asked.

"It's okay, love. You can touch it. I don't think it can be broken."

He smiled warmly at her and took the slender instrument into his large hands. He raised it to his lips.

"No!" Kayla lunged at him, alarmed. "You mustn't play it!"

He lowered it, puzzled. "Why not?"

"It could destroy the world."

Brant laughed.

Kayla was a bit offended and took the instrument from him.

"Please, Kayla. Don't put it away. Who told you it would destroy the world?"

"The king," she snapped.

"Kayla," he purred her name. His strong hands gripped her elbows and turned her around. "King Rojan is known to overreact to danger. I have heard that flute played myself. I was very young, but I do remember its tones, and I have longed to hear them again. Don't you think that if this flute was going to destroy the world, it would have done so then?"

Kayla was not sure. She, too, had heard the flute as a child and wondered the same thing. She wavered.

"Play for me, Kayla," he begged. "I want to hear those perfect tones played by your lips."

What he said made sense. Why would playing the flute destroy the world now, when it hadn't before? There was no logic to it, and she *had* heard of the king's overprotective sense of responsibility and caution. Perhaps Brant was right. What would it hurt?

But no. She'd made a promise to her king to guard the flute, to protect it and save it for The Chosen One. How could she call herself honorable if she went back on her word, just because her love asked her to do so?

"Not now, Brant," she replied, slipping into his arms. Maybe she wouldn't have to make that decision. Perhaps he would forget. Perhaps she could *make* him forget. "Maybe later."

"I can be very persuasive," he whispered in her ear. "Very persuasive, indeed." He bent his lips to hers, and his kiss made time fade away.

She broke from him after much too long. Even she was worried about the impropriety of the situation now. She had no idea how much time had passed. Lost in his kiss as she had been, she lost all track of time.

And then the dinner bell rang. That made it all too clear how long he'd been there—much too long for propriety's sake.

"You have to go, Brant. I've got to change, and I'm half-starved—"

"Okay, okay, Kayla. I get the point. I'm going. I'll meet you downstairs," he said, smiling, and kissed her once more.

"Get out of here!" She laughed, pushing away from him. "You're distracting me."

"That's kind of the point," he said, waggling his eyebrows at her. Kayla could take no more, and though she smiled the whole time, she put her long fingers in the middle of his chest and physically shoved him out the door, slamming it in his face. His laughter continued to echo down the hall as he went to dinner.

Kayla tried to pull her dress off over her head, and only succeeding in getting her laces tangled in her hair combs and jewels.

The door creaked open. "'Tis Sarali, miss. Would ye need any help afore dinner?" she asked in sweet tones that thankfully did not laugh at Kayla's plight.

"Please!" Kayla begged. Somehow the girl unwound her, got her free in record time, and continued at that breakneck pace with which she seemed to do everything. Kayla was dressed, laced, combed, and set, with hair and make-up in place in ten minutes flat, and Sarali hadn't even paused over Kayla's evahn ears. She was tempted to see if she could steal Sarali away from Brant when she finally received her title. A thought occurred that warmed her heart—Sarali might just come with the package if she married Brant.

Kayla stepped outside into the hall and pulled the door shut behind her. She took a deep breath and held it, trying to resume the mask she'd become so accustomed to wearing. It was a little more difficult today with all the joy she'd found. Still—the duchy was not yet hers. She checked her hair one last time to be sure the tops of her ears were hidden, then stepped down the stairs calmly, her head and back straight and tall.

The dining room was filled with people. Kayla stopped on the bottom step and scanned the room, overwhelmed by the bright colors and cacophony of sound. The voices echoing through the cavernous room with its massive stone walls almost deafened her sensitive ears.

There were so many voices, it was difficult to discern one from the other but for an occasional laugh that carried above the crowd. Instead of trying to block the sound, Kayla listened deeply, much as she would to a new symphonic piece. Bit by bit, the annoying grate on her ears softened into sections similar to an orchestra. The drunken gamers to her right became the deep brass and drums, while the tittering women to her left became the high wind section. It was a trick she'd learned long ago. It made these largely attended parties a much more enjoyable experience, and she'd learned a lot about the people in the process.

An annoying rumble sounded from somewhere near Kayla's midsection. The last she'd eaten had been the two sausage rolls in the square, hours ago. The tables nearly groaned with food, and her mouth watered. She took the final step into the dining room and moved almost hypnotically toward the table to her left, nearest where the cackling women stood. They silenced as she approached.

Kayla nodded as she walked past them. Their silence continued as she made her way to the side buffet and picked up a handful of grapes, grateful the duke was kind enough to put out some pre-dinner snacks. The women didn't deign to respond, but turned their backs and whispered behind their hands, eyes glancing nervously at her as they walked past toward the king's table. Few were as accepting of her half-evahn status as King Rojan and Brant's family. She never let it show, but the needles were there, pricking her heart.

Kayla was eyeballing a turkey leg when the final dinner bell rang. She snatched her hand away and faced the steward of Dragonmeer as he pounded his staff twice on the floor.

"Dinner is served," the elderly man announced with dignity, then turned himself back to the kitchen.

Brant came up behind her and took hold of her arm. "Where have you been? Everybody's waiting."

"Everybody? Brant, where are we going? There's a good spot right . . ." Kayla trailed off as he led her to a chair at the high table. Never in all her years of being Brant's best friend had she been invited to sit with his family. The high table sat on a dais just before the fireplace, framed on each side by a curved stairway leading to the second floor. It was a mark of honor to be seated there, and a thrill surpassed only by that of meeting the king and receiving the Sapphire Flute.

At the duke's side stood the tattooed Ketahean, Sarali's husband. It was the first good look Kayla had gotten at him. She stared openly as Brant pulled out her chair and waited for her to sit before he scooted her close to the table. The large chef caught her eye and gave a slight nod of his head in all seriousness. He then turned and sliced a piece of meat, taking it daintily on the tip of his knife, and presented it to the duke. Brant's father took the slice, sampled it, and nodded. The tattooed man set down the knife, placed his hand on his opposite shoulder and bowed. Kayla stiffened with surprise as she saw the spikes and swirls that lined his hand. The chef was the cowled man she'd seen twice that morning, the one who'd been in the king's presence just before her. What in the world would he have been doing there? Why would a chef meet with King Rojan?

103

The Ketahean filled the duke's plate and left the room, which seemed to signal the servants to fill plates for the other guests. Within moments, the smell wafting under her nose had her mouth watering.

Finally the duke stood, his silver goblet lifted in toast. "To Kayla Kalandra Felandian, performer extraordinaire!" He raised his cup and drained it. "To Kayla!" the room responded, though Kayla noticed that not everyone joined Duke Domanta in his exuberance. Her resolve strengthened by another notch. She would not let them ruin her night. This was *her* ball, *her* dinner, and their petty prejudice would not make it any less magnificent.

The duke sat down, picked up a roll, and slathered it with butter. That was the sign to begin. Kayla dug in with fervor. She forked a piece of steak that had already been cut and nearly choked on it. Not because it was bad; no, quite the opposite. The flavor was so intense that for a moment she could do nothing but chew and swallow the juices that overwhelmed her.

"This is delicious, Brant. What's it seasoned with?" she asked when she could finally speak.

He shrugged. "Who knows? It certainly is good, though. Chef T'Kato has certainly outdone himself this time. Most everything he cooks has a bite to it. It makes me sweat, but I can't seem to get enough." Brant took a bite from his roll and gestured with his knife as he spoke. "He's new, you know, from Ketahe." He leaned forward, lowering his voice to a loud whisper. "You should see him, Kay. He's got tattoos all over his head and down his arms. He looks entirely vicious, but he's gentle as a kitten, though he doesn't speak a word of our language."

"I know. I saw him, remember?" she added after swallowing another bit of the spicy steak.

"Oh, that's right, I forgot already. I'm always so distracted when I'm in your presence." Brant flashed a toothy smile at her. "So," he changed the subject, "are you going to play for us tonight?"

Kayla laughed. "I don't know. Are you going to play with me?"

Brant grimaced and leaned back in his chair. "Are you kidding? I can never match your ability, Kayla. You put me to shame."

"Maybe," she said, "but it sure is fun. Seriously, Brant, you're pretty good. Why not play with me? Please?" she wheedled, batting her eyelashes furiously.

Brant laughed out loud. The other members of the table glanced over at him, but went quickly back to their food and chatter.

"How can I resist that?" He winked, then took her hand under the table and squeezed it softly. Kayla's heart glowed. It would have beamed as bright as the moon, if it could.

"Kayla, *darling!*" an elderly male gushed from just behind her chair. His heavy hand settled on her shoulder just a little too hard. His falsely sweet tones grated on her ears like a beginning violinist. Suddenly, her stomach turned sour, and she wasn't hungry.

Kayla pushed her chair back, turned, and plastered a cold smile on her face.

"Why, Grandfather, whatever brings you to Dragonmeer?" she said in the same insincere tones he used. The old man despised her every bit as much as she hated him. He was supposed to be sick—he was the reason Kayla's mother and uncle couldn't come. He had something up his sleeve—he always did.

"Congratulations on your performance and pending title," he said a little too loudly. "I understand the king made you the new keeper of the Sapphire Flute."

Kayla reddened with anger. That was the last thing she had wanted him to know. Somehow she kept her mouth civil, locking her jaw just long enough to gain her composure. He saw through her; she could see it in his eyes. The man was truly enjoying her discomfiture.

It amazed Kayla that her dignified, kind, and loving mother could be even remotely related to the man. His coldness had forced his daughter to look for love wherever she could find it, thus her unapproved marriage to an outsider and resulting half-breed daughter. Kayla's mother had squirmed out from under his thumb, and that maddened the man until he came to this. Oh yes, he enjoyed every bit of torment he could inflict on them, as if punishing Kayla for her mother's choices would make any difference.

Kayla pulled her feelings back behind their walls and stood her full height to look down on him, not cowering before him as she knew he wished. She could see the spark of anger light and quickly smother in his eyes.

He's up to something, her heart whispered again.

Her grandfather leaned close and hissed in her ear, his breath bitter and smoky. "You've been working awfully hard to gain favor, little Kayla," he said, a note of nastiness creeping into his voice. "I told your mother I would be willing to bring her back into favor if you would play that darling little toy of yours."

Little *toy?* Was he calling the Sapphire Flute a toy? How dare he! Realization set in then, and Kayla saw his game. Somehow he knew that he asked the impossible of her. In his sick, twisted mind, he thought he'd come up with a way to sabotage her bid for power. Once again the responsibility for the family name was placed on her shoulders. It was too heavy to bear.

But . . . she knew how to play that game as well. She squared her shoulders and curtsied. "But of *course,* Grandfather. It would be such an *honor* to play for you. Just let me go and fetch my little *toy.*" She couldn't help the anger that crept in her voice then, so she ignored it and continued. "You wait right here like a good boy," she patted his cheek, "and I'll be right back." She turned and walked back up the stairs to her room with all the poise she could muster.

So—the gloves were off and swords were drawn. Grandfather expected her to fail. He had thought she would say no, and that was the last thing she could do. Should she listen to the king and not play the Sapphire Flute? Or play for her grandfather and prove her worth?

The question was moot, really. The answer came to her then, and she smiled to herself with anticipation. Oh yes, indeed, she would prove her worth, and not just with her abilities. She'd outsmart the fox this time, with witnesses for a change. She would defeat him in this game and send him crawling home for however long he had left to live.

She grabbed her flute case and dashed back down the stairs. Brant glanced at her face and quickly wiped his mouth before scrambling to his feet. "Ladies and gentlemen, we have the pleasure now of hearing from our guest of honor, Miss Kayla Kalandra Felandian." Brant swept his arm toward her, giving her the floor.

Kayla moved to the center of the room, took her flute from the case, and handed the box to someone nearby—she didn't know who and didn't care. Placing the flute to her lips, she took a deep breath, squeezed her eyes shut, then released her breath slowly on a high note that quickly plummeted into the depths of her range.

It was a song of sadness, determination, and triumph—a song she had never before played in public, for it was the song that opened her very self—her soul song. It was not long, nor as complex as some of the other pieces she'd done, but she played it with all the feeling in her soul. As a writer pours their heart on the page, so she put it in her breath. She kissed the flute with music once more, and when she was done, not a sound could be heard. As had her performance that morning, it brought the room to absolute stillness.

Everyone seemed to breathe together before they surged to their feet, applauding madly. The three women who had spurned her before now stood with thoughtful tears. The oldest nodded her head in Kayla's direction, and she responded in kind.

Only one did not applaud. He approached, his face red and lips drawn tight.

"That is not what I asked of you, child. Do you really think you can compete with me?" he snarled.

Kayla smiled. "Why ever would I do that? You asked for me to play my 'little *toy*,' and I did. What more could you mean?"

"I asked you to play the other flute, the special one." He leaned in close, spittle flecking his lips.

"I can't play that one."

"Ha! I knew it," he shouted. The room quieted again as its occupants finally noticed the tension between them.

Kayla could take no more. She turned to the duke's table, but brought the entire room into the conversation.

"Ladies, gentlemen, my grandfather has made a request, and I would hear your word on the matter. I am sure most of you know by now that the king has given me guardianship over a very special instrument—the flute played by his own grandfather, the Sapphire Flute."

Murmurs and gasps could be heard among the gathering. Evidently not everyone had received the news yet.

"*That* man has asked me to play it—and I would like nothing more—but I face a quandary. When King Rojan gave me guardianship of the instrument, he told me, very explicitly, that playing the flute would call C'Tan and S'Kotos down upon us, for they want this instrument desperately. Now, I would ask you, which of these two men should I heed this night? My grandfather, who tries to win me with bribes? Or the king, who is concerned for the safety of this people?"

All were still for a long moment. Then Brant's voice started a chant that was quickly picked up by the rest of the room. "The king. The king. The king," they said over and over again.

Kayla turned to her grandfather. His face changed from mortified embarrassment to purple fury.

"You can forget the offer, Kayla. I wouldn't take you in if I had no other family left to inherit. You are an outcast, a leper to me—"

Kayla cut him off. "Oh, save it, old man. I don't need you, and neither does the rest of the family. You've done nothing but taunt and torment us with your whims for the entirety of your life. No more." She spat the words at him. "What you choose to do with your inheritance is no longer my concern, but if you continue this way, you are going to die angry and very much alone."

Kayla cradled the flute in the crook of her arm and stood tall once more. "I will *not* play the Sapphire Flute for you, Grandfather—not today, not tomorrow, not ever. You are not worthy of it. That flute is a gift from the Guardians, meant to bring joy and light and life to the people. You have neither light nor joy, and I will not cower before you any longer. Goodbye, Grandfather. I doubt you'll be seeing me again."

The man's face had continued to purple throughout the speech, and finally he turned without a word and stalked from the silent room. He stopped before he left the archway and spoke over his shoulder. "Perhaps you are my grandchild after all, Kayla. Good show, child. Good show."

His words were nearly a physical blow to her heart. He was right. It was exactly the kind of thing he would have done. Set your enemy up where it causes the most harm and then watch them fall while you laugh—only Kayla wasn't laughing.

As a matter of fact, she was surprised to realize there were tears coursing down her cheeks. She wiped them away with an angry fist and wound her way through the buzzing crowd toward the stairs that led to her room. She was no longer hungry in the least. Her stomach was too full of acid and guilt.

A single person began to applaud. Kayla stopped just before the stairs and slowly turned. That one person turned into three, then three into ten, and before long the entire room was applauding and whistling nearly as much as they had when she played that morning.

People moved aside to form a path. Brant pushed his way through, still applauding, until he stopped just in front of her and let his hands rest with a final clap. He stared into her eyes for a long moment, then took her in his arms and kissed her soundly in front of the entire room. Kayla stiffened at first, very aware of the faces gaping around her, but within seconds she was as involved in his kiss as she had been that afternoon. It was as good as an announcement of their engagement. The room erupted into even louder cheers, if that were possible.

Brant pulled away, still cradling her in his arms, and shouted into her evahn ears, the room was so loud. "I'm proud of you, Kay. That took a lot of guts."

"Yes, it did," an unexpected voice came from the doorway, though how he'd heard Brant, Kayla didn't know.

It was King Rojan.

The room quieted and dropped immediately into deep bows and curtsies as he passed. The king ignored them and crossed the room to grip Kayla's arms.

"You have proven yourself tonight even better than I imagined you could. You've earned the right to a title, young or old. Kayla Kalandra Felandian, I hereby declare thee Duchess of Driane, with all the rights and responsibilities inherent therein. That should do for now." The king grinned boyishly. "Driane's been abandoned for quite a while, so you're going to have some serious clean-up to do. Some of the businesses have been running under the stewardship of the kingdom, so I'll hand those back to you. You'd better find a steward pretty quickly, child, or running a castle is going to overwhelm you."

Kayla was astonished. It was everything she had ever wanted. A title, prestige for her family and herself once more, and to be wed to the one man in her life who had truly accepted her for who she was. What more could she ask? "Thank you, Your Highness," she said, her mind still spinning. He bowed to her before turning his back and walking away. Brant immediately took her in his arms once more and hugged her tight, the crowd roaring around them.

The question echoed through Kayla's head for the next hour as everyone wanted to be near and congratulate her. *What more could she ask?*

And yet . . . her heart still lay full of longing as she thought of the silken length of the Sapphire Flute. Why could she not play it? How could C'Tan hear a flute played from distant lands, or maybe even across oceans from where she was? It did not seem possible, and yet King Rojan had explicitly told her not to play it.

Once all the congratulations had been given, Kayla found herself back in her room, caressing the Sapphire Flute and wondering what it would feel like to play it, just once. A single note couldn't hurt anything, could it?

The instrument seemed to rise of itself to her lips. She just wanted to feel it there and know what it would be like to play it.

She blew softly. There was no sound, but Kayla felt the power in the air just with the vibration her wind caused. It thrilled her in a way even Brant's kisses could not. Her entire body ached with the need to play the glorious tones this flute could produce, and yet . . . she could not.

Kayla hung her head and reluctantly lowered the instrument from her lips. She might not understand the king's reasons, but still he was her king, and she dared not jeopardize everything she'd worked so hard for. She would bow to his wishes—for now.

She laid the flute back in its wooden case, then buried it deep within her feather mattress for safekeeping. She knew if she carried it around, someone would entice her to play, and she would give in much too easily.

She quickly undressed and hung her new gown, intent only on one thing—knowing the flute was safe beneath her as she slept.

Chapter Nine

Ember dashed at the tears that hadn't stopped since she stepped out of the house and left her sobbing mother behind. She had fully expected Marda to throw open the door and chase after her, had hoped for it even, but she never came.

As the ash turned to gray mud falling from the heavens, Ember drew in a deep breath and darted across the field to the warm comfort of the barn, more grateful than ever for Ezeker's weather charm. The mage lights came up as soon as she entered, the twins having respelled them when they cast their own magelights over the field. She stopped for a moment to blink away the light blindness after the almost pitch-dark of the ash and rain-filled sky.

Brownie whickered as Ember drew near to the dark mare that had been her favorite for so long. "Hey, girl," she said as she stroked the horse's neck. "How about a ride? You feel up to that, huh?" The mare nodded as if she understood. Sometimes Ember thought she just might.

Ember's saddle was at the back of the barn resting on an old sawhorse. Reins and lead ropes hung in loops on the wall above. Ember took down the reins and threw the saddle over her shoulder before she turned back to Brownie. She had tightened the belly strap on the mare when the barn door swung open again. Ember tensed for a moment, unsure now if she wanted to see her mother, if it meant she would try to stop her from going to the trials. But it wasn't Marda.

Aldarin stepped into the warmth of the light, a satchel under his arm and a bag in his hand. He didn't say a word—just went to the back of the barn and returned with a saddlebag he packed as he walked. He threw the satchel over Brownie's rump and strapped it on, then turned and gathered Ember in his arms. "That took a lot of guts," he whispered. "You're doing the right thing."

Ember burst into tears again. She couldn't help it. Much as she and her mother disagreed and fought, she did love her, and it was tearing Ember apart to know how much she'd just hurt her. "I had to do it, didn't I?" she asked her stepbrother. "Do you think she'll ever understand?"

"Shhh," he whispered, rubbing her back. "She'll get over it. Let it go. You did what you had to—though when I told you to take control of your life, I never expected you to do it in such a grand manner."

Ember laughed and pulled away from Aldarin. She sniffed, then wiped at her cheeks. Aldarin smiled, took her face in his hands, and kissed her forehead. "I'm proud of you, Sis. Now get out of here. Ezeker is expecting you."

"What? How could he know I'd be coming tonight?"

"I told him. Just now." Aldarin tucked some small foodstuffs in the saddlebag and buckled it, then laced his fingers together and bent forward to give her a boost up.

Ember didn't move. "How?"

Aldarin gave her a lopsided grin. "I've got my ways."

She rolled her eyes. It wasn't worth the time it would take to discover his secrets. She placed her foot in his open hands and heaved herself into the saddle. She looked down to see his hand outstretched, holding a piece of white parchment. She took it, recognizing the scrawl on the front. It was the note Paeder had given her.

"Paeder wanted to make sure you read that before you left. I packed the rest of your gifts in the saddlebag and put some travel food and apple pudding in there, too." He gave her leg one more pat, then turned to go. He jumped back, startled, as Tiva ran in, nearly colliding with him.

"Father's bad, Marda needs you, can you call Ezeker?" He burst it all out in one breath, his eyes wide.

Ember moved to get down from the horse, but Aldarin turned with an outstretched hand.

"No, Ember. Now is your chance. There's nothing you can do, and you might miss your opportunity to get to the trials. Go."

"But—"

"No buts, Sis. Go."

Ember couldn't decide which part of her heart to listen to—the one that told her to help her stepfather, or the one that longed for the mage trials. Aldarin made her mind up for her when he slid the barn door open wide and pointed.

Ember chewed at her lip before giving Aldarin one brief nod. He waved and left the barn with Tiva almost as quickly as the twin had come, the side door still open and swinging in the wind. Murky gray rain spattered the hay in the entryway as Ember readied herself to go. She went to tuck the envelope in her breast pocket, but thought better of it. She held it in front of her for a long second, broke the seal, and began to read.

My dearest Ember,

I know you have loved Brownie since the night you helped me bring her into the world, and I believe she loves you every bit as much. If I know you as well as I think I do, you will not let your mother dictate your life and will be soon heading for the mage trials. Go with my blessing and love. As sick as I am, I wanted to give you a gift, a legacy that you can call your own, and perhaps remember me fondly in the process. Brownie and Diamond Girl are yours. Contained within this letter are the papers naming you their owner. Keep them safe.

Please keep in touch, daughter, and I hope that I may call you that, for daughter of my heart you are. I know that I cannot take the place of your father, but I hope I have been a father of sorts to you. I do love you, child, with all my heart, and probably even a little more than some of my rascally sons, though please don't tell them I said so.

Marda has consented to take me to see the Mage Council, and I do not know if I shall see you again, though I hope it may be so. If not, at least I can go to my grave knowing I have been loved by three of the greatest of women, and have created three of the finest of sons. If indeed you do come to the mage trials, find me. I would like to see you again before I die.

If anyone can become a mage by force of will alone, Ember, it will be you. I pray for your success so your mother might at last see you for the brilliant star you are.

Eternally my love,
Your 'other' father

Ember was in tears again by the time she reached the end of the letter. She'd always known Paeder was a good man; she'd just never known how much that affected her personally until now. She hoped and prayed she'd have the chance to see him again and tell him how much his letter meant to her. For the first time in her life, she felt like she had a real father, and couldn't stand to think of losing him so soon.

Ember wiped at her tears again, tucked the papers in her pocket for safekeeping, and gave Brownie a nudge. She didn't need Diamond Girl right now, but she'd return the first moment she could to collect her inheritance. She tried not to think on Paeder's illness and instead let her thoughts settle on his kindness and goodness.

Fortified by his love, Ember nudged Brownie forward. The horse willingly stepped through the barn door and into the muddy rain.

The high road wasn't three minutes from Ember's home, and she reached it quickly, even in the dark. The magelights that lined the highway still weren't working, though whether they had been covered by mud or if the fluctuating energy from the volcano had taken them out, she didn't know. It was darker than she'd ever seen it—so dark she could barely see the trees that edged the road.

She walked Brownie slowly for several minutes down the highway. The weather charm would keep her dry, but it certainly wouldn't prevent a broken leg or cracked head if they slipped and fell. Ember glanced at the shadows along the edges of the road and shivered. Her imagination summoned up all kinds of monsters that could attack her from the dark, and she had to fight the urge to nudge Brownie into a run. She just wanted to be safe in Ezeker's tower until morning.

Lost in her thoughts, Ember nearly jumped out of her skin when a voice hailed her from the darkness.

"Ho, the road! Would you be willing to help a traveler out? I'm looking for Horsemaster Paeder's farm. Might you know where I could find it? I can't see a thing in this weather."

Ember got her heart rate under control and chuckled nervously. "Yes, sir, you're almost there, though I must warn you, he's quite ill. I'm not sure he'd be up to a visitor tonight."

"Pity, that. Might you know if he's got a girl there, a brunette, about fifteen or sixteen seasons?"

"Why do you ask, sir?" Her heart started to race again. Why would a stranger be looking for her? Had C'Tan found her already? "I don't recollect any girls there, sir. What did you say her name was?"

The stranger chuckled, a low menacing sound that sent ice up Ember's spine. "I didn't, but judging by the fear coming off you, I'd say you're lying through your straight little teeth. Oh, yes, I can see them. Hello, Shandae. Your aunt sends her greetings."

Ember had just enough time to register his words, to realize the relationship Aldarin had implied earlier, that C'Tan was her *aunt*, before a sharp pain in the back of her head sent blackness to envelop her completely.

She awoke to a splitting head and the smell of roasting meat. The snap of the fire and the pitter-pat of rain echoed through her head with devastating effect. She wanted to moan with the pain, but held herself still, cracking her eyes open enough to see she was in a cave. A man crouched before a campfire with what looked like a skewered rabbit held over the flame. He was completely bald, though fairly young, and his muscles bulged almost grotesquely. The man was huge, nearly a freak of nature. She examined him closely for several moments but didn't move, not wanting to draw attention to herself. He said nothing, then caught her eyes with his own. They were an icy blue, so light as to be almost white. Somehow he had known she was awake.

He spoke, his voice startling her into a jump. "Get a good look-see?" He chuckled. "I thank you for your kind gifts." The man fingered the weather charm that now lay over his neck. "The sky doesn't rain mud where I come from. It was getting rather annoying. Of course, the sky doesn't send out much of anything there." The man's grin was toothy and too big for his face, much like that of a cat taunting its prey. "The horse will be a nice addition as well. Poor Neemus was getting a little worn out from all the travel."

Ember glanced past his bald head to see Brownie staked to the ground just outside the small cave. She had no idea where she was. The hills surrounding Karsholm were dotted with caves, she knew, as she'd explored a good many of them with her stepbrothers over the years, but this one was unfamiliar.

Ember didn't say anything. She tried to sit up, but couldn't move. Her hands and feet were shackled in front of her and staked to the ground just like her horse, though how the man had put a stake in the rocky ground of a cave, she didn't know. She lay in a puddle, just far enough away from the fire to be cold. She shivered.

The man noticed and grinned his toothy grin once more. "Get used to it—you're not going anywhere. The mistress wants to see you. She's been looking for you a very long time." He glanced at her hands. "You're a little young for tattoos, aren't you? I thought that was a Ketahean tradition. I've not seen many around here." Ember didn't answer. She wouldn't have if she could, but at the moment, her heart raced, her fear thick and choking.

The big man snorted and rolled his eyes at her, obviously amused by her stubborn silence. It only made her mad. She struggled against the chains that held her fast, but she was stuck good and solid. If only she could change the metal like she had changed her dress, maybe she could escape. She closed her eyes and concentrated. The image of chain turning to water was so brilliant in her mind, she could almost feel it happening. There was a build-up, a burning in her hands where the cuffs had become one with her skin, but just as she felt something was about to happen, the power trickled away to nothing—like a hole in a bucket.

The bald man chuckled, a very satisfied, smirky sound that set Ember's teeth on edge.

"It won't work, Shandae. The chains are spelled."

"How do you know my name? And who are you?"

The man shrugged. "Name's Ian. Been looking for you for a long time. We knew who you were, but not who you'd become. It wasn't until this afternoon that I finally zeroed in on Karsholm. You finally came into your power, didn't you." It wasn't a question, and it chilled Ember's stomach that he knew so much about her. She'd escaped notice all these years, and now Ian just happened to be close enough to sense the change when it came. Couldn't it have waited just one day? One more day and she would have been with Ezeker, one of the most powerful mages in the country, safe on the road to Javak, surrounded by an armed guard. One day more and she could have seen her dream fulfilled of reaching the mage trials. Instead she had the bitter taste of defeat.

Ember let her head relax against the ground, wishing with all her heart she could just melt into it, disappear as if she'd never been.

Suddenly the cold stone grasped Ember's ear as if it had sunk into mud, and she gasped, jerking upright, or at least as upright as she could with the chains holding her down. They dug painfully at her wrists.

Ian looked at her and quirked an eyebrow, turning his rabbit in the fire. Hot grease dripped to sizzle in the flames. A log popped as he spoke. "What, a mousie get you? Afraid of the dark? I'd have thought the wolfchild would be a better opponent than this. The Guardians sure didn't choose well this time around, now, did they?" He continued to chuckle to himself as Ember digested this new information. Wolfchild? Guardians? At least he hadn't realized why she had really gasped. She could live with him thinking she was afraid of mice.

For the first time since she'd awakened, Ember felt a small flicker of hope. She hadn't been able to affect the chain, but she *had* been able to affect her own body by wishing she could disappear. She didn't dare sink into the stone entirely—it might never let her go, but if she could change such a small thing as her ear to penetrate the ground, perhaps she could change herself enough to get away from this man.

A ghostly white bird flitted across the cave opening and settled on Brownie's rump. It screeched, almost sounding angry. The man looked up, then turned back to his dinner. The bird called again, and Ember realized with a start it was the same hawk she'd seen twice that day already. The bird caught her eye and sounded one last time. Ember was chilled to hear another voice join in as the hawk trailed off—a wolf howl, and close by, she was sure.

Brownie pulled against the stake and screamed.

"What . . . ?" Her kidnapper dropped his rabbit skewer and started for the cave entrance as the howling grew in volume, another wolf joining the first. Brownie pulled steadily at her tether now, Ian nearly hanging on her reins trying to hold her. The other horse started to panic as well, and Ian seemed to forget Ember in the excitement.

Now was her chance. The wolves had given her an idea, and Ember focused all her thoughts and energy into the image that had come to her. The dress and her ear had been completely accidental, but now she put all her energy into hearing the sounds of the wolves and yearned with all her heart to join them. She had watched a wolf one night as she sat on the roof, its white coat gleaming in the darkness, and now as she lay there on the cold stone, she begged her body to *become* one. It was almost easy, she found, as if she had discovered a second form that her body knew more intimately than she knew herself.

It was strange, feeling her body shrink and mold, her jaw expanding out from her face and her limbs thinning and straightening. It hurt, there was no denying that, but it was tolerable until a tail burst from her back-side. *That* hurt like nothing else. It took her breath away. But by the time she became aware of herself again, the transformation was complete. In a matter of seconds, she went from being chained and bound to the floor to shaking her white fur and scrambling out of the restraints. She tried to shake off what appeared to be chains still attached to her fur, but then realized she was seeing the shape and shadow of the bracelets that had embedded into her skin that morning. Evidently, her shift into wolf shape wouldn't take away the gray tattoos, even when in fur. She wondered if the gray pendant still marked her sternum. It didn't matter at the moment. She had to get away while Ian was distracted. She wobbled for a moment, trying to get used to the balance of four feet and a tail, but the adjustment came quickly, and she darted toward the cave entrance.

Ian yelled at her and let go of the horses to try to grab her. The white hawk swooped at his head, distracting him long enough for Ember to streak past.

Ember was clumsy at first, trying to coordinate front and back legs. She tripped several times before she found her balance and rhythm, then she took off on all fours, the wind ruffling her fur, her nose assaulted by scents she had never noticed before, her eyes finally able to see in the near dark as she darted in and out among the trees toward whatever safety she could find. The hawk screeched from up ahead, and Ember could see its glowing form flowing easily through the forest. Ian thundered through the woods behind her, much faster than she'd thought possible without a horse to carry him, but he wasn't fast enough to catch up with her. She was the wind riding through the forest, the shine of moonlight on a midnight pool.

She was wolf.

The wolves called again, and this time she not only heard, but understood. *Come run with us. Join us, wolfchild!*

One by one, the lupines darted out from amongst the trees and surrounded her, running with her in joy, guarding, guiding, strengthening her with the pack. A huge white wolf came through the group to her side, his tongue lolling out like an oversized puppy, though he was anything but. *Follow us to safety, wolfchild. We have much on which to speak.*

Chapter Ten

C'Tan waved her hand to banish the mirror, as she did every morning, and pulled her scarlet robe closed, gathering illusion around her face, creating the image, the memory of the past that walked with her each day. She hated the falseness of it, longed for the image to be made real again and to be free, but that could not be as long as she was bound to her master, chained to S'Kotos. Only the keystones could free her, and the blasted things could not be found. It infuriated her endlessly, day after day, and all she could do was continue the search that maddened her with its slowness.

She heard the steady step of the aged one long before he appeared at her door. She kept her back to him and made him wait. It was a game they had played since first she met him, when he had been the teacher and she the slave. But the roles had reversed, and she had come to live for these dangerous battles for power and position.

"You're early, Kardon," she snarled.

"I am well aware of that, mistress, but I thought you would be most anxious for my report." He stopped speaking and waited for her to respond. And so the game continued, with her issuing threats and commands, him responding with as little information as possible. Someday she would make him angry, she was sure of it, and fireworks would erupt between them, the kind of fireworks she would be lucky to survive. Until then, they continued the game.

"Report then, Kardon."

"One of the keystones has manifested itself."

That was enough to make C'Tan turn quickly and face him. "Which one?" she demanded.

"The Sapphire Flute, my lady."

Her lips parted as a slow smile spread across her face. Though any other person would have been chilled to see how the smile never reached her eyes, Kardon would not flinch. Why should he, when he was the one who had taught her the coldness, had stolen her conscience, turned her into the monster she knew she had become? It sickened her, and yet she could not be anything else.

"Well, well, well. That is news worth hearing indeed." C'Tan strutted to the unmade mess of her bed and stood staring at the blank wall for several seconds. "Is it with the king?" she asked, her back to the menace of Kardon. She knew she tempted him, but she could not help herself. Part of her wished he would someday attack and they could finally battle out the hate between them—but today was not that day.

"No, mistress," he responded in a clipped whisper. "We have yet to determine who has it, but it is within the borders of Peldane."

"Anything more specific than that?" she asked, becoming annoyed. This was too important for him to hold back. The flute was the first of the stones that could set her free.

"There are rumors, my lady, but we have been unable to verify them."

She turned then and nearly thrust her power at him, but stopped herself. No. It was not the right time. She still had need of this weak man with his dangerous games, but the anger made her voice tight.

"Well, verify them or find me a source for the manifestations, but do not come back until you can tell me who has that flute!" she spat, menace dripping from her voice like acid.

"Yes, mistress," he answered, unruffled, and turned to leave. C'Tan stopped him with his name.

"Kardon," she called sweetly and waved her hand, pulling a small knife from the air and cleaning her nails with a soft scratch. "The next time you interrupt me in the early hours like this, I'll have your heart on a plate and serve it up to S'Kotos. Do you understand me?"

Kardon met her eyes, but did not blanch under their fiery gaze. "Yes, Lady C'Tan, I understand you perfectly."

Chapter Eleven

Kayla opened her eyes and blinked to clear them. The morning sun streamed through the window at an odd angle, the light coming from above rather than to the left. The walls here were made of cut gray stone instead of thin wood panels. Still lost in a blur of foggy sleep, she wasn't sure where she was until a light tap came at the door and Sarali poked her head through.

"Are ye awake now, miss? The master sent me up to fetch ye. Breakfast be on the table."

It all rushed back then—the banquet the evening before, being seated at the high table with Brant's family, the showdown with her grandfather. She smiled, tucking the covers beneath her chin. Dragonmeer. She was at Dragonmeer.

She threw back the heavy down comforter, sat up, and rubbed her eyes. "I'm awake. Tell the duke I'll be down shortly."

"Oh, the duke still be sleeping, miss. I don't imagine ye'd be seeing his face around the castle for many an hour still. Master Brant be leading the breakfast bunch, and he sent me up to fetch ye."

Kayla grinned. It was doubtful those were his exact words. She imagined he had said something more along the lines of, "Tell

Kayla to get her lazy backside out of bed and come join me." She nodded to the servant. The girl withdrew, shutting the door softly behind her.

Kayla sat on the side of the bed for a few moments, enjoying the warmth of the sunlight and the softness of the feather bed. It was a much more pleasant awakening than she usually had. Most mornings, she awoke before dawn to her mother calling from downstairs. Content, she scampered into the lovely clothes she had worn the night before. They were a little wrinkled, but they would have to do. She had brought nothing more than that and the outfit she had worn shopping the day before, which did not seem suitable for breakfasting with the duke's household. She would rather be overdressed than under, so she laced up the dress, glanced in the mirror, and prepared to leave. She turned to the door and spotted her unmade bed. There was one thing more she had to do before she left.

She pulled the Sapphire Flute from beneath her pillow where it had slept with her during the night, and opened the case to see its glowing blue length. It had a different feel to it today, as if more alive, more aware of her and itself. It had almost a presence, as if it were a person and not an inanimate object. Chills shivered Kayla to the core. She closed the case and shoved the flute deep beneath the feather mattress so it would remain hidden even if the maids came and made up the bed in her absence. Business accomplished, she smoothed her dress, took a few moments to brush her hair and twist it into style, and marched through the door.

It was strange, circling down these particular stairs after so many years of hiding on them and watching the parties take place through the slats of the railing. She and Brant had become quite adept at crashing the duke's parties and never getting caught. On numerous occasions they had foraged for food and watched the ladies and gents as they sang and danced and performed. The dancing had been fun, the jugglers and magicians funny, but the music had always set Kayla's heart to racing. She would sit entranced for hours, listening to the sound that filled the cavernous room. It had not mattered if they plucked the soft strings of a harp or trumpeted their horns—soloists or choirs, she was pulled into a world of dreams and imagination and magic when the music struck her ears.

Brant had learned early on that if he wanted to have any kind of fun with Kayla, he had to wait for the music to end. They sat on the balcony overlooking the great hall, nibbling at their stolen food, wrapped in blankets for warmth. How she missed those years. It was nice finally to be noticed for her accomplishments, but there was something to be said for the carefree days of childhood.

It looked as if Duke Domanta was not the only one feeling a little delicate this morning. Kayla noticed many missing faces, but all that mattered to her was that Brant was there. His eyes lit when she entered the hall, and he stood, waving his arm enthusiastically.

"Come in, come in!" he called, coughing over the bite of steak he had just crammed into his mouth. Kayla shook her head at him and smiled.

"You're going to choke one of these days if you don't slow down, Brant." In answer, he cut an even larger chunk and stuffed it in his mouth, growling as if he were a starving dog.

Despite his playfulness, Brant seemed distracted all through breakfast. He was much more quiet than usual and seemed almost sad. His sense of humor only returned at the end of the meal.

"I don't know how you do it, Kayla. You eat more than most men, and you stay so blasted skinny. Can't you just try to let me eat more than you? Just once?"

Kayla laughed. "Why should I? It keeps you humble, love. You can't be better at everything, you know," she said, taking his hand and winking at him.

"Right now I'm not better at anything," he grumbled, though his heart didn't seem to be in it.

For once Kayla didn't know what to say. Despite his joking manner, there seemed to be a hint of real bitterness in his tone. She looked at him sharply, but he said nothing more. So she let it drop as he tucked her hand into his arm and escorted her into more familiar territory—the stables.

129

"What are we doing here, Brant?" she asked, curious.

"You'll see." He gave her a smug smile. He patted her hand and left her standing on the cobblestones as he went to speak to the groomsman. The old man bobbed his head and retreated inside.

"Brant . . ." Kayla called, but Brant held up his index finger in the universal sign for "wait a minute."

What was he doing? He was behaving very strangely. The answer became apparent when the groomsman led matching white horses from the stable, mare and stallion.

"What's this?" she asked, awed by their beauty.

"A little gift. Would you like to ride?" he asked.

"Of course I would, but what do you mean, 'a little gift'? From whom? Why?"

"I'll explain later, love. Just ride with me for now," he pleaded. Kayla couldn't resist and didn't really want to. The animals were beautiful. She quickly mounted and had barely settled herself in the saddle when Brant spoke. "Race you to the river?" He grinned and dug in his heels without waiting for an answer.

"Hey! That's cheating! Wait for me!" She nudged the mare, who took off like a dream.

The horse's gait was smooth, as though she was floating instead of riding, and Kayla understood what people meant when they said they were "as one" with their mounts. She felt as if she were a part of the horse, her body embedded within the back of the animal, as they flew over the hills and through the swathes of forest that dotted Dragonmeer.

She sailed over stone walls and fallen logs faster than she ever had, and it reminded her of the feeling when she played the flute—specifically *Darthmoor's Honor*. The images she had of flight were similar to the feel of racing this horse across the land. In that moment life was complete, with no battle for position, no nagging parents or loveless grandfathers, no pain, no fear, no loss—just the perfection of being joined with someone else and running.

Joy welled up in her then—an emotion she had not truly had since that moment ten years before when she had learned what her birth had meant for her mother. She felt free and wanted the moment to last forever.

But that could never be.

Much too soon, the ride was over, and Kayla met Brant at the river's edge. The two of them arrived side by side in the final leg of the journey. It had ceased to be a race long before, and instead, they rode in companionable silence, though still at the fastest speed their horses could maintain together. Kayla was pleased to see that not only did the horses match each other in looks, they also matched pace, as if they were duplicates mirrored and reversed in gender, but still moving as one.

Brant dropped to the ground, pulling the reins over his stallion's head. He helped Kayla down and immediately took her into his arms. Her head nestled against his chest as she took in the musky, sweaty smell of him. She couldn't help the feeling of wonder that came over her. Brant would be hers. It was no longer a dream she was afraid to ponder, but a tangible thing standing before her.

Their horses began to wander and pulled against the two of them, forcing the separation neither was willing to initiate. Brant and Kayla laughed, a trifle ill at ease with each other for the first time. They were alone, no one around to judge or know how they behaved or whether they kept things proper, and Kayla would have been lying to say she was not tempted to tease Brant a little and see where it would lead.

But it was wrong. She could not start their life together with that on her conscience, so when he tried to pull her into his arms again, she danced away, laughing.

"Huh, uh, uh, Brant." She wagged a finger at him. "You know the rules."

"Yeah, but rules are meant to be broken, Kayla," he said, lunging for her, his eyes gleaming.

"Not these rules, Brant. Not for us," she said, holding her ground as he slowed and stopped before her, disappointed, but thoughtful. When she was sure he understood, she moved toward him, but he turned away.

"Brant, don't be like that," she said, hurt by his refusal.

"I'm not mad, Kayla, but I don't think it's a good idea for you to get too close to me right now," he answered, his back still to her. He moved down the stream in silence, picking up rocks here and there and skipping them out across the still waters. Kayla followed after him, unable to let him go far without her. It was as if a magnet were between them, pushing and pulling, but never allowing its opposite to wander.

"My father's not happy, you know," he said.

Kayla's heart lurched. "What do you mean, Brant? I thought you said he likes me."

Brant smiled over his shoulder, then continued his walk down the water's edge.

"He does. A little too much."

When he didn't expound, Kayla blew out an explosive breath. "What do you mean?" she demanded, trying to catch up with him. He finally let her.

"I've never seen the duke as angry as he was last night, and believe me, at that moment he was '*the duke,*' and not my father," Brant said, still not looking at her.

"Why?" Surprise and worry mixed like oil and vinegar, upsetting her stomach with their fervor.

"Because our announcement was so unexpected." He sighed. "The duke does not like surprises, especially in regards to his family. I guess once people knew we were attached, they started asking him questions, and he had no answers. He said I was inconsiderate and impulsive, and that if I planned to take over Dragonmeer, I had better start thinking of other people before blurting my plans to the world." Brant stopped and faced the river, tossing his pebbles into the water with distinct kerplunks that brought fish to the surface to investigate. "I guess more than anything, he was upset that I didn't tell him first so he could plan for it. The horses are a gift from him, an outward show of his approval. You know he likes you. He doesn't disapprove—he just wishes we'd informed him first."

"I'll have to thank him," she said, relieved it was nothing more than the duke's bruised ego that bothered her fiancé. She took Brant's hand, but he shook her off, turning away and moving toward the horses.

"I'm sorry, Kayla. I'm not trying to hurt you. It's just . . ." he paused, seeming to gather courage to speak, or perhaps find the words themselves. "He's right," he continued. "I should have told him when I first came home, but I was so caught up in the euphoria that I didn't even think of it. What kind of a son am I? What kind of duke will I be if I do nothing but think of myself first?"

"Hey, now," she reprimanded. "You're going to be a wonderful duke, every bit as good as your father. You're seeing him now after decades of practice being the man he is. I'll bet you he's had his embarrassing moments and failures too. You can't live in this world without making mistakes. You just have to own up to them and be aware so you don't make the same ones twice."

Brant was quiet for a long moment. She was about to speak again when he turned to face her, a light smile playing at his lips.

"How did you ever get to be so wise, Kayla Kalandra Felandian, soon to be Domanta?" he asked, wrapping his arms around her.

"Just born that way, I guess." She smirked as she gave him a light peck on the cheek, pulled out of his arms, and turned toward the horses. "Come on." She stepped to her beautiful new mare. "Let's get back before anybody misses us and starts passing around more of those ugly rumors."

Brant pursed his lips, but before he could answer Kayla had climbed onto her mare's back and dug her heels into the flanks. She surged back toward Dragonmeer, tossing her laughter behind her like a ribbon for Brant to catch.

"Hey!" Brant hollered, echoing her earlier call, but his laughter only spurred her faster. The race was on again.

This time Kayla was clearly the winner as she dismounted breathlessly in the courtyard and handed over her mare to the groomsman. Brant barreled into the yard just as she ran toward the front door. He didn't even stop his horse before he leaped from the animal, stumbled, then charged after her.

Kayla put on speed, her slippers perfect for moving quietly through the halls as she ran for her room. She had just reached the door when Brant caught her against him, gasping and laughing, and they tumbled through the doorway to lie in a giggling heap in the middle of her floor, the door gaping wide open.

Kayla scrambled up first. "I've got to change after all that exertion, love. You're going to have to wait outside."

Brant sighed, but picked himself up and strolled to the doorway. He stopped only to brush his lips lightly across hers before he exited the room. Kayla slammed the door, flushed both from the run and his attentions. She was determined not to let him get the upper hand, though her determination faded with the chuckle that sounded from the other side of the door.

She quickly shucked off her new dress and found her lavender gown hanging in the closet. She wiped the sweat from her body with lavender-scented water and a washcloth that had been left on her vanity. How thoughtful of Sarali to match the scented water with the shade of her dress. Kayla pulled on the gown and tied the sash around her waist. She headed for the door, but spotted her now-made bed and thought of the Sapphire Flute. She had to take just one more look before she left. Perhaps she would even let Brant join her in admiring the glowing instrument.

She thrust her arm beneath the feather bed to pull the flute from its hiding place, but it wasn't where she left it.

Maybe it got moved when the servants made the bed, she thought, reaching deeper, then sweeping her arm back and forth from top to bottom and side to side. It wasn't there. She ripped the clean blankets from the bed, then pulled the mattress itself out and scrambled around inside the frame. She searched corners and down the side nearest the wall.

The Sapphire Flute was gone.

Her knees turned to rubber, and she collapsed in a heap, panicked and tearful.

Where could it be? I know I put it under the mattress when I left. Who would have taken it?

Who wouldn't?

The questions circled around in her head like a wheel on a cart. She couldn't straighten her mind enough to find any answers. She had just assumed things would be safe in Brant's home. They'd never had many problems with thievery in Dragonmeer. And how would they have known it was there? Nothing else seemed to be missing, so it was obvious they came for that and that alone.

A knock sounded at the door, but Kayla hardly heard. She sat stunned, holding back the tears that burned her eyes and choked her throat. The knock came again, louder, more insistent. Kayla roused herself, just enough.

"Who is it?" she called, emotion causing her voice to warble.

"It's Brant. What's taking you so long?"

She surged to her feet and threw open the door.

"Do you have it, Brant?" she asked.

He took a step back. "Have what? Did someone steal from you?"

Kayla's face crumpled. She threw herself against him, sobbing into his shoulder. "It's gone, Brant! It was here when I left, and now it's gone!" She clung to him, and he alternately patted her back and caressed her hair.

"Shhh, Kayla, shhh. Tell me what's missing. I need answers before I can do anything." He held her at arms' length and met her eyes.

"Someone has stolen the Sapphire Flute! Oh, Brant, what am I to do?"

Chapter Twelve

Ember lost track of all time as she ran on four legs through the forest, the wind racing through her fur like a sparrow through the trees. It was exhilarating—all her senses heightened. Even as she ran with the wolf pack, she could hear the scurry of mice and insects through the leaves and smell the musty decay of the earth and the sharp tang of pine. She never tired, her tongue lolling in joy, much like the huge alpha wolf to her left. She couldn't help the expression and didn't care what she looked like. There was a large part of her that never wanted to go back, content to stay a wolf for the rest of her life.

The pack climbed higher, and now she felt the strain in her chest and hindquarters as she surged upward through the rocky terrain. Higher and higher, until it almost hurt to breathe, then just before a rocky outcropping, the lead wolf disappeared into the mountainside. Ember followed as, one by one, the wolves vanished into what appeared to be solid rock. When it came Ember's turn, she found that it was mere illusion. The slit in the rock opened into a huge cave.

Water dripped from the heights to collect in a pool near the center of the room. The pack skirted the edge of the water and ran farther into the cave, single file now as they wound through the crack that cut deep into the earth. Finally, when the drip-drip of the rain had stopped and all she could hear was the panting of her pack, the lead wolf stopped and turned to face her. All the wolves circled and dropped to their haunches, tongues hanging, as they breathed their exhaustion.

It was the huge white wolf who spoke to her, though the words came directly to her mind, never reaching her ears. *"Who are you, little one? Why have you not been taught the ways of the Bendanatu?"*

Ember wasn't sure how to answer and had no idea who the Bendanatu were. Out of habit, she tried to vocalize her thoughts, but all that came out was a series of yips, whines, and growls. She shook herself in frustration and tried to focus her thoughts. *"Who are the Bendanatu?"* was her first question.

The white wolf looked at her as if she were mad. *"We are the Bendanatu, the people of the wolf, servants of the Guardian Bendanatu. Night walkers, wolfmen, werewolves, wolfwalkers—we have been known by all these, and you are one with us. How can you not know this?"* He sniffed at her, then sneezed, a low growl coming to his throat.

Ember's heart raced. She was Bendanatu? A wolfwalker? How could that be? She thought she was just another magi hopeful. She knew so little about magic; she had just assumed the other wolves were shapeshifting magi like herself. Was this another of those things Marda had never bothered to tell her? She had no answers and began to panic at the restless growls coming from the pack.

"I don't know! Truly, I don't know any of these things. I've never changed before today. I didn't even know I had magic until this afternoon. Please, you have to believe me." Something occurred to her then. *"Maybe it came through my father. I never knew him. He died in a fire when I was only a year old."*

The big wolf stood, seemingly surprised, and sniffed her further. He gave one last long whiff, digging his nose in the center of her chest, right about where she figured her pendant must be showing silver on her fur. When the wolf sat back, a big grin split his face. *"Shandae?"*

It was the second time that night a stranger had asked after her as if he knew her. She was almost afraid to answer after her encounter with the big, bald man. But the pack had saved her. They deserved her honesty. *"Ember Shandae, yes—"*

The wolf howled, his eyes sparkling as though they held the moon. *"Ember Shandae, daughter of Jarin and Brina?"*

Ember was confused. He knew her father, but not her mother? That made no sense. *"My father is Jarin, yes, but my mother's name is Marda, not Brina."*

The wolf chuckled, and Ember heard it in her ears and head both. It was a strange sensation. *"It is of no matter what she calls herself these days. I know your scent now. I smell your father upon you, sense his magic, and you look so much like him you could be his twin."*

"How can I look like my father when I'm a wolf?" Ember asked.

He laughed again, and once more the sound echoed in her head and ears together. *"You've taken the same form as he. It must be in your blood. Come, let me show you."*

He got to his feet and wound back through the tunnel to the big pool. Ember followed his trail, still amazed by her heightened sense of hearing and smell.

"Look," he said, as a glowing ball of pale magelight appeared over their heads. Ember yelped, startled by the light, then feeling foolish, crept forward to look into the pool as he did. She felt a sense of awe when she caught sight of herself in the water. Her fur was white, though muddied with the gray ash that ran up her legs and dotted her back. She looked smaller than the other wolves, but she attributed that to her age, or gender.

The strangest part of her appearance, though, was the brilliant emerald green of her eyes. On a normal day, they were green, yes, but a faded, muted, almost mossy-colored green, like that of sage. That had changed with her transformation. Now they were bright, the color of emeralds or spring leaves, and seemed to glow from the inside out.

Ember glanced at the big wolf beside her and realized his eyes glowed with the same green light. They also shared the same snowy fur coloring. None of the other wolves were white. They were more the traditional grays and browns, but she and this giant of a wolf were very much the same. Why?

"Would you like to see your father?" he asked.

She didn't trust herself to speak, so only nodded. How could she not want to see him? She yearned to know what he looked like.

A low muttering sound resounded in Ember's head, like listening to a crazy old man or trying to overhear a conversation from outside a closed room. Occasionally she'd catch a word she knew, though most of them she could not understand. An image began to waver in the pool, an image that looked very much like the one she saw of herself—though larger in stature, with the same glowing green eyes and broad shoulders. He and the wolf at her side could have been twins for the similarities.

Ember started to get a nagging suspicion that she had more in common with this wolf than a reflection in the pool. The image in the water shifted, and she lost her breath. The wolf that was supposed to be her father became a man, and she could see the similarities of which the white wolf had spoken.

She shared her father's eyes and brow, his nose and chin, the same quirk to the mouth that she found so often in her own mirror. If she had been in her human form, she would have cried in sheer joy and sorrow. This was her father, the man whose memory she had lost in her youth. Now, at long last, she held the image of him in her mind. She examined him carefully, knowing she would never forget, not now.

Ember turned to the white wolf. *"Thank you, but I must ask. Who are you, to know my father so well? And why do you look like us?"*

The wolf was serious. *"I knew him so well because he was my best friend and companion. He was also my brother. Welcome to the family, Ember Shandae. My name is White Shadow, but you may call me Uncle Shad."* He bowed his head to her.

All Ember could do was stare in absolute shock. She'd found her father's family at last.

Ember slept that first night in the cave, nose to tail with the other wolves, her newly found uncle Shad curled at her side. She slept warm, dry, and extremely content with the pack, and if it hadn't been for the mage trials calling her onward, she would have stayed there with her other family for a very long time. Unfortunately, her sense of duty overwhelmed her, and so she found herself restless as the darkness gave way to morning, though she only knew morning was near by the increased sound of songbirds and the smell of the rising sun.

It was none of these things which woke her. It was a dream that seemed more real than any she'd ever had and brought to mind the one she'd had the night before Devil's Mount erupted. This time Ember was absent from the dream. The focus was entirely on a beautiful woman playing a sapphire-colored flute, her hair crackling around her like static while the evil blonde woman from Ember's previous dreams dove toward her on dragonback. Even now in the stillness of morning, Ember shivered at the memory. The flute player had slightly pointed ears, and Ember guessed her to be part evahn, at least.

Only after fully awakening did she realize that the flute player had also been in her previous dream, the one in which her group had actually defeated her attacker. Was she someone important? Was she real? Were her dreams beginning to mesh with reality?

The caverns began to resonate with the most beautiful sound she'd ever heard. It was a wordless song that floated through the tunnels in a constant round so the echoes formed harmonies with the original melody.

Ember stretched and shook herself, then padded out of the cave in search of the sound, which was easier thought than done with the caverns distorting her sense of direction.

Finally she just stopped to listen. The song seemed so sad, it squeezed her heart to hear it, but she felt compelled to listen.

It was almost as if the music had become a language unto itself, and Ember knew she had to find the source.

She got up again, trying to tune everything else out, and moved forward. She listened hard, spun around and went back the way she'd come, then turned down a small side passage.

The volume continued to increase until she entered a grand cavern with multiple entrances. The roof was embedded with crystal that reflected light from the surface and looked as if it were covered with a rainbow of stars.

In the direct center of the floor, a man knelt on a boulder with a flattened top, his arms outstretched and his head thrown back. His eyes were closed, but his mouth was open in the wordless song that had drawn her. Ember slunk to the side of the cave and lay down beneath an overhang to watch him.

He was well-muscled, as if he'd worked hard and come by his strength naturally, much like a blacksmith or carpenter. He didn't seem tall, though it was hard to tell as he knelt, and her perspective had changed a bit since she'd shifted into a wolf.

His face was what drew her eyes the most. There was something tortured and yet worshipful about him, as if he were pouring his pain out to the heavens. It fascinated her. She didn't know why, but she couldn't go until the song was done.

Ember closed her eyes and listened, letting the music carry her much the way the wind had as she'd run in wolf form. It was every bit as exhilarating, and gave her a glance into his true soul. She was sure he would not have sung if he'd known he had an audience. The moment seemed so private, but somehow she felt close to him in spite of it—or maybe, because of it.

Eventually the music wound to an end, the echoes of the tuneless theme coming back to her one more time. The singer's head fell forward in benediction and stayed that way for several seconds before Ember released a sigh of regret.

His head snapped up at the sound, and he scanned the room, finally stopping on her glowing eyes beneath the overhang. There was no use hiding now. She got to her feet and came forward, then bowed her head in his direction, a gesture of gratitude and praise before she turned to go. He nodded back, his blue eyes a little guarded, but not unfriendly.

Ember didn't want to scare him, not sure if he knew the wolves personally or not, so she walked slowly toward the tunnel she'd come through.

"Are you one of them? I haven't seen you around before." His speaking voice was every bit as beautiful as his singing voice had been.

Ember turned, unsure how to communicate with him. She whined and nodded her head.

"What's your name?" This time she watched his face and realized he hadn't used his mouth to say the words. He was mindspeaking, just as the wolves had, but it was so clear, it sounded as if he were vocalizing.

"Ember," she said. *"Who are you?"*

"DeMunth. I'm a friend of Shad's. I asked him to accompany me to Javak."

"Javak? You're going to Javak? For the mage trials?" Ember couldn't help the excitement that crept into her mindspeech.

"Yes and no. I've got a meeting to attend there. It just happens to coincide with the mage trials." He cocked his head. *"Why do you ask?"*

"That's where I was going before I turned into a wolf." She laughed. *"I still need to get there somehow, much as I'd like to stay. The only problem is, I'm not sure how to get back to my human form. This is a first for me."* Somehow it was easy to talk to this man. She felt as if she knew him. Perhaps it was the music.

"That does sound like a problem. I'm sure Shad can help you. The journey to Javak will be challenging in this weather, especially for a lone wolf." DeMunth cocked his head and looked thoughtfully at Ember. *"Perhaps it is the will of the Guardians for us to meet this way."* He bowed when he said it, bringing his hands together in front.

Ember wasn't sure what to say, so she said nothing. She'd ask Uncle Shad about changing later, but right now, she wanted to find out more about this man who fascinated her so. *"Why don't you sing words to your song? It's beautiful as it is, but I want to know what it means."*

DeMunth didn't answer for a long minute. He seemed to be examining Ember, searching her soul before he would give her the answer she sought. Finally he opened his mouth to speak and made sounds, but no words came forth. It was just a wordless stream of "oohs" and "aaahs." Ember took a step closer, confused, until the light from one of the crystals struck his open mouth and she could see the problem.

DeMunth had no tongue.

Ember's hackles went up, not in anger at the man, but at whoever had done this to him. It was obvious he had not been born that way. Someone had sliced his tongue out and left him mute, except for the wordless songs he sang. When he saw she understood, he closed his mouth and quieted. *"I sang words, once. Not long ago, I was a priest of Sha'iim. I spent my days in song and prayer, serving those around me and finding peace in my life. Now I sing the only way I can. At least I have my voice. It could be worse."* He bowed his head and put his hands together again. Ember wondered if it was a form of respect or prayer to this Sha'iim. She'd never heard of him, but evidently DeMunth considered him some kind of deity.

"Good morning, DeMunth," came a mindvoice from the tunnel behind her. Ember jumped and spun, a yip bursting from her before she could stop it. She'd not heard a sound as Uncle Shad came up behind her. *"I see you've met my niece, Ember Shandae."*

DeMunth looked startled. *"Little Shandae? The girl you've been searching for so long?"*

"One and the same. She nearly fell into our laps last night. Transformed herself into a wolf while captured and spellchained to stone, with no experience whatsoever. The girl is gifted." Shad walked to DeMunth and rested in front of him. DeMunth reached down and scratched behind Shad's ears and around his neck. The big wolf's eyelids half-closed, and he sighed in contentment. Ember snickered to see him so dog-like.

"*Very good, Shandae. Most shifters bungle their first transformation in dangerous ways,*" DeMunth said. "*Or would you prefer that we call you Ember?*"

She shrugged as best she could in wolf form. "*Ember is what I've always gone by.*"

"*Ember it is, then,*" the singer said, scratching beneath Shad's chin, then patting him on the shoulder before he got to his feet. He picked up a pack Ember hadn't noticed until then. "*Isn't it about time to go, my friend?*"

Shad sighed heavily, though it seemed to be done in fun. "*Yes, I suppose it is. Ember, where may we take you? I'd really like to speak with your mother before I leave the area.*"

Ember shook her head. "*You don't want to talk to her right now. She's pretty mad at me, and my stepfather is sick. Really sick.*" Paeder's smell invaded her senses. Funny that as a wolf it was memory that triggered scent, rather than the other way around. She sincerely hoped Ezeker had persuaded her mother to take Paeder to Javak. That gave her an idea. "*Actually, they're going to Javak to see the Mage Council about healing him, so you can talk to her there.*" She desperately hoped he'd accept, but it was not to be.

"*I'm afraid that's not possible. It's rather urgent. Besides, if she's going to Javak, we can travel with her and provide some protection. I'll have to change into my human form to speak with her, though. Your father never did get around to telling her he was half-wolf.*"

Ember was surprised at that, though she shouldn't have been. She was pretty sure Marda wouldn't have been so antagonistic toward magic if she'd known her husband was a shapeshifter by nature. She sighed with resignation. "*Well, can I at least stay a wolf while you talk to her?*"

Shad laughed. "*Why would you want to do that?*"

"*So she doesn't see me. She really doesn't want me to go to the mage trials. She might try to keep me home, and I've got to go. I have to!*" Ember was starting to feel panicked. She couldn't afford to let Marda ruin things for her now, not when she was finally free and discovering so much.

Shad shifted into human form right then, so quickly that Ember hardly saw the stages in between. He was wolf one moment and human the next, and somehow he was a fully-clothed human. Where had his clothes come from? For that matter, where had hers gone when she'd shifted?

The wolf, now human, crouched down in front of her and held her head in his hands, forcing her eyes to meet his. "It's not going to happen, little one," he said with his actual voice this time, though strangely accented. "I'll make sure your mother does not interfere. The mage trials are part of your destiny. I'll get you there, but I need your help in speaking to your mother before it's too late. You have no idea the danger she is in—that you're both in."

Ember searched his face and found only truth and fear there. She nodded, closed her eyes, and tried to shift herself back.

Nothing happened.

She opened her eyes in frustration and not a little fear. *"I don't know how to change back, Uncle. It was so instinctive before—I don't know what I did."*

Shad chuckled. "The first time is always the hardest. Start slowly. Change one thing at a time. Start with your fur, perhaps. Imagine yourself a naked wolf."

Ember looked at him, not sure if he was joking, and decided he was. *"Ha, ha. No, thank you. Why don't we do the fur last."*

Shad shrugged. "If that is what you wish. Perhaps you can imagine yourself standing on two legs." Ember closed her eyes again and pictured it. She wanted to make it real, but nothing happened.

Come on, change! She tried over and over again, but nothing happened. Evidently she was going to stay a wolf for a lifetime after all. It wasn't nearly as appealing as it had seemed earlier. She missed being able to talk. She growled in frustration and looked up in time to see DeMunth put his hand on Shad's shoulder.

"Perhaps we should let this go for now. We'll have plenty of time to practice on the road. Time is wasting and can't be brought back."

Shad nodded. "You're right. I'm sorry, Ember. I'll work with you on it. I'm not sure where the block is, but we'll figure it out."

146

Shad scratched his head, then shrugged. He glanced down at her front legs and paused. "What is this?" he asked, kneeling before her and lifting her paw to inspect the threads of silvery gray that ran up her legs. Ember shrugged, not wanting to explain at the moment. She had enough on her mind as it was. Shad let her paw go and stood up. "It appears you've got your wish. I still need you to take me to Marda, but you're going to do it as a wolf." He shifted back into wolf form himself and mindspoke. *"Will you lead the way back to your home?"*

"If I can figure out where I am, I should be able to get you there." Ember hoped that would be true. She knew most of the caves, but not all, and she hadn't recognized the terrain they'd scrambled through last night.

"If I can get you back to familiar territory, will you take us the rest of the way?"

Ember was reluctant to agree, but finally she bobbed her head in assent. Shad turned and ran back to the sleeping room, Ember hard on his heels. He called the pack to order, and they filed back out the way they had come in the night before.

There must have been an exit on the other side, because shortly after they left the cave, DeMunth met them on a huge stallion, bigger than any horse she'd ever seen. She was sure it would flatten her if it ever decided to do so, but strangely, it didn't even stir in the wolves' presence. It acted as if they were nothing more than a pack of hounds.

Shad went to the head of the group, glanced over his shoulder, then took off in an easy run that had them leaping over boulders and across the rocky face of the mountain.

Ember was sure she was going to lose her footing and tumble down the mountainside at any time, and under other circumstance she probably would have. She was usually a rather clumsy girl. But not in wolf form. She seemed to know instinctively where to step, which stones would hold her, and which would give. It was an exhilarating, amazing feeling.

After a while, the territory seemed familiar, and as they approached the roaring waterfall above the lake near her home, Ember got her sense of direction back. She howled and put on a burst of speed that took her to Shad's side, then edged ahead of him. He pulled back a bit and let her take the lead, and within a matter of minutes they were at the edge of the forest that lined Paeder's property.

There Ember stopped. She was about to lead the pack through the wooden fence and across the field when Tiva and Ren came out of the house with Paeder supported between them. He looked like a walking corpse, and it nearly broke Ember's heart to see it. The boys guided Paeder to the covered wagon they'd parked in the courtyard. It looked like the boxcar would be making the trip to Javak after all. Ember wanted to feel resentment, but her heart held nothing but gratitude. The wagon would give Paeder a controlled, warm environment in which to travel. He'd never survive the trip to Javak otherwise.

Marda came from the house, a large bag settled on her shoulder. She looked as if she'd aged ten years overnight. Her face was pale, her eyes lined and exhausted, with deep purple rings below them.

Again, Ember was about to lead the wolves across the field when Ezeker and a dozen of his guards rode into the courtyard.

"Marda! Where is Ember?" Ezeker demanded as he threw himself off his horse. It was obvious he was angry, and Ember detected a bit of worry there as well. She gathered herself to leap through the fence and race to him to let him know she was okay when a hand on her shoulder halted her. It was DeMunth. She growled, but stopped to watch.

Marda stopped. "She's not with you?"

"If she was, do you think I'd be standing here, asking?" he said. His voice softened a little.

Tears started to leak from Marda's eyes. She put her hands over her face and sank to the ground with a moan. Ezeker knelt with her, his arm across her shoulders. Ember growled and tried to push past Shad, but paused at his words.

"Now is not the time, child. Do you think she's going to welcome a wolf with open arms when she's missing her daughter?" The force of Shad's stare was powerful. Ember whimpered, but sank to her haunches. Her heart chilled as a man entered the courtyard.

"My pardons, folks, but I came upon this horse and was told it might be your'n." Ember's hackles rose, and a low growl came to her throat at the sight of her attacker from the night before.

Tiva rushed around the wagon and inspected the horse. "It's Brownie, all right. What happened to her? What did you do with our sister?" he demanded, his body nearly shaking with anger. Ember was surprised at his reaction, though she didn't know why. Tiva was her brother, after all, or at least he'd been raised as one.

"Easy there now, boy, I don't rightly know what happened to her," the kidnapper said, taking off his hat to scratch his bald head.

"Liar!" Ember would have yelled it if she could, as her growl increased. Too bad he couldn't hear it.

"I found this horse wandering by the side of the road and asked around. Somebody told me it might belong to you. I'm just returning what's rightfully yours. You got a girl missing, you say?" He scratched his head again, all calm nonchalance. "That's a pretty awful thing to have happen, especially when the master isn't feeling so great. I'd be happy to help you look for her, if you wish."

Marda finally found her voice. "That's kind of you, stranger, but she'll be fine. We know where she's going. I'm sure she'll get there safely." Tiva nodded his agreement.

"Good instincts, girl," Shad whispered.

Unfortunately, the others disagreed. Paeder called from the wagon. "Let the man help! There's no point in turning down assistance when we're so short in numbers. If Ember's in trouble, she needs all the help she can get." The coughing took over then, and his speech stopped.

Ren, Ezeker, and Aldarin all nodded. Marda's shoulders slumped in defeat. Ember wished with all her heart she could change into herself and tell her family how dangerous this man was. They were teaming up with a viper, an agent of C'Tan. But even if she had been able to turn back into herself, she knew she couldn't go. Exposing herself would only endanger her family. She would have to stay out of sight until she knew he was gone for good.

"Well, since you all know where she's headed, why don't I travel with you, and I'll scour the forest for her as we go? I've got my own food. I won't be no trouble—I just want to help."

Marda snorted, and Ember smiled at her mother's reaction, though her heart still raced.

Ren took Brownie and tied her to the wagon. The stranger climbed up on his horse and waited for the rest of the family to settle. Ezeker gathered his small army around the wagon—evidently they were all traveling together. There was no way Ember could get past them to see her mother. It looked as though Shad would have to wait to talk to Marda until they got to Javak after all.

"We sure do appreciate your help," Ren said to the kidnapper. "What's your name?"

"Ian. Ian Covainis," he answered as he threw his hat back on his head and looked around. He glanced behind him, his gaze stopping on the wolves at the edge of the property. A slow grin crept across his face. He lifted his hat in salute, tipped his chin, and nudged his horse forward as the wagon began to move.

Chapter Thirteen

What do you mean, the flute's missing? The Sapphire Flute?"
Brant asked in disbelief. Kayla nodded, unable to dam the flow of tears.

He stood perfectly still for a long moment, then cursed under his
breath and moved into the room, shutting the door behind him.

"Are you sure it's missing? Where have you looked?" he asked,
taking in the mess she'd made.

"Everywhere!" she wailed. "It was under the mattress when I left
for breakfast this morning, and when we came back from our ride,
it was gone! Why, Brant? Who would have done this?"

Brant did not answer, but instead began his own search of the
room—a search that, Kayla was reluctant to admit, was much more
thorough than her own had been. He moved the bed, the dresser,
the wardrobe, and the chairs. He rolled up the carpet and pulled
down the tapestries. He even scaled the wall to look in the window
ledge, and he found exactly the same thing Kayla had.

Nothing.

He stood in the middle of the room, chewing at his lip and
staring into space, then without a word he began to put things back
in order. The tapestry baffled him for a moment, but, making up
his mind, he headed for the door.

"Where are you going?" Kayla asked, uneasy about his leaving.

"To get a ladder," he replied, seemingly distracted. "I'll be right back."

Kayla didn't answer, but continued the job Brant had started. She was putting her clothes back in the dresser drawers when she found something that didn't belong.

On the top of the dresser was a note—with her name scrawled across its folded back.

For a long time she could do nothing but stare at it, afraid to touch it for fear it would disappear much as the flute had, but finally she had to know what it said. Hand shaking, she reached for the parchment and opened it.

> *Why did you play the flute, Kayla? You were warned, and yet not even a full day went by before you breathed life to the instrument. We have claimed the flute until you are worthy of it. We will protect it, and Dragonmeer, if you will not. Prove yourself worthy, and it may be returned, or spurn your duty and lose it forever. The choice is yours. Speak through the stone.*
>
> *Thenari Kafato Topuini*
> *Hand of Klii'kunn*

Kayla sank to the floor in shock. Stolen because she had played it? But she hadn't! No sound had come from the instrument—she knew that with her heart and soul. How *dare* this Thenari claim she was not worthy? How dare he take it from her when the king himself had given her guardianship of the flute? Anger took over now, where fear had overwhelmed before. She read the note again and again, trying to decipher the message. She would find out who this Thenari Kafato Topuini was and claim back what was rightfully hers. She'd show him that she was "worthy" and take it back by force, if necessary. She was no weakling to be pushed around and threatened. With the name and identity of the thief, she had gained a purpose and would not give up until the Sapphire Flute lay in her hands once more.

The main thing that confused her was the last part.

"Speak through the stone," she whispered. "What does that mean?"

Brant chose that moment to open the door and manipulate a ladder into the room. He got the ladder through the doorway and propped against the wall when he caught sight of her face.

"What? What happened, love?" He was at her side in an instant.

Instead of answering, she handed him the note. He read it, growing more tense with each sentence. It affected him just as it had her. By the time he reached the end, his face was red with anger, and he seemed to have forgotten both ladder and tapestry.

"Who does he think he is? He speaks as if he is guardian of the flute, and not you! Who is this 'Hand of Klii'kunn'? Do you know?" he demanded.

"Of course not. If I knew, don't you think I'd have reclaimed the flute already?" She took the letter from his hand and answered with a set jaw. "I don't know, but I intend to find out."

"How?" he asked. It was a very good question, and one for which she did not have an answer. Instead of answering, she asked him a question in return.

"What do you think this means—'Speak through the stone'?" She pointed at the sentence on the paper. Brant read it again, chewing his lip in thought.

"I don't know. Was anything with the paper? Where did you find it?"

"It was on the dresser." She walked to the dark bureau and rested her hand on its surface. She'd already moved the few items from the top and found nothing of significance. She had no idea what the thief was talking about.

Brant got on his knees to search the floor. "We have moved things around a bit . . ." he muttered as he ran fingertips along the baseboards, following the wall toward the bed.

"What are you doing?" Kayla asked.

"Looking for something," he mumbled, his head and half his body wedged beneath the bed.

"That's obvious, but what?"

"This," Brant said, backing out from beneath the boxy frame with a small item clasped in his right hand. He stood and opened his fingers. At first Kayla was not sure what she was looking at—it appeared to be a plain old rock until Brant turned it over. Kayla took in a sharp breath and released it slowly. It was a scriptstone, a reading rock, a message stone—it went by many names, but Brant was right—

"He wants us to communicate with him," Kayla whispered.

"It appears so," Brant said, still fuming. His eyes flashed when they met hers, but Kayla's anger had faded. All was not lost. She just had to find this man or woman who had taken her flute and somehow prove she really was worthy to have it. She didn't care what it took or how she had to humble herself, she would recover the instrument.

"It's okay, Brant," she said, not quite able to smile, but at least she was no longer crying. "We'll figure it out, and we will get the flute back." Her promise seemed to do little to relieve his anger. He still paced the room, his hands flexing in agitation, but at last he nodded. He was willing to help.

Kayla sat down and tried to compose a letter to the thief, this Thenari Kafato Topuini. That was a mouthful of a name, both to write or to speak. She decided to call him Thenari. It was easier and the most normal-sounding of the three. Mostly she wanted to call him "thief," but had the feeling that doing so would not help the situation. She had to have the flute, and she had to get it before she saw the king again. There was no way she could lie to King Rojan if he asked about the instrument. If that happened, she could forget about her duchy, her mother's restoration to nobility—and she could especially forget about her upcoming marriage.

"Brant," she said as he tried to hang the tapestry again on his own. He wasn't having much luck.

"Yeah," he snarled.

"You aren't going to tell anybody, are you?"

He paused in his attempt and let the tapestry drop to the ground, then turned to face her while standing ten feet up the ladder.

"Of course not. What kind of person do you think I am?" he said, a little of his frustration aimed at her, but she didn't take offense. She was too relieved by his answer.

"A smart one," she said, giving him a weak smile. "I just had to be sure we were on the same page. I should have known."

"Yes, you should have," he snapped, then softened. "I don't blame you for voicing it. I probably would have done the same in your shoes."

Kayla nodded at him, then turned back to the blank paper and began to write:

> I do not know who you are or why you have done this, but your accusations are false. I did not play the instrument. It had no voice from me. I am its guardian, determined worthy by the king, and I will not stop until it is back in my hands. Return the instrument to me and there will be no repercussions. Keep it, and you will have all the wrath of Peldane against you.

Kayla did not bother signing the letter. The thief would know who sent it. She set aside her pen and ink and sanded the paper. Once she knew it was dry, she set the scriptstone in the center and waited.

Nothing happened.

"Brant," she said, and he immediately came to her. "It's not working."

"Did you tell it to send?" he asked.

"I didn't know I had to."

"Hold your hand over the stone and say 'send.' It will do the rest," he explained, and went back to his labor of rehanging the tapestry on the wall.

Kayla cupped the rock in the palm of her hand. "Send," she croaked, and immediately a rainbow-colored light burst forth and pulled the ink from the paper. She sucked in a breath of surprise. She had not realized that a scriptstone would actually steal the ink from the page. It was strange. Very strange indeed.

The letter was sent. She'd done what she could. Now she must wait.

In the meantime, Kayla helped Brant with the tapestry, and they got it back in place without too many mishaps and only one broken vase. It was slightly crooked, but Kayla figured no one else would really notice, and if they did, they could fix it. They were done—and none too soon, for at the same moment Kayla saw another flash of rainbow light, a knock sounded at the door. Kayla wasn't sure where to go first, though her heart tugged her toward the writing desk and the now-full page that lay waiting for her response. But in order to keep a low profile, she had to answer the door.

"Yes," she called after a second knock.

"'Tis Sarali, Miss Kayla. Would Master Brant be with ye? His father be needing him right away."

Brant groaned and climbed down the ladder.

"Don't do anything foolish while I'm gone," he whispered to Kayla, his eyes pleading.

"Of course not," she answered. "I never do."

He raised his brow at her, both of them remembering too many incidents where she certainly *had* been foolish, but Brant said nothing, letting a sigh of resignation escape his lips before opening the door.

"Yes, Sarali, I'm here, but I'm kind of busy right now. What does Father need?" He leaned against the doorframe and ran his hands through his tousled hair.

"He wouldn't be telling me that, sir, just asked me to fetch ye," Sarali replied with a wink and a smile.

"Tell him I'll be there shortly," he said, but Sarali shook her head.

"The master insisted that I not return without ye, sir. 'Tis very important,' he said."

Brant grunted, obviously disgusted, and gave Kayla one last warning glance before he left. "All right then, Sarali. Let's get this done. I've got work to do."

"Yes, Master Brant," she replied as she pulled the door shut. The instant they were gone, Kayla ran for the paper.

You speak untruth, Lady Kayla, for I heard the flute calling in my sleep last night. The flute cannot speak unless given your breath, thus you have played it. If you wish to have the flute returned, threats and lies will get you nowhere. Prove yourself.

"Prove myself? How?" she asked of the air, throwing her hands up in frustration. Prove herself. Prove herself. It made no sense. What more was there to prove? How could she persuade this person that she truly had not played the flute?

Left with no other options, she decided to be completely honest and sat down to write another letter.

Sir, I do not know what you want of me. How may I prove myself and have the flute returned? I will do all that you ask, but please, return the flute to its rightful guardian. I swore to my king to protect it with my very life, and so far I have failed in that task, as you have been able to remove the instrument from me. I know not what more to say. Tell me what to do, and it shall be done.

Kayla sat and waited for a response and received it within minutes, though its message chilled her to the bone.

Meet me in the cellar and thy worth shall be proven. Do not respond. Go now while Brant is away.

How could the thief know Brant was away? Only if he were watching her room or knew that Brant had been called to his father.

And then it clicked. The thief knew because he had sent his servant to fetch Brant. The thief knew because he was a trusted member of the household and had a name she knew, a name that, when contracted, became one she'd heard several times that very day.

Thenari Kafato Topuini.

T'Kato.

Sarali's husband was the thief.

Chapter Fourteen

Ember watched her kidnapper ride away with her family, her hackles up so high it was almost painful. Ian Covainis had effectively cut her off from her family and those who could be of help to her at the mage trials.

He was with her *family*. A low growl rumbled deep in her chest as she tried to push past Shad to get to the man, but Shad moved with her, and after several attempts she tried to bull her way through. He rammed her to the ground and pinned her as easily as he would a pup, holding her there until she'd quit thrashing and biting and finally lay still. *"Are you done?"* he asked.

Ember didn't want to answer. She wanted to throw him off and run after her family. They had no idea what kind of man Ian was. She had to warn them before something happened, but Shad wasn't budging. He was getting heavy, and Ember couldn't catch her breath with his weight on her.

"I ask again, are you done?" Shad's snarl started low in his throat and rumbled across his chest.

Ember could feel the vibration as he pressed her into the ground. This was one battle she couldn't win, so she answered. *"Yes."* She sounded as sullen as she felt.

"Good." Shad scrambled backward and faced her, wariness evident in his lowered head and motionless tail. There was no question he was waiting for her to try running off again, and Ember would have been lying to herself to say the thought hadn't crossed her mind. But Shad made it pointless. It was obvious he wasn't going to let her go anywhere. *"You need to think before you charge off like that. Do you have any idea who that man is?"*

"Yeah, he's my kidnapper, and he works for C'Tan." Speaking C'Tan's name gave Ember chills. The woman was well-known for her ruthlessness, and it made Ember's skin crawl to know they shared blood.

Shad snorted. *"That's putting it mildly. Ian Covainis is second only to Kardon in C'Tan's legions. It is rumored that he is the son of Kardon and C'Tan, though there is no proof of it. The man has no conscience, child. Leave him be."*

Ember felt sick. Everyone she cared about was in the company of that monster. *"But he's with my family! They don't know how much danger they're in. I've got to warn them."*

Shad shook his head. *"So long as he doesn't find you, they'll be fine. He needs to keep himself from being noticed at this point. If you warn them, it puts them in more danger. I know for a certainty that Ezeker and Marda can take care of themselves, and with the guard and your brothers there as well, they could not be much safer. Covainis may be powerful, but even he cannot take on an entire regiment without injury."*

Ember didn't want to listen, but it seemed she had no choice. She nodded reluctantly and bowed her will to that of her uncle.

"Good girl. DeMunth!" Shad called to the mute singer who had left their side somewhere in the scuffle. DeMunth rode up from behind the pack at the mental call. *"Ember's kidnapper is riding with her family, trying to pass himself off as a do-gooder. I need you to keep an eye on him. Find out what you can and meet us at the big willow."*

DeMunth nodded and turned his mount back to get some distance. The horse gained speed, racing for the fence, and just as

Ember was sure he would ram through it, the huge animal gathered himself and leaped over the wooden railing as if it were nothing more than a bush.

As soon as DeMunth was in the pasture, he dug his heels into his stallion, and they ran even faster. Even in her wolf form, Ember was amazed at the speed of his horse. She'd quickly discovered the night before how fast four legs could take her, but DeMunth's mount made her long for that kind of swiftness. She watched until they hurdled over the gate on the other side and faded out of sight in the gray rain, headed for the high road.

Shad turned to her. *"Are you ready?"*

Ember nodded, not trusting herself to speak quite yet. She was still too angry at Shad's interference, whether well-meant or not. Her stomach roiled with worry for her family, but it seemed there was nothing she could do without making things worse for them.

The pack ran, Shad and Ember in the lead, the other dozen or so loping behind or fanning out to the sides as they wove in and out of the trees around Paeder's farm. The rain had lightened earlier, almost non-existent in the morning, but the muddy deluge had returned, making footing treacherous. Each bound forward threw mud behind them until those in the back of the pack were covered nearly head to paw in the gray muck, and Ember struggled to resist stopping to lick herself clean.

For most of the day they ran, their senses dulled by the constant rain and the need to pay attention to the slick surface. Most of the pack ate on the run—they stopped for a mouse here, a rabbit there, but Ember couldn't quite bring herself to accept the blood lust that gnawed at her belly and made her mouth water. The logical, human part of her was revolted by the thought of raw meat—especially rodents.

It was near dark when the pack burst through the thick woods into a clearing dominated by the biggest willow tree Ember had ever seen. It was taller than Ezeker's tower, almost as wide as Paeder's house, with branches that spilled from the top to sweep the ground. The pack darted through the wiry branches, settling beneath the sheltering tree. Ember sank to her haunches in exhaustion. Running on all fours came rather naturally to her, but it still took a lot of effort, and she was more tired than she could ever remember. She panted, her tongue hanging low, her chest moving so quickly with her breath that she felt like a hummingbird.

The long branches of the tree channeled the rain down their lengths, leaving the open space near the trunk nearly dry. The branches were so thick, she felt as if she were standing behind a living curtain. For the first time in nearly two days she felt safe, hidden, and protected from a hostile world. At least, she did, until several wolves dropped rabbits at her feet. They nudged the animals toward her, then backed away. Ember looked at Shad, but he wasn't laughing.

"You need to eat. You are expending a lot of energy with this kind of run. You won't last if you don't feed." Shad tossed what looked like a gopher through the air. It landed with a thud in the dirt next to the rabbits.

Bile rose in Ember's throat even as her mouth watered. The two sides of her nature battled. She sniffed at the rabbits, picked one up in her mouth and bit down gently. The coppery taste of blood filled her mouth, sending a wave of revulsion over her. She dropped the rabbit and backed away, whimpering.

"Ember, eat. You'll get used to it." Shad came around and bumped her from behind. She parked herself and wouldn't budge.

"I can't eat that. I'd rather go hungry."

"You'll do more than go hungry if you don't eat. You won't survive. You don't have a choice." He said it so matter-of-factly that, for a moment, it didn't register. She was going to die if she didn't eat a raw rabbit?

Ridiculous.

"There are other things to eat." Ember's stomach growled.

"Like what?" Shad was obviously humoring her.

"Berries and stuff. Grass. Roots. Anything's better than that." Ember lowered her head toward the dead animals and sneezed.

Shad seemed almost offended. *"Wolves don't eat berries. Wolves eat meat. Red, raw, bleeding, still-warm meat. You are wolf, whether you*

162

want to be or not, and until you can shapeshift back into your human form, this is it."

That gave Ember an idea. "*Speaking of shapeshifting, do you think we can practice that again? I think I can do it this time.*"

"*You're changing the subject. You need to eat.*" Shad's set jaw was almost human. It reminded Ember of Aldarin in his most stubborn moments.

"*I know I need to eat, but I won't eat that. If I turn human, I can cook it first. I just can't do the slimy raw meat thing.*" She shivered in disgust.

Several chuckles sounded around her. Shad rolled his eyes and shook his head. "*It's not as bad as you think, though your father also had a hard time with it. Very well, then, we'll practice shape-changing, and in the meantime I'll have the pack roast your meat for you. Will that suffice?*"

Ember nodded, relieved.

"*Good. Now, I've had some thoughts, especially now that Ian Covainis is in the picture. Your safety is of the greatest import, no matter the inconvenience. Would you not agree?*"

Ember nodded again, not sure where he was going with this. He seemed nervous as he paced back and forth.

"*Since shape-changing is now an option, or at least it will be once you figure out how to change back, it would make sense to use that as a way to disguise yourself, yes?*" He didn't wait for her answer before he continued. "*The best way to disguise you is to present you in the way Ian is least likely to expect. Obviously you need to be human, but I am afraid he will search all females in the city looking for similarities. He would be much less likely to find you if you were much less female.*"

Ember was confused. "*I am female. How am I supposed to get around that?*"

"*By disguising yourself as a non-female.*" Shad cleared his throat, obviously embarrassed.

"*What? Non-female? But that means . . .*" Realization dawned. "*You want me to look like a boy?*"

"*Er, yes.*" Shad at least had the decency to shut up after that.

Ember was appalled. *"No. Absolutely not. Dressing like a boy, fine, but I will not make myself less female by shape-changing."*

Shad sighed and stepped closer, his head almost touching hers. *"I know it's hard to grasp, but it's the last thing he would expect. Most people don't understand that as a shapeshifter, any form is possible. You wouldn't technically be a boy—you would just look like one. You know, make yourself a bit bulkier, narrow the hips, thicken the jaw, and add some stubble, shrink your chest—"*

Ember interrupted him there. *"Whoa, whoa, whoa! Just hold on. I can't even figure out how to become my normal self again—how do you expect me to do all that? Even if I could, I wouldn't. I can see the need for changing my face, but there is no way I am going to shrink my . . ."* She stopped. If she'd been in her human skin she would have been several shades of red. *"Well, I'm just not, that's all."*

"I'm going to have to insist. Your safety is of the utmost importance. I'm not going to let you endanger yourself just because it makes you uncomfortable. You will change your face and form, Ember. Accept it, or I will not help you learn how to shift back, nor will I take you to Javak."

Shad turned to walk away, and Ember's panic set in. Like it or not, she was going to have to do as he asked. She *had* to be at those mage trials. *"Okay, okay, I give up, you win, but I won't shrink my chest. I'll bind it up if I have to, but I'm not going to change anything that makes me female, understood?"* Too many years of being teased by the village girls about being flat-chested made Ember all too aware of the differences between boy and girl.

Shad looked at her for a long moment, his head cocked as he thought. Finally, he nodded once in assent and beckoned for her to come with him to the other side of the tree. Several of the wolves had shifted into human form and carried loads of rocks to the center of the clearing. Ember was curious what they were doing, but learning how to shift back into herself seemed more important, so she left with one last glance over her shoulder.

Once Shad and Ember were in a semi-private spot on the other side of the tree, he stopped and sat down. *"I've been thinking—"*

Ember interrupted. *"It sounds like you've been doing a lot of that today."*

Shad chuckled. *"Actually, yes. More than usual, anyway. So, I was thinking, maybe we're looking at this the wrong way. Maybe breaking the transformation down into steps is too much detail for you. When you changed into a wolf, you did it quickly, almost instantly, correct? You didn't stop to think about what to do with your clothes or how to change the color of your eyes, did you?"*

Ember hadn't thought about it, really, but he was right. When she'd transformed in the cave, it had been an emotionally spurred act. She didn't think about it, she just did it. She thought of what needed to be and made it happen. It had been the same with the dress. She'd visualized it, wanted it very badly, and suddenly it was. Could it really be that simple?

Shad continued. *"How do you best see magic?"*

"With my eyes closed, or at least, that's the way I saw the green swirls and spikes yesterday. When my eyes were open, everything looked normal, but when they were closed, I saw green everywhere."

The wolf nodded his head thoughtfully. *"Let's try something here, shall we? Close your eyes. Keep them closed and tell me what you see."*

Ember complied, though she saw nothing.

"What do you see?" asked Shad from beyond the darkness.

"Nothing," Ember answered. Even she could hear the frustration in her voice.

"Good. You weren't supposed to. That was a check. Now comes the important part. Pay attention."

Ember strained against the darkness, but there was still nothing for what seemed forever. She was about to call out to her uncle in frustration when a sullen green light sprang to life in front of her. She gasped in surprise. It was a wolf-shaped image that started to stretch and pull like taffy. She could see the flares and spikes as energy surrounded what had to be Uncle Shad, and somehow, on a deep, magical level, it clicked. As she watched him, she suddenly understood how it worked, though she could not have told someone if they'd paid her. It was so basic as to be instinctive—there were no words to describe it. She watched with her magic eyes until he became a man, then opened her eyes.

Uncle Shad was more handsome as a human than she'd thought he would be. Ember hadn't really taken the time to see him that morning, but now she did. His dark hair was short, his eyes the same murky green as her own. He was shorter than she'd imagined, but powerfully built, though not in a grotesque way, as the kidnapper Ian had been. He was just a nicely built man with not a bit of fat on him. He smiled, and her heart melted. He had dimples that creased his cheeks and sparkles in his eyes, the kind she knew identified him as a big tease.

"All right, your turn," he said, his voice a melodic baritone. It was strange to hear him speak aloud after all the mind-speech they'd shared in the past day. "Remember, try to turn yourself into a boy. Take the picture of someone you know, or better yet, parts of people you know, and combine them into a whole. It's your best defense against Covainis."

Ember nodded. The idea was repugnant to her, but she didn't see any alternative. Closing her eyes, she created the image in her mind of the perfect man. Dark eyes, hair as black as raven's wings, a strong chin, and full mouth. She made it as perfect as she could, then wished for it with all her heart. There was a searing pain in her paws, and then her entire body felt like it had been caught between the horses. She was smashed, stretched, and molded like clay, all of her fur disappearing into the clothes she'd worn before she transformed. She'd wondered where her clothes had gone—evidently they became her fur. Strange.

Glancing at her hands, Ember was relieved to see long fingers instead of furry paws. She felt her face. She still had her same nose and rounded cheeks, but her jaw and mouth felt different, and what hair she could see in the twilight seemed pretty black.

With a snap of his fingers, Shad called up a mage light and examined Ember's face in the blue glow. A slow grin spread across his face as she panted, still fighting with wolf reactions despite her human face. "Good. Very good. I was right." His laughter was contagious, and she smiled, despite the residual pain that still sparked through her body. "Next time go a little slower. The pain will be less, but you've got the idea. A few finishing touches and you'll be set." He looked closely at her nose and ran a thumb along her jaw. "Your nose is too dainty for your face. I'm sure it would be beautiful for a girl nose," he qualified when he saw she was about to object, "but for a boy, it's too pretty. Make it bigger here, maybe a little thinner there," he touched her nose, "and give yourself some stubble."

This was the part Ember had been dreading. She closed her eyes again and imagined a bit of peach fuzz lining her upper lip and chin, much like Tiva and Ren had at the moment. It felt strange to feel hair sprouting from her pores, and she only hoped things would go back to normal when she was herself again. She didn't want to go through life as a bearded lady.

Next, she concentrated on her nose. She found it helped to actually touch it as she worked. She imagined it thinner through the bridge and wider through the nostrils, and finally settled on one similar to Aldarin's. He had the perfect male nose—very dignified, but not overly hawkish.

When she felt she was done, Ember opened her eyes to gauge Shad's reaction. He nodded his head, his lips pursed as he examined her face in the light. "Not bad, my dear, not bad at all. Now, are you *sure* you won't flatten your chest a bit? You're rather, umm, how shall we say, obvious as a girl."

Ember was shaking her head before he had finished. She closed her eyes one more time and attempted to bulk her body up as he'd suggested earlier, hoping that it might better hide her assets. The mass in shoulders, arms, and chest increased, her hips thinned, and her hands expanded a little to look more masculine, though she didn't dare increase the size of her feet or she'd never get her boots back on. She thought about flattening her chest, but she just couldn't do it. For some reason, it felt wrong to her. Instead, she asked, "Do you have anything I can use to bind myself? I think with all the muscle, I can hide things pretty well."

Shad looked leery, but he didn't object. "I'll give it some thought and see what we can come up with." He cocked his head, very wolf-like, and nodded approvingly. "You've done a marvelous job. It would be a miracle if Ian found you in this disguise. Are you hungry yet?" he asked, completely changing the subject.

Ember's stomach growled loudly, answering his question. He put an arm around her shoulder and thumped her on the back. "Then let's go eat." Ember took several steps forward before realizing Shad wasn't with her. She stopped and turned. He was looking at her as if he wasn't sure whether to laugh or pull out his hair. "What?" she asked, feeling self-conscious.

"We've got to work on the way you move."

"Why?"

"You walk like a girl," he said, his dimples starting to show.

Ember flipped her hair and strolled away. "Well, I certainly hope so. I *am* a girl."

Shad threw back his head and laughed. "Not today, you're not. I wish you could see yourself." Shad simpered past her, and if that was anything similar to what she looked like, he was right. Her walk definitely needed help. Ember snickered and shook her head. For having had the morning from helar, the day hadn't turned out so badly at all. At least now she could eat.

Chapter Fifteen

Kardon was at C'Tan's bedside when she awoke, the red light from the windows high above streaked across her black walls. It was a perfect reflection of her mood. She had not heard him enter, and only became aware that Kardon was there when he touched her, awaking her with a start.

"Kardon!" she spat, raking her fingers through her illusory hair. "Has your memory left you so quickly that you have forgotten my words of this morning?"

"No, mistress," he answered. "I remember both of your threats quite clearly, but since I am not disturbing you early, you have no reason to carve my heart and serve it to our master, as you promised you would."

She snarled. "I ought to flame you where you stand."

"As you wish, mistress, but you may want to hear me before you decide to turn me into a human barbecue."

C'Tan fought the urge to laugh. It was not like Kardon to joke. For him to make such a comment meant he had very good news for her indeed. His face remained an expressionless mask, seemingly molded from stone, so cold and still was it. The only thing that showed he was truly alive was the movement of his eyes and mouth and the slight flaring of his nostrils with each breath. She had wondered many a time if he were not a simulacrum of S'Kotos sent here to torment her, but he had proven the humanity of his physical form often enough to convince her that his body did indeed live, even if his heart did not.

"Oh, very well then," she sighed, bored, though she was anxious to hear his apparent good news—important enough to wake her from the small amount of sleep she was able to get.

"We have found the flute," he answered, still not smiling, though his eyes held a small amount of excitement for once.

"Yes, so you told me this morning. Have you nothing more for me? I do so want to get some sleep before the moon rises."

There was a flash of annoyance in his eyes, and C'Tan smiled, though her face didn't show it. Finally, she had gotten to the old man.

"This morning the flute manifested itself. Tonight we discovered who has possession of it."

C'Tan stilled. Her heart skipped a beat at his words. "Tell me more," she purred.

"The flute is held by one Kayla Kalandra Felandian of Darthmoor. We have tracked her location, and she is currently staying at Dragonmeer, the keep of Duke Domanta. Rumor has it the youngling is engaged to the duke's son. What are your wishes, my lady?" he asked, obviously pleased with himself.

"Kay-la . . ." She drew the name out like a caress. "What a common name for such a special little girl. What do we know about her?"

"She is not well accepted there, mistress. Her father was evahn, and her mother is a disinherited noble."

"This could work in our favor. Perhaps the people of Darthmoor will send her to me with only a small amount of persuasion." She smiled coldly and threw the silk blankets from her. She waved a hand in the air and pulled her riding clothes from the same insubstantial place where she stored her mirror. The red leather and silken cape suited her well. She pulled them on, disregarding the man still standing in her room as if he was of no matter, and truly he was not. They both knew he was no threat to her.

"Well, then, we'd best saddle up the dragons and pay her a visit, hadn't we, Kardon? See to it."

The ageless man bowed and backed his way from the room.

"It shall be done."

Chapter Sixteen

T'Kato was the thief. Kayla never would have thought it possible. He didn't strike her as the type of man capable of pulling off such an act. Actually, he seemed the kind of guy that would bash your head in and take what he wanted without subtlety. Evidently there was more to the tattooed chef than anyone had realized. Now that she thought of it, he made everyone in Dragonmeer believe he didn't speak their language, proof of his duplicitous nature.

And then there was Sarali to consider. Kayla was extremely disappointed that the servant she adored so much had played her for a fool. It hurt and made her angry, though she had known the woman with the beautiful brogue less than a day.

Kayla looked at the darkening window. The hours had raced past since the flute's disappearance. She'd missed lunch and probably dinner as well, and had not heard the bell announcing meals. That was not like her, but the thought of food was repulsive. The loss of the flute tightened her stomach with nausea and fear.

Her thoughts turned back to T'Kato, Thenari, thief—all applied, and she couldn't distinguish between the three names. They had become synonymous.

"The Hand of Klii'kunn," she muttered to herself, remembering the last phrase in his note. What did that mean? Klii'kunn was one of the Guardians who created Rasann, or so legend said. The glowing flute was supposedly cut from the mountain whole. But questioning the legend of deity did not answer the *real* question: what did T'Kato mean when he claimed to be the Hand of Klii'kunn?

Legend said Klii'kunn was one of six Guardians who remained behind after Rasann was nearly destroyed. He was the Blue Guardian, responsible for the blue magic dealing with wind, sound, and air. Okay, that made sense, since the flute was powered by air, but why the Hand? The hand was the extension of the body, the tool of the mind. So . . . maybe Thenari was like . . . a prophet? No . . . that didn't seem right, but something along those lines, as if he were the Blue Guardian's greatest tool, his servant, a disciple perhaps. Disciple, yes—that word made sense to her, whether true or not, and would explain his seeming possessiveness where the flute was concerned. It helped somehow to label him. He wanted the power of air to be used properly, wisely, though why he would not just come and talk to her about it, she wasn't sure.

Something in that last train of thought nagged at her, though she couldn't quite grasp it.

The power of air . . .

What was it Thenari had said? Kayla pulled the note from the folds of her dress and read it aloud.

> . . . *You were warned, and yet not even a full day went by before you breathed life to the instrument* . . .

Breathed life to the instrument . . . the power of air . . .

Could it be? Kayla's stomach clenched, her heart stopping at the thought. Surely not—but, what if . . . ?

The power of air—

If the flute was the blue keystone, and if it truly had been created by the Guardian Klii'kunn, the Guardian of sound, wind, and air . . .

Could her breath alone have brought the instrument to life?

Somehow that was exactly what had happened. Kayla knew it without doubt. She was tempted to give up right then. How could she prove herself worthy when she truly *was* guilty of T'Kato's accusations? It seemed hopeless.

But it was not in Kayla's nature to give up.

She stiffened her spine and stopped sniffling, then swallowed the lump in her throat. She would not let him beat her, no matter who he thought he was. *She* was the flute's guardian. Somehow she would prove her worth and get it back. She had to.

She just didn't know how.

The sun was going down quickly, and Brant still had not returned. Thenari was waiting in the cellar. Kayla quailed at the idea of going down alone. Anything could happen, anything at all. What if T'Kato was something worse than a thief? What if he was a murderer? What could she do then?

In the end, she decided it didn't matter. She would rather die than face King Rojan without the flute.

And so, just as the light of the sun was brightening to sunset, with streaks of pink flashing across her wall, Kayla left her room in search of a thief and went to meet T'Kato, the tattooed Ketahean chef, in the darkness of the immense cellars.

She walked down the hall, stopping to look at the statues and portraits of Brant's ancestors that seemed so out of place on the bare stone walls of the castle. Only the tapestries brought lightness and life into the castle, and Kayla found herself admiring them as she wound her way downstairs.

Despite her resolve, she was in no hurry to reach the cellar. Few people wandered past—a servant activating magelights and lighting torches, a young whispering couple cuddling in a corner, a pack of giggling girls she easily avoided. Kayla sincerely hoped Brant would find her so she could let him know where she was going. Mentally she kicked herself for not having left him a note, though if T'Kato truly was what he claimed, even Brant could not help her. She would have to fix this one herself.

Kayla finally reached the main level and meandered through the kitchens. The servants still bustled about, almost oblivious to her as they snatched their dinner between dishes and cleaning duties. The smell of food still made her sick, so she moved quickly through the noisy room, arriving at last at the great door leading to the cellar.

With a hand on the knob, she hesitated, listening with faint hope for Brant's footsteps that would keep her from this insanity. But all she heard was the faint clatter and laughter echoing from the kitchen. Here there were no footsteps, no voices to which she could cling. She stood at the border between safety and the unknown blackness before her, suddenly terrified to open that door and descend into the musty darkness she had loved as a child. In those days of games and adventure, the monsters had been innocent, make-believe. Now the terror was real. The man down there had stolen her beloved flute, and only she and Brant knew of it. Was this a trap, or a legitimate opportunity to claim what was hers by right? Honestly, she didn't know, but she couldn't miss the chance. She had to try, and could only pray that T'Kato spoke the truth.

With shaking hands, she pulled open the heavy door and slid into darkness, the wood whispering closed behind her.

She stood for a long moment, her back secure against the thick oak, hands behind her ready to push it open in an instant, but no monsters came from the dark. No one jumped at her, no one called, nothing moved. Her ears could make out the scurry of rats and the faint drip-drip from the wall closest to the moat. These sounds were familiar, an echo of the past that relaxed her enough to calm the shaking consuming her.

She stepped into the darkness.

There were twelve steps to the basement. As her eyes adjusted, she made out the faint outline of the pillared, boxy rooms. The last of the evening light disappeared through the slits that marched along the tops of the high wall. If it had not been so close to sunset, Kayla knew she would have been able to see fairly well. As it was, she was guided more by memory than by her eyes.

She had no idea where she was supposed to find the thief. All the note had said was to meet in the cellar, but the cellar was an awfully large place. It ran the entire length and width of Dragonmeer.

Kayla had spent many hours as a child playing in the rear portion of the cellar. There were some fascinating old costumes and furniture back there. It seemed as good a place as any. Thenari would probably want to meet where discovery would be least likely.

Of a sudden Kayla's nerves got the best of her, and she stopped, unwilling to go farther into the deep recesses of the dungeon without even a lantern or magelight to guide her. Instead she quietly pushed her way into one of the small rooms that stored root vegetables and hid behind the open door. Her pulse quickened and her knees trembled. The door didn't offer much protection, but the solidity of the oak between her and the unknown, the crack that allowed her to scan the room, did a lot to make her feel better. She gathered her nerve and breath and called out, "I'm here, Thenari. Show yourself."

Kayla waited. There was no response.

"You asked me to come, and I have come," she yelled a little louder this time. "Will you torture me with your games? Show yourself, and bring me the flute."

Still there was no answer, and Kayla began to grow desperate. "T'Kato! Show yourself! Please!" she begged.

Her heart nearly stopped at the soft chuckle that sounded from just outside the room. "You're smarter than I thought, Kayla. How did you figure it out so quickly?"

Her heart pounded so loudly she couldn't think, could hardly hear. Finally she got her nerves under control enough to answer, though her voice still quavered. "You said to come while Brant was gone, and I couldn't think of any other way you would know he'd left unless Sarali told you. Then I looked at your name and saw how it contracted into T'Kato. It wasn't hard," she said.

The quiet chuckle came again, and a soft blue magelight appeared, floating just outside the door. There was the scrape of leather on stone as the giant of a man approached the door and peered through the crack at her, then gently pushed the door open and stepped into the room. She cringed and wanted to scream, being inches away from the man with swirling blue tattoos that made him look hideously ferocious.

If it wasn't for the soft sadness of his eyes, Kayla would have cowered, shrieking at that moment, but she remembered her mother telling her that the eyes could not lie. *"You can tell a lot by a person's eyes, Kayla. Always remember you can judge the man by the windows to his soul."* She had never forgotten, and those words had led her unerringly through the years. The eyes of this fierce-looking giant said, *"trust me."*

And she did.

Kayla met his eyes, the color of the Sapphire Flute, and let him see into the windows of her own soul. He seemed troubled by that, a little confused, but eventually a gentle smile settled, and he withdrew from the door. She stepped from her hiding place, no longer afraid, though the man had to be near seven feet tall and broad as an ox.

"I didn't mean to play the flute," she said, her face red with shame. "I didn't think I had, since no sound came from it. I didn't know my breath alone would bring it to life. I'm sorry, T'Kato. I really didn't know, or I never would have done even that."

T'Kato was silent. He looked at her, troubled, then stared into the distance, lost in thought or prayer or . . . something.

After a long moment, he spoke. "I believe you, Kayla, though I had not expected to. You show your wisdom, not only in admitting your wrongdoing, but in understanding *why* it was wrong." He was quiet, then continued. "Do you know why I took the flute?" He leaned against one of the great stone pillars, his arms folded across his chest.

"Only by what you said in the letter, though why you didn't just come and speak to me about it, I don't know," she answered.

"I probably should have," he said, looking slightly embarrassed. "But I truly thought you had played the flute purposely, selfishly, and were undeserving of it. I misjudged you, and I was wrong. I'm sorry."

Kayla was very surprised by his admission, though she shouldn't have been. The face she presented to the world was only an act. Few knew the real Kayla, she kept herself so well hidden. If his judgment of her came from the banquet dinner and the confrontation with her grandfather, it was no wonder he had jumped to conclusions.

"Thank you." She leaned against the door jamb, relaxing further in his presence.

"Lady Kayla, this flute is more than just a beautiful, magical instrument. It is a key, *the* key . . . the sapphire keystone."

She nodded in understanding, and he continued.

"The keystones were created by the Guardians themselves to knit our world together after Mahal and S'Kotos nearly destroyed it with their battling. C'Tan wants those keystones more than anything. As long as they are inactive, she cannot find them, but once they live . . . they call to any who will listen, and she is listening very, very hard."

Kayla thought about that and suddenly understood why she was not to play this instrument. "So when I breathed upon it, I awakened it, and now C'Tan knows where it is."

The Ketahean nodded gravely. "That is why I had Sarali take the flute. I felt it awaken, and in order to protect it and all our people, I had to shield it from C'Tan. I only hope it was done soon enough."

"Shield? As in magic?" she questioned, pushing herself away from the door.

Again T'Kato nodded. "I am the keeper of records and protector of the keys within Ketahe. I was told to come here and await the Sapphire Flute."

"By whom?" Kayla demanded, but the large man only shook his head.

"That I cannot tell you." He paused and looked her over, seeming to assess her strength before he continued, guarded and compassionate.

"If you wish to save these people, you must leave here. We will protect you and keep the flute safe until the player comes to collect it."

"The player? I thought *I* was the player."

"You are its guardian, but player you are not."

We'll see about that, she thought, then focused on the rest of what he'd said. "Wait, you want me to leave with you? What are you talking about? Leave Dragonmeer, or Darthmoor?"

"Leave Peldane, Kayla," he said, voicing her worst fear.

"Peldane? You want me to leave the country just because I breathed on the flute? Isn't that a bit much?" she asked.

T'Kato shook his head before she even finished.

"If you care for your home, you will get as far from here as you can. I have done my best to shield the flute, but it is possible that C'Tan can sense it even so. At the very least, she may know where it was last held and come to Dragonmeer. We must get you to a place where it can be shielded indefinitely. Until the player comes, we have no choice."

"Can't you just take it?" she asked, a little desperate. She couldn't leave now. Everything had just been righted for her family. She was getting married, for goodness' sake. She could not leave!

"It must be thus, holder of the flute. It is tuned and tied to you, as it was you who breathed it to life. Only you can carry it, and until the player comes, you are the only one who can use it. You must come away with me."

"I think he's right," said a familiar voice from the darkness.

"Brant! You found T'Kato's note!" She rushed to him. Brant took her in his arms and gave her a quick squeeze, then held her hands as he faced her.

"Much as I hate to lose you right now, you must look to the good of our home first. That's what leaders do, Kay," he said, giving her his haunted smile. "My father was in agreement."

"Your father? You told him? Brant, how could you?"

"I didn't, Kay. Sarali did. Father wanted to speak with me about it. He has to look at what's best for his home and country too, you know. I'm only grateful this didn't happen on purpose. I know it was an accident, that you were not informed well enough, and so do my father and the king—"

"King Rojan knows, too?" Kayla groaned.

"My father had an obligation to inform him. He feels badly that he didn't give you a better idea of what rules apply to the instrument, and he accepts responsibility."

"But it's not his fault!" she defended.

"Nor is it yours, Kayla," T'Kato broke in. "Lord Brant is right. You were not well enough informed before being given such a gift, and with your love of music . . . well, no more need be said."

Kayla hung her head. They were right and she knew it, but part of her still wanted to take the blame. The other part was still trying to process the fact that she was leaving Dragonmeer and Darthmoor all because she was idiot enough to breathe into the flute.

She looked longingly at Brant. "I can't leave you when I have barely found you," she whispered.

Brant chuckled, though she thought she detected tears lurking in his eyes. "Kayla, the last thing I want is to lose you, but we can't afford to have C'Tan flaming down on us. When the danger has passed, or you have what you need, or the flute has been passed on . . . come back. I'll wait for you."

Kayla was desperate. She didn't want to go, but she knew in her heart she had no choice. She slowly nodded her head in agreement. Brant put his arms around her again, held her for a long moment, then let her go.

She turned to T'Kato. The big man took her shoulders in his giant hands, giving her a surprisingly gentle squeeze. "You choose well, little one—very well indeed. Let's find a place for you to sleep. We'll have someone retrieve your things from home. We leave at dawn."

Chapter Seventeen

Dinner was without salt and season, but still was one of the best meals Ember had eaten in a long time. The wolves had shifted to human form and laid down a base of stones, put the animals on it, then covered them with more stones. They heated the rocks magically, baking the rabbits in the middle as well as any stove. Ember ate a whole rabbit on her own and would have taken more if there had been any left.

After she'd eaten her fill, and her packmates had shifted back to their natural form, they curled together near the base of the willow. For some reason, all the wolves but Shad seemed more comfortable as wolf than man. Once everyone was settled, Ember sat across the fire from her uncle and finally had the chance to satisfy her curiosity. Shad sat in the dirt and leaned against a log with a satisfied sigh.

"Uncle Shad, what was he like?" Ember asked as Shad extended his feet toward the soggy fire. He seemed to know exactly who she meant.

"He was a good man and a great friend—the best. I've met a lot of people in my life, child, an awful lot, and I have yet to find one who is as caring, responsible, trustworthy, and talented as he is . . . was," he corrected, his voice catching. She was silent, hoping he'd continue. Shad stared into the small fire, huddled for warmth as they sat protected beneath the giant willow. "I remember the first time I met him. It was supposed to be this big secret between my father and me, but he wanted me to meet my human brother. He said we were a lot alike, and I think he had regrets about leaving Asana."

"Asana?" Ember asked. "Who's that?"

"Your grandmother." Shad glanced at her, then let his eyes be drawn back to the fire. "She's a strong woman, feisty as could be, but with a lot of love to give. I've met her a time or two. You'd like her," he said, giving her a half-smile. "I know my father cared for my own mother, but he never loved her the way he did your grandmother."

"Then why did he leave?"

He shrugged. "Political reasons. The chief of the Bendanatu passed away, and Bahndai, my father, was next in line. The Elders finally convinced him he needed to return home and lead us, for the good of the people, though it wasn't something he wanted. He just happened to be chosen." He shifted on the log that looked even more uncomfortable than the rock where Ember sat.

"Chosen? Why?"

"It's the eyes. The Bendanatu believe that our Guardian will show the sign of his favor through the eyes of his Chosen One."

"What do you mean?" she pursued.

"The Chosen's eyes are different in color than the rest of the tribe."

"Really? I thought all wolves had brown or gold eyes."

He shrugged again. "Usually they do," he answered, not really paying attention to her as he began to snap a twig into little pieces and throw it into the fire.

"But your eyes are green," she said.

"Nice of you to notice," he answered with a hint of sarcasm lacing his voice.

The realization of what he said sunk in. "So does that mean you're the next Chosen One?"

"Unfortunately, yes."

"Unfortunately? Why, Uncle? Don't you want to be a leader?" She was surprised. He seemed so capable and wise, even if he was a jokester.

"It's not that, Ember. Of course I want to help my people however I can, but . . ." he spread his hands in a helpless gesture. "It's a big job. My father is a great example of the sacrifices leaders must make. He gave up the love of his life to marry a friend, because that was the 'right' thing to do, and he did my mother no favors by it. Much as I love my parents, there's a part of me that wishes he had stayed with his human love and found a way to make it work."

"I didn't know wolf life was so complex," she said, leaning back against the log.

He rolled his eyes. "You have no idea, Ember, absolutely no idea. Human life is no picnic, but wolf life is extremely complex, with prejudice everywhere one looks."

"Now that's something I do know a little bit about," she said, trying to make light of the painful subject. Shad gave her a sympathetic grin and continued his previous story.

"Jarin was about five years old when my father took me to see him. For some reason, I thought of him as my little brother, though he was actually the elder. The Bendanatu age differently than humans." A half-smile quirked Shad's dimples to life. "He was little for his age, but he thought he could do anything. I've never seen such foolish courage, old or young, since then. He thought that if he could run fast enough and flap his arms really hard, he could fly."

"You're kidding!" Ember laughed. Shad painted a wonderful picture—it made her father seem so real and pulled him off the pedestal on which she'd kept him most of her life.

"Of course he didn't succeed," Shad continued, smiling at the memory, "but it quickly became a game with us. We'd run and chase each other back and forth, and pretend we were flying. When we tired of that, we just raced across the fields and through the trees. He was the elder, but I still beat him—until he took to riding me." Shad chuckled then. "He became the wolf master and I his wolf, and he was small enough that I could carry him on my back without harm."

Shad was quiet for a long moment then, seemingly lost in thought, and Ember found her mind wandering, imagining her father so young and innocent.

"That was the first day Father taught him to change into wolf form so he could run with us," Shad spoke again, startling Ember out of her reverie. "It was exciting. It had been great fun playing with Jarin as a human pup, but as a wolf cub he truly became my brother. We spent the time rolling and running and sniffing until Asana called him home. She never knew we came to see him, didn't know her husband was so close. Believe it or not, she never knew her husband was a wolf."

"No!" Ember gasped. "How could she not know?" She sat forward in surprise. The fire popped, spitting sparks, and she leaned back again, away from the flame.

"He didn't choose to tell her. In her eyes, he just disappeared one day, with no explanation. He was gone for two years before he came home for her. It had taken him that long to convince the council to accept a human amongst them, but when he showed up on her doorstep to explain, she would not speak to him. The stubborn woman sent him packing, wouldn't even listen, and so he returned to the Bendanatu, and they haven't spoken to each other since. The pride between the two of them . . ." Shad shook his head. "I've been trying for years to get one or the other of them to take the first step, but they think it's too late, despite the regrets. They won't even try."

"That's so sad."

Shad nodded slowly, staring into the glowing coals. A comfortable silence stretched between them for a long while, long enough that Ember lay down in the grass near the fire, close enough to stay warm, but far enough to keep from being caught by sparks. The flame seemed to know she was named for it and was sending an invitation. Shad continued to stare into the fire as if he could see things beyond Ember's ken.

She was drifting off to sleep when he spoke again.

"Your father showed an incredible talent for magic when he was very young. He was six when I caught him milking the goat without hands, seven when he learned to fly."

"Really? My father could fly?" Ember sat up, astounded.

"Oh, yes, that man could fly like a bird. You should have seen Asana's face the first time she saw him. I couldn't stop laughing—it just about gave her a heart attack," Shad chuckled at the memory.

"He apologized, of course, but it wasn't long before Asana took him to the academy in Karsholm to get some training."

"At seven? Isn't that a little young?" Ember wasn't sure, but it seemed most magi started between eight and twelve.

Shad nodded. "Yes, it's very young, but it was either that or tie him down. Asana couldn't keep his feet on the ground once he learned to fly, especially once he could shape-shift into hawk form. Oh, he was beautiful. I never could do the bird shift, but he was a natural at it. Almost preferred hawk to wolf form, which is near to unheard of. In fact, it *is* unheard of—except for him—at least among the Bendanatu."

Ember chuckled at the image of her father tied to the ground. If he was anything like she was, that would have been next to impossible. What a treasure of memories Shad gave her. This was exactly what she'd always wanted from her mother and never received. The thought of her mother brought back her longing and fear, now that Ian Covainis had entered the picture. She changed the subject to keep her thoughts from dangerous realms.

"How did you and DeMunth meet?" she asked. Her thoughts had continued to linger on him and his wordless song throughout the day.

"DeMunth? That's a long and strange story. In short, I found him wandering the woods one day, delirious, and I took him to your grandma Asana to clean him up. She was the only person I could think of at the time who might care enough to help. I've kept an eye on her over the years, though she doesn't know whose son I am." Shad fiddled with a loose string on his sleeve. "She took a real liking to DeMunth, healing what was left of his tongue and nursing him back to health."

"What happened to his tongue?"

Shad met her eyes across the fire, his lips drawn into a thin line. "That's not my story to tell. You'll have to ask him." The silence stretched between them for a moment before he continued. "Your grandmother treated him like her own son, and he treated her like the mother he never knew. I haven't seen a closer relationship between two people that weren't kin. He helps her around the house, doing all the physical things that age makes difficult for her, and she keeps him healthy and fills his emotional needs. It's a good situation for both of them." Shad shifted against the log and pulled off another twig to feed the fire.

"Every once in a while, the two of us go to Javak and check in. Asana sends some of her best mage stones with him to sell. Since the trials are in session, the people we need to see are there. It seems easier to travel together, and we enjoy each other's company. He's quiet and laughs at my jokes, and I give him a living pillow at night," Shad grinned.

Ember's grandma mined mage stones. What a thought. She wondered what it would have been like to be raised with grandparents in her life. She'd not really thought about it before, but now the absence left her aching from one more loss.

"Will I ever meet my grandparents, do you think?" Ember thought aloud. She knew she must be getting tired, with her thoughts popping out of her mouth as they were.

Shad thought about it for a minute. "I don't know, lass, though I hope so. I think they would love and welcome you. Neither of them has seen or heard from your father in over twenty years." Shad threw the last of the twig into the fire before scooting to the ground and putting his back against the log. "It's incredible we've met like this, but the Guardians have reasons for all the things in our lives. This was meant to be."

Ember wasn't sure about that, but she found herself open to the idea. She knew of the Guardians, of course, but had thought of them only as legend or myth, not as real, living beings watching out for and guiding her throughout her life. It was a strange thought, yet somehow comforting. She wrapped her arms around herself, shivering with the drop in temperature the dark had brought.

"You know, you'd sleep a lot warmer in wolf form. I was about to change myself. Care to join me?" He grinned at her and began to slowly shift his body back into his natural shape.

Ember tried to follow him, attempting to recreate what she had done at the cave. Shad stopped his transformation at a patchy half-bald look, not quite human or wolf, to laugh at her attempts.

"Lass, you've got to let your clothes absorb into your skin. Change the color. Right now you have clothing-colored fur."

Ember looked down and was appalled. She had a brown breech-shaped bottom half and a sage green top. She must be quite a sight indeed, and that would have to change immediately. She imagined the fur white, as his was, and it slowly faded into the same snowy shade.

"Good," he applauded with paw-shaped hands. "Let's continue."

The change was gradual—first hair, then body, then limbs and face and teeth. Ember learned about halfway through the process that if she stopped thinking about it and simply tried to feel her way through the change, she was more successful in her attempts.

At last they were done.

For the second time that day Ember felt at ease in her wolf body, and thankfully warm. Her senses went back to their heightened state, both smell and hearing aware of every minute sound and scent within the forest, down to the steady tread of a beetle crawling across the clearing and the scent of various animals around the woods marking their territory. She had to adjust to the greater sound before she could sleep, but just as the nose adjusts to a familiar scent, even when overpowering, she found her awareness of noise slowly fading. Once she got used to it, she sauntered over to join the pack, circling to find a comfortable position. She finally settled, curling her nose around to meet her tail in typical canine fashion. It seemed a natural and comforting way to sleep.

Then she had a thought. *"Uncle?"* she yipped in wolf speak.

"Yes?" he answered, half-opening a single emerald eye.

"Did my father ever sleep with you under the moon like this?"

Shad smiled in his wolfish way, tongue lolling, and sighed, sadness oozing from him like a reopened wound. *"Every chance he got. When your father and I ran, the moon was our best friend, the night our ally. Song was our hearts, and sleep our souls. Wolf was life. Being wolf was sheer joy when we were together."*

Ember could understand that sensation. Never before had she felt so comfortable in her own skin. No more awkwardness, no more questions about who she was or what she should do. Things were clearer, simpler. There were no more lies about her family and past. She might not know everything about who she was or where she had come from, but she now had a start and a source of information. She had a feeling she and Uncle Shad were going to be very close indeed, and it was a relationship no one would be able to sever.

Not even her mother.

And with that happy thought, she faded into sleep.

Chapter Eighteen

"Bless you, Joyson. Your help has been invaluable," Kayla said to the boy as he dropped her trunk in the middle of the cellar.

"T'was no problem at all, miss," he replied, winded. "The other servants had all your things packed afore I even knocked on the door."

Kayla nodded at him, not really paying much attention as she knelt in front of her trunk and unbuckled the leather latches. She raised the lid and let it fall back with a muted thump on the dusty stone, pulling the hovering magelight closer.

"Yes, it looks like it's all here," she mumbled and smoothed the top gown, a vivid blue with lace cuffs at wrist and neck. By the depth of the dresses, it looked as if the servants had packed three or four of her best, as well as socks, underthings, and two more pair of good, heeled boots. She buckled the leather straps and stood.

"I hope you'll be having a pleasant mornin'." The boy bowed awkwardly and turned to leave.

"Joyson, thank you," she said. "You're an asset to this household and bring honor to your family."

"No trouble, miss," he said. "Happy to help." He nodded his head to her once more and headed up the stairs in that long-legged stride of his. He was a kind soul. Brant was lucky to have him.

T'Kato chose that moment to enter from the far reaches of the back rooms. In the faint blue glow of the magelight, Kayla was surprised at his changed appearance. The apron had been replaced with trousers so loose they were almost a skirt, and he wore a cream tunic caught at the waist with a wide purple sash. It was not a color she would have imagined for this intense hulk of a man. His boots were knee-high leather that rippled with his muscles.

"Did you get your things?" his deep voice rumbled quietly at her, eyes flicking up and down to appraise her dress. He shook his head slightly in dismay. Kayla was not sure what to make of that. She had thought her new dress would be perfectly acceptable.

T'Kato rubbed his temples, then dragged his hand down his face, the sound of his whiskers scratching loud in the stillness of the room. "Did anyone see you come down?" He sounded tired and a little exasperated.

"Just Joyson. He brought my trunk."

"Joyson can be trusted," T'Kato said in that gravelly voice of his that sounded as if it boomed from the depths of a cave. "He won't speak, I'm sure of it."

Sarali stepped lightly down the stairs and joined them.

"'Tis nearly dawn, Kato. I've brought a bit of food for the journey. Would you like me to divide the stores between us?" She held a bulging sack in her right hand.

T'Kato nodded, then turned his attention back to Kayla. "Have you got anything useful in that trunk of yours?"

"That depends on what you consider useful. I've got two pair of good boots, several dresses and underthings, some books, a knife . . . what is so funny?" she demanded of the snickering Sarali, who got herself outwardly under control, though her eyes still sparkled. T'Kato glared, dismissing his wife with a sharp gesture of his head.

"Does she have issues with me?" Kayla asked, surprised by the change in the servant girl she had liked so well the day before. It was interesting to note how uncomfortable she was having Sarali treat her as an equal instead of a superior.

T'Kato ignored the question.

"Would you please open your trunk so we can see these 'good boots' of yours?" he asked politely, though Kayla had the feeling he would not accept no for an answer.

She knelt before the chest and threw back the lid. She was almost embarrassed by her finery and unsure how to deal with the emotion.

T'Kato bent in half to reach inside her trunk with his huge hands. He pulled out her boots, snorted, and tossed them in the corner.

"Hey! What are you doing?" Kayla started toward the outcast boots, but T'Kato grabbed her arm and forced her to stay at his side without offering a single word. The feelings that washed over her then were overwhelming. She felt helpless and a little scared and definitely angry, standing next to this gorilla of a man she did not know and had to trust. What did she really know about him, anyway? Was she making a mistake? She couldn't answer that, but felt she had to take the chance.

T'Kato pulled her dresses out one by one and tossed them into the corner with her boots. He sorted through her books and set two aside. The rest joined the growing pile. He tossed all the frilly underthings but one. When he had emptied her trunk, he took the knife from its jewel-encrusted sheath and examined its edge with his thumb.

He snorted. "This thing wouldn't cut butter, lass. You ever use it?"

Kayla didn't trust herself to speak, so only shook her head.

"A gift, by the look of it," he questioned her with brows raised.

"My father," she spat, still fuming over his dismissal of her best clothes.

"And his name would be . . ." he waited.

She considered not answering. What business was it of his, anyway? She wasn't comfortable talking about her father with people she knew, so why should she talk about it with this stranger who alternately terrified and soothed her? In the end, his silence won out.

"Felandian," she answered, barely giving him what he asked for.

T'Kato's eyes showed surprise. "Felandian the evahn? Of the Kingdom Fashan?"

Kayla was startled. "You know my father?"

T'Kato's eyes showed new respect. "I do," he said, moving to the pile of clothes he had tossed in the corner, gathering them up in one arm and dropping them back into the trunk. He closed and latched it quickly before Kayla thought to object to the mess he was making of her dresses. She'd be forever ironing when she returned.

"What's Felandian doing, fathering a human child? That's not like him." His words cut sharply into Kayla's heart, and she had to blink back tears she would not allow herself to shed.

"I don't know, and frankly don't care. He left when I was young. I barely remember him."

"And you're how old? Seventeen? Eighteen? That would have been about the time his grandfather died. It was hard for him. They were very close. I hadn't known he'd taken up with a human, though. Interesting."

Kayla wasn't sure whether to spurn the man for his insensitivity, or thank him for the knowledge. She had known nothing of her father but his name and race. She had a few scraps of memory. He never seemed happy, and now she knew some of the why. Kayla only wished he had involved himself with her rather than leaving her behind like worn-out rags or dirty laundry. She turned her back on T'Kato so he would not see how much his words pained her.

She could hear him rummaging about, then the soft scrape of metal on stone. She looked over her shoulder to see what he was doing. He had her small knife and was honing its edge on a dark whetstone. He licked his finger and slid it across the blade, making a rasping sound as his calluses caught at the sharpened steel.

"If this thing is evahn-forged, it should hold its edge once sharpened. At least he left you a gift to show you some kind of favor, though I'm sure that's pennies to your heart with the ache he must have caused."

Kayla turned her head again to stare at the slits, brightening with the rising sun. How keenly this man knew her, and she knew him not at all. Sarali's soft footsteps startled her out of her reverie.

"I didn't know me da either, Kayla. He left when I was but a wee babe, and it breaks me heart still these thirty years later to think on it. Never did know what became of him." She gave Kayla a moment to collect herself, then thrust an armful of clothes at her. "Here. These ought to fit yer needs a bit more rightly than those dresses of yours. A dress is fine for the dances and such, but when it comes to traipsing through the forest, they do nothin' but slow ye down, and I can promise ye, the dresses wouldn't be fine for long."

Kayla took the clothes gratefully. She was not sure what to expect from T'Kato's wife. It unsettled her. The woman noticed and laughed.

"Ah, don't mind me, miss. I'm a bit put out that I have to leave this place when I just came to like it. Been here longer than most, and Dragonmeer feels a lot like home."

Sarali took Kayla by the arm, leading her into the small room where she had spent the night on an uncomfortable straw mattress.

"It's goin' to be an adjustment for ye, but we'll do our best to lead ye along and find that player of yours, miss."

"I don't understand why the king would make me guardian of the flute and yet I'm not its player. I'm having difficulty with that." Kayla tugged at the laces on her corset.

"I wouldn't know much about that, only what me husband has seen fit to share. We'll help ye find some answers somewhere, and T'Kato can keep ye safe if anyone can. The man's a beast with a sword, he is." With that, she turned and left Kayla to dress herself.

There was only one problem.

"Sarali?" she called before the woman could leave. "Could I trouble you for some help? I've got this darn corset on . . ." she waved her hands helplessly, and Sarali laughed.

"Sure, sure. Never could fathom why a woman would want to wear one o' them things meself. Nothin' but misery, pure misery."

Kayla grimaced. "I would agree, but unfortunately this particular society demands them, and I've had to spend most of my life living by their rules. I didn't have much choice."

"There ye be wrong, Kayla. Ye always have a choice. Ye just need the courage to take the chances when they come."

Sarali punctuated her words with sharp pulls at Kayla's laces until she was free and able to breathe deeply. It felt good. *Really* good.

Kayla stepped out of the dress and turned to the heap of clothes Sarali had given her, not sure where to begin. They were all so foreign. The sash she could figure out, but the blouse and trousers had no buttons—just flaps and small laces that seemed to criss and cross endlessly. Sarali laid the individual pieces out on the straw bed.

"Here. This is what we use for bindin' ourselves up, instead o' the corsets yer women wear." She handed Kayla a cloth that looked like two thick circles joined together, with straps that went around and tied together in the back. It was fairly comfortable compared to the corset she was accustomed to wearing, though she felt almost naked. It would definitely take some getting used to.

The pants fit snugly around the ankles, were extremely baggy, and much too long in the leg, but Sarali showed her the trick to them by rolling the top down several times, then securing the inside flap with a lace that traveled through loops and tied in the front.

Sarali pulled the laces running down the outside of the leg, knitting them in a series of 'x's. It was actually quite pretty to look at by the time she was done, and the pants fit as though they had been made for her. Sarali tied the ends around Kayla's ankle. After the pants, the blouse was easy.

A wide sapphire sash, wrapped around her waist twice and tied in the back, ends tucked inside the sash itself, finished her attire. It was mind-boggling how at ease Kayla felt in such strange clothing, and not just physically but emotionally, almost as if she were born for these clothes.

T'Kato knocked on the partially closed door and entered the room with a large leather backpack, Kayla's knife, and tall, black boots. He had added to his outfit since she'd left him, and now wore a leather breastplate, with metal guards on his forearms. He tossed the backpack on the bed and dropped the boots at her feet.

"Here's your knife. I gave it a new sheath. The other one was just begging for stealing." He held the knife out for her to take. "I'll teach you how to use it later. It would be a good fighting knife, and not likely to break."

"Oh, no, I couldn't," Kayla objected, putting her hands behind her back.

"Oh, yes, you will," T'Kato said in much the same tone. He knelt and tied the knife to the x's on the right side of her pants. Kayla watched his nimble fingers, impressed by his dexterity despite the size of his hands.

"Is that too tight?" he asked, looking up. Kayla bent at the knee and leaned forward, flexing her thigh. She could feel the knife, but it was not uncomfortable.

"No, it's fine, but what I'll ever use it for besides cutting fruit . . ." She trailed off at the look on his face.

"It never hurts to be safe, Kayla. I'll teach you a bit about using that thing when we're out on the road, and I hope you'll never need it. Now, I took measurements from your other boots and shrunk a pair of mine down for you. Try them on and see how they feel, and we'll adjust them as needed."

T'Kato knelt, and Kayla slid her foot into the boot. She balanced on her left foot and slid the other into the buttery leather, stamping down once to settle her foot.

"How's that feel?" he asked as she stomped around the room in one boot.

"Pretty good. There's a slight chafe in the heel, and it's a little too wide, but overall they're great. How do you shrink down a pair of boots?" He didn't answer at first, just prodded at her foot to find the spots she mentioned. Kayla looked at the embroidery around the upper edge of her boot. Blue again. She was afraid blue was going to be known as her signature color, now that she was becoming known as the guardian of the flute, but she didn't really mind. It was one of her favorite colors, though it would be nice to have a little variety.

"Well, we can fix that easily enough, though Sarali's touch is a bit softer than mine in the details." The big man folded his arms and leaned against the wall, watching as his wife knelt at Kayla's feet and prodded with deft fingers.

"Yes, I feel the air where it shouldn't be. We'll fix that right and proper. Just hold still for a bit, would ye, lass? That's it now." Kayla felt a surge somewhere in her soul. The boot tightened slightly on the sides and flared at the heel to fit her snugly, like a second skin. It was incredible. A practical use for magic! She'd never thought much of the application other than for keeping her room warm or cool, or for exchanging notes like she had with T'Kato.

"That's amazing!" Kayla blurted, bringing chuckles to husband and wife. She reddened, but continued. "I've never had a more comfortable pair of boots in my life."

"Good. Ye'll be doin' a lot of walkin' in them, so they'd *best* be comfortable," Sarali said, helping Kayla into the other boot and repeating the process.

"Walking? We're not taking horses?" Kayla was dismayed. She thought of her new cream-colored mare while balancing on her other foot. The duke's gift had been a dream to ride, almost like flying, and the thought of not being able to ride made her very aware of the reality of her banishment. It felt like she was being punished for something she hadn't meant to do. Her stomach was sick with the thought.

T'Kato chuckled. "No, lass. Can you imagine a horse that would fit me? We'll find mounts for the three of us elsewhere, but I had planned on following water wherever we can. Perhaps a boat would serve us better."

He looked down at his wife, and something passed between them, though Kayla wasn't sure what it was. There was some special significance to his words, she was sure of it, but she shrugged and let it go. They'd tell her or they wouldn't.

"We'd best be headin' out, T'Kato. It's nearly full light. Both flutes are packed in the bag, lass, along with the pretty sheath you can use for barter, one change o' clothes, and a bit o' food. Do ye have any money?" Sarali asked, walking through the doorway and shrugging herself into a hooded cape.

"A little," Kayla responded, wary. After all, she hardly knew these two and had only their word as to the truth of the flute. A shiver of fear went through her. What if it wasn't true? What if they were taking her to the slave traders? Or were going to ransom her to her father? Her thoughts must have been apparent on her face because Sarali snorted at her.

"We aren't going to rob ye, girl. We've got a bit o' money, but it won't be enough to get far. If ye've got some to pitch in, let us know, or we'll have to work for food, more than not." She stepped through the curtain and donned her backpack.

Kayla realized that if she was going to leave with these two, she had to trust them or it would be a miserable journey for all. She could not go halfway. For a brief moment she wavered in her determination. It was so tempting to forget about the danger, forget about her guardianship, and return to the old life, but there was that stubborn part of her that said no. She would not run away from her duty to the flute any more than she had run from her duty to her mother. She would trust these two and go.

Kayla dug in the waistline of her underthings and untied the money belt she had hidden there, then moved through the doorway and offered the money bag to T'Kato. He froze in mid-shrug and stared at her, surprise registering on his heavy, hair-free features. He slowly shook his head, a soft smile tickling the corner of his mouth.

"I don't need you to give it to me, Kayla—we just needed to know if you had any. I'll trust you just as you trust us, though we'll have need of that, I'm sure." He settled the backpack on his shoulders, adjusting the straps, then came forward and held Kayla's shoulders in his great hands.

"Thank you for trusting us. We'll not lead you astray." The tattooed man looked around the room. Kayla's eyes followed his glance toward the trunk standing in the corner. She had one final twinge of regret for her dresses, but the comfort of her new clothing made it easier to leave the old things behind.

"Let's go."

T'Kato moved forward into the dark, pausing only long enough to let their eyes adjust as they went deeper into the bowels of the cellar. He took the lead and walked with measured steps tailored to the shorter stature of the women, though he still moved quickly through the darkened rooms.

"There's a passage down here that tunnels under the moat and emerges at an abandoned cottage outside of Dragonmeer. We'll exit there and make our way across the fields toward the forest," T'Kato said over his shoulder.

Kayla blinked. A hidden passage? She wondered if Brant knew of its existence. She wouldn't be able to ask him now—not until she returned. Her heart ached at the thought of her fiancé. She was going to miss Brant and hoped he truly would wait for her, but she was surprised to realize that of all the people she was leaving behind, it was hardest to say goodbye to her mother.

Kayla had asked Brant to deliver a note to Lady Kalandra before the sun began to kiss the eastern peaks. She only hoped her mother would understand, and Brant had promised he would explain things to her. He had also reassured Kayla that the king promised that her title would be waiting for her when she came back. It would not be rescinded, despite her mistake with the flute, and for that she was extremely grateful. Her mother would be cared for, no matter what happened.

The sound of dripping water got louder, and at last T'Kato led Kayla and Sarali into the farthest room. There was a large mirror in the wall—so large that as children, no matter how Kayla and Brant had tried, they could not get it to move. They'd always thought it strange to have something as frivolous as a mirror in this forsaken corner of the cellar, but nobody could answer their questions, and after a while it no longer mattered.

T'Kato pressed the bricks to the left and right of the mirror in what seemed a random pattern. When he pressed the last one and stepped back, the mirror and part of the wall sank inward and slid aside.

The secret passage.

A thrill of fear and excitement shivered through Kayla. She'd never been down a hidden passage before, but the adventure soon wore off when she realized that it was a hall like any other, except it was much wetter.

The puddles rose to mid-calf and higher—dirty water that stank of unspeakable things, debris floating across the top. She was reluctant to take a close look. Rats paddled by, nibbled at the legs of her boots, then left upon finding she was not edible, though she still jumped every time one bumped against her.

The tunnel seemed to go on forever, but eventually sloped upward, leaving the smelly water behind. They reached a rickety wooden ladder. T'Kato gestured for Kayla to go first. The wood looked half-rotten with age and ready to collapse at the slightest bit of pressure, but when Kayla put her hand on it and gave a testing pull, it held. She climbed quickly to the top, stepping onto a landing and near the back side of another hidden door.

T'Kato placed his eye to a small hole in the wall. He scanned left and right, then pressed his ear to the wood. Evidently satisfied, he pulled a latch to his left. The panel slid open to reveal a dusty bedroom with moldy blankets and a ceiling full of cobwebs. The windows were boarded up, but still the light beamed into the dust-filled room, motes dancing in the rays. Kayla coughed as the dust stirred. She looked around to get her bearings, and everything clicked into place. She knew where she was.

The haunted cottage.

Children always avoided this place except on a dare, and though Kayla had never entered it, she now knew why the youngsters thought it haunted. The place was old and creaky. The wind howled through the tunnel and sounded very ghostly to a childish imagination.

T'Kato led the two women through the bedroom and pried the boards from one of the empty window frames, then helped Kayla and Sarali into the open air. He didn't attempt to board the window back up, and somehow that bothered Kayla, though she knew it was silly.

The sun was now fully up, and the field stretched out before them, a long distance from the trees. T'Kato looked over his shoulder at the two of them, checked their backpacks, and motioned with his head that it was time to go. He took off at a slow jog and picked up speed quickly, Sarali and Kayla following. There was no way Kayla could keep up with his long-legged sprint for the trees, and she fell farther and farther behind. Sarali stayed with her for a while until Kayla waved her on, and the serving girl took off in a lope that was astounding. No one should be able to run that fast.

Just before she reached the tree line, Kayla had to stop and suck in some air before she fell over. She was not used to such physical exertion, and she had to learn how to breathe all over again.

She gulped in and out, trying to slow her pounding heart. Eventually it began to work. She knelt on the ground a few minutes longer, enjoying the smell of the morning dew evaporating from the field, then stood, filled with excitement and fear. It was a new beginning—a change that both thrilled and terrified her. She had a feeling the flute was either going to bring her great success or terrible pain. Of course she hoped it would be the first, but even the threat of the latter held a kind of thrill. She was no longer held by the rigid rules society had forced on her. She was her own woman, sacrificing comfort and success to save her small world. It helped to think that.

Kayla looked over the tall grass, trying to spot her guides. She caught a glimpse of Sarali standing just inside the line of trees, T'Kato at her side. They beckoned, impatience and fear obvious in their near-frantic waving.

Kayla gathered her breath and stretched against the pull of the pack. She was about to run and join the others when she caught a sound she could not quite identify—snapping, like the wind-filled piñons high on the keep walls, but lower, deeper. Or footsteps snapping rotted wood, or the banging of water inside a trough. Kayla looked up, but saw nothing. Clouds had settled so low in the sky, she couldn't pinpoint the sound's origin.

There was no one near, but the sound continued. Chills traveled up and down her spine, an eerie tap dance of ghosts upon her soul. Something bad was coming. She could feel it in her very bones. The dread she felt was so strong, it gave her the energy she needed to finish the run. With a burst of speed, she took off for the trees and the new friends she could see waving to her from the forest's edge.

Chapter Nineteen

For the second time in as many days, DeMunth woke Ember with his wordless singing. His voice haunted her dreams in the best of ways, so when her eyes cracked open, it was with a wolfish grin and a lightened heart. She lay in silence, watching and listening as he knelt in the same position as the morning before, his arms outstretched and head thrown back. In anyone else, it would have seemed a prideful challenge to the heavens, but in DeMunth, it was an attitude of humble servitude, as if he were giving every piece of himself to the Guardians through his song.

Ember was more than a little fascinated with him. She hated to admit it, but just being near him made her stomach jump. He was handsome enough, she guessed, but it was his energy, the intelligence, and talent he kept hidden except in praise, that drew her to him. He reminded her of the best parts of Aldarin and Ren, with something uniquely his own added to the mix. Too soon, his song was done and Ember sighed. She hated to have it end.

She closed her eyes as she looked at him, then snapped them open again just as quickly, a sharp yip escaping her as she jumped to her feet. There was more to DeMunth than could be seen with eyes alone. He stared at her now, his face a mixture of confusion and fear as she immediately went to full defensive mode, a low growl rumbling in her chest.

"What is it?" Shad asked, all calmness with still-sleepy overtones.

"He glows," she answered, not sure how to express what she'd seen. The man was a miniature sun. It hurt to blink in his presence, though why she hadn't noticed it the day before, she wasn't sure.

Instead of answering, the two men laughed. Ember's hackles rose higher with the indignity. DeMunth slowly got to his feet and approached her, his hands open and out, a sign that he meant no harm. Still, her fur stood on end as he came close. She couldn't calm the uneasiness that settled over her at the sight of his glowing form.

"There's nothing to fear," Shad answered. *"DeMunth, you might as well tell her. If she's anything like her mother, she won't trust you until she understands."*

What was that supposed to mean?

DeMunth settled on the log in front of Ember and began his story in his clear mind-speech. Again, he sounded as though he spoke with his lips, but Ember watched and was sure they never moved. His mouth drew down at the corners, his brow furrowed just a bit. Evidently it was a painful subject. She sat down slowly and waited.

"At the age of five, my mother took me to the priests of Sha'iim to be raised as one of their own. Why she did this, I am unsure, and it does not matter. I had not one father, but seventy-three, and nearly one hundred brothers. I had no time to miss my mother, nor did I often feel the lack. I was well cared for, loved, and rose quickly in my studies.

"By the time I turned fifteen, I was in training to become a full priest and taught classes to the young acolytes. It was predicted that I would become Father of the order by forty, and it may well have been, if not for the dream."

Completely immersed in the story, Ember didn't even bother to scratch as a beetle climbed slowly up her leg. DeMunth continued.

"At seventeen, I had a dream, but it was unlike any other dream I'd known. A man came to me as I slept, a man who wore sunlight the way

I wear clothes. He shone so brightly, it would have burned my eyes had I been awake. I doubt I would have survived the experience if he had not changed me in some way." DeMunth's face shone, not with light, but with peace and joy as he relived the experience.

"*He spoke of a breastplate I was to find and protect. It was a keystone created by the Guardians to hold Rasann together after the battle between S'Kotos and Mahal nearly tore our world apart.*"

This was all new to Ember. Evidently that was obvious, for DeMunth addressed her directly then, pulling himself from the story. "*You do not know of the teachings? Have you not heard of Mahal, Klii'kunn, or Hwalan?*"

Ember shook her head. The names were foreign to her. DeMunth sighed deeply. "*Your education has been much neglected. We will rectify that. The Guardians were the creators of our world, brothers, all of them. There were a hundred to begin with, but after the fall only seven remained, one of whom became The Destroyer. S'Kotos.*" DeMunth nearly spat the name.

"*It was Lahonra who visited me that night. He is the Guardian of Light, father of all Guardians, holder of the yellow magic, and it was his creation that lay in peril—the Golden Breastplate. He told me where it could be found, and as soon as the light faded from my dream, I awoke with the knowledge of where to find it, and how it could be retrieved.*

"*In the basement of the monastery I found a hidden room, accessed only by the highest of the priests. I found it quickly, guided by my dream and the voice speaking to my heart. It told me of a hidden latch and taught me what I must do to enter. The breastplate was there. It glowed when I entered the room, as if it was waiting. It spoke to me.*"

Ember drew back at that, and he was quick to explain.

"*Not in words. It spoke peace to my heart and sent an invitation which I readily accepted. I removed my tunic and donned the breastplate. Strangely, the armor embedded itself in my skin and sank beneath it. I know it is hard to believe, but it is that which you saw when I sang my praises.*"

Ember had chills on top of chills. The breastplate sank beneath his skin? That scene was too familiar for comfort, and she really didn't like the implication for her own situation. The bracelets sank beneath her skin just the day before, but she found it hard to believe it was Guardian magic. Hadn't Ezeker said they were made by her father? Or had she just assumed?

DeMunth continued. *"Unfortunately, the head priests found me and did not understand my vision. They tortured me in the hopes of getting the breastplate back, and finally resorted to cutting out my tongue so I could never speak the 'lies' which kept me from returning what I had stolen. Rather than take my life, which would have been against the laws of the priesthood, they set me free to wander in the forest alone. That act nearly killed me. If it had not been for your uncle carrying me to your grandmother, I surely would have died."* DeMunth placed his hand on Shad's shoulder and affectionately scratched behind his ears.

Ember finally understood the closeness they shared. She also understood what it was she had seen. She wanted to know more about this keystone, but she had so many questions, she didn't know where to start. She sat in stunned silence for a long while. Shad and DeMunth began to look at each other nervously, fidgeting where they stood, growing more impatient with each passing moment.

Unable to organize her thoughts well enough to project them, and frustrated with the limitations of her wolf body, she shape-shifted back into her boy form. It was less painful than the night before, and she did it almost instantly.

"So, this breastplate, did it leave any kind of mark on your skin? Can you see it with your eyes open?" she asked. DeMunth stared at her in shock, though Ember wasn't sure if it was because she looked like a boy or had shifted so quickly. She couldn't hear his thoughts unless he sent them to her, and all she felt from him was astonishment. Shad chuckled appreciatively in his mind.

Visibly shaking himself, DeMunth answered. *"No, not so much as I can tell. Why?"*

Ember didn't answer. "Can I see?"

DeMunth cocked his head, but slowly pulled his tunic up. Ember's heart fluttered at the muscles rippling across his chest, but her stomach knotted with imagined pain at the scars across his arms and neck. She took a step closer and bent her head to his chest to see better.

There was a faint shimmer to DeMunth's skin, but not much more than would be had by a shirtless walk through a pollen-filled meadow. She looked closer. The shine stopped in a distinct line at his shoulder and neck. There were also no scars on his torso. One particularly bad burn scar severed exactly on that line. On one side it was waxy, shriveled skin, and the other perfectly normal, if softly glowing. The hair on the back of Ember's neck stood up as she traced the lines. DeMunth shivered and pulled away.

"There is a line. Right here," she traced it again, "and here." DeMunth squished his chin downward. Shad stepped forward to look.

"Well, look at that. She's right."

"Where?" DeMunth asked, straining to see.

"Just trust us. It's there. How did you know?" Shad asked, turning to Ember. She pulled up her sleeves and showed them her tattooed wrists and hands, then opened her collar and showed them the pendant tattooed into her sternum.

"Yesterday these were silver, a gift from my father." Shad's nostrils flared as he sniffed at her arm and examined the bracelet as closely as she'd examined DeMunth's chest. DeMunth glanced at the scrolling lines and smiled, then grabbed her wrist and pulled her into his arms.

Ember's breath caught in her throat. The pull she felt from DeMunth was not just physical. There was some kind of connection between them that she didn't understand, but could not deny. The smell of him was intoxicating. A mixture of sunshine, horse, and some kind of herb. He smelled good, and not just as in "pleasant." He smelled of goodness, strange as it sounded even to herself. She took a deep whiff while his arms were wrapped around her. She was in his arms, her heart racing—but it couldn't be. It wasn't right.

She pulled back quickly. She was a girl on the inside, yes, and there was not a thing wrong with liking this handsome, strong man, but outside, for all intents and purposes, she looked like a boy. It was tempting to tell Shad she had changed her mind and was going

207

to be female no matter what, just so she could continue to feel safe and protected. But it was silly and she knew it. Her safety was at stake here, and not only her own, but that of Shad and DeMunth as well. She had to bury her feelings or things would not only look bad, but if Ian found her, they would *be* bad.

Ember sat down heavily on the log behind her, Shad sitting on his haunches at her feet and DeMunth beside her. "I'm not sure what all this means," she said, "but Ian saw the tattoos when he had me in the cave. He's going to recognize me, whether I'm a boy or a girl, if he sees these." She raised her arms from her lap again. "It would be nice if my new magic would let me cover them, but what am I supposed to do? Grow another layer of skin?" Ember had tried doing just that the night before, but it had been like trying to move a house with her bare hands.

Shad shook his head and didn't answer. DeMunth took his time before he mind-spoke to her, his eyes staring into hers with great intensity. *"Did you have a vision when you received the bracelets?"*

Ember shook her head.

DeMunth sighed. *"Then I am unsure whether it is a gift from the Guardians, or magic created to imitate it. Either way, it is powerful, and nothing to be toyed with. It also needs to remain hidden. My story alone should convince you of the danger these things can bring when the wrong people know of them."* He scraped a hand through his hair, then spoke to Shad. *"Do you think perhaps you could use your gifts to create a similar bracelet to cover up the one on her skin?"* DeMunth asked, tracing the pattern of the bracelet on her hand for a brief moment, giving Ember goosebumps.

Shad nodded. *"Yes, I think I can. The only problem is finding materials. I obviously don't have anything on hand to make such a thing."*

DeMunth jogged to his saddle bag and pulled out a sack that chinked as he threw it to the wolf. Shad shifted to human form almost instantly and plucked it out of the air. He opened the neck of the bag and spilled a few coins into his hand, a mixture of silver and copper. Shad looked up at DeMunth, and the mute shrugged.

Something passed between them that Ember didn't understand, but Shad sighed and got to work.

He separated the coins by type and placed them in small piles on the log, one to each side of him. He took one of the copper coins in his hand, closed his eyes, then pushed at it with his thumbs. The copper stretched like clay. Ember gasped, then watched transfixed as he proceeded to stretch it into long threads that he snipped and curled into small chains, using only his fingernails. He melted the chains into the edge of one of the larger copper coins, then put his hand out.

"May I?" he asked, nodding toward her hand. Ember rested it in his lap. Shad measured the length of the chain and width of the coin against the dark silver lines on her hand, then nodded approvingly and resumed working.

DeMunth tapped Ember on the shoulder. She turned, reluctant to tear her eyes away from Shad's creation, only to have a bundle thrust at her. *"Shad told me about your decision not to change . . . certain things about yourself."* DeMunth reddened. *"I thought this might help with your disguise."* It was hard to remember that DeMunth didn't speak with his mouth. Even staring him in the face, she almost heard him with her ears.

She took the bundle as he turned away, his ears still red. Ember tried to hide her smile. She'd feel the same in a similar situation. It was one more thing she liked about the man.

She found a semi-private spot behind some bushes back in the woods. She unraveled DeMunth's bundle to find not only clean breeches and a baggy cream shirt, but a leather vest, some boots, and a roll of bandages.

Relieved, she pulled her shirt over her head and wrapped the bandage around her chest, pulling it tight, for once thankful for her modest size. Uncle Shad was obviously not completely human to think she was well endowed. That had *never* been her problem. It made hiding her gender much easier.

Once dressed, she sat down to pull on the boots. They were huge, almost twice her normal size. She almost put her others on, then thought twice about it. If she wore her own boots, her feet would be completely out of proportion to the rest of her body. How many men had feet as small as hers? She'd never met a one.

She sighed in resignation. If she was going to pretend to be a boy, she might as well do it all. Well, almost all. She glanced down. It would be pointless to have gone through the pain and challenge of changing her appearance only to have her identity given away by something as silly as the size of her feet.

Grasping her foot, Ember closed her eyes and sent a surge of energy from heel to toe. Her foot grew slowly, growing pains accompanying a deep ache that throbbed through her feet and brought tears to her eyes. When she thought she might be done, she held the boot up to the bottom of her foot, but it was still too big. Whose boots were these, anyway? She shook her head and sent more energy into her foot, expanding the size another couple of inches before she stopped and looked. They were bigger, yes, but they still looked feminine. What was it that made boys' feet look different? Ember tried to remember Aldarin's feet. Veins bulged across the top, and his toes were extremely hairy. Maybe that's all it was. She experimented with it, actually coming to enjoy the finite details that truly made her feet look masculine.

Pulling the boots back on, she was relieved when they fit just right. She gathered her old clothes into a ball and walked back to the big willow tree to find that DeMunth and Shad were the only ones left.

She scanned the woods before asking, "Where's the pack?"

"They returned home. There is no need for them to travel to Javak, and most of them are not comfortable in large cities."

Shad handed DeMunth the nearly empty coin sack. The mute promptly tucked it into the side of his saddle bag, then strapped it across his stallion's rump. Shad continued. "We're only an hour away from Javak. DeMunth says your family's group was planning to travel through the night. If we leave now, we should just beat them there. Running with the pack has certain advantages, one of which is speed." He reached inside one of the old coin sacks and pulled out one of the bracelets he'd spent the last half hour making.

"Here." Ember extended her arms and let Shad slide the ring on her finger, then the bracelet around her wrist. The lines matched up perfectly. "How did you do that?"

He shrugged. "It's part of the stonesculpting gift. Perfect visual recall." Shad glanced around the clearing. Evidently finding everything to his satisfaction, he strolled to the curtain of branches, parted it, and turned to Ember. "Come. There's no need to shift shape and scare the locals." His eyes twinkled.

"If we're so close to Javak, why didn't we just go there last night?" she asked.

"Multiple reasons, but primarily because they collapse the pipes at dusk." Ember gave him a questioning look and he laughed. "You'll see when we get there. Come on." When Ember stepped through the curtain, Shad took her bundled clothes and handed them to DeMunth. "It would have been pointless to camp on the rim of the city when there's a perfectly good spot here under the willow. Besides, it was raining—did you forget already?"

Ember grimaced. "How can I forget when it hasn't stopped?"

Shad laughed, and continued to laugh as he stepped to DeMunth's side and led the two of them to the road.

It was actually less than an hour before they arrived in Javak, the city of magic. Ember could hardly believe she had arrived. It was a deep valley with sides that looked as though they had been cut, smooth and perfectly straight—sheer rock that led to a valley of water and life. The city lay before her as though a giant had planted his walking stick here. She had never seen any place so green and lovely. It was breathtaking as a whole, but her eyes were drawn time and again to the water as they walked the cliff's edge and headed toward a line of people. Shad escorted Ember to the back of the line and stood with her in silence while she took in the view.

Five waterfalls cascaded into the bowl, and it was a wonder the valley hadn't flooded with the sheer volume of water that pounded from the mountains. Somehow it had been diverted into a large river that circled the city and exited the southern end of the valley, while the largest and most beautiful of Javak's buildings thrust up from the water itself. Ember watched the people from a distance, appearing antlike as they moved on the floating bridges and paddled through the water to reach their destinations.

Ember felt a nudge in her side, and she looked ahead to find the line had crept forward. She glanced at her grinning uncle and took a step to catch up. She wasn't sure if the constant grins were part of his nature or if he was extremely happy to be with her, though she suspected the former.

It was strange, traveling with men she didn't know. Ember had been with Shad and DeMunth for less than two days, and yet she connected to them on a subconscious level that rivaled the strength of emotion she held for her stepbrothers. She could understand it where Shad was concerned. He was blood, after all, even if she had just met him, but her feelings for DeMunth confused and overwhelmed her. She didn't know where those feelings would take them, or if he even felt the same way, but she certainly hoped she'd have the chance to find out under better circumstances.

She turned her thoughts from the mute and instead let her mind wander back through the last forty-eight hours and the changes they had brought. A tale of dreams, it seemed. Her father, a wolfwalker and a mage. And now all these years later, finding family she didn't know she had in Uncle Shad and a grandmother she longed to meet.

It seemed forever before the line crept forward again, and then Ember was at the front, staring at a large man who looked quite at ease behind a small, square table. It was obvious he was used to taking charge. He glanced up at her with a pinched, bored smile.

"Name, please," he asked.

"Ember Shandae," she said before thinking about it, then mentally kicked herself just as a voice she knew very well called from behind her. It took all the willpower she had not to jump with guilt as she heard it.

"Step aside, councilman coming through," Aldarin yelled.

Ember moved as far from the table as she reasonably could, her heart racing like DeMunth's horse. The people around her grumbled, glaring at Aldarin and Ezeker for cutting to the front. If they recognized her, not only would her plans be ruined, but all their lives could be in danger. She couldn't take that chance. She ducked her head and hid herself behind Shad, though she peeked upward to watch as the old mage and her stepbrother approached.

They stopped right in front of her. Ember held her breath, trying to swallow her stomach as it had somehow managed to lodge itself in her throat. She put her hands in her pockets to hide the shaking. Shad put his hand on her shoulder, and for the first time, mind-spoke to her in human form. *"Calm yourself, child. You'll do none of them any good if your nerves give us away."*

"I know," she said, blinking back tears of frustration. *"I keep telling myself that, but my body isn't listening."* She expected him to laugh, but he didn't.

"Deep breaths. Just keep taking deep breaths." He withdrew from her mind, but kept his hand on her shoulder and breathed with her. Her heart rate began to slow. She closed her eyes to better concentrate. She had just reached the point where she felt she could handle the situation when a hand touched her elbow and her heart raced back to its previous pace, her eyes snapping open.

Aldarin's head tipped to the side, his eyes troubled. She'd blown it—he'd seen through her disguise, and her family was going to pay for it. She pleaded with her eyes, and had just opened her mouth to say something when he spoke.

"Are you all right? You look a little pale." Shad tensed and sent a questioning thought her way. Ember shook her head in his direction. Oblivious to the exchange, Aldarin continued. "I'm sorry we had to cut to the front like this, but my father is dying. We have to get him to the council right now." His eyes teared up. He blinked hard, then leaned over Ezeker's shoulder and whispered something to him. Ezeker nodded. It bothered Ember to see his long, white beard caked with ash, turning it a dirty gray. *What happened to his weather charm? Surely he didn't give it away.* She shook her head. Obviously he had, and probably to Paeder, no matter that her stepfather was protected in the wagon. It was just the kind of thing Ezeker would do.

Ember sighed, almost collapsing with relief that they hadn't recognized her.

"Sir, your papers?" the waiting guard said to Aldarin. He turned and accepted the packet with a nod, then stopped as he caught sight of Ember's face. He cocked his head and really looked at her.

"Do I know you?" he asked.

She shook her head, not trusting herself to speak.

"Strange. You seem so familiar. Any family up Karsholm way?"

Ember wanted to laugh at the question, but she didn't dare. She shrugged her shoulders and nudged the ash with the toe of her boot.

"Huh."

She watched Aldarin from beneath her lashes as he caught his lip in his teeth and examined her. How he would puzzle out her identity, she didn't know, but she was sure he would if he had enough time with her. He hadn't become captain of Ezeker's guard merely because of his ability to lead—he was smart and very observant. She tried not to shrink under his gaze, though it was difficult. More than anything she wanted to throw herself into his arms and confess the truth, but she couldn't take the chance. She hadn't seen Ian, but she was sure he would arrive before long. Ember scuffed her boots in the ash and waited for the guard to call her forward again.

"Who?" Shad asked in mindspeech.

"Aldarin. Brother," she answered, and at his confused look, clarified, *"stepbrother."*

Ezeker saved her from Aldarin's questioning when he turned and walked across the clearing to Paeder's boxy wagon. He opened the door and spoke to someone inside. Aldarin followed with a shake of his head and a final questioning glance in Ember's direction. She tried hard to appear as if she wasn't aware of every step he took.

Shad chuckled, but it had an edge to it.

"All right, who's next?" the man at the table called.

"I'll be right back," Shad whispered. She felt him leave and someone step into line behind her. She paid very little attention as she checked in with the guard at the table and received instruction on the mage trials and a cloth bag containing all orientation material, as well as food chits. Ember turned to go, still examining the contents of the bag, when she ran smack into a very hard stomach. She looked up in surprise, her hat hitting the dirt about the same time her jaw fell open in shock.

Ian had been standing behind her all this time. She stared, searching her brain for anything to say, but all she could do was stare at him and stammer. "Sorry, so sorry, sir. My apologies."

"That's fine, boy," he said with a smile, though his eyes remained hard and cold.

Ember backed away and reached for her hat, her sleeve pulling back to expose the bracelets Shad had made just that morning. In a flash Ian took hold of her hand and examined the workmanship. Ember's heart had raced earlier, but now it froze at his grip. She didn't dare even breathe, though her eyes frantically searched for Uncle Shad in the throng that surrounded her.

"Where'd you get these?" he asked, suspicion lacing his gravelly voice.

"A-a- boy on the road made them, sir. Bought 'em off him just this morning. Said he was goin' to make a fortune at the trials, he did." Ember scrambled for the first thing that popped into her head and hoped he bought her story.

Ian snorted. "Slave bracelets? You bought slave bracelets from a vendor? Why would anyone want those?" His eyes seemed to see right through her.

"Slave bracelets? They're just pretties, sir." Ember shrugged and raised her hand, pretending to examine the workmanship while watching Ian from beneath her lashes. *Pretties? Oh, that was just brilliant, Ember.* She groaned inwardly. He was going to figure out the truth for sure.

The man squinted at her and pursed his lips, then leaned close and spoke quietly. "I'll check out your story, but if you're who I think you are, I'll find you."

It took everything she had not to run right then. Instead she schooled her expression into confused terror, which wasn't too far off from what she really felt. How could he sense the fear and deceit in her? The man must have some kind of gift. She remembered the night he'd taken her, and how he'd known her heart rate and seen her teeth in the dark.

"Sir, they're just pretties. Please, can I have my hand back?"

She trembled, but hoped it added to her disguise rather than exposing her. Ian gave her one last searching look before letting go. "Bah! Off with you, boy. I'll be seeing you again, I'm sure."

Ember scrambled to the end of the line of people waiting to use the transportation pipes. She had never seen anything like it. Where were the stairs? Ladders? A path leading down the cliffside? Anything had to be better than the suicidal ride before her. A large pipe gaped before her, a dark opening that looked more like a mouth waiting to eat her than anything else. Her turn was coming up fast, and Uncle Shad had not returned. The girl in front of her took a running start and dove into the darkness, squealing. Ember turned her back on the pipe and scanned the clearing for Shad, but there was still no sign of him or DeMunth.

"This way, sir," a young guard said, taking her by the elbow.

She pulled back. "I'm waiting for my uncle. It's okay, I can wait." He beckoned her forward and patted a large rug that was placed on a smooth, flattened area before the pipe. "He'll meet you at the bottom, I'm sure. Sit here, lean back, and have fun. This is the best part of the journey. You'll see," he said, grinning at her like the youth he was. It reminded her a bit of Tiva's lopsided smile, and suddenly she missed him. It surprised her. She hadn't missed the twins while they were gone to school, but now she did. She didn't want to think about it. Besides, her brothers were on the way down to Javak as well. She'd seen their horses led away as Paeder's bed was lowered down the side of the cliff. She might even run across them at some point, though they wouldn't know her from a stranger.

Ember looked around one last time, then realized her real identity would be revealed pretty quickly if she didn't stop acting like a girl. She sat on the rug, legs extended, with her small satchel resting in her lap. She clutched it impulsively as the boy got behind her and, with no warning whatsoever, shoved her forward. She flew through the gaping hole and screamed as the bottom dropped from beneath her. She knew it didn't sound masculine to scream, but she couldn't help herself—it just burst out as her stomach sank and she flew down the pipe, twisting and spinning and bumping her head on every turn.

It was a long spiral, down, down, down. Ember rocked back and forth around the tunnel as she slid forever toward the ground, seeming to defy gravity—and then it occurred to her that the trip might be easier if she lay back. Immediately her pace increased, though she was better able to steer herself. That marginal feeling of control allowed her body to relax. She was almost enjoying the ride when, suddenly, she was upside down and falling feet first out of the pipe, where she stopped, half-way to the ground. Ember looked around at the laughing faces as she hung in midair.

One of the men reached out a hand, and Ember gladly took it. He pulled gently on her arm, and she floated to him as if she were a skater gliding on ice. It was a rather odd feeling, as if the air itself had thickened to hold her weight, and it was only that which held her down. It seemed that at any moment she might just float away like a magic carpet. But the farther she got from the opening, the more she sank to the ground, her body regaining its weight. She had never been so grateful to feel dirt beneath her feet.

"Thank you, sir," she said breathlessly to the handsome ruffian who had helped her.

"Not a problem, boy, not a problem at all. Happy to oblige a new candidate."

She was saved from further conversation by familiar voices coming from the space behind her, though still completely within her head, continuing the conversation they'd had for the past hour. She had tuned it out shortly after they began talking about vortexes and wavering power lines. It made no sense to her.

"I tell you, someone is playing with the mage lines, for the power to go out in the area like it has. An eruption alone would not be enough to draw that much to it. Someone has been feeding that mountain and disabled most of the spells in the area," DeMunth ranted.

"Oh, hush for a bit, Munth. We can talk about it later," Ember's uncle responded.

DeMunth snorted, though whether in laughter or disgust, Ember wasn't sure. Once the two men had their feet on the ground, Shad took charge.

"Come on then, let's get you to the council house." Uncle Shad propelled her forward with a hand he quickly dropped from the small of her back.

"The council house? What's that?" she asked.

"It's home for the next few days. Not exactly my idea of a comforting cave, but one does have to make sacrifices." Shad laughed as he led her and DeMunth westward.

The town was set up in a grid. They wandered down the avenues created by the stores and vendor stalls. Most of the stores were actually canvas or silk tents—temporary storefronts that could travel wherever business was best.

There was a carnival atmosphere here. People dressed in bright and bold colors, with gauzy veils and shawls for the women, colorful vests and knee-high boots for the men. And hats. Many, many hats. Tall hats, brimmed hats, pointed and round hats. There were caps, and turbans, and a little beanie hat that barely covered the top of one gentleman's oversized head. It made Ember smile. The place was a cacophony of sight and sound as they made their way due west, with vendors calling and laughter bubbling as people browsed.

The scent of roasting pig, sausage rolls, and fruit pies assailed Ember's nose. Her stomach growled in protest. Last night's rabbit dinner had been long ago, and she found herself suddenly famished. She was also penniless and not about to ask her uncle for money after all he'd used up making her bracelet. Breakfast would have to wait.

Most of the people wandering the streets seemed to be there more to experience the sight, tastes, and smells than for any real business. Ember's mother would have called them "rubber-eyed" because they bounced from place to place and never bothered to settle. Marda hated how people wasted their time like that, as she had lost many an afternoon presenting horses to potential buyers who browsed the stalls just for entertainment. Ember could understand a small measure of her mother's feelings, seeing desperate vendors who were consistently passed by.

Seeing them reminded her of the conversation with Ian. "Uh, Uncle? Can I talk to you about something?"

"Certainly," he said, obviously distracted as he scanned the booths to both sides, then stepped to the nearest food vendor and purchased three turkey legs and a large bowl full of vegetables. Ember's mouth watered as he handed her a portion, but she didn't eat.

"This is serious. Can we stop for a second?"

Shad cocked an eyebrow, but nodded. She and DeMunth followed as he stepped between two tents and turned to face them. "Speak, but quickly, please. If we're to get decent rooms, we must hurry to the council house before it fills up. I don't know about you, but I'd like a private shower."

Ember's skin began to itch at the mention of a shower, so she spoke fast. "I literally ran into Ian up there, and he saw the cuffs." She relayed her conversation with Ian, finishing with, "I said the boy was planning to make a fortune selling his 'pretties' at the trials, and Ian would be able to find a booth selling them." Ember watched as Shad's eyes widened.

"You told him you got them from a vendor? They'd be sold here?" She overheard him processing in his head how long it would take to make enough bracelets to sell at a place like this. DeMunth laughed out loud. Shad's eyes flashed, rueful.

"I'm sorry. It just popped out before I had a chance to think. What are we going to do?" Ember pulled at her lip in agitation.

Shad dragged a hand down his face, his stubble scratching with sound, then nodded. "We might be able to use this to our advantage. If people start to buy and wear the bracelets, even if we further change your appearance, he will be less suspicious. Besides, it will grow our monies as well. Don't worry—I'll take care of it. Is that it?"

Ember nodded, relieved her uncle wasn't mad at her for messing things up.

"What magics have you manifested yet? Any of the orange?" he asked, taking Ember completely by surprise.

"Orange? There's orange magic?"

Shad sighed and shook his head. "Your education has been decidedly lacking, my dear."

Ember blushed, but laughed. He was right.

The issue of Ian and the bracelets resolved, Ember finally dug into the food that Shad provided, her stomach thanking her for the sustenance. The three of them left the privacy of the alley and made their way toward the large building Ember had spotted from the top of the cliff. She could smell the water in the air as they got closer to the western wall of the Javak shelf, and by the time they left the alley of tents, the sound of a waterfall greeted her ears like nature's music.

As they stepped clear of the buildings, Ember's mouth dropped open in awe at the sight before her. The largest building she had ever seen thrust up from the water, like an island reaching for the sky. It was U-shaped, with the base of the U facing the cliff and the sides nudging against the rock face.

The building looked to be made of light-colored stone with marbled streaks of pale and dark blue slashing through it. The stone was beautiful, but it was not what caught Ember's breath. The thing that held her was the waterfall that leaped and tumbled down the sheer side of the mountain and, with a thunderous roar, poured into the building itself. It was the most amazing thing she had ever seen.

A bird screamed overhead. She glanced up, stunned to see the white hawk from Karsholm circling over what appeared to be the council house. There was no doubt in her mind it was the same bird.

It was the only white hawk she had ever seen or heard of. Somehow magic marked the hawk. How else could all the color have been bleached from it? Shivers flowed over her.

Was it following her? For a moment, she wanted to be afraid, wondering if perhaps it was through the bird C'Tan had found her, but true fear would not come. The bird always seemed to be nearby, but it had never harmed her, not once. It seemed more of a guardian than anything.

A deep growl came from the right. Ember glanced over in time to see a dog staring at Uncle Shad, teeth bared and hackles up. She stopped, heartbeat jumping to high speed once more.

Shad snorted. "Stupid dog. They catch the scent of wolf and go into defensive mode." He stopped and glared at the animal, a growl coming to his own throat that sounded strangely canine for his human form. The dog's head lowered, but it held its ground. A man came up behind the animal and scratched its head, a menacing smile creeping across his face. He turned to speak to someone behind him.

Ember caught just a glimpse of Ian stepping into the alley before Shad grabbed her arm none too gently and guided her toward the council house. "Come on. Let's get you someplace out of sight before he verifies your identity. We need that booth set up soon to get him off your trail."

Ember nearly ran across the floating path and into the council house.

As they stepped through the double doors, a flowery man greeted them from behind a massive desk. He was all movement and bobbing, like a sunflower in the breeze. "Welcome to the council house, Councilor White Shadow," the man said, stepping around the corner and bowing to Uncle Shad. "Councilor DeMunth."

"And how are you faring, Siedow?" Shad asked, extending his hand to the houseman as if what happened outside was of no matter.

"Doing well, thank you." The man took Shad's hand with his fingertips. "And you?"

"Fine, indeed." Shad released his hand. "Might you have some rooms available?"

221

"Certainly, councilors. Follow me, please."

Ember's mind was still trying to wrap around the implications of what their greeter had said. Her feet seemed to have rooted to the ground, and everyone had taken several steps before she was able to catch her breath enough to follow them. They were *councilors*. Uncle Shad and DeMunth were part of the Mage Council? That knowledge completely pushed aside her worry about Ian and the dog.

She shook her head as she trailed behind them. This explained a lot about their business here, but made her feel rather insignificant. And how did a shapeshifting wolf and a mute ex-priest end up on the Mage Council, anyhow? No wonder they had brought her to the council house. This really was their home away from home. Ember felt smaller with each step she took. What was she doing here?

Their greeter and guide walked very lightly, with a swish to his hips and fluttery hands. He seemed everything a good houseman should be—gentle, soft-spoken, and he had an excellent memory, as shown by remembering Uncle Shad and DeMunth's names.

The houseman led them to two rooms at the end of the south wing, one right next to the other. "I apologize, but we are out of rooms with a private bath, though the public bath is certainly available. Will that be a problem?" He looked at Shad and DeMunth, completely ignoring Ember. She shrank a little further into herself.

'Uh, no," Shad said, glancing at Ember apologetically. "We'll manage, thank you. This is my nephew, Emben. Might you have a guest room available for him?"

Siedow examined Ember, his head cocked to the side as he pursed his lips and looked her up and down. She fought the blush that sprang to her cheeks. The man noticed and smiled, not unkindly. "I believe we have room just down the hall. Here for the trials?"

Shad nodded, and Siedow's smile grew.

"Wonderful! Follow me then, Emben. We'll get you settled in no time." The man moved off without giving her a moment to say goodbye. She glanced nervously at Shad. He nodded and motioned for her to follow. *"I'll meet up with you later. Don't worry, we'll find you a bath."*

Ember nodded, and in no time at all had come to her own room. It was small, but very nice, with intricate wood carving on the bedposts, mirror frame, and around the door.

"Do not lose this," the man said emphatically, and touched the satchel she still held from registration. He took it from her hands, opened it, and dumped the contents on the bed. He separated them: a map, a timepiece, her meal tickets and store chits, paper and a charcoal stick, and a clear, flat stone. He held the last up to her.

"This is the most important item in your bag, Emben. All your messages and summons will come through this stone. It can vibrate, speak, and even write messages in its depths. Always keep it with you. The time for your trial will come quickly, with very little notice, and there are no second chances here. You make it to your assigned trial, or they send you home."

That was all the man said before he showed her around the room. She had a private sink and toilet, but no bath. Ember knew Shad would figure out a way for her to bathe, but she was still a little worried. She was caked with ash, and the smell emanating from her was very much akin to that of a wet dog.

Before leaving, the man showed her the small, square panel just outside her door, made of the same material as her clear stone.

"Place your hand here, please." Ember did as she was told, her fingers spread across the width of the cool stone. It warmed slightly and shone a pale yellow before it faded back to its transparent state. "You and I are now the only ones able to enter this room. If you wish any others to have access, please see me for imprinting." Siedow left, and Ember reentered the luxurious suite that had everything she could ever dream of having in a room.

Everything except a bath.

She sighed wearily, pulled off her muddy boots and travel cloak, and lay down on the bed to rest. She was asleep before she had time to regret her decision to become a half-man in a world of men. She had entered her dreams, and there it didn't matter.

Chapter Twenty

C'Tan ground her teeth in frustration and instructed her winged mount to circle Dragonmeer. The dragon's wings snapped and popped in the wind as he glided through the low clouds that hid the castle from her sight. So close, so very close, and the flute had disappeared. Well, she wasn't going to let a thing like that set her back. She knew where it had been last; she'd just start there and track it, though there would likely be few standing when she was through. She'd take her frustration out on the very stones of the ancient keep if she had to. That flute was hers. Hers! And no mere shielding would keep it from her again.

Dragonmeer. She could feel it near now. There! A break appeared, and C'Tan guided the great black beast into a steep dive through the mist above the granite castle. She circled it slowly to get her bearings and to determine the greatest entrance effect. She could come in flaming, but that would accomplish nothing except to ease her frustration and send people screaming into the safety of the walls. No. She needed something more subtle—something that would get the best results with the least effort.

She was inspired at the sight of carriages winding their way from the keep. She guided her mount away from the fluttering piñons, over the gated drawbridge, and onto the winding road. The drake landed with huge beats of his wings and settled her softly in the midst of the darkened road. Three more dragons landed behind her and discarded their passengers. Kardon, as usual, approached the instant he dismounted.

"Mistress. There are three sub-humans heading into the woods. Should we delay them?" he asked in his ageless rasp.

C'Tan glanced to the line of trees and saw a lone figure plunging into its depths, most likely a traveler who had run in fear of her and the huge dragons. She snorted in contempt of her old master. "No, Kardon."

"But mistress, they may have the flute," he continued.

She turned the full force of her chilling gaze on him.

"But? Did I just hear you say 'but' to me?" Kardon's eyes never left her face, nor did he show any fear, though wisely he did not answer. She crooked her finger to draw him near. He stepped slowly forward until he was within arms' length. C'Tan reached her perfectly manicured fingers with their blood red nails out to tip his chin. "Never say 'but' to me. My word is law, is that clear?" she hissed as her face pressed close to his. A spark of anger flashed in his eyes, but was suppressed as quickly as it arose.

"Yes, mistress," he snarled, never moving.

"Good." She flicked her fingernail along his chin, drawing a small bead of blood which he quickly wiped away. "Forget the sub-humans. We're looking for a flute."

"Yes, C'Tan," he said. He bowed himself back to his own drake, where he took comfort in the scaly head of the beast.

C'Tan scratched under the chin of her mount. She looked at the dragon thoughtfully. More than a mount, she realized, chuckling, as she whispered into the dragon's ear hole.

Drake nodded his great head once in agreement and began to shift. He shrank in size—his wings pulled into his shoulders and disappeared. Crooked legs and claws straightened and fused while his long tail pulled into his hindquarters and sprouted thick hair. His head squared and teeth flattened. Where seconds before a massive black dragon had squatted, now stood a midnight stallion pawing at the ground. C'Tan heard startled exclamations from around her, and the other dragons shifted themselves to match her mount. She sauntered to her changed friend. She patted him on the shoulder, then ran her hands down his well-formed legs.

"Beautiful," she murmured in his ear. He threw his head and snorted, making it clear he was unhappy with the change. "It's just until we reach the city. You're perfect, my love." She stepped into the stirrup he had provided and sat astride his massive shoulders. He fit her exactly. All the years of riding together in one form or another, and he knew how to fit her body like skin on a drum. It was exhilarating. What power she held, that even her mount would change himself to suit her needs.

C'Tan did not need to turn in the saddle to know that Kardon and her soldiers were ready. The stillness as they waited told her all she needed to know. The dragonmount moved forward at a trot, then ran down the path leading to Dragonmeer and the Sapphire Flute. She'd wring the truth from the duke's people with fire if she had to. The flute would be hers if she had to take every life in Dragonmeer to find it. C'Tan's lips twisted in grim expectation as hooves echoed across Dragonmeer's bridge.

Chapter Twenty-one

Kayla reached the edge of the wood, and panting, turned in time to see a wing of dragons glide to a landing in the field. She held her breath, aware of the relatively short distance between the beasts and herself, terrifed that at any moment they would turn and see her. Crouched in the thick brush, she watched the dragons and their masters as they gathered together to talk.

Kayla watched as an old man slid from dragonback and approached a beautiful blonde woman. He spoke to her, pointing toward where Kayla and her companions had just pressed into the forest. Whatever he said angered her. The woman gestured for the man to come closer, and despite her small size, her fury dominated the man. Kayla held her breath as she watched the exchange. She was immovable in her position, too terrified to move. Had they seen her run into the woods?

Kayla strained to hear anything the group might be saying. She turned her head and stilled herself even further, wishing her heart would stop pounding so she could hear better. She was so focused on the woman with the dragons, she barely noticed when her ears began to ring and spots swam before her eyes. She focused even harder when she saw the blonde woman's dragon begin to shrink.

Kayla's body demanded attention when her chest began to burn with an urgent need.

T'Kato hit her back hard. Kayla gasped and only then realized she'd been holding her breath, almost in a trance. The ringing and spots stopped immediately, but her back stung with the sharp slap the man had landed.

Kayla glared. "Don't do that." Granted, he had kept her conscious, but there had to be a better way to do it than by hitting her.

"Would you rather I let you pass out?" he asked, calm and rational. Kayla was beginning to hate that about him.

She decided not to answer and turned to watch the dragons, gasping when she saw they were gone. In the short minute she had faced T'Kato, the black dragons had disappeared and been replaced by an equal number of midnight horses. The leader pulled herself astride her mount. T'Kato gasped and shoved Kayla down to the ground.

"What—" she started, unable to finish with T'Kato's hand over her mouth.

"Don't talk. Don't move. Don't even breathe if you can help it."

Kayla's heart hammered in her chest. First he hit her to *make* her breathe, and now he was telling her *not* to? She felt T'Kato gesture with his chin toward the group as they entered the gates of Dragonmeer astride great stallions.

"If you value your life and the safety of that flute of yours, you must do exactly as I say." T'Kato kept his hand over her mouth until she nodded, then slowly pulled it away.

Kayla tried to breathe shallowly, repulsed by the salty taste of his sweat on her lips. She licked them anyway, grimacing. "Who was that?"

T'Kato didn't answer for a long time, and Kayla thought he had not heard her. She was about to repeat herself when he answered. "C'Tan." His voice was expressionless.

The name sent chills down her spine.

Kayla immediately jumped to her feet, running faster than she ever remembered, pressing as deeply into the thick woods as she could. She had no idea where she was going, and it didn't matter, so long as it took her as far from the dragonriders as possible. Fear became a tangible thing inside her, a voice screaming in the hollows of her soul. She knew only to run, beyond thought, beyond reason. She had to get as far from C'Tan as her feet would allow.

Sarali caught up with her as they entered an almost circular clearing. The maid took hold of her arm, pulling her to a stop.

"Wait," Sarali whispered, holding up an open hand as she apparently listened intently for signs of pursuit. Kayla leaned over to better hear, her heart hammering in her chest. Sarali really was tiny, Kayla realized in that moment. Small and lithe—like a cat. "T'Kato wants us to rest here while he scouts about. Relax, lass, the mage won't find us here anytime soon." She sank to the ground, her back propped against a tree for support.

Kayla followed her example, though not nearly as gracefully. It felt more like she thumped and creaked in her weary bones. It had been too long a day—two days, even—and she felt every bit of the strain. She leaned back and closed her eyes, taking a small amount of pleasure in the whispering of the wind through the quaking leaves. The trees spoke to her in ways she could never understand—they spoke in feelings, not thoughts, part of the evahn heritage she'd never had a chance to explore, though perhaps she would still have that opportunity. T'Kato said he knew her father—maybe she'd get to meet him at last. She only hoped Darthmoor would be safe while she was away. Her family was there.

C'Tan was there.

Kayla tried to calm her heart and rest, but her stomach was sick. There was only one thing that could have brought C'Tan to Dragonmeer—she'd traced the flute. Dragonmeer was in danger, and it was all Kayla's fault. She felt like a coward. If only she had listened to King Rojan. If only she'd had more thought in her head when she picked up the flute. She'd been so beguiled by the flute's beauty and the yearning to play, she had given no thought to the consequences. The people of Dragonmeer would pay for her mistake, not Kayla, and it wasn't right. She should be with them, standing with the flute in defense of Brant's home. If anything happened to any of them, she would never forgive herself.

The guilt and panic continued to build, then burst when screams sounded through the forest.

"No! No, miss, I don't know nothin'. Put me down! No!" an adolescent male voice cracked and yelled. It was a voice she knew.

"Joyson!"

Her heart was full of dread. What would they want with the boy? He'd done nothing wrong and was too young to know anything. Unless . . .

"He was with me. Oh no, Joyson. What have I done?" she whispered. She was up and running for the line of trees before she even realized it, startled shouts coming from behind her. She crashed through the underbrush, muttered curses coming from T'Kato and Sarali as they tried to catch up, but she felt as if her feet had wings. She had to know if it was the boy.

Her mind raced, though no definite thought formed there. It was too overwhelmed with a mish-mash of emotion that swarmed over her like ants, devouring all thought and will. She could do nothing but run.

Somewhere in the dash back toward the dragons, Kayla pulled the Sapphire Flute from her bag, and it miraculously appeared in her hands, minus the case. She didn't remember doing it, just found it there, glowing a deep midnight blue, almost black—maybe even an angry blue, if there was such a color. It buzzed and hummed and throbbed in her hands like a living thing, as if it breathed in her anger and need and pushed it out before her like a shield.

Kayla skidded to a stop when she reached the bushes that marked the boundary of Dragonmeer. The sun was just rising from behind the eastern mountains, the fog and clouds strangely absent, and she was able to see the horror of the situation before her.

Dragons surrounded the city.

A single dragon hovered about thirty feet off the ground in the direct center of the field, the blonde woman on his back, her face hard and cold—beautiful like marble, but immovable as granite. The dragon's body was snakelike, with thick shoulders and leathery wings that sprouted from his shoulders and snapped as piñons in the wind.

That was what she had heard while crossing the field. The realization of how close they had come to finding her was terrifying. If she had waited any longer this morning, it would have been too late. They would have been captured . . . just as Joyson was.

Kayla's eyes widened with horror when she realized that the twisting thing hanging beneath the dragon was actually the boy, clutched within its claws. He scrabbled at the dragon, looking for a handhold of any kind, but just as he would find purchase, the great midnight beast would scrape his hands away with a talon. The boy whimpered and sobbed in terror.

Kayla raised the flute to her lips, inhaled, and held it as she felt the prick of a knife at her throat, held in place by a tattooed hand. Her eyes widened in desperate fear. She didn't move, frozen in terror as she watched the dragon play with Joyson. She couldn't let him die—but with a blade at her throat, what could she do? Frustrated, conflicted, she did nothing.

"Don't do it, girl," T'Kato growled.

Kayla hesitated a long moment. Joyson had to be saved, but she had no trouble believing the tattooed man would slit her throat if it kept the flute safe. What choice did she have? She released her breath slowly, careful not to make any noise on the glowing instrument.

Kayla's resolve hardened, knife or not. "I can't let her hurt him."

"Yes, you can," T'Kato answered with surprising tenderness.

"No!" she cried.

"Kayla, you must. Sometimes we have to sacrifice one in order to save many. C'Tan must not hold that flute!" he hissed in her ear. "It is your *duty* to guard it, Kayla Kalandra, and right now you are on the edge of handing it to C'Tan in a golden bowl. You might as well walk out there and say, 'Here you go, C'Tan, I've decided I don't care if you destroy the world, you take the flute.' Do you care about Rasann, or not?"

Kayla was angrily silent.

"Well?" he asked again.

"I care," she snarled.

"Then put that thing away and come into the woods."

Kayla hesitated a moment longer, then lowered the flute, but she did not move. She had to watch.

"Kayla!" Sarali snapped. "Come, girl, we must go if ye wish to survive the day."

Kayla still did not move. She watched as C'Tan's great dragon suddenly beat his leathery wings and pulled himself higher, clawing into the sky until he was but a speck above her.

Suddenly one speck became two, one hovering high overhead while the other plummeted toward the earth, screaming and thrashing about in terror. Kayla choked down a cry as she watched Joyson appear to grow larger and larger. She closed her eyes when he was about twenty feet above the ground, unable to watch the horror of his body slamming into the meadow floor. She waited for the thud she knew would come . . .

But it never did.

She opened one eye and saw the dragon hovering about fifteen feet above ground, holding the terrified boy in a claw once more. They were close enough that she could hear C'Tan's voice this time.

"Where is she, boy? Where's the one they call Kayla?" she asked in the sweetest tones, so out of place with the position in which she held him.

"I don't know!" he sobbed. "I really don't, miss. Please let me go."

The great claw opened, and Joyson started to fall. He screamed, and the dragon's back claw reached out and plucked him out of the air again.

"Are you sure you want me to do that?" C'Tan asked. Joyson shook his head emphatically, still sobbing.

"Oh, quit your blubbering, boy. Just tell me where the girl is, and I'll let you go. Simple as that." C'Tan leaned over the side of her dragon and snapped her fingers.

"Please, miss. I don't know where she went. I carried her bag to the chef's quarters just like Master Brant asked—"

"Brant!" She stopped him. "Duke Domanta's Brant?"

Joyson bobbed his head so hard, Kayla was afraid it was going to pop off his shoulders. "Yes, miss. Brant. He and Miss Kayla were great friends. Maybe he knows where she wennnnnaaaaaahhhhh!" Joyson screamed as C'Tan's dragon released the boy to fall the last twenty feet to the ground.

This time there was a thump and a groan, but Kayla dared not go to the boy. He might have broken his leg or ribs, but he should survive a drop like that. The ground was still soft from the morning dew.

Her fear now was for Brant.

"Kayla!" T'Kato took her shoulder and pulled. "We have to leave!"

"No!" She shook him off. "I can't go until I know Brant and my family are safe!"

T'Kato balled his fists, then moved away to converse with his wife. They murmured back and forth for a long time, Sarali shaking her head with her arms folded.

Kayla ignored them, her heart in her throat with fear for Brant. If the woman would torture a serving boy like Joyson, what would she do to the duke's son—to Kayla's husband-to-be? She'd never felt so helpless. It made her feel much differently about those who spoke so often of depending on a higher power. There was nothing for her to do but watch and offer up a sincere prayer to the Guardians.

Please don't let them find Brant! Please keep him safe. Don't let them find him! Don't let them find him! Don't let them find him don't let them find him don't . . .

But they found him.

One of the other dragons dipped into the city and came up with a struggling figure—one Kayla knew even from that great distance. The one person outside of her family she truly loved was now in the clutches of C'Tan.

The dragon carried Brant to the middle of the field. Kayla nearly screamed when he threw Brant in a great arc toward C'Tan, whose dragon lunged and caught him by the shoulders, one of the talons piercing through.

Brant howled with pain. Kayla shrieked along with him. Somehow she found herself on her knees and could do nothing but watch in silence as the questioning began once more. Over and over again, C'Tan asked Brant where Kayla was, and each time, he answered her with silence.

Kayla was so proud of him, her heart was about to break. And then the torture began.

Up, up, up C'Tan's great dragon flew, until the beast was so high it seemed the size of an ant in the heavens. Then Brant would fall, tumbling toward the earth without any scream or thrashing about as Joyson had done. Brant would assume different positions each time he fell, sometimes on his back, other times spread-eagled. He would go head first, feet first, and even repeatedly somersaulted end over end. He looked as though he was enjoying himself, but Kayla knew it was all for show.

Finally C'Tan retrieved him one last time just before he hit the ground. The woman clenched her jaw, and Kayla knew Brant's time had run out. The overwhelming anxiety and fear, the mind-numbing terror that had held her captive, was suddenly washed away to be replaced by a calm understanding she had never felt before.

It was as though the spirits of her ancestors or the life of the woods had reached out to her and spoken to her heart of hearts, the very center of her being. Never before had she understood these trees, these birds, this life all around her—but now they chanted the same thing over and over again, and Kayla knew what she had to do.

"This is your last chance, Brant. Where is Kayla?" C'Tan demanded. "This time I will not stop your fall, and you will die here in this field with your people watching."

Brant responded, his voice laced with the pain he would not express.

"Then so be it, C'Tan. I will never tell you where she has gone. I hope she plays that flute and destroys you with it. It doesn't matter whether I live or not. You've lost." He said it so matter-of-factly that Kayla at first didn't believe his words, couldn't register that she heard him speak aloud the words the trees chanted.

"Play the flute . . ."

C'Tan screeched her fury at Brant, and the great dragon tensed his grip, sending talons through the joints of both shoulders now. Brant screamed in agony, but did not beg for mercy. The dragon climbed in the sky again, pulling itself higher than it had been before.

Kayla stood, barely aware of the rocks that clung to her pants or the slice in her arm from her hurried flight. All she was aware of was the sight of her love being carried high in the sky to be dropped to his death, and the chanting of life around her—chanting that filled her up and silenced her fears.

"*Play the flute . . .*"

But the flute was not hers to play! Hadn't she been told? She was its guardian, not the player. What good could she do? She was only a half-evahn runt, not wanted by the people from either side of her heritage.

"*Play the flute, and you will see . . . Play the flute, and you will see . . .*"

The chant changed. Kayla's eyes were still glued to C'Tan and her great beast as she became a speck, a flea in the sky.

And then Brant began to fall.

"Kayla," T'Kato said in concern, trying to take her arm—but he could not touch her.

The tingling energy of the flute surged through Kayla's blood and muscles, making her hair stand on end. She radiated blue light that sent waves of air swirling around her, picking up the leaves and twigs and stirring her hair into a charged blonde mass that seemed to have a life of its own. T'Kato tried to touch her again, and an arc of blue light shot between them. He flew backward and lay still, stunned and pinned against a tree.

But T'Kato didn't matter right then. Her eyes were all for Brant as he tumbled and grew larger in the sky, and still he did not cry out.

Kayla raised the flute to her lips, closed her eyes, took a deep breath, and released it on the purest, most vibrant color of sound she had ever heard or felt. It was one long note that pulsed and twined with the wind in the leaves and the rustling grass. It sang chorus with the cicadas and the eagle and the sun. It was the song of life. Kayla played that one long note, then segued intuitively into the song she had played the day before.

Darthmoor's Honor felt different now. It was as if the strength in the stone and the dream of an eagle's flight brought power to the music it hadn't held before. Kayla felt her will, her soul, reaching out to her falling love and embracing him in her woven sound until she could see the rate of his descent slow. His face split with a grin as tears streamed down his cheeks.

One great discordant shriek came from high above. Kayla was aware of it, but dared not stop playing until Brant was safe. She had to keep him safe, as she couldn't Joyson.

The black speck that had been high above grew rapidly, too rapidly. Kayla had to speed Brant's descent, but she was not sure how. There was no understanding in her action. It was all intuitive as she continued to play and send her prayers heavenward. *Fast, but safe, fast, but safe . . .*

"Kayla!" T'Kato screamed at her. "Let him go! Let him go now, or all is lost! She is nearly upon us!"

Kayla watched in increased fear as C'Tan grew from flea, to ant, to dog, to horse, to dragon-size—all within a matter of seconds. Brant was still too far from the ground, much too far, but Kayla had no choice.

She let him go.

"I'm okay, Kayla! Run while you can!" Brant screamed as he fell those last twenty feet.

C'Tan headed straight for Kayla, a grin of triumph slashing her face. The black beast reached his back talons forward like a hawk coming in for the kill.

Kayla lowered the flute, waited until the last possible second, then dropped to the earth and rolled. The great dragon swooshed past her, taking the tops of several trees along with it.

C'Tan cursed.

"Kayla, come on!" T'Kato yelled. He sprinted away, Sarali loping catlike at his side. This time Kayla did not hesitate.

She ran.

Chapter Twenty-two

Ember awoke with a start, her eyes snapping open. She'd dreamed again. This time the dream didn't have a happy ending. She'd been in a group the same as in her vision of the night before, but it was the wrong group of people, and the dragon lady had killed them quickly.

Not the dragon lady—C'Tan, Ember reminded herself. She knew who the woman was now. If Ember didn't succeed at the mage trials, if anything interfered and she was unable to learn magic, the dream would become reality, and she would die. Her life was forfeit unless she could learn.

She closed her eyes, turned over, and wrapped her arms around one of the pillows. She sought comfort in sleep, but it eluded her despite her best efforts. She was too distracted by all the new smells. At first, she had been confused by the odor of her new room. It wasn't unpleasant, but rather than the dusty smell of warm wood she was used to, there was the scent of fresh soap and the mineral tang of stone. She'd stayed curled up for a long time, analyzing the differences without the use of her eyes.

It was a new experience for her, one made interesting by her sharpened wolf sense. She'd never paid much attention to the scent of things, not unless they were overpoweringly strong, but she certainly noticed now.

She'd quickly come to realize it wasn't her sense of smell alone that had changed—taste and hearing were much sharper as well. Curious, she stretched and tuned her ear to the smallest sound she could hear—a heartbeat that seemed to come from almost in front of her. Ember strained to catch each tharump-ump and finally opened her eyes. Shad's chin rested on her bed, his face inches from her own.

She scrambled back and squealed. To his credit, Shad didn't laugh, though it looked as if he were biting his tongue to keep from doing so.

Ember scowled, then glanced at the open door.

"How'd you unlock the door?"

"Magic," he said, wiggling his fingers.

Ember snorted, but part of her worried he might be serious. The look on her face must have given her away, for Shad snickered.

"No, no, I'm only teasing, little Shandae. I had the deskman let me in. He knows we're together. You slept so soundly I didn't want to wake you, though it's almost time for supper."

Ember looked at her orientation bag in a panic. What if they'd already called her to trial and she'd missed it? Again, Shad read her mind. "Your number has not come up yet. Don't you worry, I won't let you miss your chance. Now, while you were out like a magelight, DeMunth and I have worked hard. What do you think?" He tossed a cloth sack on the bed. It hit the mattress with a chink.

Ember untied the drawstring as Shad settled against the dresser, arms crossed, a smug look on his face. She upended the sack and dumped the contents on the bed. She whistled in appreciation at the slave bracelets and ring chains dangling amid the cuffs. Ember held more wealth on her bed than her family had seen in ten years of work. The detail was exquisite. She quickly untangled and examined each piece.

The pure copper cuff was identical to Ember's, but the others were different. Three of the cuffs were made of silver, with different animals instead of her wolves—a stag, a large cat, and a bear. The last bracelet was made of gold, with a fierce dragon head on the ring. If she hadn't seen her uncle design her bracelet that morning, using only his fingers, she would have thought each item had taken months of labor by a skilled craftsman. Well, he was skilled—just not in the traditional way. Shad used magic where most used tools.

"So, what do you think?" he asked again, obviously fishing for praise. Ember didn't disappoint him.

"What do I think? I think they're beautiful, phenomenal, amazing, and every other good word I can't think of right now."

Shad's smirk grew, though he did seem genuinely pleased. "Good. I'll get to work duplicating them. We found a boy who was willing to run the booth for us, and I manipulated his memories a bit to 'remember' meeting you on the road. The few cuffs we made are selling like your grandmother's apple pie at the yearly fair, so we've got to restock as quickly as possible. Duplication seems the best option."

Ember eyed the bracelets, and her eyes grew round. "You mean, you can create gold out of nothing? How is that possible?"

Shad had the decency not to laugh for a change. "I would that it were so. No, I still need raw materials. I only take the 'map' of the finished product and imprint it upon the metal so it duplicates the original. There is more energy expenditure, but it's worth it for the speed. Ian has already found the booth and questioned the boy we hired. He seemed rather frustrated when the boy's story matched yours." Shad's eyes sobered. "I'm glad we took the time to imprint his memory before setting him up in the booth. Ian pounced on him within the first hour."

The hair on the back of Ember's neck stood up. Ian was getting too close, and she had the feeling he wouldn't be fooled easily, despite Shad and DeMunth's best efforts.

Ember's uncle gathered up his handiwork and put it back in the satchel. "Is everything okay here? How's your room? Are they treating you well?"

Her dream came to the front of her mind. Goosebumps prickled her arms at the remembered terror, but she didn't say anything. Shad could do nothing for now, but he would support her when it came time for the battle with C'Tan. He'd promised her. For now, it seemed best to keep her fears to herself, though her stomach knotted with nerves. "Everything seems to be fine, though I could sure use a good soak. Does your room have a private bath?" Ember asked, desperation oozing from her sweaty, wolf-tinted pores.

Shad shook his head. "Sorry, I don't. And none of the residents were willing to share their bath with you."

Ember groaned and slid sideways down the wall, collapsing almost on top of the bracelets. "I can't go to my trial smelling like a wolf and covered in mud. What am I going to do?"

"It's very simple, Ember. You go take a bath." He pulled the drawstring tight and threw the satchel over his shoulder.

"I can't!" she snapped.

"No! You won't." Shad leaned against the doorjamb and crossed his arms.

Ember glared at him.

"Look, Ember, why is this such a big deal? You just go to the public baths when they are empty, wash, and get out. No problem."

"But it's the *boys'* bath. I can't go in there. And what if they call me for my trial before I get to bathe?"

"So bathe earlier. Bathe now, if you wish."

"I can't!" Ember reddened just thinking about it.

Shad sat down on the bed beside her and put his arm across her shoulders. "All you have to do is put some shorts on. Nobody will see a thing."

"But I'll still have to see *them*! And I'd feel stupid with shorts on. I won't be like them, and that will draw attention to me, which is the last thing I want. I don't have the same parts they do, Uncle. I need to blend in, be the same."

"Then make it so," he said, shrugging.

"Huh?"

242

"If you're so worried about not having the same parts, then make yourself some. If you can shapeshift into a wolf and change your own body, you can change that too."

Ember was too shocked to respond at first, and when she did, her words were a gut response and sent out with all the feeling her body possessed.

"Ewwww!"

Shad started to laugh and could not stop. Ember scowled. "Uncle," she said, rolling her eyes when he didn't stop immediately. He doubled over in hilarity until finally she got off the bed, shoved him, and shouted.

"Uncle!"

Shad swallowed his laughter and hiccupped at her, but he did stop at last. "Sorry," he said, not sorry at all, she was sure. He took a deep, shaky breath and put his arm back around her.

"The way I see it, Em, you've got only two options if you're that desperate for a bath. Either you go ahead and bathe with the boys, no matter how you decide to do it, or you go and bathe with the girls."

"How can I do that? Right now I'm neither boy nor girl."

"So, change yourself fully into one or the other," he said with a nonchalant shrug and a squeeze of her shoulders.

"But what about Mum? I can't really afford to—"

"I didn't mean forever, Ember," he interrupted. "Just to take a bath. If you're not comfortable being all boy, then be a girl again and go bathe . . . before the rest of the building smells like your room. Please." He waved a hand in front of his nose.

Ember was so surprised by his suggestion she didn't even notice his insult. Change back into herself to bathe? Yes, there was a chance her mother might see her, but it was a slight one. At least she'd be clean and make a better impression for the trials. It was worth taking a chance. There was only one problem.

"How?" she asked. "I've only changed into a human twice, and then it was to turn into a boy. How do I go back to my normal self?"

"Ahhh, now that's a good question. Focusing on the solution and not whining about the problem. And," he said, one finger pointed skyward for emphasis, "it's a simple one to solve. Changing back is always the easiest because it's the most familiar. Your body knows what you did, Ember—just follow the paths you have already opened, like listening to your blood when you changed into a wolf. Open yourself to it and trust it. I'll guide you as best I can."

Ember nodded, though doubt filled her. What if something went wrong? What if she couldn't duplicate the process?

But what would it hurt to try?

Shad pulled away and propped himself against the dresser opposite her. Ember watched him for a long moment before she sat gingerly on the edge of the bed. His nodded reassurance did little to soothe her rapidly frantically twitching nerves, but she took a deep breath, closed her eyes, and began.

First she imagined her face as it truly was, the image she had seen in the mirror every day for sixteen years, then she let her fingers explore.

At first nothing happened. Her fingers prodded at her nose, and she could feel the difference, could see in her mind how it should be, but nothing happened until the frustration built to the breaking point and in desperation she whispered—

"—change!"

And it did—with all the accompanying pain of two days before. Ember gasped and groaned for a long moment, her fingers gently massaging the familiar shape of her true nose as it ached through her cheek bones and eye socket and all the way into her head.

"Good," Shad commented, "but do it slower this time. Remember, it's the abrupt change that causes the most pain. Mold it like clay, Ember. Mold and shape and pull to achieve the best effect."

Ember nodded, not really sure what he meant, but she took him at his word and pictured the change in her jaw and chin being more gradual. She tugged gently at her chin and could feel it pull forward with a deep ache, but it was not the excruciating pain she'd had before—more like a well-used muscle and less like a boot in the face.

244

Next, she used her fingertips to gently massage and pull her eyes wider. She changed the color, lightening her brow and smoothing her lids until she felt nearly herself again. Her lips filled and widened, and at last she moved on to her body. All the changes made the day before returned to normal—her hips and arms narrowed, her ribcage thinned. It was painful, but bearable, and didn't leave her gasping as before.

Finished, Ember opened her eyes and met her uncle's tear-filled gaze.

"Beautiful," he whispered, no longer leaning casually against the desk, but instead kneeling at her feet and staring into her face. "You look so much like your father, it's uncanny. You have his eyes and nose and forehead. I can see your mother in you too, but you favor your father. Ah, how I miss him."

Ember couldn't help herself. She leaned forward, put her arms around her uncle, and squeezed him tight. Shad wrapped his big bear arms around her and hugged back. Their embrace lasted only a moment, but she thought it probably did both of their hearts good.

"Now, if I can only avoid Mum while I'm myself, I might be able to get through this in one piece." Ember chuckled and wiped away the beaded sweat from her forehead with the sleeve of her shirt. "Some days, it seemed like she'd stop me from becoming a mage at all costs, that she'd do anything to keep me her slave."

"She has her reasons, Ember, and I am sure that to her, they're good ones. But you're right to pursue this dream of yours. You're meant to be a mage, though of what kind, I'm not yet sure. Your magic is like none I've ever seen."

"What do you mean?" she asked. "I thought you said I had the shapeshifting ability like my father and yourself."

"You do, lass," he answered, taking her hand, "but you don't use the land magic alone to make your shift. Your color of magic is like a pallet of paint that's been mixed and swirled together, and it's all faded pastels, not the vivid color magic usually gives."

"I'm not sure I understand, Uncle. Doesn't all magic show green?" she asked, puzzled.

He shook his head. "No. Why would you think that?"

"Well, so far that's the only color I've seen. Aldarin had green around his hand, and I saw green around the plants, so I just figured magic was green."

Shad chuckled. "You also saw the golden yellow of DeMunth's breastplate, remember? No, Ember, there are actually seven colors of magic, each reflecting a color of the rainbow. Let me give it to you in short, though you will learn more once you reach the mage academy. You have heard the stories of S'Kotos and Mahal, and the breaking of Rasann?"

"No," she answered, leaning forward eagerly.

Shad rolled his eyes at her, but said nothing derogatory and began his tale.

"Long ago, there were a hundred Guardians who watched over Rasann, but there were two who were the greatest. They were twins—Mahal, and one who became known as S'Kotos, the Destroyer. Mahal and S'Kotos battled on Rasann and nearly destroyed our world. There were great cracks in the earth. Water rushed in to drown whole cities, mountains covered entire nations, and still other places were covered with ash and lava. It was Helar on earth, child, and when it was over, ninety-four of those Guardians were so distraught, they left the heavens to walk among the people of our world, healing it as they could, and joining the peoples of those they could not.

"Only six Guardians remained in the heavens, and their father stood with them. They held Rasann together, netted with magic, until one could be found from among mankind to heal her again. Mahal was afraid that if he stepped upon Rasann, she would rise up in rebellion against him and destroy herself entirely, so injured was she. And so the seven remaining Guardians stood in the heavens and divided the white magic among them." He seemed to be reciting to her, but then the far-off look left his eyes and he met hers again.

"Have you ever seen a prism, Ember?"

"Huh?"

"A prism," he stated again. "Cut glass that reflects light into a rainbow of color."

Ember understood then. "Yes."

"Magic is like that prism. Once, it was all together—white and pure—but the Guardians divided it into its individual colors to better bind Rasann. Each of the Guardians took charge of one color, until only Mahal remained. He was to take the red, the color of fire and heat, but S'Kotos stole it from him. All that was left was a small bit of the white, and so Mahal took charge of the binding of colors again. It is He who will lead the Chosen One to heal our world. It is He who will bring forth the next white mage."

"Wow," Ember sighed, enthralled with the story. "I've never heard of a white mage, and never understood what a green or red mage was, until now. They each focus on something different, then? Are there people who can do more than one kind of magic?" She leaned back on the bed and tucked her knees beneath her chin.

Shad hesitated. "Yes, but they all tend to be best at one type. To have three colors of magic is considered phenomenal. A white mage has all."

"Wow," she said again, unable to find a better word to express her awe. "How many white magi are there?"

Shad met her eyes, all seriousness. "None, Ember. Not for three thousand years. There are no binders to weave the magic of our world. I only hope we can find one soon, for we need a white mage before it is too late for all of us—before the magic completely unravels and Rasann is destroyed."

"Rasann destroyed?" she whispered in shock.

Shad nodded, all sadness now. "Why do you think our world is rising against us—Devil's Mount spewing all that ash and lava, the spells coming unraveled? You may not have heard of it, but there have been disasters among the water folk as well—entire cities consumed by great waves, denizens of the deep thrust from their home to perish on dry land." He shook his head. "Rasann has never been healed, only temporarily patched and mended—but those patches are a little threadbare after thousands of years of use and abuse.

"But this is a conversation that can be continued later. If you are going to bathe before your trial, young lady, you'd better go now. I'll escort you to the women's quarters, but from there you're on your own. Take your stuff with you, just in case they call while you bathe."

Ember gathered her bag and a change of clothes, and took his arm. "More than ready, Uncle."

"Whew, you can say that again." He twinkled at her, waving away the not-so-imaginary stink once more. Ember didn't bother shoving him again. She was grateful for his solution, and it just felt too good to be in her own skin. One last thought occurred to her.

"But what about Mum?"

Shad shook his head. "Think about it, Ember. You changed into a boy. Don't you think you could shift your face enough to be unrecognizable?"

Ember felt stupid. She should have thought of that. She covered her face with her hands as Shad took her arm, and they walked together out the door.

The bath was amazingly wonderful. Ember sat beneath the waterfall on one of several boulders apparently placed there for that very purpose and let the falls pound away the tension in her neck and head while rinsing the soap from her hair. She'd never bathed in a warm waterfall before. They were usually ice cold.

"Marvelous, isn't it?" a familiar voice asked. Ember started, then looked to her right to see her mother standing under the falls, washing her hair just as Ember had done. She immediately buried her hands in her hair to hide the tattooed bracelets, then, remembering her pendant, pulled her hair forward to cover it. She was tempted to slip off the boulder and bury herself in the water, but feared it would appear too obvious.

Marda continued as if Ember's behavior was perfectly normal. "I'd never admit it to my husband, but the falls are the one thing worth coming to Javak for. Or they would be if I weren't here for more pressing reasons." Marda's eyes clouded for a moment as she sat on the adjacent boulder. "I need the water massage after the week I've had."

Ember felt a pang of guilt. She didn't dare speak, as she was afraid her voice would give her away.

"You look familiar. Have we met?"

Ember groaned inwardly, her heart speeding up in preparation for the lie she was about to tell. "Sorry, no." The pain in her mother's face was raw. Ember turned away, unable to face it.

"You look so much like my daughter, it makes me miss her." Marda wiped at her eye. It wasn't just water she swept away, Ember was sure of it. Her stomach clenched at her mother's pain. She almost told her everything then.

"Are you . . . all right?" Ember asked, hands behind her back, still hiding them, but not able to face the hurt she knew she had etched in her mother's face overnight.

Marda gave a forced chuckle. "Oh, I'm fine. That daughter of mine ran off to the trials, and I haven't seen her in two days. I'm sure she's all right." She sounded like she was trying to convince herself.

Unable to stand the guilt any longer, Ember opened her mouth to admit the truth, but before she could say anything, Marda changed the subject.

"Did you know the magi created these falls? They redirected the flow of a hot spring to cascade over the cliff. It's beautiful and very nice on sore muscles, but it's as fake as a lead coin."

"Really? I never knew." An uncomfortable moment came between them, though Marda didn't seem to notice. After several quiet minutes Ember excused herself. "It was nice meeting you, ma'am. I've got to go now. My number will be coming up soon."

Marda opened her eyes. "You just be careful, child. The magi talk pretty, but they don't always live up to their promises. Watch yourself."

Ember didn't know what to say for a long moment. How would her mother know that? She seemed to speak from experience she'd never had, so far as Ember knew. Instead of answering, Ember nodded once and slipped into the water, feeling Marda's eyes on her

as she swam to the far end of the pool and pulled herself up onto
the side. Ember took two towels, wrapped one around her, and
stepped into a small dressing area.

Ember looked around. The baths were near empty. She smiled and
made a note to remember to come here about this time each day.

She was toweling her hair dry when she felt a hand touch her
own. She stopped the brisk rubbing and peeked from beneath
the confines of the oversized towel to meet the dark eyes of a
bath servant.

"Are you Ketahean?" she asked in a light whisper.

Ember shook her head, puzzled.

The women reached tentatively for Ember's hand and drew it in
front of her, inspecting the embedded color and weave of the bracelet
and ring Ezeker had given her just two days before. The woman
traced the lines across the back of Ember's hand, rather wistfully,
Ember thought.

"I have not seen marks like these since I was a child. I know of
no other people who mark themselves this way." The woman looked
at Ember questioningly.

"It was a gift," she stated, she hoped without emotion.

"Ahhh," the woman answered as if that made all the sense in
the world.

Ember retrieved her hand and continued to towel her hair.
Nothing more was said about it. She moved into a curtained stall,
took her clothes from the girl, which had been washed and dried
while she bathed, and dressed herself in the nice things DeMunth
had brought her. She gathered her bag and turned to go.

"Was that also a gift?" the woman asked.

Ember sighed and turned back to answer. "What, this?" she
asked, pointing to the wolf charm embedded in her neck.

The woman nodded.

"Yes."

The bathgirl quirked her head and reached for the tattoo.
"May I?" she asked just before she touched it. Ember hesitated
only a moment before nodding.

Her fingers were light, and the wolf eyes pulsed spring green at her touch. The girl gasped and moved in for a closer look.

"It is excellent, miss. I would guess from the Bendanatu. It holds great power. My father once sold pendants with markings such as this, but no more. Still . . ." she tilted her head further and blew once upon the charm. The girl's warm breath tickle Ember's skin. "I do not know much, miss, but this has a feel similar to a protection charm my father once sold."

A cold chill traveled down Ember's spine. She knew very well from whom it protected her.

The girl took a step back, put her hands together, and bowed slowly to Ember. "Thank you for allowing me the familiarity, miss. It is good to see pieces of home now and again."

Ember glanced at her wrists. She understood what the girl meant. Gaining the bracelets had given her a piece of history she hadn't known was missing. Even with the trouble it caused, she wouldn't trade the gift of the bracelets or the necklace for the wealth of the world. She was indebted to the girl for the information. Ember tied her hair back, then fingered the pendant tattoo. A piece of her life's puzzle clicked into place. She had learned more about her past in two days than she had during her previous sixteen years.

Ember nodded and smiled at the girl, receiving a shy smile in return. She then left the facility, crossing the narrow bridge that passed over the lake waters. There was a copse of trees where Uncle Shad had said he would meet her, and sure enough, he stood as she neared the center of the grove.

"Well, it took you long enough. I didn't think you were that dirty," he said.

Her crystal chose that moment to chime at her.

"Looks like your turn for trial." He folded his arms and leaned against a tree as she frantically dug in the pouch for the small clear stone she had been given earlier that afternoon. She found it on the bottom and looked into its depths. It glowed with faint light, much like moonlight, and the words written there were thrown at her and magnified clear as day.

*Orientation and first trial scheduled for seven
hours after noon in the central auditorium.*

Twelve minutes remaining.

The stone glared at her and died, now that it had delivered its message.

"Twelve minutes? What do you mean, twelve minutes?" Ember shouted at the stone. She shoved it in her pocked and looked at Shad. "Uncle, how can I have only twelve minutes? I thought they'd give me at least an hour."

"They probably did, but you were drowning yourself and didn't hear. Well, there's nothing to be done about it now. You're going to have to make this shapeshift a quick one, because it's going to take you a good five minutes to get to the auditorium from here."

Ember panicked for a moment, her stomach jumping with nausea, then took a deep breath. Panic would solve nothing. She took another breath to steady herself, then instead of sending the image just of her nose as she had before, she decided to try something new and sent the image of her entire male face, attempting to merge it with the old. She could feel the ache settling into her bones again and would have known it was working even if she hadn't felt the shift beneath her fingertips. Finally finished, she let go of the breath she held and wiped the sweat from her brow.

"Very good, Ember. Oh, marvelously done," Shad applauded.

Ember moved on to the rest of her body. She divided the change into three sections: torso, chest, and limbs. When finished, she glanced at the stone once more, its light reflecting on her face.

"Four minutes left, Uncle. What should we do?"

"That's easy. We run." With that, he shot out of the trees, and it was all Ember could do to follow him. They twisted and turned among the buildings and tents, first right, then left, then straight on to the very center of the city. Ember thought she was going to pass out long before she arrived, but just as she thought she could go no further, Shad stopped, and, with barely a gasp, said, "There it is. Just head through the big double doors and check in with the guard, find a seat, and let the fun start." He winked and turned to go.

"Wait!" she gasped. "Where do I find you?"

"You won't. I'll find you. Trust me, Ember," he said, and loped away.

Ember was alone.

She stumbled forward, her legs rubbery after the long run, and headed for the large double doors that fronted the round building. There was a young guard just stepping out to close them. Ember found the strength somewhere within her and bolted for the door just as it was pulling closed. She slid through the narrow opening and grinned at the guard, then stopped when she realized who it was, not sure whether to back up or keep going.

It was Aldarin, and he wasn't alone. He and Tiva stood arguing just inside the door, the other guard looking on without a smile.

"I'm telling you, Aldarin, Ember's here somewhere, and if Marda would relax a bit, she would show up. Marda needs to focus on Da right now, not her daughter."

Aldarin let his breath out in a rush. Ember knew that sound. It meant he was holding onto his temper by a sliver. "I know, Tiva, but you aren't going to convince her. Drop it. We know where to look. She'll show up sooner or later. Just do your job and shut your mouth."

Ember stood still as a mouse, staring at the two of them as they argued. Aldarin looked over Tiva's shoulder and met her eyes, a look of puzzled recollection crossing his face. "You're the boy I cut in front of at registration, right?"

Ember nodded, her eyes darting to the door behind him. She had to get in there. The alarm was going off in her bag.

Aldarin's eyes followed the noise, then met hers as it stopped. He smiled at the panic on her face, but what he did not know was that her panic was two-fold: one, that she would miss the trials, and two, that he'd recognize her—though how that was possible, she didn't know.

"It's okay, boy, you're not in trouble. They haven't started yet, though you'd better find a seat or you'll miss the best part. Give the guard over there your name, and he'll find you a place."

Ember didn't trust herself to speak, so only nodded at the one person she had ever really trusted until yesterday. Now she had Uncle Shad and DeMunth to add to that small list. She smiled and turned to the young guard, whispering her real name since she'd so stupidly given it to the guard when she'd registered for the trials. He checked his list and marked her off.

"Right through there, boy. Find an empty seat and listen. Good luck!" he said with a lot more enthusiasm than she felt. Ember turned and darted through the doors.

There were not as many people as she had anticipated. She'd figured on hundreds showing up for a trial like this, but there were maybe thirty or forty people between the ages of eight and fifteen. Everyone was clumped together at the front. She spotted a seat in the middle section on the far right side and turned to make her way along the back row, but ran smack into somebody who stood in the shadows.

"Oomph," she said. She pulled back from the iron stomach, looked up, and froze.

It was Ian. He looked at her, his hand on her shoulder, a slow grin spreading across his face as he saw through the disguise, through all of the work, to the very heart of herself. "I told you I'd find you, Shandae," he whispered as he took a stronger grip on her arm.

Ember wanted to scream, but her throat closed off. She looked around, panicked. She was in a room full of people—surely there had to be a way to get out of this without anyone getting hurt. She tried to pull away from him, but his clasp was like a vise.

Just then Aldarin came around the corner, bringing in another young candidate. "Excuse me, sir, can I help you?"

"No, you cannot. I am escorting my son from this trial." Ian took her arm and tried to push past, but Aldarin blocked the path. He pointed down the aisle for the candidate to find a seat. The boy seemed oblivious to the growing tension and darted toward the front of the room.

Ember's head spun. She looked at Aldarin with pleading eyes. Her heart seemed to squeeze itself into a tight ball. More than anything, she wanted to throw herself at Aldarin and beg his protection, but she could hardly breathe, let alone speak.

"Is that your wish, boy?" Aldarin asked.

Ember shook her head, still not trusting herself to say anything.

Aldarin met Ian's eyes then, finally recognizing who stood before him. His eyes hardened. "Let him go, sir, before I call the guard."

Ian seemed dumbfounded. "What?"

"I said, let him go. The boy has preference here. You are in the realm of the magi. If the boy wishes to go to trial, he is allowed to do so, despite parental wish or country's call. It's in the accords."

Ian slowly let go of Ember's arm as the guards continued to gather behind Aldarin. He fumed at her. "This isn't over yet," he whispered in her ear. "I know your face now, and I've known your heartbeat since that first night. I'll find you again."

Ember stilled at his words. He would be waiting, just as he had that morning when he'd sent the dogs in search. There was no escaping the man. Strangely, instead of losing hope at his words, she felt even more motivated to learn the craft of magic. She must pass this trial. Relieved, she watched as he turned and stormed from the building. She wanted to throw her arms around Aldarin, but didn't dare. "Thank you," she muttered instead, letting her eyes show just how thankful she really was. Aldarin seemed dazed by her look for a second, then slow understanding dawned on his face. He finally grinned, gripped her arm as he would greet a brother, and escorted her down the aisle to the very front row. He squeezed her arm before he left and leaned over to whisper in her ear.

"I'll let her know you're okay. Your secret's safe with me."

How he'd figured it out, Ember didn't know. Aldarin always had been very intuitive. Her eyes welled up with tears. "Thanks, Dari," was all she could whisper in response. He rested a hand on her shoulder and pressed softly before joining the rest of the guard at the back of the room.

Ember directed her attention forward. The room was dominated by a large stage, and though only one person was there, he seemed to fill the space. His graying hair was cropped close, and he wore a purple cape that fluttered around him like a flag on a pole, very ostentatious. His eyes flicked over the whispering crowd of youngsters, quieting them as his vision passed over each one. When everyone was settled, he began.

"Good afternoon, candidates, and welcome to orientation and first trial. Thank you for taking the time to attend and being willing to help us with this great work of service in magic, though it is not a livelihood for everyone. Even those who have the gift are sometimes not able to make the sacrifices required in this vocation, and thus we have created orientation for candidates before your first trial. It gives one a chance to change their mind if they feel this is not a job they are willing or able to do. There is no shame in that decision. There are many reasons why one would be unable to fulfill the calling to magic: family commitments, illness, death . . ." The audience chuckled. "All of these are valid reasons for not answering the call. Magic is a life-long commitment, candidates, so you must be prepared to devote the rest of yours to the work we do.

"Many young people, perhaps even you," he said, pointing to a smug-looking young man sitting to Ember's left, "are under the mistaken belief that magic is all about power, glory, and fun. There are moments of joy and glory and even reward, yes, but it is hard work. Often, it is a thankless job. Many magi have given their very lives in the service of the Guardians and our world Rasann. Don't be mistaken—it could happen to you," he said, pointing to a young lady on the end of the row this time.

"Let us begin." He extinguished the mage lights with a wave of his hand. The class squirmed in darkness for a long moment, the sound of rustling cloth and giggles reaching Ember's ears. A slight glow came from the center of the stage before her. It grew until it became a large ball of blue light with strange, squiggly formations, like a map pasted to a ball. The mage's deep voice echoed from the darkness.

"This is Rasann, as seen from the heavens—as the Guardians see it," the mage said. "She was deeply wounded by the Great War of the Guardians, and so the Guardians stitched her back together as best they could."

Lines of rainbow light began to criss-cross the globe to form a giant net around their world.

"The Guardians bound Rasann together with the colors of magic, and it is the duty of all magi to keep those bindings in place. Each day of a mage's life is, in part, spent repairing the damage done to those ropes of magic. It has continued daily for thousands of years.

"You are the next line in the defense of our world. It is exhausting work, and there are many who spend their lives doing nothing else—nothing but the work of knitting our world together. We are used where our talents are greatest, and for some—the healers in particular—their lives are used in giving the gift of themselves."

The mage lights came slowly back up. "Now," he said, "I know there are some of you who are not willing to do this, for once you commit yourself to the order of the mage, there is no turning back. You will be called where you are needed with very little choice in where you go and what you do, but," he raised one long finger, "the benefits are worth the inconvenience for some."

The audience murmured in appreciation.

"You will always have a home, food, and clothing. Society, for the most part, is respectful of the mage order and usually grateful for those tasks we perform to ease their lives.

"I would ask you to now determine if this is a way of life you would choose, and if not, feel no shame in escorting yourself from the auditorium. I shall wait for two minutes while you decide." The head mage stepped to one side of the stage and waited, still as a statue.

"Excuse me." The boy next to Ember stood to make his way past. She wasn't surprised to see he was not alone, though the number of people who filed out surprised her. A good third of the occupants left the room.

The tall man stepped forward again once the door closed behind the deserters. "There, that looks better," he said, "Now, before we continue, are there any questions?"

"Yeah," said a gruff-looking boy just behind Ember. "Do magi ever get married? Because the mage in our village is really old, and I don't think he's ever had a wife."

The tall mage nodded. "Most definitely, young man, and not always to another mage. I myself have been married for forty years and have five children and sixteen grandchildren. There are no laws or rules against marriage or dating, though we do ask you to be respectful and chaste in your dealings with one another. It's only courteous, and courtesy *is* one of the primary rules of our order.

"Any other questions? No? Then let us proceed with your contracts and testing. Please take a sheet of paper from beneath your seat and set it upon the desktop in front of you. Has everyone done that?" He waited for a moment until the rustling died down, then continued. "Good. Now, take your timestone and lay it upon the paper," he said, steepling his fingers in front of his nose.

Ember dug the timepiece out of her satchel and laid it in the middle of the paper. Almost immediately, deep black ink seeped into the parchment. Ember heard gasps and thumps around her as startled initiates jumped in their seats, and their stones fell to the floor. She held her breath as the ink spread across the page, then she began to read.

This is to certify that I, Ember Shandae, agree to the following . . .

Ember repeated the words, shocked at seeing the ink continue to spread across the sheet without pen to guide it.

It was a straightforward and simple contract, stating that by signing this paper, she committed herself to attend each of the trials and, if selected by the committee, would accept the calling of mage in the order of color determined by testing. Ember had no objection to signing the paper. It was what she wanted to do anyway, and she fully expected to be part of the order of the green since she'd already shown an affinity for that color.

She put her thumb to the bottom of the contract and held it while her thumbprint and name were taken in lieu of a signature. Papers were passed to the right and picked up by one of several gentlemen wearing black capes. The youngest of the assistants took the entire stack to the presiding mage, who placed the pages beneath the prism that had cast the image of Rasann. *Very symbolic*, Ember thought.

"The first thing a mage notices when coming to power is the color of magic surrounding a person or thing."

The men who had collected the papers assembled themselves across the front of the stage and stood with hands behind their backs in a relaxed, but attentive position. Without warning, they shrugged the capes from off their shoulders to pool about their feet in a nearly perfectly synchronized act. The colors beneath the capes were as varied as the men wearing them, but all of them had one thing in common. They were bright and gaudy and hurt her eyes to look at them.

"These gentlemen have consented to assist me. All of them are journeymen magi of differing colors. It is your job today to assess which color of magic belongs to which mage. Those who are correct in their assessments will move on to round two. Those who do not are free to return home. You will be notified of your status by morning. Take another piece of paper from beneath your seat and place your timestone upon it."

Ember did as asked and waited expectantly. Color began to bleed into the paper and she watched, her stomach bubbling with excitement, as images of the eighteen men assembled across the front of the stage suddenly appeared on paper. Their clothing was all of varied color and style, thus it was easy to determine who was who, even without detailed facial features.

The mage continued speaking.

"Place your index finger on each figure and think of the color you see. You will know you have locked it in place when the figure

259

disappears from the page. Give the page to the assistants in the aisles when you have finished. Watch your timestones, as results will be posted by morning. You may now begin."

Ember studied each of the men standing across the stage. For a moment she was afraid she would be unable to see their magic color, but as she closed her eyes to think, she could see the auras glow about them—rainbow-colored figures twinkling in her magesight. She sighed with relief and put her index finger on the first picture on the left. In reality, the man was dressed in red, but his aura showed yellow, just like DeMunth, so Ember pictured bright vivid yellow. She opened her eyes and looked down. The picture of the man faded away before her.

She moved to the next man, dressed in black pants and a vibrant purple shirt. When she closed her eyes, his aura was a clashing scarlet. Again, she held her finger on the paper representation, and the figure disappeared. Ember followed the same steps for all eighteen men until at last the paper was empty.

Opening her eyes, she glanced around the auditorium at the sweating initiates. A few more seats had emptied since she'd first looked at her contract, though whether it was because more of the audience had left or had finished their test ahead of her, she wasn't sure. One of the black-caped young men caught Ember's eye and beckoned to her.

Standing, she managed to move past the others on her aisle without mauling too many toes. She reached the end of the row and handed in her paper. He didn't even look at it, and she wasn't sure whether to be grateful or insulted. Her nerves were acting up again, now that she was finished. She hoped Aldarin or Shad would be close to the entrance. She did *not* want to run into Ian again.

"Are you finished?" the boy whispered, pulling Ember from her thoughts. She nodded in response.

"Great! You're the first! Good luck, candidate. I hope you make it." He lightly touched Ember's arm.

She gave him a nervous smile, then turned and made her way up the aisle and into the refreshingly cool air, grateful the testing was done at last. Aldarin and Shad stood side by side waiting for her. Ian was nowhere in sight. Relief washed over her as she approached the men.

"How'd you do?" Shad asked. Aldarin wrapped an arm around her shoulder.

Freed from her anxiety over Ian, Ember's thoughts turned to the test, and she shared her experience with the men. She yawned as the sun pulled the last of its rays behind the mountain and prayed she'd be able to sleep as she hoped for good results in the morning.

Chapter Twenty-three

Kayla ran at full speed, adrenaline surging through her veins as she pounded through the forest with T'Kato and Sarali just ahead, as if they were a herd of deer chased by a mountain lion.

Only it was not a mountain lion they fled, but a roaring dragon that snapped the tops off the trees and shot great gouts of flame into the sky overhead, though it was not the dragon they feared the most. The greatest danger sat astride his back.

Kayla had no room for anger at the moment. The peace that came with the song of the woods was gone, and now fear laced her veins like icy fire.

T'Kato slowed. Kayla pulled even with him very quickly.

"We've got a choice. The path branches up ahead," he yelled. "We can either run for the mountains and find a cave, if we're lucky, or head to the sea."

"That's not much of a choice," Kayla answered between gasps. She was really beginning to wish she had been more active in the past. She wasn't sure how much longer she could run at full speed like this. "Which one is closer?"

"The mountains, but there's not much cover, and the going is steep. I can't promise we'll make it, or that we'll find a cave when we do." He didn't show any of the bitterness she would have felt in a similar situation. After all, they wouldn't be in this mess if Kayla hadn't played the flute. But in her heart of hearts she knew she'd had no choice, and felt no guilt. T'Kato seemed to understand that.

"I'd say mountains, but I'm not the leader here," she said, and stumbled.

T'Kato caught her elbow and steadied her as they ran. "Yes, you are," he mumbled, then pulled ahead to speak to his wife.

What did he mean by that?

C'Tan's dragon had taken to pulling branches off the trees and hurling them like giant javelins at the fleeing threesome. Now their flight could no longer continue in a straight path, and they zigzagged through the forest, creating some distance from each other to make harder targets. Evidently it worked, because the dragon quit throwing the trees and backed off a bit. The snapping of the dragon's wings faded in the distance, the beast screaming its fury at being pulled from the hunt.

Kayla staggered to a stop and bent over, nearly vomiting with her need for air. T'Kato was not in much better shape, though Sarali hardly broke a sweat, and her breathing had only accelerated slightly.

"How do you do it?" Kayla gasped at her.

Sarali grinned. "Lots o' practice. 'Tis the nature of me people to be active." The longer they were in the woods, the more cat-like Sarali became. Her movements were even more lithe and graceful than usual, but there was a dangerousness menace about her that made Kayla ill at ease. The woman was obviously comfortable here, as if she'd come home.

"Can't rest long," T'Kato said, breathing hard. "She'll be back with reinforcements. Any suggestions?" His fear showed for the first time.

That sent a chill through Kayla, and she straightened quickly. If T'Kato was afraid, there was real reason for fear. As if her racing heart wasn't enough, her hands began to tremble at the realization.

"What about the river, Kato?" Sarali asked.

"Kayla wants to try the mountains," T'Kato answered her with a warning glance, though Kayla caught it.

"But the lass doesn't know all her options. Give her more, T'Kato, while we've got a bit o' time to breathe."

The tattooed man shook his head. "Sarali, there's no point—"

"It'll be savin' her life, man! Of course there's a point!" Sarali snarled and turned to Kayla. "Look, girl, we won't have much time here, so it might be best if I just show ye a thing or two. You'll need to watch me for this, but don't be afraid."

Before Sarali finished speaking, her face had begun to change. The already narrow, feline-type face grew more pronounced, her eyes slitted, and she sprouted whiskers and hair. Sarali crouched, her body changing and thickening until what appeared to be a great blonde cat sat on its haunches before her. It spoke, and Kayla jumped, wanting terribly to rub her eyes in disbelief.

"Now ye know the truth and me secret, Kayla. My people aren't entirely human now, ye see. We are shapeshifters, much like the wolf people, but we're more than that, too. We're MerCats, masters of the waterways and lords of the sea." She grinned a feline grin, tail twitching back and forth, and it was all Kayla could do not to run screaming at that very moment. She knew of magic, of course, had just performed some, in fact, but . . . not like this. What this woman had done was supposed to be impossible. People could change their appearance by illusion, but only the white magi were able to change physically, and there hadn't been any around for thousands of years.

And MerCats? Really? Kayla had heard of mermaids, but cats were supposed to *hate* the water. How could an entire race of people exist, whether underwater or not, and there not be a single legend or rumor about it?

"What she's saying, Kayla," T'Kato continued for her, "is that the waterways offer a very definite chance for survival."

"My people would be willing to help, I'm sure of it. They've got no love for S'Kotos or C'Tan, and would be glad to put it to 'em now and again. We can swim the waterways and be safe. The dragons cannot travel with the MerCats. The fire in 'em fades in the water."

"And with my luck, I'll probably drown," Kayla said, fear getting the best of her and pushing her into sarcasm.

"Nay, lass. Not with me. I promise ye can breathe in the wet just like the cats themselves, if ye'll let me help ye."

It became apparent Kayla's time was done when a fireball burst through the trees and exploded not ten feet away. Immediately the three of them were on their feet and running again.

"What's it going to be, lass?" Sarali asked, loping beside her.

What's it going to be? Kayla asked herself, unsure of the answer. The mountains lay closer. She could see them through the trees now, jagged and rocky, with switchbacks climbing the cliffs. But if they continued to the left and downhill, they would reach water and, according to Sarali, be safe. There *was* no promise in the mountains. They could just as easily strand themselves on a mountain top, sitting ducks for the dragons, as they could find a cave and hide in the depths of the hills. Kayla was more impressed by the odds of a water survival.

"Let's try it. Take the water," Kayla gasped, racing among the trees as fireballs continued to explode from the dragons above them, causing not only danger from the balls themselves, but also danger from the spreading fire and falling trees that were blasted in the passage.

Sarali loped to T'Kato. "She says water," she called to her husband, loud enough for Kayla to hear.

"I hope you know what you're doing, Sari," he said, but the feline only smiled, showing sharp teeth, and ran to the front to lead the way.

Kayla thought she could run no faster until Sarali took the lead, and then it seemed that if she held out her arms, she'd take off in flight. They tore down the mountainside and toward the water where they could hear pounding against the rocks far below.

The ground raced beneath her. She wove to avoid fallen trees and tumbled rocks, then fireballs and more falling trees, and finally a wave of fire that slowly gained on them.

The dragons changed tactics then, sending wave after wave of flame to feed the wall that chased the fugitives so they no longer zigzagged their path, but ran a straight course toward the water Kayla could now smell. They had just to stay ahead of the raging wall of flame.

They came to a dead stop as they entered an open meadow, with a hovering figure waiting for them in its midst.

They were trapped.

Kayla's heart sank, and her stomach rose as the fire crept closer, the heat pressing in on them. C'Tan's humorless smile slashed her face. Those eyes were cold—colder than the frosty wind that blew from the eastern mountains, colder than anything Kayla had known. They froze her heart and stilled her soul as she stared into them and knew there was no way to escape.

"Give it up now, Kayla, and I may let you live," C'Tan said, her voice sickeningly sweet.

"Like you let Joyson live?" Kayla snapped before thinking.

"The boy has suffered no irreparable harm. He'll live, Kayla. You, I am not so sure. Give me the flute, and I'll consider it," she said, her hand outstretched.

For a brief moment Kayla was tempted to give in, to just hand it over and escape this mess, but . . .

She couldn't.

It was wrong, and she knew it. Not only would she then be responsible for handing over one of the keystones to The Destroyer, but she would be shamed, and her family with her. They would lose their place in society forever. She could live with that for herself, but not for them. Not for Mother, and she could not live without Brant—so she responded in the only way she truly could.

She answered with her heart. "No," was all she said, but it was enough to harden C'Tan's features.

"Give me the flute, Kayla," C'Tan demanded again, her voice not so full of sweetness this time.

"And I said no." Kayla held the flute close to her chest.

"Give me the flute!" C'Tan yelled.

Kayla was shaken. C'Tan's wrath was terrifying. Red light flickered around her hair, almost like lightning. In that moment she no longer looked human, the beautiful image flickering to show a scarred monster behind it. Kayla balled her fists to keep her hands from shaking, but still she refused. She crossed her arms over her chest, chin jutting in her stubborn posture. She shook her head.

"I will never give you the flute, C'Tan. I am its guardian, and I will defend it with all the strength of my body and every breath I take. It shall not be yours, even if I have to destroy it to keep it from you. Now move and let us pass, and *I* may let *you* live!" she threatened, not really sure if she could live up to that reckless promise, but determined to try.

C'Tan screamed in rage. Her dragon reared back and lunged, a huge tongue of flame preceding him.

"Run for the river!" T'Kato yelled as he shoved Kayla aside and ran in the opposite direction. They were split by the flame and hidden by it at the same time. Kayla dove beneath the reaching dragon and ran with everything she had. She had no idea what she ran toward or where she was going; she only followed her heart and senses, running blindly through the unknown forest.

The trees were speaking to her again. *"Left, Kayla, left. Run to the river . . ."*

The leaves rustled louder. The roar of dragon wings sounded as if they snapped directly above. She dared a quick glance over her shoulder and wished she had not. C'Tan was bearing down on her, dodging between the trees to follow her straight through the woods, barreling through the small saplings that got in her way so they snapped behind her, moaning in the pain of death. The forest groaned around her, and it was no wonder. The fire still burned there, still pursuing Kayla as relentlessly as did C'Tan.

Her only safety lay in the water. She had to find the river, but where was it? She didn't know these lands, and now she ran alone.

"Follow the trail . . . we'll light the way . . . follow the trail . . ."

Of a sudden, the moss that grew on the trees began to fluoresce, but in an obvious pattern that led in a straight line just to Kayla's left—a line that couldn't be correct. It led upward, not down. Water ran down. The river had to be down, not up!

"That can't be right!" she called to the trees, but they continued to pulse their faint silvery-green glow, leading her up the hill. Kayla didn't know what else to do, so she followed the trees, her breath increasing with the extra effort of fighting against gravity, and her pace slowed.

Just enough for C'Tan to catch up.

Kayla heard the dragon before she felt it, but not soon enough. She leaped forward, intending to hit the dirt and roll, but only succeeded in coming up underneath the great beast and impaling herself on one of the outstretched claws. The talon penetrated her right shoulder just below the collarbone, and Kayla felt it snap, the muscles beneath tearing and shredding on the razor-sharp claw. She couldn't help herself. She screamed.

The agony was exquisite as the dragon grasped her other shoulder and lifted her high above the trees. It bellowed triumphantly to the other dragons. The wing of beasts roared an answer and made a beeline toward C'Tan.

The dragons formed up around her, a bubble of black curves and wings in every direction. It would have been a beautiful sight if she were not nauseated by the pain and height. So close! But not close enough.

She had tried. What more could they ask of her? She'd been handed guardianship of this instrument. She hadn't asked for it, and she'd received no training. How was she to know what she could and could not do? And now, so much destroyed. She wished C'Tan would drop her to her death and end the agony of body and soul. The failure was almost more painful than the injury to her shoulder.

Kayla reached her hands up to grasp the dragon's claws as it climbed higher, angling away from the forest and over the water. T'Kato and Sarali leaped from the cliff face and into the sea just below her. One of the beasts broke formation and dove after them, but they didn't resurface.

Two more minutes and she would have been with them, would have been safe. Now here she was, pinned and captured, flying above the water and heading who knew where.

Kayla wanted to give in to the darkness that threatened to overwhelm her, but something within her fought and could not—something inside buzzed and throbbed with power and the *want* and *need* to be free.

Something musical.

Suddenly, just like before, the fear was gone, the pain left, and Kayla was filled with the music of power, the song of the flute. She reached across her body to grasp the instrument she had tucked inside her tunic when she ran. It was still there, but how was she to play it with an injured arm? And what good would it do if she could? If C'Tan dropped her, she would fall hundreds of feet to her death on the rocks that lined the shoreline, or drown in the depths of the sea, unless . . .

Unless she could somehow get near her friends and fall there. Hadn't Sarali said she could enable Kayla to breath beneath water? Hadn't Sarali said her people would care for her? It was a slim hope, but it was more than she'd had an instant earlier.

Kayla tried to pull the flute to her lips, but the dragon's legs were in the way, and her right arm was practically useless with the damage done to it. She may have been momentarily free of pain, but that did nothing to restore the torn and damaged muscle, nor repair the broken bone. She tried again to raise the flute, to bring even one note from its length, to no avail. She sobbed with frustration.

Sarali and T'Kato finally resurfaced and treaded water, watching as C'Tan banked closer to the surface, probably to mock them in their defeat. Their faces were filled with horror and fear. Kayla was grateful they cared—whether for herself or the flute, it didn't matter. That one thing empowered her to try once more.

She raised the flute to her lips, took in a breath—

—and lost it with the wind.

The dragon hit some turbulance, causing him to spin and rock back and forth like a boat on storm-tossed waters. Kayla tried to grab hold of the dragon's leg with her good arm, and in that instant, a large gust caught them and tore the flute from her grasp.

"No!" she screamed as it tumbled toward the waters below. Instinct claimed her then. She reached her hand for the flute, even though her mind knew it was useless, grasping for it with all the strength of her will and being, and nearly fainted as a result.

The flute halted its fall in mid-air like a glowing blue hummingbird. It was beautiful. She reached for the flute, but C'Tan laughed.

"It's mine now, fool," she taunted.

The blonde witch leaned over the side of the dragon and reached for the flute, just as Kayla had. Slowly it ascended toward the dragon, and Kayla's heart fell. Surely C'Tan would claim the flute from her now. She had failed, miserably failed. Still, she held her hand out, hoping against hope that the flute would hear her heart and come to her.

The flute continued to rise inch by agonizing inch. Kayla's arm began to tremble with the effort. The flute tickled her fingertips, just out of reach, then paused, and to Kayla's great astonishment, moved itself not to C'Tan's outstretched hand, but her own.

C'Tan shrieked in frustration and leaned farther over the side of her mount, trying to grab Kayla, but she was safely beyond C'Tan's reach. *Well, not safe,* she thought as the waves below her seemed to rise and fall an eternity away, but she was not helpless. She had the flute. It had chosen her. She raised it to her lips and this time, instead of trying to play it, she merely hummed into the mouthpiece, a perfect middle-range note.

The flute began to vibrate and pulse, sound and energy expanding from Kayla's body to touch the dragon's legs. It sparked a shocking wave of blue, and the huge dragon bellowed its pain.

"Hold on to her, you beast!" C'Tan shouted.

Kayla was stunned when the dragon spoke. "I can't, mistress. It pains me," he said in a deep bass.

"Dragon, if you let her go—" C'Tan began to threaten, but in the end it did not matter.

The flute would not be held.

Nor would it allow Kayla to be held against her will. The great blue arcs of electricity stunned the black dragon enough that he loosened his hold on Kayla as he lost consciousness.

"No!" C'Tan wailed.

"Yes!" Kayla hollered in glee as the dragon released her, and she fell toward the waters below.

The pain pounded at her then, the moment just before she hit the water with enough force to knock the wind from her— enough force to knock the flute from her grasp—though it did not.

Kayla clung to the flute with a death grip, and even as she floated on the top of the water, the salt stinging her wounds, even as she faded toward unconsciousness, her hold on the flute was as cement.

No one would take it from her.

No one.

Chapter Twenty-four

Ember awoke to pounding on her door somewhere near the midnight hour. She rolled out of bed and stumbled across the room to crack open the door.

"Ember Shandae?" a gravelly voice said from the hall.

She rubbed sleep from her eyes and nodded. "Yes? Is something wrong?" she answered before thinking, then cringed. Fear and sleep had made her careless. Only her uncle and the people in charge of testing knew who she was and where to find her.

"We've been sent by the Mage Council to escort you to the hall. They wish to discuss your test results," the wizened guard answered her, with no emotion on his worn and scarred features.

At twelve o'clock? Wow, when the council said they would let her know before morning, they really meant it. "Just give me a moment to change and gather my stuff—"

The guard shook his head and pushed the door open wide. "I'm sorry, but the council made it clear that you were to come immediately. There is no time." The man stepped into the room, three other guards fanned out behind him.

"What? You won't even give me time to change?" Fully awake, her heart jumped in her chest. Why would the council need to see her this late at night? It made no sense, but she wasn't used to the way of things here. Maybe this was normal.

She turned back to her bed and bent to retrieve the satchel she'd been told to keep with her at all times.

"Let me just get my bag—"

"You won't need that, sir," the lead guard said, placing a hand on her shoulder. He turned Ember around and clapped an iron cuff around her wrist. "The council only requires your presence at this time. If they need anything more, someone will be sent to retrieve it." He pulled her along and snapped the other bracelet on her left wrist so her hands were tied together, forming a T. There was no room for movement. It hit her then that she was not a guest, but a prisoner of these four men.

They had Ember through the door before she could gather her thoughts enough to say anything. About that time they passed Uncle Shad's door. Ember dug in her heels and pulled against the leader, but another man stepped forward to take her other arm.

"Wait, wait! What are you doing? What did I do? Where are you taking me? Uncle Shad! Somebody, help me!" she screamed and let her legs collapse so all her weight hung from those two strong arms. It did not seem to faze the soldiers a bit; they merely lifted her by the elbows and carried her down the hall. Nobody answered, not a word. No doors opened to her cries, not even Uncle Shad's.

Ember was on her own.

"Please," she begged. "Can't you just tell me where you're taking me? What did I do?"

"We're only following orders, sir," said the guard to her right. "Our apologies for the discomfort."

"Who sent you for me? Was it Ian?" She put her feet beneath her again, tired of holding her legs up like a chicken.

"The council sent us, sir. We're only following orders," the same guard repeated.

As they stepped from the building with Ember thrashing between them, another group of men approached. "Release the girl," said a voice she knew, a voice that sent chills down her spine. Ian had caught up with her after all. "She is to be put in custody of the city guard for crimes committed against the city of Javak."

"That's a lie!" Ember screamed.

"Silence!" The pockmarked guard demanded. Even the crickets stilled at his volume. He turned to Ian. "By whose authority do you claim this *boy*?" he said, to make the point that Ian couldn't even get her gender straight.

"Police Chief Naedar," Ian said, impatient as always.

The guard shook his head. "I am acting on behalf of Councilmember Laerdish. His authority overrides that of the police chief. The boy remains with us."

Ian growled, frustrated, as he ran his hand over his head. He glanced back at his men, then at the group that surrounded Ember, as if he were weighing his chances against them.

A voice whispered in Ember's mind then, a voice she'd never heard before, yet was strangely familiar and carried with it the tingle of lightning before a storm. *"Drop to the ground, now!"* The voice was so powerful that her body responded immediately. She let her weight sag, and this time the guard let her go. She hit the hard dirt face-first just as her keepers drew their swords and Ian let out a pained scream.

She rolled over and out of the way to watch.

The first thing that caught her eye was a white blur arcing into the sky away from Ian. It screeched as it banked to the right, and Ember recognized it as the white hawk that had been watching her. She noticed bloody streaks across the top of Ian's gleaming head as he searched the sky for his attacker.

Her mind raced at the implications. The white hawk could talk; it must have been the one who told her to drop. It was also becoming increasingly clear that the bird really was a guardian of some kind— but what was it? A spirit? Another shapeshifted animal? And why would a guardian bother to protect her?

275

The answer lay only with the bird, and he soared quickly away from her.

The men who stood behind Ian divided themselves between watching the sky and nervously eyeing the guards who surrounded Ember with glowing swords.

Ian wiped at the blood dripping into his eyes and put a hand on the hilt of his sword. The men behind him looked at the guard and to a man standing just behind Ian. The man chewed his lip for a moment, then gestured a retreat with his chin. The group disappeared into the dark.

"I wouldn't if I were you," the guard to Ember's right said in a deathly quiet voice.

When Ian still didn't remove his hand from the sword, the guard spoke again. "Look behind you, man."

Ember's kidnapper scowled, refusing to move until the captain sheathed his own weapon. Ian sneaked a glance over his shoulder, then surprise and frustration flashed across his face, only to be replaced with cold fury. He faced the scarred captain and glared, first at the guards, then at Ember as she lay in the dirt. "This isn't over yet," he said, then stormed to his horse. He threw himself across its back and galloped toward the council chambers.

The pockmarked guard reached down and took Ember by the elbow, pulling her to her feet once more. "You certainly are the popular one tonight, aren't you, boy?"

"Why are you doing this to me?" Nobody answered. She kicked herself for not escaping while the guard was distracted, but there was nothing to be done about it now.

Ember did everything she could to slow the guard down, hoping Uncle Shad would come to her rescue, or that she'd see Aldarin, or Ezeker, or even Tiva along the way. She dug her toes and heels at the dirt, tried to squirm her way loose, kicked, bit, and spit at the guards, but it was no use. They held her fast. In the end she had to be satisfied with being dead weight and letting herself be carried and dragged all the way through town and into the building she had tested in that very evening. If they were going to take her without cause, she wasn't going to help them.

Instead of going left into the auditorium, the guards turned to the right and, pulling aside a curtain, dragged Ember up a hidden stairway. As the passage narrowed, two more guards stepped forward and lifted Ember to their shoulders. She traveled feet first, staring at the ceiling as if being borne to her own funeral.

Why, oh why, did she ever think she could be anything different than what she was? Why had she resisted her mother's attempts to keep her safe? Riding atop these guards' shoulders while clapped in irons, she would have given anything to be sitting at home with her mother. Drinking spiced cider and debating over the crops or the care of the newest foal would have been plenty of excitement. She would rather be anywhere but here, and that feeling only intensified when the guards stopped and lowered her to her feet in front of the grand double-paneled doors.

The four tall men brought themselves to attention as the doors swung wide with apparently no hand to open them. Ian strolled from the room and tipped his hat to her. Somehow in the short time since she'd last seen him, he'd found a bandage for his head and retrieved his hat. Ember had the feeling he'd just made her situation much, much worse. Two of the guards took her elbows once more and pulled her forward.

The fight left her as she saw the silent crowd waiting, some glowering and others with fearful expressions.

The room was huge. Ember felt like an insect under a looking glass. The ceiling domed high above with triangular windows. Magelights bobbed around the walls, their odd blue glow casting shadows that seemed strange and twisted. She shivered.

The men and women of the council sat on tiered bench-style seats forming a half-circle around the room, rising from ground level up twelve or more layers. The seats were nearly full, and the hush that settled over the group at Ember's entrance was loud to her overwrought nerves.

The center of the room was beautiful. A star of inlaid stone sat in the middle, a circle surrounding the points. The guards led Ember to the circle, then backed away to take positions on four of the points of the stars, a fifth guard appearing to take his place on the remaining corner. A streak of lightning arced between the five of them and quickly disappeared. Ember wasn't sure what that was about, but the sinking feeling in her stomach told her it was nothing good. She stood quietly, though her eyes flashed at the silent crowd facing her.

One man stood. He was wider than any man she had ever seen, and his clashing robes billowed about him like silken sails on a ship. It almost hurt Ember's eyes to look at him, but look at him she did. She was not going to let them beat her down, not even when she stood helpless in chains before them. She was sure it was a misunderstanding that could be cleared up quickly.

Unfortunately she never had a chance to talk. Their minds had already been decided, no matter what logic might tell them.

"Brothers and Sisters of the Council, I give to you Ember Shandae," the large man said, throwing his arm toward her and spinning slowly toward the council like a great thespian. He then turned back and met Ember's eyes. She was surprised by the intelligence and hate there. What had she done?

"*Ember.*" He said her name like it was a joke of some kind. "Do you know why you are here?"

"No." She tried to hide her emotion, but her voice quavered. "The guard said you wanted to talk to me about my test results, but that's all I know."

"Ah, yes. Your test," he said, smirking at her with angry eyes once again. "Did you know that no one has perfectly passed this test for three thousand years? Did you know that it is next to impossible to get every single answer right?"

Ember shook her head.

"It's true. The test has been designed so you can see only the colors you can use with your power. Three thousand years full of one-, two- and three-color tests. A four-color every now and then, but six? Seven? Never. Not in three thousand years. And yet you have managed to do exactly that this evening, Ember Shandae. Would you mind telling me how it is possible that you could do this thing that no one has done in all this time?"

"Because I could see all the colors," she said, anger chasing away her fear for the momement. Her heart beat fast in her chest.

"Liar!" he screamed, spittle flying from his mouth. His face reddened with the intensity of his emotion. "You cheated!"

"I didn't cheat!" she yelled back at him. "I've never cheated at a thing in my life. I saw all those colors, whether you want to believe it or not. I don't cheat, and I don't lie."

The room stirred with voices. Sleeves fluttered as the council members turned and whispered to each other.

"Silence!" the lead councilman demanded. The room immediately quieted. "You do not cheat and you do not lie, you say? Perhaps then you can explain to us the discrepancy we find with your name." He gave Ember a gloating type of smile. The man had some kind of plan, one she wasn't going to like, Ember was sure of it, but she didn't know what to do. She just stood and watched as he beckoned to a sixth guard who had previously gone unnoticed. The man nodded to the councilman, leaned inside a curtained alcove, and muttered to someone there. They waited for a moment, and when he pulled aside the curtain, a woman stepped forward. Ember's heart surged at the familiar face, and then fell with sickening dread. She knew where this was heading and could kick herself for her stupidity. The flamboyant councilman was watching and smiled at her discomfort.

"Someone you know then, I see. Let's hear from her, shall we? Mistress Rikash, do you know this boy?" he asked the woman Ember had met at the baths that afternoon, the woman from Ketahe who had been so interested in Ember's tattooes. The woman she had spoken to while she had been a *girl*.

Rikash shook her head. "I do not know this boy, no."

"And yet the girl you spoke with today was one Ember Shandae?" he asked, watching Ember squirm from the corner of his eye.

"Yes, I signed her in to the baths this afternoon."

"Could you describe her to us, please?"

"Yes, sir. She was small—slender and short, with shoulder-length brown hair and green eyes. She had tattooed wolves and fine chains on her hands, and a wolf pendant embedded in her breastbone. It was quite fascinating."

"Tattoos like these?" he asked, reaching for Ember's hand. He pulled off the bracelet Shad made for her, exposing the embedded chain and pendants that had been absorbed into her skin. "A pendant like this?" He pulled a small knife from his belt and ripped the shirt DeMunth had given her from neck to mid-chest, exposing the pendant. He jabbed it with his finger, the wolf's eyes flashing at the intrusion.

Ember gasped and tried to yell for the man to leave her alone, but her mouth was frozen. She could not move, could not speak—could only watch in horror as the pendant her mother had told her never to remove, the pendant she had been told was a protection to her, slowly rose through her flesh, transformed back into solid metal, and fell whole—chain attached—into his hands. She felt as if a piece of her very soul had been torn away. How had the man overcome her father's magical tranformation to take it off?

Anger, fear, and something else surged up inside of her— something that battled with the constraints that kept her from speaking or moving, that kept her bound to this spot of earth. Heat rose and blinded her for a long moment, so that she missed part of what was said.

When she came back to herself a few eternal seconds later, her pendant was in the woman's hand. She examined it very closely.

". . . very much like the one I saw this afternoon, yes. If it is not the original, it is a very good copy, though it feels much the same as the other did. Yes, I would say it is the same pendant."

"So how would you explain the difference here, Rikash? You very clearly saw a young woman going by the name of Ember Shandae with these tattoos and this pendant in the bathing room, and now standing before us, having taken the test, getting one hundred percent of the questions correct, is a boy with the same tattoos and pendant. Girl in one, boy in the other. So who is the real Ember Shandae?"

The woman shook her head. "I cannot say, sir. I only know that which I saw this afternoon. The two of them do not look much alike, so I cannot even guess that one is disguised as the other."

Ember wanted to shout at them, *I am the real Ember Shandae! I am both!* but she could not get her mouth to work. She stood frozen, a living, breathing piece of marble that could not speak or move. She fought it with all she had, even tried calling on the magic within her, but she was bound tighter than with chains and rope. She was completely within their power.

The only person who had seen her as both boy and girl was Uncle Shad, and he hadn't heard her calls earlier. She realized there had to be a certain level of physical proximity for mindspeech to work, but she called to him anyway. He still didn't answer. If she could have cried, she would have. It seemed hopeless.

"I'll tell you what happened, Mistress Rikash, council members. It has come to my attention that C'Tan herself has taken an interest in our academy. I have it on good authority that she has been trying to infiltrate by placing an agent amongst our apprentices—an agent who very much fits the description of this young man here. I believe she prepared this boy and somehow has found a leak in the system, providing him with the answers that would make him seem too good to be true . . . a new white mage. Here is a sketch of the agent, provided me by one of our own spies."

He held up a piece of parchment for the council members to see, then set it on a small table and placed a clear pink stone on its face. The rest of the council picked up papers that had been replicated just like her test that afternoon. They glanced at the sheet and at Ember, then stared harder. Surprised and angry mutterings came from the crowd. The head mage picked up the paper again and turned around to Ember, holding it before her.

"Look familiar, boy? It should. It's the face you see in the mirror each and every morning. Thought you could get away with it, did you? Well, you're about to see that the council of magi is much smarter than your mistress gives us credit for. She will pay for her treachery, and so will you, boy. Oh, so will you."

Ember would have screamed if she could have, for the image staring back at her was indeed her own, the male face she had created beneath the giant willow, a face pulled from her own imagination and brought to life at Shad's urging.

Chapter Twenty-five

C'Tan screamed as the girl fell from her grasp. She'd had her in the palm of her hand, and because of a little pain, the dragon had let her go.

"Stupid beast!" she yelled at the winged dragon beneath her. She pounded on his armored back, though she knew it would not even faze him. "Get her! Get her now!" she howled as the dragon gathered itself and shook. C'Tan clung tight to the mount and cursed him silently. Too moody, too sensitive, these dragons. Too soft for her taste, but all she had to work with, all her master would allow. He was too partial to these beasts, she felt, but could not, would not ever say it.

"Get her!" she shrieked again when the dragon had calmed. C'Tan was pleased to see the girl had landed awkwardly when she hit the water. The pain must have been pretty awful, and might even slow her down a bit. She wished Kardon was nearby. She would have loved to throw the useless old man in after the girl and watch him flounder. She was certainly not going in to retrieve her. The water was too hard on her riding leathers, let alone the dampening effect it had on her magic.

The dragon still had not moved, so C'Tan kicked him in the sides with her spiked heels. The beast bellowed with pain and turned a long, sinewy neck to glare at her with one baleful eye. He hissed, and she snarled back, wearied of the battle for power she went through with him every day. Why couldn't S'Kotos have selected a more obedient animal when he chose his totem? She glared at the dragon, and finally he turned his head back with a last hiss.

C'Tan was determined to capture the girl before she escaped, and then realization hit her. She laughed. Where could the girl go? It's not like she could breathe in the water. All C'Tan had to do was persuade her dragon to move, and she could pick Kayla up. The flute would be hers and hers alone! No half-evahn runt was going to take the blue keystone from her; she'd worked too hard to find it.

"Toast them or pick her up, but move, you stupid beast!" she yelled at the dragon, who listened to her at last, tucked his wings, and dove.

He belched several balls of fire, but missed the runt, of course. C'Tan had better aim with a rock than this beast had with his fire. She tried to wait patiently, but patience was not one of her virtures and never had been. It disappeared completely when the tattooed Ketahean swam toward the girl. She didn't know what he was capable of, but something told her that only trouble came with this trio— trouble for her.

"Go and get her, beast!" The dragon dove and got hold of the girl's satchel, which was strung across her back. He started to lift her from the water. It was slow-going with the added weight and nearness of the water, and the drake had to struggle for every inch of height he gained.

He sagged again when the Ketahean grabbed the girl and climbed up her body high enough to reach the dragon. C'Tan watched in satisfied horror as the tattooed man pulled a great knife from his belt and stabbed the dragon between the toes, then sawed at the straps. They parted, giving way strand by strand, until the last few broke all at once, severing the bag's strap. She felt no pity for the beast, but lost her treasure once again as the girl was freed and fell to the water once more. She did not resurface. C'Tan waited, growing more agitated with every passing second.

It didn't take long for her to realize the girl was not coming back up. C'Tan howled at the loss. Furious, she sent spikes of lightning flame surging into the water. She sent wave after wave, hoping she would hit the half-evahn called Kayla and could retrieve her body from the flotsam dotting the surface, but the girl did not come. C'Tan realized her defeat.

"No!" she screamed at the dragons that now huddled around her, waiting for orders. It would be easy to end it now, to give in to the failure, go home, and await her next chance, but she could not stand the bitter taste of defeat in her mouth, nor would her master be pleased that she had come so close. He would not blame his dragon for the error. No, he would hold *her* responsible, and the last thing she wanted was more of her master's unwanted attention. She shivered at the thought and made up her mind. She *must* have that flute! There had to be a way she could enter the water without losing her flame.

And then it hit her.

The tunnels.

She yanked on the reins of the midnight dragon and turned him south, despite his pain-filled howling.

"Shut up, Drake. We'll take care of you later. Right now we've got an entrance to find."

He quieted, though tremors still shivered through his body. "What do you mean, mistress?"

C'Tan spurred him forward. "We're going after them, Drake, and you're going to help me."

"But I cannot enter the water—" he started, but she cut him off.

"I know that, fool. We're not going in the water. We're going to go *through* it—if we can find the entrance to the waterways. Now move it, before I remove your wings with my teeth."

The dragon snorted at her useless threat, but flew south. He flew fast, for he knew of what she spoke. The waterways that ran beneath the oceans of Rasann were made long ago, and few still knew of their existence.

Drake knew. He knew them well.

Chapter Twenty-six

Kayla sank deep and fast. At least the flute would be buried in this vast, watery grave. C'Tan would not have it. Kayla readied herself to give in to the darkness, was about to breathe in her last, when she felt hands on both sides of her.

To her left, T'Kato, and to her right, a creature that seemed a cross between cat and beaver. Kayla wasn't sure whether to be thankful or scared, but at the moment wasn't sure she even cared; she was in too much pain, and her lungs felt near to bursting.

The cat smiled, and Kayla recognized the toothy grin and flashing eyes of Sarali. Strange that she looked different in the water than she had on the land. The MerCat leaned close and exhaled directly into Kayla's face.

To her amazement, a bubble about the size of a grapefruit formed around Sarali's mouth. She blew out again and the bubble grew to the size of a melon, then again until the pocket of air was the size of a boulder.

Sarali released the bubble and grasped it with her paws, much as a child would a ball, and pushed it into Kayla's face. Her nose punctured the skin of the bubble, the texture much like that of gravy skimmings. It spread across her face and then past it until her entire head was completely encased.

Kayla opened her eyes, lungs still burning, and met Sarali's eyes. "Breathe!" The cat woman mouthed.

Kayla shook her head, afraid she would dislodge the air and perish in the sea.

"Breathe!" Sarali mouthed again, her eyes concerned.

Darkness tinged Kayla's vision, bright flashes pulling her sight upward, but she dared not take a breath. If she was going to die, she preferred it be a nice, quiet drowning. That was what she expected, not this last surge of hope that was too fragile to hold.

T'Kato goosed her backside, and Kayla gasped, arching forward in surprise. She inhaled huge lungfuls of air for a moment, astounded that she could actually breathe underwater. She only wished T'Kato had found a more dignified way to get her to do so. She turned and glared at the grinning man—but she was breathing, and he had saved her life, after all, so her glare was half-hearted at best.

Kayla was afraid her air would completely disappear if she couldn't slow her breathing, but the bubble held—though it shrank marginally with each breath. Now that she could breathe, she became aware of the constant flood of tears that leaked down her face. The pain from her injured shoulder was horrid. Never in her life had she known such misery. She wanted to lie down and die, would be thankful to drown just to end the torment.

Sarali pointed downward and Kayla nodded, not sure how she was expected to swim in her condition.

T'Kato wrapped an arm around her good side and pulled her downward. He was a strong swimmer and somehow was able to manage himself and her . . . all without breathing. She finally noticed the frills on his neck that surged open and closed, water flowing through, like the gills of a fish. She quit worrying about him then and relaxed her upper body, kicking only her legs to assist him on the journey down.

But the fight was not over yet.

A lance of lightning-colored flame came from above, searing through the water before it caught her arm, leaving a black streak of char on the outside of her bicep. Kayla shrieked, her voice echoing strangely inside the air bubble. Another streak fell and caught T'Kato in the shoulder, and a third singed Sarali's fur. T'Kato did not stop. He pulled harder until at last they were out of reach.

C'Tan had found a way to attack them while they were buried beneath the sea, shooting fire or lighting at them from the air. Kayla should have known that a little water wouldn't make C'Tan give up her quest for the flute. This was a battle for life—and not just Kayla's own. It was a battle for the life of her planet and not something she could afford to surrender, though pain made it very, very tempting.

The pressure began to build, her bubble of air growing smaller, her body able to take in less air as the pressure grew on her chest. It seemed Sarali was guiding them to the very bottom of the ocean, though at the moment it seemed bottomless—a neverending expanse of ever-darkening blue.

A long line of glowing light gleamed up from the depths. It grew larger the closer they swam. Sarali headed directly to the light and beckoned for Kayla to come to her. T'Kato dragged Kayla forward until it seemed she could reach her hand out and touch it.

Sarali pointed at the light and then at Kayla, trying to tell her something, though Kayla was so befuddled by her injury that she wasn't sure what. She shook her head, not in denial, but in questioning. Sarali touched the light, then pushed her foreleg through. Sarali's hand was on the other side, claws extended and retracting as she wiggled her paw. She pulled it back, then pointed back to Kayla and again to the bubble.

Suddenly Kayla understood.

T'Kato pulled her forward a few inches more as she reached her hand out to the glowing light and pushed it through. Immediately her hand felt lighter, water dripping from her arm. Kayla was so astonished that she did not move for a long moment, just held her arm through the skin of the bubble and felt the air caress it.

Air.

At the bottom of the ocean—a tube of air. Kayla couldn't wrap her mind around the idea, but despite that, she pushed her other arm through to experience the same effect, and then leaned forward and let her nose puncture the air tube the same way it had around her hand. The oxygen tickled her nose as she pushed the rest of her face forward: brows, chin, and then her entire head dripped water inside the tube.

Kayla opened her eyes and gasped in astonishment. The sand at the bottom of the tube was completely dry, such as she would find while walking on land. The flowing air was crisp and clean, and was apparently the only thing holding the walls of water away. Kayla shivered. It was creepy in a way, but she was so thankful for it, she pushed the rest of her body through the skin and immediately fell to the dry tube floor, unable to stand. She lay there, spread-eagled on the cool sand, breathing in the moist air. She would have slept that very instant if not for the pain in her shoulder and the burn on her arm. They throbbed and ached as if someone were eating away at her with acid-filled teeth. She groaned and sat up, clutching her shoulder with a hand that came away damp. At least her shirt was not stuck to the wound, but pink water and red blood dripped from her elbow and fingertips to stain the ground.

Help arrived in the form of T'Kato and Sarali, now changed back into the human forms Kayla knew so well. They entered the tunnel about ten feet down from her and approached quickly, kneeling to each side.

"How are you doing, Kayla?" T'Kato asked.

"I'm still alive," she responded, "though I'm not sure if that's a good thing or bad right now."

"I'd be sayin' good, lass." Sarali said, "but I think we need to take a look at that shoulder."

"Just be careful," Kayla answered, willing to accept any help she could get. When Sarali unlaced her blouse, Kayla did not object.

She thought nothing of modesty at that moment, though thankfully T'Kato did. He took himself some distance down the tunnel, keeping his back to her.

Kayla glanced to the water wall and would have been fascinated under other circumstances, but at that point she was nearly unaware of the closeness of the fish and long, multi-limbed squid. All she knew was pain as Sarali pushed and prodded, inspecting the injured shoulder.

It seemed an eternity before she was done and called to her husband. "T'Kato, come set your eyes to this, man. I need your opinion."

T'Kato came back, though it did not seem he was anxious to do so. Sarali beckoned him onward.

"Hurry, man, this is no time to be shy! I need your eyes and hands."

T'Kato settled down on Kayla's left, his eyes meeting his wife's, and Kayla thought she detected a hint of red under his coloring. Could this giant of a man be embarrassed? Granted she was half-undressed, but nothing of import was showing above her bindings—just her shoulder and collarbone.

Sarali jabbed at Kayla's shoulder, lightly, though it felt as though an iron rod drove through her skin. Kayla gasped in objection.

"Sorry, lass," Sarali apologized. "Here, T'Kato, what do ye make of this?" She pointed to the broken bone that jutted from the mangled flesh. "Do ye think we could be binding this with a bit of power until we can get her to a healer?"

T'Kato leaned in close then, forgetting his embarrassment. He prodded the bone lightly, then held his hand over the wound without touching it. He closed his eyes and seemed to feel. Not with his hand, but more an inner feeling. Kayla felt heat and a tightening tingle beneath his hand, and somehow it soothed the pain. She found herself reluctant to have him move away, but eventually he did. He looked at his wife and slowly nodded his head.

"I think it can be done—enough to keep it clean and in place, yes. The energy is still there and flowing in the proper patterns, so we need only to align the bone with energy, and it should heal itself. The flesh is a different matter, though. I don't think I can do much with that. I know some herbs and salves we could use to speed the healing if we were on land, but here—" He shrugged and left his sentence unfinished.

291

Sarali looked thoughtful for a moment. "There be some things like that in the water world, too. Maybe I could make a short trip back to the waters and fetch a wee bit for the lass?" She looked questioningly at her spouse.

He nodded again. "Let's fix this bone first, though, Sari, and let her rest while you're getting them. She's probably even more tired than I am. We could all do with some sleep."

It wasn't until he mentioned how tired he was that Kayla realized that her pain had not returned to its previous level of intensity. Evidently the magic used to probe had relieved some of the pain already.

Sarali did not answer, only smiled at the man and touched his face tenderly for a moment. They joined fingers and both placed their free hand over Kayla's collarbone, much as T'Kato had before. The heat intensified this time, much more than she would have imagined by only adding a single person. The tingling itched until it was almost painful. It was all Kayla could do to keep from reaching up to scratch the raw wound.

She clutched the flute to her chest to keep herself from moving, and realized the flute glowed its bright sapphire blue again, the color flowing into the joined hands of T'Kato and Sarali, their eyes closed in concentration.

Her eyes followed the flow of energy to her shoulder, and she gasped in surprise. The hands of her healers were encased in the blue power of the flute, and not only were the bones knitting back together, but the flesh and muscle were joining and healing as well. These two were healing her with the help of the flute, despite their belief that they could not.

But why was the flute helping her? Did it need her whole? Were they now bound and joined in some odd way? Watching her body being healed from the inside out, she felt the urge to learn all she could about this blue keystone. If she was to be its guardian, would it not make sense for her to learn as much about it as possible?

Kayla's eyes were wide and teary by the time the two fell back, exhausted, and lay on the sand, breathing as heavily as if they had just finished their run from C'Tan. They did not even open their eyes to look at their handiwork. But Kayla inspected it carefully. She pulled her blouse back and took her arm from the tattered sleeve to examine it.

What had looked like shredded meat was now whole, with only three slashing scars covering her shoulder as evidence of the injury. She moved the limb around, twisting and turning it, back and forth, her grin growing broader with each move. She was healed, only a little sore, as if she had been lifting sacks of potatoes or bales of hay.

Suddenly she wanted to be clean and rid of the smell of blood and fear. She stood and moved down the tunnel a short distance, then pulled the blouse from her shoulders to thrust it through the wall of air and into the water, leaving her dressed only in the baggy trousers and the strange binding Sarali had given her. Kayla's hands immediately chilled, but she didn't care. She swished the shirt through the sea, thrilled by her unexpected healing.

The two finally became aware as she stood with her arms elbow deep in the water.

"What are you—?" Sarali started, and then gasped as Kayla turned and grinned at her, holding the dripping blouse up to inspect it. Sarali immediately rushed to her side to examine the scar. She pushed, prodded, moved Kayla's shoulder and arm, and finally sat down hard in the sand, completely shocked, without the strength to stand.

Kayla laughed at Sarali's expression—a laugh of pure delight at the astonishing experience. It had become obvious that somebody was watching out for her, though whether it was the flute or one of the Guardians themselves, she was not sure. All she knew was that she was healed.

"What happened?" T'Kato finally asked, confusion on his face.

"Between the two of you and a little help from the flute—"

"The flute?" Sarali asked, surprised. "The flute did this?" Her face showed a little disappointment.

Kayla knelt before her friend and took her hands. "You and T'Kato healed me," she answered, meeting Sarali's eyes in thanks. "The flute merely added power and direction to your efforts."

"But—" the small woman began. Kayla would not let her finish.

"*You* did this, Sarali. Don't doubt it. It was the two of you who healed me," she continued, squeezing Sarali's hands. The flute pulsed brighter, as if in agreement, and Sarali slowly nodded.

Kayla put the cold, dripping blouse back on, grateful for the ability to do such a simple thing as that. She was still weak from blood loss, but felt strangely ennervated after the experience of healing. She laced up the blouse in silence, letting her thoughts and feelings wander until she was through.

"So where are we?" she finally asked, and that seemed to break the awe-filled silence that had settled over them.

"Would ye laugh if I told ye it was a secret passage through the ocean?" Sarali asked.

Kayla blinked. "Really?"

"Passages criss-cross the oceans the world over, lass. The land walkers have lost the memory of these things. Not many souls find a way to enter, and not a one has a map—but my people know. We've been navigating these passages for hundreds of years. I know where to go. Just name a place, and I'll be getting ye there."

Kayla was quiet for a long moment.

"Can we go to the evahn? Can we go to my father?" she asked, a faint ray of hope shining in.

T'Kato and Sarali met eyes, questioning one another, and then Sarali turned. "I don't see why not, lass. And it may be he'll have a bit o' advice for ye about the flute. The evahn have many a scroll and book that none o' our peoples have had access to for a very long time. If any man can tell ye where to go to find the player, that'd be the place to start."

Kayla grinned, a sudden wave of butterflies fluttering up from her already unsettled stomach. Excitement and fear mingled, but she knew where she needed to go now, and it was no longer just a childhood dream, a fantasy.

She was going to be reunited with her father at last.

Chapter Twenty-seven

If Ember could have run from the council chambers, she would have done so without a thought, but this time it was fear that motivated her rather than the willful defiance of the past. She was immobile—frozen by some unknown magic she could not counter, facing a gathering of the most powerful magi in the land, and they accused her of being a cheater, a liar, and now a spy, and she could not even speak to defend herself.

The council members argued. Ember caught snatches of their conversations, some in agreement with the head mage and others arguing for Ember to present her side of the story. Still others whispered the possibility that she truly was a white mage—perhaps even the wolfchild.

Ember had no idea what they were talking about, but she definitely wanted a chance to speak her piece. They were *wrong,* and she could prove it, if she could free herself and change to her own form. If Uncle Shad or DeMunth came, they could tell the council. She'd even welcome the sight of her mother at that moment.

As if the thought had been somehow plucked from her mind, the head mage began to speak again, making his case against her.

"Proof? You ask for proof? Then you shall have it. Let them in!"

The flamboyant fat man again nodded to the sixth guard, who leaned out the big double doors and was nearly pushed over by the entrance of Ember's diminutive mother, her rage giving her strength she wouldn't normally have. The one person she had been avoiding, the woman she'd tried to evade with her disguise, was now standing not ten feet away and all Ember wanted to do was call out to her—and she was denied even that.

"Where's my daughter?" Marda demanded angrily, her hands on her hips and chin thrust forward as if to batter the head mage with it.

"Sister Brina. The council welcomes you back to its midst." The eye-popping mage sneered at Ember's mother.

"I haven't been your sister or Brina for fifteen years, Laerdish, and I'm not here by choice. Where is my daughter?" she asked again.

Ember had a memory of Shad calling Ember's parents Jarin and Brina. Was Laerdish really her brother? Or was it figurative? And why would he welcome her back to a council she'd never joined? Ember's thoughts scrambled, looking for sanity in the nightmare her life had become.

"Don't you recognize her, Brina? For the one going by her name is standing right before you." He swept his arm toward Ember, and her mother's gaze was on her, burning holes through her soul.

Ember wondered what in heaven's name she had been thinking when she wished her mother would come. She'd forgotten just how piercing her mother's eyes were in the short few days she had been gone.

"No. I do not see my daughter here. What game are you playing?" She glared at Laerdish.

The fat man grinned maliciously at her. "This boy took the mage test in Ember's name while wearing this. I seem to remember Jarin had something similar." He handed the pendant to Marda.

She took the pendant, shock and horror on her face as she realized exactly what it was she held.

"Does it look familiar to you?" Laerdish almost taunted.

Marda cried out and rushed toward Ember with a despairing yell. She reached the edge of the circle where Ember stood and was thrown back by an energy field. She scrabbled at it like a crazed woman, screaming incoherently.

Ember watched, stunned. She hadn't thought her mother really loved her. She'd spent a lifetime trying to squirrel out from under her thumb, but the panic and near insanity of her mother's actions made it clear that Marda loved her very much. Ember's mother pounded against the invisible wall and shrieked through her sobs.

"What have you done with my daughter?"

The instant the question was out of Marda's lips, Ember found herself able to speak once again. She took advantage of it while she could.

"Mum! Mum, I *am* your daughter! I turned into a wolf to get away from Ian Covainis when he tried to kidnap me, and then Uncle Shad taught me to turn into a boy so Ian couldn't find me, and then Uncle Shad found me a room, but I couldn't bathe with the men because I didn't have boy parts, so he told me to change back into a girl to get a bath, and so I did, and I *saw* you there, I *talked* to you, and then I changed back into a boy for my test, and now nobody believes I'm Ember because I look like some spy of C'Tan's. Can you believe that?" Ember spat it all out in one breath as fast as she could.

Marda looked at her like she was crazy. "You're Ember." She laughed a little hysterically, then stopped as suddenly as she began. "Don't you think I would know if my daughter was capable of this kind of magic? Wouldn't a mother know?" Bitter tears rained from her eyes. Marda wiped at them with a closed fist.

"It only started the day I left. Remember when I changed the dress? I didn't even know I could do things like that until that day, and then I was so scared when Ian caught me, I changed all of a sudden, just like Da—"

"Stop!" Marda covered her ears. Ember suddenly found her mouth frozen again. She wanted to grind her teeth in frustration, but she was denied even that pleasure.

"I would have known! I don't know how you learned about the dress, but you are not my daughter! You can't be! Now tell me where she is, and I may be able to convince the council to go easy on you, but if you do not tell me where she is, and right now, I will be there when they sentence and punish you, and I'll be cheering them on and demanding more. Now, where is my daughter?"

"I *am* your daughter!" Ember cried back, freed again by the question. "Please, Mum, it's me. Tell them to release me for just a few minutes, and I'll change back to my real self. You'll see it's really me. I can prove it to you."

"Or you might be a spy, trying to trick us so you can escape," Laerdish answered for Marda. "We are not foolish enough to do such a thing, boy. You will stay bound until your guilt is proven."

"Or innocence, perhaps," another familiar voice responded. Ember's fear eased with his arrival.

It was Ezeker, Aldarin at his side. If anyone would know her from the inside out, it would be these two. Aldarin had already guessed the truth—maybe Ezeker would as well.

Laerdish spun to face the newcomers, his face reddening under Ezeker's accusing eyes, but he controlled his expression and yielded the floor to Ezeker. He bowed himself back to his previously abandoned seat.

"But of course, headmaster," the gaudy man fawned. "That is what I meant. Until guilt *or* innocence are proven."

"You have overstepped your bounds, Laerdish. You had no call to begin this council without my presence," Ezeker said in a low tone.

"I only stood in your place until you were found. I was assured you would be here shortly. Now that you have arrived, the floor is yours."

Laerdish sat daintily despite his bulk, but Ember saw him glower at Ezeker when the headmaster's back turned.

Headmaster. The meaning finally occurred to Ember. No wonder he had pushed her all these years—he was head of the mage academy, and she had never known, never even suspected. She wanted to ask him about it, but again the spell left her speechless and frozen until she was questioned.

"Just in case this truly is Ember Shandae, why don't we return the pendant to her." Ezeker did not make it a request. He stood next to Marda, his hand out, waiting.

"That is not my daughter, Ezeker, and you know it!" Marda snarled at him.

"I know no such thing, Marda, and if you'd let your heart get out of the way of your head, you'd know the same. Now give me the pendant."

"But—" she started.

"Give me the pendant," he demanded, more forcefully.

Marda glared, then threw the pendant into his hand and stormed away to stand by the door.

Ezeker turned and nodded to the two front guards, who nodded in return. They pulled their swords and put the tips of them together on the floor, forming a "V." There was a flash where the tips met before they pulled the swords upward to man height, and then apart, leaving a glimmering shield of blue between them. It stood as a portal through the shield that kept Ember separate. Ezeker moved purposefully toward that glowing blue doorway despite the objections sounding behind him, led mostly by Laerdish.

"Sir, I must insist—" the large man shouted, clambering to his feet.

Ezeker stopped in the doorway, one foot on Ember's side, a snarl of crackling energy surrounding his leg. "Let things be, Laerdish. I'm safe enough here. You wouldn't let anything happen to me, now, would you?" he said over his shoulder. Laerdish didn't respond, though he continued to advance. Ezeker took two steps forward, the energy surrounding his body for a moment so his hair and beard stood out around him. Once he was inside, the guards quickly lowered their swords back to the floor, and the portal collapsed. Laerdish stood on the other side, glowering but unable to get through.

Ezeker approached Ember, his eyes wary, but hopeful. "Is it really you, child?"

His question freed her from the spell, and she nearly sobbed with relief. "Yes, Uncle Ezzie, it's me! Please get me out of here. I can't move or speak unless someone asks me a question, and it makes it awfully hard to defend myself. Mum doesn't even believe me."

"It's the manacles, child. They dampen your magic and will. The only problem is proving to the council that you are indeed the Ember Shandae I know and love. They won't accept your word for it, nor mine either, I'm afraid, and most things you could say to prove your identity could have been received from another source. Is there anyone who has known you as both your male and female self, child?"

"Yes! Uncle Shad has seen me, but I don't know where he is. He was staying in the council house, but he didn't come when I passed his room and screamed at him."

Ezeker seemed startled. "Shad? You mean White Shadow of the Bendanatu? You've met him?"

Ember nodded vigorously. "Yes, Uncle Shad saved me when I escaped from Ian Covainis after he kidnapped me and I turned into a wolf. He's traveling with a mute named DeMunth—"

Ezeker threw back his head and started to laugh. Ember was not sure why, and it offended her.

"Ezeker! This is no time to be laughing!"

"No, child, you are wrong. This is the perfect time to be laughing. Aldarin! Come here, my boy!" Ezeker called out to Ember's stepbrother, who stood silently by the doorway. He came quickly, his armor clanking. He winked at Ember when he got close enough for her to see. Ezeker gestured for the guards to open the portal, and once more they created the glimmering blue doorway with their swords. The old mage stuck his head through the wall and whispered to his captain of the guard. In a matter of seconds, Aldarin was grinning from ear to ear.

"As you wish, master." He nodded once and backed away, bowing, then turned and strode purposefully through the double doors.

Ezeker stepped back from the portal as it dissolved, and turned to Ember. "I cannot take those manacles off until a majority of the council approves it, and at this moment, that is not the way things stand. Laerdish has done some damage to your reputation, but that is something we may still be able to repair. We can free you and get you into the academy in one swoop. Will you work with me?"

"Of course, but why do you believe me when even Mum doesn't?"

Ezeker stepped forward and put the pendant around her neck, then winked at her as it sank beneath her skin once again. "Because I know you better than any one thinks, Ember. I know your potential, I know your spirit—and I know you are the only person alive who would *dare* to call me 'Uncle Ezzie' without pause."

Ember grinned back at him, relief washing over her. "So tell me what to do, Uncle Ezzie, so I can get out of here."

"First, I need you to read the colors of all the magi. It will be a lot of work, but I need you to prove that you are capable of being that which your test claims."

"Which is?"

"Why, a white mage, of course," he said.

"A what?" she asked, her mind just now grasping the impossible, though why she hadn't connected the thoughts before, she didn't know. "But Uncle Shad told me there hasn't been a white mage for three thousand years. Nobody knows anything about them, so how can I *be* one?"

"We know a little. We know they are able to do all the magic—and we have the test in place that tells us how to recognize one. If you are truly able to see all the colors of magic, as the test shows, then you are a white mage." He watched her closely.

The room spun around her for a moment, and Ember reached out for something to steady herself before the floor got too close. Ezeker took her arm and held her up until her vision cleared.

"I'm a white mage?" she said, her mind still trying to grasp the implications.

"But of course. What else could you be, child?"

"I don't know. I just didn't . . . I mean, I never really thought about it, I guess."

"Well, you'd better think about it now, Ember, because the potential is definitely there, and it is something you need to learn quickly. Not only does our world need your help in healing, but until you understand your capabilities, you are in danger—and not only from the followers of S'Kotos. There are many who will wish to undermine or destroy you for what you are—not because you are a threat to them, but because your power is greater and your experience less. They will destroy you out of envy and spite. Think now and think hard, Ember, because what you decide will change your life and anger a lot of people. You can choose to become a mage and harness the power you've been given, or you can choose to deny it and close yourself to the world of magic. The one makes you free, but the other is much, much safer. There is a whole other world out there waiting to be discovered and used. Perhaps even . . . well, we'll go there later. Right now I am asking only three things of you. One—tell each of the council members the colors you see around them. Two—decide whether or not you want to be a mage. And three—trust me."

Ember was overwhelmed by his requests. They seemed so simple, and yet they were not. She didn't think identifying the council members would be difficult, and trusting Ezeker was never an issue, but deciding whether to become a mage or not scared her. She had thought she wanted nothing more than that, but her experiences of the past hour had shown her a different side to the mage world, a place where you could not automatically trust someone just because they were a mage, a place where people would use you to elevate themselves, or put you down because they couldn't stand the idea of your power. Did she really want to be a part of that world? Did she really want to give up the life she had known to live and study amongst people like this?

Ember pondered for a long moment, searching her heart and soul to feel which way was best, and in the end it all came down to one thing.

The magic.

For Ember, the magic had nothing to do with power, stature, or political maneuverings, and had everything to do with helping people and soaring free.

She could not be anything different than what she was.

She was a white mage.

Ember nodded slowly to Ezeker.

"I will accept, Uncle Ezzie. I'll do as you ask."

He didn't smile. "Are you sure, child? This is a serious commitment, a thing you never can run away from, and it will change you forever," he reminded her, placing a gnarled hand on her shoulder.

She straightened and met his eye.

"I know. It's worth it, Ezeker. It's what I've been waiting for my entire life. It's who I am. I have to do this, no matter where it leads me."

Ezeker smiled then, a soft, proud smile, and squeezed her shoulders tight in a grandfatherly hug.

"I'm proud of you, child," he whispered in her ear and let her go.

At that moment the big double doors swung open again, and Ember's champions swaggered into the room, looking none too happy.

"Have I missed the party?" Shad asked the assembly, slamming a menacing-looking cudgel into his oversized hand. DeMunth looked deadly beside him with a drawn sword and glowing golden armor shielding him. "Because I hate to miss a party, and it seems you left my name off the list." Shad glared at Laerdish. "Let her go."

Chapter Twenty-eight

Kayla shivered and pulled her damp woolen cloak closer about her shoulders. It did no good, but instinct made her try. She trudged down the tube of air that carved itself out of the ocean's bottom, feet dragging and sinking into the sand with a light swish. What had begun as an exciting adventure, a journey to the home of her father, had lost its excitement and interest for her not even thirty minutes into it. There was nowhere to go but onward, and she was sick of even the glimmer of faint blue light that guided her steps. She was about to fall to the creamy sand and refuse to take even one more step when T'Kato called a halt.

"Hold up, Kayla. Let's rest for a bit." He dropped the satchels and squatted down.

Kayla didn't have a bag to drop, thankfully or regretfully—she hadn't decided which yet, but she did collapse to the sand, her knees giving completely out about halfway down. At that moment she couldn't have cared less; she was too grateful for the break. She only wished she could stop her chattering teeth and trembling hands. Her fingernails were turning a faint blue, or so she thought. It was hard to tell, with the dim sapphire-tinted light that sifted through the water surrounding them.

She pulled her knees to her chest and wrapped the cloak around her legs, trying to trap even a marginal amount of body heat in the closed wool. It helped a little, and the shaking in her hands seemed to decrease.

Sarali squatted by her then, her hand outstretched. "Eat a bit o' this, lass. Tisn't much, but it will be strengthenin' ye a wee bit, though the taste leaves much to be desired."

Kayla reluctantly took the soggy-looking mess Sarali held out and sniffed. It didn't smell any better than it looked—oats, nuts, and berries pressed into bars, now more resembling a badly-made bowl of porridge than anything else, and if there was anything Kayla hated, it was porridge. Still . . . it *was* food, and she had eaten nothing in who knew how long. She had lost track of the hours in this dark and never-ending tunnel. She took a tentative bite, chewed slowly, and had to agree with Sarali. It certainly didn't taste good— soggy oats with all sweetness washed away, and only the nuts and berries to give it any flavor. She ate it anyway and had to admit that she did feel better with something in her belly, a bit more energized, though not quite ready to move. She wasn't sure if she'd ever be ready to move again, she was so tired.

"Sip this," T'Kato said, handing her a small cup. Kayla almost spilled it with a sneeze. It smelled awful. Vile. She tried to give the cup back to T'Kato, shaking her head, but he pushed it back.

"It's not as bad as it smells. It will warm you up, trust me." He helped lift the cup to her lips.

She tried to take just a teeny amount, but T'Kato tipped the cup, and Kayla's face would have been washed with the mixture if she had not opened her mouth and gulped it down. The mixture burned all the way. Even when she stopped drinking, her mouth burned. Tears sprang to her eyes, and she couldn't close her mouth with the fire that seemed to be pouring from it. Finally she caught her breath enough to gasp, "What are you trying to do, poison me? What's in that?"

T'Kato smiled. "It's a chili drink my people favor, made from certain warming herbs and hot peppers. It's not much for flavor when you drink it straight like this, I know, but it will keep you warm and stop those shivers."

It wasn't exactly the way she had wanted to warm up and was nothing compared to a cozy fire and bear skin rug, but it would do under the circumstances—though she couldn't quite bring herself to thank the man. He had tricked her, after all, asking her to trust him. She'd think twice before doing *that* again.

Kayla leaned her head on her knees and closed her eyes to rest for a moment. It was hard to comprehend all that had transpired in the past three days.

The emotion and longing that swept over her was like nothing she had known before. Tears leaked down between her knees, and she tried to hide the sniffles. It was childish to cry like this. She knew it, but could not stop the stream of tears.

All she wanted at that moment was to be held in Brant's arms, or to feel the warmth of her mother's smile. She didn't even know if either of them was still alive, and not knowing was hardest of all. What if Brant had died from his fall? What if C'Tan discovered her mother's identity? *What if, what if, what if . . .* it circled in her mind like a vulture, but no matter how she tried, she could not seem to shake the questions or the feelings that attacked her in waves.

Kayla felt a hand on her shoulder, a small hand, light and petite. Sarali, she knew, though she did not look up from her huddled misery. Somehow the cat woman seemed to know her feelings and sat beside her, not saying a word, slowly caressing her back, up and down, up and down, like Kayla's mother used to do at bedtime. It was soothing, comforting in a way no words could have been. It pulled her mind from her troubles and sent her drifting into sleep.

Dreams hit Kayla with force. Some part of her knew she was sitting huddled in the sand, with Sarali at her side, but her mind and heart left that misery to speed ahead and down the tunnel that protected them from C'Tan.

Kayla's dream-self twisted through the worm-like tunnels, left, then right, then left again until it flew with the speed of an eagle.

In an instant she was at a large cavern made of water, but domed and smooth as if made from rock, and in that room stood a man.

Her heart leaped as she saw him, for his was a face she had known in her dreams for ten years. He stood tall and straight, with hair that fell past his shoulders in dark, wavy rings. His face was long and clean-shaven, with a sharp chin and nose.

It was his eyes that drew her most: crystalline blue, more pure than water from a birthing spring. His eyes stared through her as he stood in the center of the cavern as if waiting for her, which seemed strange, even in her dream state. How could he be waiting if she was dreaming?

"Hello, Kayla," he said. Startled, her shoulders twitched in her sleeping body.

"Hello, Father," she responded, guarded, but longing to run to him, to let him take all the pain away and make it better . . . but she knew it could not be. Her heart ached to admit it, but he had never taken away the pain before—why would he start now?

"I know why you are here, and I wish I could help, but there is danger behind you and danger ahead. You cannot come here, Kayla. You must go back to your own people." His face barely showed emotion, though his eyes reached out to her.

"But . . . you *are* my people, Father! I have nowhere else to turn!"

"You are my seed, Kayla, and you are my family, but my people do not accept that bond. To them you are impure, made worse by my sin of wedding a human," he answered, lips twitching in irony. "Love matters not to them, only honor and duty. There are many places you can go—but not here."

"But I want to be with you!" A petulant tone crept into her voice.

"And I you, but your coming will destroy my people. You must not come."

"What? How could I—" she started, and then it hit her.

C'Tan. The woman would not give up until she had the flute, if she had to destroy everything in her way to get it.

Kayla's eyes teared. Was there no place she could go that was safe? No one who could teach her the secrets of the flute? No way to protect herself or hide the instrument that now called death down upon her?

Her mind raced, but she said nothing.

"You understand, I see. There *is* no place that is safe for you, Kayla. No place to hide, except in havens of strong magic. They interfere with C'Tan's ability to sense you and the flute. But there are few havens left within our world, and she knows most of their secrets.

"That flute has been in the hands of my people for generations," he continued, "and there is much anger over it now being in the hands of a human, half-evahn or not. If you come to us, not only will you bring C'Tan down upon us, but the evahn people will do everything they must in order to recover the flute. Find another way, child."

"Another way? Where, Father? Where else can I go? T'Kato says nobody knows more about the flute than you do. How can I research without books or scrolls? How can I learn without a teacher? Please, Father, it is your job, your responsibility to look out for me. Don't you think you owe me that after all these years?"

Felandian's eyes were sad. Kayla could see her words hurt, though he knew the truth of them. He shook his head.

"If I could be there in person, I would. You are my blood, and I would never have left you if the need had not been tremendous. My father is dying, and the care and guiding of my people has fallen to me. I cannot even leave long enough to teach you in person. For now, we may only speak in your dreams, but I shall do that as often as I can.

"Find the flute's home—its birthplace—and you will find your answers. The flute can teach you as no human can. Trust it, Kayla, more than you trust any person or thing, and it will never lead you wrong. Do you hear me, daughter? Trust the flute!" he emphasized each word, his eyes drilling into hers.

"I'm not letting it out of my sight, Father, but how can I find its birthplace? Does anyone know where it came from?"

"The Guardians know, but they won't be able to help right now. They're preoccupied with the wolfchild," he answered.

"The wolfchild? He has come?" Her heart pounded in her chest. Kayla was beginning to wonder if the wolfchild was the player of which T'Kato spoke. She felt a compulsion to find him, though her heart battled with her head. She knew she needed the boy, but *she* wanted to be the player. She *was* the player, she told herself again.

Felandian grinned. "Not he. She. The wolfchild is a female, not much younger than you."

Kayla was floored. A female? And young? She'd always imagined an elderly male, many years trained in music and magic to take possession of the instrument. How could someone so young know how to use it? She took a deep breath and tried to set that aside to ponder later.

"Tell me where to go, Father," she said, putting her trust in this man who had left her ten years before.

He was quiet for a long while, chewing on his lip as he pondered her question.

"It is rumored—*rumored,* mind you—that the flute was birthed in the mountains behind the city of Javak, but I can be no more specific than that. It is a beginning."

"Javak? The city of magic?" she asked, and he nodded. "That's a long way, Father. How do I get there with C'Tan following me through the magic of the flute?"

"You must find a way to hide the flute from her, Kayla, though I cannot say more than that. Ask the flute."

"Ask the flute? But—" Kayla stopped as a look of alarm crossed her father's face. He stared into the distance behind her, his brows narrowing in concentration. His eyes widened in surprise.

"You must go now," he said, fear tightening him like a drum.

"But—" she objected.

"Kayla, I'll see you again. Go. Go!" he yelled, then added the one phrase that gave impetus to her departure. "C'Tan comes," he whispered.

Kayla didn't even say good-bye. She jerked awake at his last phrase and did not even have time to think about what she had just dreamed, for she could hear in the distance the sound of a horse racing through the tunnel. She scrambled to her feet and awakened her companions, who had both fallen asleep in the sand.

"Get up! Get up! We've got to go," she yelled, shaking T'Kato and then Sarali, running back and forth between the two of them until they were alert enough to hear. It took more time than they could afford.

The pounding of hooves increased. Kayla looked down the tunnel and could see a speck of black that grew larger with each passing second.

"Wha . . . what?" T'Kato finally mumbled, turning over in alarm.

"C'Tan is coming! We've got to go!"

"That's imposs . . ." The tattooed man's voice faded as he listened to the rhythm of the stallion's hooves digging at the sand. He scrambled up and took the two bags over his shoulder in one toss, then started to run. Sarali was at his side, Kayla lagging behind, all of them running for their lives once again as C'Tan pounded down the trail.

"How did she find us?" Kayla shouted.

"She must have found the entrance to the tunnel," Sarali called over her shoulder. "It wasn't too far from where we went in the water."

"I thought you said dragons don't do well in water," Kayla said again, projecting her voice ahead of her.

"They don't," Sarali answered. "Somehow she's coerced her mount down here, but chances are he's not happy about it. We may be able to use that somehow."

"There's not much I can do here, Kayla," T'Kato called out to her. "See if there's anything you can do with that flute of yours. She's already found us, and the flute is awake to your touch, so use it."

"Me?" she squeaked.

"Who else is there? I certainly don't play, and I don't think Sarali ever got good enough to do anything with it, so it's up to you to save us this time."

Kayla didn't respond. It was up to her to save them? How? She didn't know how to fight, not much more than a little wrestling and archery. Her mind churned with fear as the hoofbeats grew ever louder behind them.

She didn't know what made the flute work. When she desired something strongly as she played, it had come to pass. Was it her will? Or the wish? Or the tune she happened to play? She was not sure, and didn't have time to puzzle it out.

The tunnel ahead of them still had no end in sight, and C'Tan was gaining fast, so Kayla did the only thing she could think of.

She stopped and turned.

Kayla faced her enemy as C'Tan raced toward her. She scrambled in her waistband for the flute she had tucked away so carefully before. Despite the cold water and air, despite the hard conditions here, the flute was warm in her hands with not a scratch on it. Kayla put the flute to her lips . . .

And froze.

What could she play? What did she plan to do? Kayla had no idea. Her mind was completely blank, and C'Tan drew closer by the second. She couldn't collapse the tunnel because then they would be washed away. She wasn't sure if she could, anyway, with the strength of the magic that held it open. She had nothing with which to make a wall, nothing to shoot at her enemy. All she had around her was water, cold, and air, and what could she do with that?

Her mind spun, faster and faster, panic setting in as her heart pounded against her chest like a woodpecker. Water. What could she do with water?

And then she knew.

Kayla smiled to herself and began to play a soft, slow melody, a song about the river that her mother had sung to her as a child, pulling the water into her music and closing her eyes to block out the distraction of the mage bearing down on her with her charging stallion. Water and cold and air. Water and cold and air.

Kayla tugged at the water, thickening it like clay, then pulled it in to form a wall across the tunnel. She opened an eye and was amazed to see a shimmering wall of water in front of her. She stopped playing for just a second, the surprise making her breathless.

The water began to fall. Kayla started the melody where she left off and strengthened the water before her, thickening it inch by inch. First it was finger-thick, then wrist, elbow and shoulder. When the water was as wide as she was tall, she knew it was thick enough.

The song changed, a breathy whisper of sound, like the wind over the mountains picking up the cold and ice of the snowy peaks. There were no mountains here beneath the sea, but the ocean, the water, the depths themselves where sunlight barely reached, were cold enough to turn her fingers blue. If she could concentrate that cold into this place, the water would solidify. It might be enough to hold C'Tan for a time.

Kayla pulled the cold together into a ball in front of her. It became almost painful, and it was all she could do to keep her teeth from chattering. She stepped back and opened her eyes once more to watch the process as she continued to play.

There, floating before her, was a writhing, white ball of ice that pulled the moisture and cold from the air. Kayla pushed it forward with her will and embedded it into the center of the shimmering water.

The ice crystals spread.

Snapping crackles sounded from the water as the ice expanded to form a huge wall of transparent water. It was as if a six-foot glass pane had sprung between Kayla and C'Tan, and it was none too soon.

C'Tan's midnight stallion reared up and dumped his mistress in the sand. The woman sat pummeling the ground in frustration, and Kayla could hear the screams of rage even through the thick ice between them. In that instant, the picture of the beautiful blonde woman changed. It was as though a blanket dropped, exposing a beast. Instead of luxurious hair that caressed her shoulders and a face that seemed to be made of silk and dew, C'Tan was bald and scarred as if she had been burned by flame. She was two sides of the moon— one bright and lovely, the other dark and loathsome.

Illusion. C'Tan carried with her a vain illusion of beauty.

She was hideous.

The scars flared across her cheek to curl around one of her glaring eyes, like a red flame licking at her skull, almost as if it had been shaped to that form by a magical hand. Kayla stared at the woman as she changed before her eyes.

C'Tan ran at the wall then, pounding the ice with her fists, nearly foaming with fury. She stepped back and blasted fireballs at the wall, but Kayla kept playing, strengthing the ice with her will. Blast after fiery blast pummeled the ice, but it would not budge. Kayla asked it not to, and it stayed, becoming steel-like. The wall would not move unless Kayla willed it so, and she would not.

C'Tan bombarded the wall with fire, alternating between great gouts of flame and surging balls time after time, but the wall held strong. Kayla could still see C'Tan clearly, and though the scarred woman was tiring, there was no surrender in her.

For just a moment Kayla felt sorry for C'Tan. What desperate need drove her for the flute? Surely it could not be power alone that pushed her like this. There had to be something more, but what, Kayla could not even hope to imagine. In that moment she could no longer stand to look at the face of her enemy, which was desperate with wrath and anguish.

She turned her back and walked ahead, meeting T'Kato and Sarali. They had stopped to watch as Kayla built the wall of ice to protect them, ice that did not melt nor burst, ice as strong as steel. Their eyes showed awe, but Kayla did not revel in it. She was pondering the questions in her mind and the strangeness of the dream of her father.

"Shall we go on to the evahn, then, lass?" Sarali asked, but Kayla shook her head.

"No, Sari. The answers don't lie with the evahn," she answered, still lost in her own thoughts.

Sarali looked surprised, but took the change in stride. "Where, then, would ye wish to go?"

Kayla looked behind her at the woman still trying to burst through the icy wall. Her thoughts solidified, just as the ice had, and she turned back to her friends, for friends they were, having given up the comfort of their own lives to aid her. She smiled at them, despite the muffled curses coming from behind her.

"Javak, Sarali." Kayla hoped she'd find what she needed there. She would know soon, one way or the other, and hoped she could avoid the wolfchild in her search for the flute's birthplace. There was still too much to do, and she needed the flute to do it.

Sarali looked at T'Kato. He shrugged. Together, the three moved away from the still-howling C'Tan and toward the answers they sought—the answers that lay in Javak.

Chapter Twenty-nine

Ember beamed at her Uncle Shad's entrance. She could not have imagined a better rescue than the performance he put on. It was worth the discomfort of the past hour to see him like this. Laerdish was not pleased, though, which made it all the more enjoyable for Ember. She'd taken an instant dislike to the fellow, for obvious reasons, and it had absolutely nothing to do with his size.

As soon as the doors slammed open and Shad invited himself into the council's "party," Laerdish had surged to his feet.

"There are no weapons allowed in this room, and you were not invited to these proceedings. Guards, seize those weapons, and if the men put up a fight, throw them in jail."

Shad started to laugh, and Ember was startled to hear DeMunth join him, then Ezeker and the guards themselves.

"They can't seize me, Laerdish. You know darn well we have as much right to be here as you do." Shad snorted, chuckling all the while.

Laerdish reddened, his lips thinned in fury. "You shouldn't be a part of this council, no matter the votes that got you here. You're not human and DeMunth has no voice. You are no more a part of this council than that boy." Laerdish snarled and pointed to Ember, losing control in his anger.

Shad instantly sobered, eyes hardening, and sneered wolf-style. DeMunth seemed not to be bothered by the words. He stood calmly, but sheathed his sword as if he had nothing more to worry about. It seemed clear DeMunth felt he belonged.

"You go too far, Laerdish," Shad snarled at him.

"Yes," the large man said, "so I've been told, but truth is truth. I speak it as I see it."

"Too bad you're half-blind," came an anonymous voice from somewhere in the council.

Laerdish spun and glared, but aside from a few snickers, no one would claim responsibility for the comment.

"That 'boy' is my niece, and I'm here to ensure she gets a fair trial." Shad stepped menacingly toward Laerdish.

"Pish-posh. There is no way you can prove it, White Shadow. I know for a fact you did not meet this child until recently, and you only have his word that he is Ember Shandae." The large man receded to the safety of his padded bench, but Shad kept coming.

"I know and can prove it." Shad stopped between the guards that held the mage shield in place around Ember.

"How do you propose to do that, when Ember's own mother won't claim this boy as her child?" Laerdish demanded.

"Brina doesn't want to believe what her ears and heart tell her." Marda startled, her eyes jerking to meet Shad's. "If this boy is her child, then it is the undoing of her life's work, keeping Ember away from magic, away from what she sees as sure death. Can you blame her for her denial?" Shad questioned the council in general, ignoring Laerdish now. Many heads nodded in agreement.

"Now, wait a minute—" Marda began angrily. Shad's eyes narrowed, and she did not finish. She glared at him for a long moment, then doubt crept into her eyes, bit by bit, until at last it left, and she remained silent.

Ezeker stepped back through the shield, a hand on Shad's shoulder showing support for Ember's uncle.

"I sent Aldarin out for our fellow council members—White Shadow of the Bendanatu, also known as Shad, and DeMunth, previously of the brothers of Sha'iim. They have seen Ember's transformation, and thus, know that it is indeed genuine. They have spoken in depth to Ember Shandae, and know her to be what she claims: a girl who is able to alter her appearance and become a wolf, or a boy."

The council murmured at that.

"Now, brothers and sisters, just because we ourselves are not capable of this feat does not mean it is impossible. Remember, the power of white has been lost to us for three millennia. Ember has already shown her potential, and if you will allow her freedom here within the confines of this room, I have asked her to prove her abilities to you each on an individual basis," Ezeker concluded. "Please, fellow council members. Allow her to prove herself to you. Let the magic speak for itself."

The council was silent for a long moment, apparently deep in thought. Laerdish was the first to break the silence.

"Oh, this is ridiculous. It's obvious the person before us is a boy. What need have we for this? I vote to sever his magic ties and send him out. It's already been proven he's a spy—"

"Oh, shut up, Laerdish. Nobody's proven anything," said a tall woman in her middle years. "We only have your word that C'Tan sent a spy here, and only a sketch from *your* spy to prove it. Maybe *you're* the spy. We have about as much proof of one as the other," she added flippantly, but Laerdish's eyes hardened at her words. Wisely, he kept further comments to himself.

The woman then spoke to Ezeker. "I call for a vote on the matter of the alleged imposter of Ember Shandae. Free the child and let the magic prove itself."

"Aye . . . yes . . . I agree," voices called from around the room. Ember's heart lifted to realize there were many agreeable to Ezeker's plan.

"A vote then," Ezeker called loudly. "All in favor of allowing the child to prove herself, say aye."

"Aye!" came thunderously back, many hands shooting in the air. Aldarin took a quick tally and wrote down the results.

"Those opposed?" Ezeker continued.

Laerdish gave a vocal "Nay!" Few followed his example. He glowered at the obvious desertion of his co-councilors.

"The ayes carry it. Release the prisoner." Ezeker said. He and Shad turned, smiling at Ember, who was almost weak with gratitude. The guards sheathed their swords and stepped out of position on the star points.

Immediately the air felt different—Ember could feel the shield drop and breathed a deep sigh of relief. The pockmarked guard stepped forward and unlocked her manacles.

Ember rubbed her wrists for a moment, then looked at the faces of the councilors before her. Suddenly her stomach was aflutter. What if she couldn't do it? What if she couldn't transform under pressure? There were so many eyes watching her. Shad and Ezeker stood expectantly, confidence and love shining from their eyes. Shad winked, as he usually did, but that didn't alleviate her fear. It built and built until she was frozen with it, bound as if she were still locked in the manacles that blocked her speech and magic. She searched around, almost desperate for a breath of air, a place of refuge.

And then she found it.

A pair of eyes, doe brown and soft like she had never seen them, met her own—eyes that exuded love and sadness, confusion, hope, and despair. Eyes that begged to be proven wrong, and hoped against hope that they were right.

Her mother's eyes.

Suddenly Ember felt calm and peace. She knew her mother did not want to believe it was she, but those eyes told her that it was because of fear—fear that she might truly have the magic she so hated—but not because of love—never because of love. Her mother's eyes held more love at that moment than Ember had seen since she was very young, and suddenly Ember wanted those eyes to be proud of her.

With eyes locked with her mother, she began the change.

Ember took a deep breath and held it, picturing her face as it should be—green eyes, brown hair, button nose, and strong chin. She saw the image all together, and then as she released her breath, she let the magic flow into her skin like mud between her toes. She felt the shift with only a slight ache to accompany it, and was pleased with the lack of pain.

The most satisfying moment was the gasp that echoed through the marble chambers as the council saw her face reshape itself like clay molded by an unseen hand. The hardest was the gray pallor that crept over her mother's face as Ember changed. Tears streamed down Marda's cheeks. Her head shook back and forth.

Ember had become sensitive to others' feelings. She could read the emotion oozing from her mother. Marda didn't want to believe what her eyes told her, didn't want to see that her baby had become everything she feared, everything she had tried to prevent—afraid to see that Ember had grown up.

Ember ached for her mother, but knew this had to be. She closed her eyes, gathering her strength for the next change. Again she took a deep breath and held it while she pictured her limbs as they should be—shorter, thinner, with softer lines and less hair, though no less strong. Her body continued to shape itself to her demands.

Finally she moved on to her torso, adjusting shoulders, narrowing waist and hips.

Ember tried to slow the process, but it seemed her body wanted to be normal again, and pushed beyond her ability to control it.

When the transformation was complete, she found herself on hands and knees, panting, tears seeping from her eyes, dribbling onto the marble floor. She breathed hard for several moments, the entire room silent around her. Nobody moved nor hardly breathed as they waited for her to stand. She gathered her feet beneath her and staggered upwards, then proudly thrust her shoulders back and stared defiantly at the council.

They were all stunned, staring at her in absolute awe, including Ember's grieving mother who had forgotten her anger and fear long enough to admire her at her best. That moment, that look, made the pain worth it, and was a memory Ember would treasure for a long time.

Of course it was Shad who broke the silence. "Any questions?" he asked the council, as blasé as could be.

The silence stretched on for a few seconds longer before Laerdish cleared his throat and spoke. "So what?" He seemed to be shaken, despite his words. "It still proves nothing. Your people do it all the time—"

"Have you no eyes in your head, man?" Shad rounded on him. "This girl can do that which hasn't been done in at least three millennia. Can you change your face like that?"

"Of course I can." Laerdish held his head high.

"Not illusion, Laerdish. Can you actually mold your skin the way she has done?"

Laerdish said nothing.

"I thought not. It's just not done," Shad continued until Laerdish interrupted him.

"Regardless of whether it is real or illusion, it can be done. The Bendanatu do it, as you know, as well as the MerCats and Phoenixians. The *animals* have the ability, and we already know her blood is corrupted by it."

"What?" Marda jerked and faced Laerdish, but he ignored her.

"Besides, it's all semantics, White Shadow," Laerdish continued. "If we haven't seen a white mage in three thousand years, how can we hope to train one?"

Shad was quiet for a long moment, the room waiting expectantly for his answer.

"I hate to admit it, but you pose a good question there," Shad finally responded.

Laerdish gloated.

"So I put it before the council. The mage laws require us to train this girl. How?" Shad continued.

No one answered for a long time, though the conversation buzzed around them. It was the woman who had spoken against Laerdish who finally spoke up. She stood, awaiting recognition.

"Yes, Sister Shiona," Ezeker acknowledged her. "You have the floor."

"It would seem that before we can decide what to do with the child, she must first prove her ability, with no opportunity for dishonesty. I propose her second trial be right here amongst us."

Ember's heart beat fast. A second trial? She'd already forgotten. She was so exhausted by lack of sleep and having changed her appearance so many times in the last twenty-four hours, she wasn't sure how much more she could do. What if she failed?

"And how would you propose doing that?" Ezeker asked, but Ember could see the twinkle in his eye. Suddenly she knew what was coming. This was something she could do.

"Perhaps if she took the time to read the colors of magic within each of us, it could be proven that indeed she *is* a white mage," Shiona continued as if she had come up with the idea. Maybe she had, but Ember had the feeling that Ezeker had put her up to it.

"Excellent idea, Sister Shiona," Shad seconded the motion.

"Preposterous!" Laerdish objected. "The child's integrity has already been called into question once. There is no way we can know whether she is being fed the answers."

Shad growled and would have lunged for the man if DeMunth had not physically held him back.

"Are you crazy, man?" Shad demanded.

"White Shadow! Call yourself to order!" Ezeker turned on Laerdish. "And that is quite enough from you. A motion has been put forth, and it has been seconded. We will test Ember and let her show her merit. Perhaps to alleviate Brother Laerdish's fears, we should have silence in the chamber during the trial. Only Ember Shandae and her current examinant will speak during this time, and I will appoint Aldarin to notate her answers—unless there are any objections?"

There were none, though Laerdish looked ready to chew nails.

"Good. Then let the testing begin," Ezeker finished and turned to Ember. "Test me first, child, and speak your answers for the council to hear."

Ember looked at the rows of people before her and suddenly felt overwhelmed by the daunting task. "I thought eighteen was a lot of people to read, Uncle. You really want me to do all of them? There must be at least a hundred people up there," she whispered.

Ezeker laid his hand on her cheek and smiled tenderly. "Tonight there are only seventy-three, but, yes, all of them, child. It is the only way. Good luck." He waited patiently for her examination of him to begin.

Ember shook her head, but there was no getting out of this one. She took a deep breath, closed her eyes, and began to examine the aura that surrounded one of her dearest friends. Uncle Ezzie had a rainbow glow about him that took in five of the seven colors of magic. All he lacked was the red and white, but the strength of his colors was neither even nor high. They wavered and merged together, the strongest being blue and green. Ember found herself speaking her thoughts aloud, then opened her eyes and met Ezeker's gaze.

"Kind of disappointing, isn't it, child?" Ezeker asked, his eyes twinkling, but saddened.

Ember shook her head, but had to admit to herself that he was right. He was the greatest mage in the area, and his color was weak.

Ezeker chuckled. "You are kind to an old man. It is all right. We are used where our talents take us, Ember, and my talents lay more in teaching and the administration of the academy than in the actual work of magic." He sighed. "I can do what is required of me, but I would not have the strength to weave the net of magic around Rasann day in and day out, the way many of our members do. I am needed elsewhere. Now, who is next?" He raised his voice as he turned to face the council.

"I am," a surprising voice came from Ember's right. She was stunned to see her own mother step forward, a strange mixture of resignation and pride battling on her face.

"Mum?"

"Just do it, Ember. You'll understand," Marda said, and it seemed those words held much regret.

Ember shrugged and closed her eyes. They instantly flew open again, her mouth hanging in stunned amazement.

She closed her eyes once more, just to confirm what she thought she saw. She wondered if she had lost her mind somewhere during these trials, because what she saw seemed impossible.

Marda had an aura.

And not just any aura, but a rainbow of vibrant greens, blues, and yellows in a dance of magic. Marda was a mage, and a strong one. It astounded Ember as nothing else could have. She was utterly speechless. She stared at her mother for a long time—long enough that the council became restless, shuffling in their seats, long before Marda finally spoke.

"And now you understand," she whispered, sadness dripping from her like water from a willow.

Ember shook her head. It made *no* sense, not with all the prejudice her mother seemed to have against women magi, not when she had discouraged Ember from even *trying* to become a mage.

"I don't understand, Mum. You made me believe it was bad to be a mage, and yet here you are with color swimming around you. You wouldn't even let us have magic around the house!"

"It was for your protection, Ember. I thought I was doing the right thing, but I'm beginning to see that I cannot fight destiny. You were chosen long before you were born to become that which we are starting to glimpse now. The Guardians have been connecting people and trying to create you for millennia, since the beginning of time, but . . . I'd already lost your father. I couldn't stand the thought of losing you, too . . ." Marda trailed off, fighting tears.

"I'm trying to understand, Mum, really I am, but this is so hypocritical." Ember tried to hold her temper in check.

"I know. You're right," Marda responded. "I saw no other options at the time, but I was wrong. I'm sorry."

That was the last thing Ember ever expected to hear come from her mother's mouth, and once again she was struck speechless. Marda? Sorry? It just never happened. Not in her entire lifetime had her mother apologized to her. Her childish anger fought with a growing adult understanding. She could not resolve the two, but somehow she found her voice.

"I'm not sure how to deal with this right now, Mum, but thanks for telling me the truth. I'll think about it, and maybe . . . we can talk later?" Ember asked hopefully, raising her eyes to her mother's.

Marda smiled at her daughter and nodded her head, seeming to fight emotions she did not want to share. It was enough.

Ember looked up at the council. "Okay, who's next?" she prompted them, rubbing her hands together. Several arms shot up at once. Ember found herself having to choose from among the greatest magi of her country, the leaders and healers of Rasann, as they all sat patiently waiting for her to test them. Ember chose the tall woman who had come to her defense earlier.

"Shiona?" she asked, hoping that was indeed the woman's name. "I'll take you next."

The tall woman smiled and stood, all dignity and grace as she flowed down the steps to Ember. Ember had known she was tall, but she hadn't realized exactly how tall until the woman stood before her. Ember cricked her neck trying to meet the woman's eyes. She didn't say anything, but the woman must have sensed Ember's discomfort.

Before Ember could do a thing, the woman was on her knees in front of her. They were now nearly eye to eye, her head just below Ember's. Ember smiled in gratitude, honored by the trust this woman showed. It was very humbling.

She closed her eyes and began the process once more, to be repeated time after time over the next three hours. The results were consistent in every instance. Ember was able to read each color within the members of the council, including Shad and DeMunth.

In the end the only mage remaining was the rebellious Laerdish, who refused to come forward. He objected one last time.

"This is ridiculous, Ezeker. The girl has proven herself. There is no need for her to read me. I'll give my vote to the will of the council," he grumbled, not happy at all.

"No, no, Laerdish," Ezeker said with obvious glee. "I insist. You were the one who put up such a fuss over her credibility; we must all be united in allowing her to prove her abilities. Please step forward."

"I won't do it, Ezeker. I disagree with this entire process . . ." Laerdish burst out. Ember interrupted him.

"It's okay, Uncle Ezzie. I can read him from where he is. There's no need for him to get any closer," she said sweetly.

Laerdish paled.

Ember did not understand why he was so afraid of her, but fear oozed from him like stinky cheese. She closed her eyes and looked at his aura as he headed toward the large double doors.

"Laerdish, I demand that you wait!" Ezeker said, his brows drawn together in fury. Ember glanced at him, then looked away, fascinated by the inconsistencies in Laerdish's aura.

"You are not what you appear to be, sir. Your colors are . . . patched, full of holes. Mostly red, very strongly red with some flashes of orange and yellow, but . . ." Ember paused, trying to describe the difference she saw in him compared to the rest of the councilors. It was almost like . . . rusty metal with mud showing through, or a mouse-eaten quilt, only instead of batting showing through the holes, there was darkness, black, color-eating, life-eating in its intensity.

"Your magic is layered. There is color on the top, but it is becoming holey, like a moth-eaten quilt, and underneath it is only black," Ember finished. "Why is it black?" she asked, turning to her uncle, but he seemed not to hear.

The council stared in horrified fascination at the large man as he shook and trembled with rage. He fumed at Ember. "You've ruined it—ruined it all, you good for nothing . . . changeling! Impure blood, and you've ruined me! Do you have any idea how long it has taken to get where I am today? What I've gone through, what I've done? S'Kotos does not take on his priests lightly, and I've had to prove myself time and again to my master. How dare you, child of a misbegotten wolf? Not even a half-breed!" Laerdish was actually foaming at the mouth.

327

Ember watched with growing horror as the fat man shredded his clothing in insane fury. Beneath the robes lay not the large belly Ember had assumed, but a grotesque pair of bat-like wings wrapped around his fleshy torso. Unfurled, they hovered behind him as he stood, frothing.

The entire council stood motionless, watching, as Laerdish tried to control himself. *Why don't they do something?* Ember wondered. Her heart seemed to stop beating for a moment, then resumed as if it belonged to a racing horse and not the small, almost-woman she was.

"Well, it won't happen again, child. You can meet my master in the great beyond!" he screamed, suddenly flinging his hand forward, a great fireball hurling through the air directly at Ember. For a brief moment she froze and time slowed. The great ball grew larger as it traveled. She saw her mother lunge, but too late to block the flame. Shad, DeMunth, and Ezeker were all a fraction of a second too late to stop the pumpkin-sized ball from reaching her. Ember didn't know what to do—but something inside her did.

Without knowing exactly how, she reached deep inside herself to a forgotten center, a place of wind, rain, and light—a place that spoke peace to her soul and pushed it outward. Just before the great ball of fire would have burst Ember into flaming cinders, it halted in mid-air, flared briefly, and died.

Ember had stopped the flame—and had no idea how she'd done it. She didn't care. She was alive and breathing. She took a menacing step toward the hovering Laerdish, but got no further.

The winged beast-man gave a howl of defeat. Ember's hands immediately flew to her ears before her eardrums burst from the sound. The man who had once been Laerdish leaped, wings clawing at the air to gain height hard and fast. He sent a great flame skyward that obliterated one of the beautiful triangular windows and much of the frame around it, then burst through the opening and into the darkness beyond. Ember heard him bellow his defiance one last time amidst the tinkling of glass and thumps of falling stone, then he was gone.

She pulled herself out of her instinctive crouch and looked around. Every person in the room had their eyes trained on the ceiling in horror, anger, and fear.

Everyone, that is, but Marda. Her eyes were glued to Ember's, and Ember thought she detected a hint of a smile playing around her mother's mouth. It was enough for a sob of emotion to escape Ember's fragile control, and that was all it took for Marda to take the last few steps across the room and gather her daughter into her arms.

Where she belonged.

Chapter Thirty

C'Tan continued to pound the ice wall with fire long after Kayla had gone. She lost all control when the group walked away without even a glance behind them. The anger and desperation drove her over the brink of sanity, and rationality left along with the Sapphire Flute. There had to be a way past. There had to be!

She'd had it, had been so close to ridding herself of her master's chains, and she'd lost it. The flute was gone.

She sagged in defeat. The fire drizzled from her hands into the sand, warming it to an almost comfortable degree. The water that walled her in sizzled and evaporated with the heat, and still the ice remained.

Gone. What now? Wait another month? Two? A year? How much longer could she continue in servitude to The Destroyer? She had no answers, and all she could feel was despair, fury, and fear.

She was not sure what alerted her to his presence, whether it was the shift of sand beneath his feet, or his breath—perhaps something else. Whatever it was, C'Tan stiffened and rose, almost afraid to turn—but how could she not? His mere presence called her to him, and though internally she fought with what small will remained, he had chained her soul long before.

Compelled, she turned to meet his flaming eyes. Her heart fluttered when she saw him. In appearance, he was everything a woman could desire. That was how he had turned her to him in the end, with his dark hair and lips that could kiss moisture from a rose.

The master called.

"C'Tan." His voice, soft as feathers, smooth as molasses, but with an undercurrent of . . . what? Nails? Iron? The buzz of a wasp or hiss of a snake? Something menacing, dark lay beneath his voice, like jagged stone below still water.

"Have you failed me again? Have you lost the blue keystone once more?"

C'Tan trembled, but stayed on her feet, silent in his presence, defiantly keeping her illusion down. Let him see the ugliness he had created.

"And where is the wolfchild? Have you found her yet? We can't afford to have her wandering around where she might cause trouble, now can we?" he continued in his falsely sweet voice.

C'Tan could not answer. Her tongue was frozen, her mouth dry, her breath nearly ice in her chest.

"No answers for me, Celena Tan?" His flawless lips quirked in a smile. She continued to stand before him in silence, defying him in the only way she could, though she trembled doing it.

"Perhaps Kardon would serve me better after all," he threatened, and suddenly the man was there, staggering in the sand, having been pulled from whatever task he'd been doing to appear at his master's side.

A wave of terror washed over her, and she hated herself for it. He knew just how to manipulate her. She both hated and adored him. C'Tan found her voice. "No, Master. I serve you. I have lost them, yes, but only for a time. I will find them again."

"Be sure that you do." He smiled then, his eyes cold and expressionless.

C'Tan turned hard eyes on Kardon, her former master, once again in the presence of the *true* master, a smirk floating across his face. It infuriated her. She would not let the conniving old man take her place again. She would not be chained to two men. One was horrid enough. She gathered fire to her, and S'Kotos stepped aside, smiling.

Kardon knelt, head bent before the Guardian of Fire in quiet reverence, then turned his adoring face upward. C'Tan pulled heat from the air and the sand, and created a flaming ball that grew from grape, to cantaloupe, to watermelon-size, and still she fed it with heat.

Without realizing it, a growl started in her throat. Kardon looked up at that, his eyes expressionless, much like the master's, though she detected a note of bitter glee in his voice.

"Has it come to this at last then, C'Tan?" he asked without moving from his humbled posture, only turning his head to gaze at her with disgust.

C'Tan's heart stilled, but she dared not let him know how he affected her even after all these years. The man she called slave was truly in the image of his Guardian, S'Kotos, much more than she would ever allow herself to be. The look in his eyes, the darkness of his soul mirrored his master. It repulsed her, terrified her in ways nothing else could.

The fireball shrank, the heat settling back into the air and sand around them.

"Not yet, Kardon. I am too tired to battle you now. Perhaps another day." C'Tan let the emotion empty from her as water from a bucket. Then she changed the subject. "Why are you here?"

"I received a report from Laerdish. I thought you would be interested. Perhaps I was wrong." Kardon pushed for the confrontation they both knew was coming. He was like an incurable rash.

When C'Tan said nothing, S'Kotos spoke for her. "Oh yes, please continue," the Guardian of Fire purred, his half-smile suddenly malicious.

Kardon cleared his throat. Even he was a little unnerved by The Destroyer, she was glad to see. It evened the bar between them.

"Laerdish has been discovered and fled, but he wished to send word that Shandae will be accepted into the mage academy and should enter within a few days."

S'Kotos growled and turned away from the kneeling man. He sent a fireball of his own toward the ice wall, but it continued to hold.

"That is terrible news," he said, spinning back toward C'Tan and a still-kneeling Kardon. "I should roast you for delivering such unhappy tidings to me this day. Haven't I had enough disappointment?" he asked, his eyes beginning to smoke.

"Master, I disagree," C'Tan said. There was another way to salvage this. "We already have agents in place within Ezeker's academy—agents who can lead her to our side, perhaps?"

"And a fifth has been accepted into the class with Shandae," Kardon chimed in.

S'Kotos thought about it and began to smile. "I see what you are saying, children. Yes, indeed. This can be turned to our advantage if handled properly. Are these agents of yours trustworthy, Celena Tan?"

The force of his personality made her tremble again. "Yes, master, the best that I could find. Two of them are of the Mageguard—another, an instructor. My own daughter has been in place for three years already. The fifth will be a fellow student. I have turned him back from his previous age so his young body carries adult memories and experience. He is shrewd and already carries a hatred for the girl. He will find a way if no other can."

S'Kotos chuckled. It was not a pleasant sound. "Good. Perhaps we can take down the academy and turn the girl at the same time, but what of the flute? And the other keystones? When will you retrieve those for me, C'Tan? I grow tired of your excuses."

"Master," Kardon answered for her. "The girl will go to the evahn, I am sure of it. Her father is there. But," he held up one finger, "I am quite certain they will turn her away. They dare not infuriate C'Tan or yourself at this time. Their position is too precarious, and they have taken a stance of neutrality in this war. My best guess is that they will send her to the birthplace of the flute."

"Which means we can destroy them all in one act," C'Tan finished for him, angry that he had taken even that much of her master's attention. She hated the weakness in herself that craved and detested her master all at once.

S'Kotos began to laugh. His head tilted back, and his entire body shook with his mirthless roar. He stopped as suddenly as he began, and in an instant, he went from laughter to silence. He stepped forward and placed his hands on the heads of each of his servants as an act of benediction. A crowd of whispering voices invaded C'Tan's mind, along with instructions from the Guardian. Going suddenly from warm to hot, sweat streamed down her face to puddle in her collar. She was pleased to see the master's touch had the same effect on Kardon. The Guardian of Fire removed his hands, nodded his head briefly to both of them, and disappeared in a blaze of fire.

C'Tan met Kardon's eyes, and for once emotion burned in them, though she could not quite name what she saw there.

"You owe me," was all he said as he raised himself to his feet. C'Tan did not respond, unsure what he referred to.

"Gather the troops," she commanded. "We're going home."

Chapter Thirty-one

The council stared at the fragmented ceiling in silence. Pieces of stone and glass continued to fall from the edges of the gaping hole with sharp pings and heavy thuds. Marda gave Ember one last squeeze before she released her.

"Well, that explains a lot," Marda said.

That broke the shocked silence, and everyone spoke at once, some demanding answers, others talking to themselves, some weeping quietly, though whether it was at the destruction of the beautiful ceiling or Laerdish's betrayal, Ember was not sure.

"What do you mean, Marda?" Ezeker called to the woman. The room quieted, waiting for her response.

"Just what I said. Laerdish's exposure explains a lot of things. You know we went to the academy together." She glanced at Ezeker, who nodded his head. She continued. "He just . . . I don't know how to explain it. He was never part of a group. He never swam in the crystal lakes, or took in a roommate. He insisted on having his own quarters, though no one else did. Little things that never really fit the image he tried to project. Sometimes he was nice and friendly, and other times, the very soul of contention. How long has he been a part of the council? Twenty years? In all that time, has he ever made a friend?"

No one answered. They all stood looking at each other thoughtfully.

Marda turned to Ezeker. "Is that normal? In twenty years, not to become close to a single person with whom you work daily? I never trusted Laerdish, and now it's obvious my heart lead me correctly. I only hope he hasn't damaged us more than we know."

Ezeker looked alarmed. The tall thin councilwoman, Shiona, spoke up. "Explain yourself, Marda," she demanded. Ember couldn't tell if she was angry or afraid when her voice trembled.

"A man can do a lot of damage in twenty years' time. How much do you think he's undermined the cause of the academy? How many apprentices has he allowed in who don't belong there? Or worse, who belong to C'Tan?"

The woman paled noticeably. She was not the only one disturbed by Marda's questions.

"So what do we do?" asked a short, bearded council member, turning to Shiona.

"We need some help, that's obvious," the tall woman answered. "I never suspected."

He gave a short bark of laughter that held no humor. "Help? Oh, yes, but who to trust? Trust will be in short supply after this fiasco. Are we to believe there are no others among us who have sided with The Destroyer?"

"One who recognized the darkness is hiding in our midst," Ezeker said with a twinkle in his eye. "One who sees beyond that which blinds us, who has suffered enough heartache at the hands of C'Tan that she will never let her guard down."

He looked steadily at Ember's mother. Marda raised her chin and glared.

"Someone like Marda, wouldn't you say, council?" Ezeker asked, and faced them directly.

There was silence in the room for a long moment as the council looked at each other, pondering Ezeker's words. Councilwoman Shiona nodded somberly at Ember's mother.

"I think that's a marvelous idea. Laerdish has just left a . . . vacancy." She glanced at the gaping hole in the ceiling. "There's no reason Marda can't fill his seat immediately."

"Aye!" the council responded together. Most of them seemed relieved.

"It's settled then. Welcome to the council, Sister Marda," Ezeker said, throwing his arms around Ember's mother.

She stiffened and pushed him away. "Now wait just a minute. I can't accept—you know this, Ezeker. Paeder is—" she choked up and couldn't continue, her eyes welling with tears. She took a sobbing breath and continued. "I can't leave Paeder. You know how ill he is, and I can't allow Tiva and Ren to quit school to run the stables or the farm, and there's no way they can do both. Someone has to be there, and my leaving wouldn't be fair to the boys. Nor Ember," she added, glancing at her surprised daughter.

"But we need you, Sister." Shiona said. "Is there not some way we can persuade you to assist us? Perhaps we could find someone to help until the boys graduate. Or you could donate the farm to the academy, and we can run it for you. It would still be yours, and would be returned to your care upon the twins' graduation."

Marda chewed at her lip thoughtfully, then shook her head once more. "I can't. The farm means everything to Paeder. Giving it to the academy would crush any dreams he ever had for the place. I just can't do it."

"But—" Ezeker started.

"I said no, Ezzie." Marda mimicked Ember's name for the old mage and placed her hand on his cheek, then patted it. "Thank you for thinking of me. If things were different . . . perhaps. For now, I'll spend what time remains with my husband. Are you sure there's nothing more you can do for him?" Her eyes pleaded with the council.

Shiona shook her head. "I am sorry—we've done all we can. He is too far gone. It will be a matter of days before he returns to the Guardians. We shall make his passing as easy as possible." An awkward silence gathered around the room. Shiona bowed slightly in Marda's direction. "The offer will stand until you are ready to accept it."

Marda held herself tall, though the ache obviously brooded beneath the surface. Ember took her mother by the elbow and pulled her gently toward the door. "Come on, Mum. Let's go see Paeder."

"Ember, a moment, please." Shiona grasped Ember's shoulder with surprisingly gentle strength. "I think the council is in agreement that you have more than proven yourself to us. Wouldn't you agree, councilmembers?" She spun the both of them to face the crowd. "What say you? Shall we welcome Ember Shandae into the Academy of Magi? Shall we invite the first white mage in three millennia into our midst?"

With glass and pebbles still dropping from the jagged edges of the hole in the ceiling, the council responded.

"Aye! Aye! Aye!"

"Looks like you're now the Step of Mahal upon Rasann, child," Ezeker leaned over and whispered in Ember's ear.

Shiona turned to face Ember. "Welcome, Ember Shandae, and may Mahal guide and bless you in the quest for healing our world," she said softly. From her pocket, she pulled a copper necklace with a round medallion hanging at the end, then dug in her pocket once more and came up with a white stone. She set the stone in the center of the medallion. A quiet surge of energy bound it to the metal.

"This will mark you as one of the incoming initiates and indicate your mage color. It is wonderful to see the white amongst us once more. We have much hope for you, Ember Shandae. Much hope." Shiona placed the charm around Ember's neck and gave her a brief hug.

With tears in her eyes, Ember looked at the tall woman, then at Ezeker. "Thank you," she whispered, then turned back to her mother and escorted her across the litter-strewn floor and out the double doors.

No words passed between them as Ember and Marda strolled arm-in-arm through the city of Javak away from the Mage Council and toward the council house. It wasn't until they passed the houseman and were near the back of the building that Marda stopped and turned Ember to face her.

"I know you had reasons for leaving as you did, Ember, and I know you were angry with me. I'm sorry. I was wrong—but please don't leave me like that again." Tears welled up in Marda's eyes, and her chin started to quiver. "I thought I'd lost you, not once, but three times this week, and my heart has nearly exploded with fear because of it. Please. Will you just speak to me from now on?"

Ember cocked her head. The anger she'd had for so long began to fade with the pain she saw etched in Marda's eyes. The ache she'd held in for so long began to ease. "I love the idea of that, Mum, but will you listen?"

Marda paused, then offered a timid smile. "I'll try. Please understand, I only wanted to keep you safe. I know I went about it the wrong way, but I truly did have your best interests at heart. I hope in time you can forgive me." She took a step toward a door on the right, but Ember grabbed her arm before she could go any further.

"I can forgive you right now if you'll promise to listen and trust me. For me, dreams are more than a way to process. They are glimpses into the future and tell me things I need to know. They're not imaginary. They're not something I can forget. Can you learn to trust my dreams?"

Marda opened her mouth to answer, then paused, gnawing at the corner of her lip. Finally she closed it and shrugged. "I want to, truly I do, but that's going to take a little more time. Can you be patient with me when I get stubborn?"

A little more of the ice melted. Her mother's honesty was more important to Ember than blank agreement. She chuckled. "Well, that's what I've been doing for sixteen years—it shouldn't be that hard to continue. At least now I know I can talk to you about it. I love you, Mum. I just wanted you to know that." She looked down, scuffing the toe of her boot along the smooth marble floor.

Marda placed both hands on the sides of Ember's face and lifted her eyes to meet her own. "I love you too, my dear. I haven't said

341

it often enough, I think. You handled yourself well tonight. I'm proud of you."

Ember threw her arms around her mother and squeezed, tears running in rivulets down her face to dampen her mother's shirt. "That's all I've ever wanted, you know," she managed to get out.

Marda squeezed back and said nothing, just kissed the top of her daughter's head before she gently pushed her to arm's length and changed the subject.

"Paeder has been desperate to see you. Why don't you spend some time with him alone tonight and let him know about all your adventures? He'd love to hear the story." Marda cradled Ember's cheek in her hand one last time before she moved past Ember to the door. She put her hand on the clear square, and the door opened with a soft click. She pushed it open and beckoned for Ember to enter.

The room smelled of sickness, and Ember's heart clenched with sorrow and regret. Paeder lay on the single bed, Ren holding his hand. They both smiled as she walked in, and her half-brother stood and patted the stool he'd been sitting on. Ember gripped his arm as they passed and settled in the same position he had been in, with Paeder's big hand in her own.

"We're right next door if there's a problem," Marda said before she smiled with tear-filled eyes and closed the door, leaving Ember alone with the dying man.

"You came," he whispered, and squeezed her hand without any strength.

"Of course I came. How could I not, after your letter? Thank you, not only for Brownie and Diamond Girl, but mostly for your beautiful words. They meant the world to me—Da."

The words felt awkward on her tongue, but she meant them with all her heart. Paeder was the only father she'd known. He deserved the respect of being named as one.

Paeder's breath caught as a tear trickled down his cheek to bury itself in his hair. Ember wiped it away for him. "Hey now, none of that. You need happy memories to live by now."

"There is none happier than hearing you call me 'Da,'" he said before he began coughing.

Ember wasn't sure what to do. The bottle of medicine that was usually at his bedside at home was missing. She stood to get Marda, but he grabbed her wrist with surprising strength. "I'm fine," he choked out. "Stay. Too stuffy in here. Maybe you could open the window?"

Ember nodded once before moving to the large glass. It took her a moment to figure out the mechanism, but shortly the window had been shoved upward, and a sweet breeze wafted in.

Paeder took a breath and the coughing fit passed. Relieved, Ember sat again. This time he reached and took her hand. "Tell me about your adventures since last I saw you." His voice was rough from the constant coughing, but more alive than she'd heard it in a while. A bubble of contentment rose to envelop her heart. It was a small thing she could do to make him happy, and so she began with her departure from the house and meeting Ian. She told him about her ear sinking into the stone, and changing into a wolf. She told him about Shad, running with the pack, DeMunth and his singing, the mage trial, and finally about her evening with the Mage Council and Laerdish's betrayal.

"They want Mum to join the council to see if she can't weed out any other betrayers."

"Really?" he asked, his eyes alight. "I didn't even know she could do magic. I can't believe she kept that from me all these years, though I do understand her reasons. She was pretty broken up after your father died." He began to cough, sounding worse than ever. When he stopped and caught his breath, he continued. "Jarin was the love of her life. I knew it then and I know it now, but she and I have our own kind of love, devotion thing. She's a good woman, your mother." Paeder's voice fell to a near whisper. "Hang onto her and do whatever you can to get her to accept that offer. She needs them as much as they need her." His energy seemed to fade with every word. Ember's heart squeezed with fear. She hadn't realized talking would tire him so easily.

"I will, Da. Why don't you rest now?"

"No, no. I don't want to miss a moment with you, my dear. You were the best thing that ever happened to our family. You've kept us bound and made us a true family, though we don't all share blood. Keep them close, Ember. Don't let the boys drift away. I worry for Tiva—" Paeder started coughing again, and after the third round he expelled all his breath and didn't take another one. His eyes stared blankly at the ceiling and slowly lost their light.

"No. No, no, no, no!" she whispered, the strength taken from her at his sudden passing. "You can't be dead, Paeder, you can't! Da, come back!" Her voice never reached the door, it was so quiet. She laid her head on his stomach, wrapped her arms around him and sobbed, her heart breaking. She'd been sure the council would find an answer for him. How would the family go on without him? How could the farm survive? Tiva and Ren and Aldarin needed their father. She *needed* a father. She'd lost not one father, but two, and her grief was almost as much for her birth father as for this man who'd raised her.

Vaguely, she heard a flutter of wings at the window. She glanced through her tears to see a white blur perched on the window sill. It was the white hawk that had followed her from Karsholm.

"Why don't you help him?" She glared at the bird. "You can protect me, but not save him? How am I supposed to go on when I've lost my father, again? I need him, so you just go back to whomever keeps sending you and tell them to bring him back!" Her voice broke on a sob. All the anger and fear had built to bursting. It hurt so much, she thought her heart would explode with it.

The hawk chirped, hopped once, then gathered itself and took off from the ledge. For a brief second, Ember thought he might be able to do something, that he might have understood and really would go for some heavenly help.

Almost instantly she reprimanded herself for being so silly, so childish in her belief. A bird? She was asking help from a bird?

Ember snorted, then stood. Somebody had to tell the family what had happened, and the responsibility was on her shoulders alone.

She took a step toward the door, then spun as wingbeats returned. The white hawk soared through the window, circled upward, then dove directly into Paeder's chest. At first Ember wasn't sure she had seen right. The bird had aimed right at him, but had disappeared on impact. It was nowhere to be found.

Ember sat back on the stool for a moment, weary with disbelief and grief. Was she going crazy? She glanced at the still form of Paeder, and her heart stopped beating for a very long instant.

Paeder's chest was moving. Up and down it went, harder and faster, almost as if there were a battle taking place within his body. Black ooze began to seep from his mouth and nose, thick and tar-like. It crept down his cheek and stained the pillow beneath him.

Once the stream stopped, Paeder's skin began to glow—softly at first, but the brightness increased until Ember could hardly bear to look at him. She threw her arm over her face to protect it from the light, her heart hammering in her chest as if it would thump its way into her throat. She backed away from Paeder's body, unsure what was happening, when suddenly the light stopped, and Paeder took a gasping breath.

Ember lowered her arm, incredulous. Her body felt wave after wave of chill bumps. Had she just witnessed a miracle?

Paeder continued to gasp, his back arching to get enough breath. He gave a strangled groan before he collapsed back onto the pillows, and the white hawk burst from his chest. The bird stood on Paeder's stomach and shook itself. At first Ember was afraid the bird had blasted a hole in Paeder, but there was no blood. Evidently the hawk was of a spiritual nature.

Paeder seemed to have passed out or fallen back to sleep. His breath continued steadily, stronger than she'd heard for a very long time. Ember hardly breathed as she watched her guardian spirit hop from Paeder's stomach, to the bed, and finally the stool.

His form shimmered, lengthening, until it solidified and a man sat upon the stool. He stared at Ember, a soft smile playing across his lips, his green eyes twins to her own.

"Hello, Shandae," he said, his voice a rich baritone that sent thrills through Ember's heart. She knew this face, but it couldn't be!

"Da?" she whispered, still not believing what her eyes told her to be true.

He nodded.

"Da?" she asked again, and rubbed at her tear-swimming eyes.

"Yes, my sweet."

"You mean, it's been you all along, and you never told me?" Ember demanded in a hurt tone.

Jarin chuckled. "I'm afraid so. There are rules, you see."

"But—I thought you were dead!"

"I am."

Ember's heart sank again. For a moment, she'd thought she might get to have both of her fathers back.

Jarin continued. "At the moment of my death, I was given a choice. I could join the spirits who dwell in paradise, or I could stay and be changed in order to do Mahal's will. I chose the latter. I couldn't stand to be away from you, my dear. I would have died a thousand deaths to keep you safe."

"I only wish I'd known it was you. I have so many questions—"

"It will have to wait for another time, Shandae." Ember tried not to let her feelings be hurt as he continued. "I have a message for you, your family, and the council. Call them, please."

"But—"

"Ember, there is little time. Your questions will be answered at a later date. For now, I have things that need to be said." He glanced upward and grimaced. "And time is about finished." He glanced to Paeder and then Ember. "You must serve as my messenger, my love, you and this blessed man who has watched over you when I could not." He reached a glowing hand to Paeder's forehead and pushed his hair back from his face, much as a father does his child. He then covered Paeder's eyes with his fingers and gave a single command.

"Awake."

Immediately Paeder's eyes snapped open, and he sat up, the blanket falling to his waist as he turned to face Jarin. "Who are you?" Paeder's voice had vibrant strength resonating through it that took him by surprise. His hand went to his throat, then his chest. He took an experimental deep breath and grinned like a little boy when he found he could breathe without coughing.

"I am Jarin, father of Ember and once husband to Brina," he said.

"But, you're dead!" Paeder said, paling.

Jarin glanced at Ember and chuckled. "Yes, quite." He cleared his throat, a very unspirit-like sound. "I have a message for the council, and very little time in which to deliver it. In exchange for your service as mouthpiece—and as thanks for raising my daughter—I have given you healing and beg you to deliver my words to the council. They are the words of my master, delivered to you as they were given to me."

Jarin cleared his throat once more and began, his voice resonating like sound through a cave. "I am Mahal, Guardian and Creator of Rasann, Eldest of the Hundred Guardians and Master of the White Magic. The time has come to show my face upon Rasann, though my foot touches not her shore. Clean your house, masters of the magic. Cleanse the darkness of S'Kotos from among you, for the wolfchild is come. The time of healing is at hand."

Jarin turned to Ember. "Would you deliver a message to your mother for me?" His voice sounded normal once more.

Ember nodded, awed by his presence. She couldn't get enough of his face and stared until her eyes burned, almost afraid to blink.

"Tell her I still love her and will continue the work of my life on the other side. Tell her I am a father forever and will watch over you. For you, my dear, dear child—know that I love you. Believe in yourself as I do. I shall never be far."

Ember ran to him before he could fly away and threw herself into his embrace. He wrapped very real arms around her and held her for just a moment before he evaporated into mist and disappeared.

"Believe in yourself as I do." Jarin's words echoed through Ember's head and heart. She wished he had stayed longer. She had so many

347

questions, so many things she wanted to know and no chance to ask them now. Her heart swelled. He wouldn't be far away. She'd get the answers from him one way or another.

In the meantime, she had her other father, healed and whole, with a family still unaware. She had witnessed a miracle and couldn't wait to share it.

Her eyes streaming, she left the room and banged on Marda's door. It flew open quickly, Marda on the other side. She took one look at Ember's tears and collapsed. "No!" she sobbed, hands covering her face.

"No, Mum. It's not what you think." Ember knelt beside her, a comforting arm across her shoulder.

Another voice came from the room next door. Ember glanced over. Paeder stood in the doorway, chuckling. "Marda! I am healed!"

Marda's head snapped up. Her jaw dropped in astonishment. Slowly she got to her feet, her knees shaking and giving out beneath her with each step, until she stood in front of the man she had thought dead. She reached one tremulous hand forward to caress his warm and living flesh.

"But . . . how?" she choked.

"You won't believe it, Marda. I was healed by a dead man, given life from a ghost. A man we all thought dead, but somehow has been brought back." He laughed out loud then and danced about in glee. "Jarin did it, Marda. Ember's father, Jarin—he healed me!"

Marda's knees gave out a second time, but Paeder kept her from falling. He wrapped an arm around her shoulders and gave her a solid kiss. Ember's heart lifted, seeing the two of them. Marda glanced at Ember for confirmation and Ember slowly nodded her head. "It's true. Paeder was dead, Mum. Da brought him back to deliver a message to the council, though I honestly think he used that as an excuse."

Marda snorted. "That would be just like him. Well, if you've got a message to deliver to the council, we'd better go before they dismiss." Ember nodded and fell into line behind her parents, Paeder shirtless and shoeless with an arm around his wife. Marda leaned into him as if she couldn't get close enough.

Aldarin, Tiva, and Ren rounded the corner and stopped in astonishment at the sight of their father. Paeder ran to them and threw his arms around his boys. Their voices tumbled over each other with laughter and tears as Paeder told them right there in the hallway what had happened. One by one, the doors around the family opened and people stepped out to listen to the story. Before long, a large crowd had gathered around Paeder.

At the telling, they cheered, lifting Paeder to their shoulders to convey him to the council chambers, Ember and her mother following arm-in-arm behind them.

Their cheer was a sound Ember would never forget, a sound that stilled her heart and filled it, a sound that meant all her dreams were fulfilled . . . and yet had only just begun.

Sneak Preview

The Armor of Light

Book Two
The Wolfchild Saga

Prologue

The girl called Shadow crept into the glade, the mage lights of Javak shining their unnatural blue glow over the city. Unlike a true fire, the mage lights never flickered. They were unwavering, neither hot nor cold—and yet the glow seared into her eyes, leaving floating balls of blind light impressed on her retina long after she turned away to hide in the shadows of the forest. The girl blended into the darkened lengths of shade cast by the tall pines in the moon's glow. She faded into nothing, an extension of the natural balance of light and dark, unnoticed, unseen.

The teacher came next, the one called Dragon. Careless, he was fully into the meadow before he slipped the dragonhead mask over the top of his head and let it rest there, his face exposed to view. C'Tan would be furious if she knew.

Shadow was stunned at his true identity. Had she not seen Dragon's face, she would not have believed, so great an actor was he.

At the mage academy, Dragon was the kind teacher, always willing to take time to help a student. Shadow had never heard him express anything but full support for Ezeker. But here in this glade, he was always harsh and bitter, full of fury and hate for the academy and for Ezeker in particular. Dragon at last pulled the mask over his face, the dark contours of the black drake leaving all but his eyes hidden. He leaned against a tree to wait.

The guards came together, Magnet and Seer, male and female, their faces already covered by the plain helmets that hid them— but Shadow knew them. She had known since the first meeting.

There was no mistaking Seer's terse alto tones, and Magnet's rich baritone, as familiar to Shadow as her own—a voice she both loved and despised.

The voice of her father.

The three masked figures watched each other warily, never trusting. Absolute silence descended over the glade with their presence, as if the very insects could feel their malice.

They stood in silence until the deep beating of wings coming from the east pulled all eyes up to watch the descent of the mistress, current owner of their souls, by rule of their true master, S'Kotos.

C'Tan flew in on her dragon. Behind her sat a young boy, his arms wrapped around her torso. The black beast back-winged, stirring the pine needles and dust into a frenzy about the group, hair whipping in the wind.

Nobody moved. They waited stone still until C'Tan dismounted the dragon and leapt to the ground, leaving the boy to slide down the black scales on his own. He did so, as if he were born on a dragon, and stood at her side, his stance too mature for his years.

"Who is the child?" Seer asked.

C'Tan did not answer, but instead threw her words to the darkness where Shadow hid.

"Show yourself, Shadow."

"Yes, Mother," the girl answered, fading from darkness to a semi-transparent gray that still left her face and figure a mystery.

C'Tan grimaced. "I have asked you not to call me that, girl. Do you wish to give away our plans with a slip of your tongue?"

"And who is there to hear, Mother? They already know that—" Shadow stopped with a grunt of pain. Her shadow cover wavered as she collapsed to her knees and looked at C'Tan in astonishment. The blonde woman's arm was outstretched, hand hooked in a claw-like motion. Shadow's insides felt as if they were about to burst. She fell to her side, the pain was so great, but she refused to give her mother any further satisfaction. The pain stopped immediately when C'Tan dropped her hand. Shadow sucked in a deep, sobbing breath and scrambled to her feet.

354

"Do not question me, child," C'Tan spoke in a deadly whisper. "There is too much at stake. Do as you are told."

"Yes, Moth . . . mistress." Shadow faded back into darkness.

There was silence for a long moment as C'Tan glanced at each person, then to the boy at her side. The child couldn't have been more than eight or nine. He grinned up at C'Tan with cold eyes. Shadow felt a pang of envy for the boy who stood so close to her mother, but she squelched it quickly. There was no use in longing for that which would never be.

C'Tan finally spoke. "The Chosen One has come."

She didn't need to say anything more. Everyone stood a little sharper, the intensity in the glade increasing.

"Laerdish has failed us. His true nature has been discovered, and he has fled with barely his life. But he has managed to get us some useful information. The Chosen One has been accepted to the academy."

Now their voices leaped over one another, asking questions. C'Tan quieted them with a single motion.

"Her name is Ember Shandae, and she will arrive with the next intake, but . . . ," she paused, her eyes gleaming. "I have a plan. I believe you all know Ian Covainis?" She gestured to the boy and was greeted by stunned silence as the boy stepped forward and bowed.

"You must be joking," Shadow's father, Magnet, growled.

"Have you ever known me to joke?" C'Tan quirked an eyebrow in his direction.

Magnet scratched his nose beneath the helmet. "Actually, no, I have not."

"Nor do I joke now. Ian, tell them," she demanded of the boy.

Shadow had to admit there were certain similarities between this child and the man she knew. The protruding ears, the shape of the nose, the tawny eyes—yes, it could be, though it seemed impossible.

"I found Ember, outside of Karsholm. I captured her and planned to bring her to the mistress, but she shapeshifted into a wolf and escaped with a pack. I didn't find her again until I arrived at Javak and discovered that she had shapeshifted into a boy. I alerted Laerdish, and he tried to make her look like a fraud, but it backfired on him. She can read all the colors of magic, people. Every one." The silence around him spoke for itself. "The mistress thought it might be good if an agent could be implanted into her class— someone who can get close to her while she's vulnerable. And since I've had the most experience with her, C'Tan age-regressed me so I could hide in plain sight." Ian's young voice was at odds with his tone and words. "Much as I might wish, I cannot do this alone. The girl is smart and trusts very few. We'll need to work together if we hope to succeed, and I can't do that with your anonymity. It has served its place, but now is the time to let yourselves be known."

Ian waited in silence. Nobody moved or spoke. The boy shook his head and ran a hand through his wavy hair. "All right then, if you won't trust me with your identities, we need to have an alternate way to contact one another. Any ideas?"

Seer snorted. "And why should we help you?"

"Because I said so," C'Tan answered for Ian. Seer glared from beneath her helmet, but said nothing more.

"Let's use the sending stones and establish a password in case we need to meet in person," Magnet said in his deep voice.

Shadow shivered.

"A password? Such as?" Ian asked.

"Wolfchild," Dragon growled. "Make the code 'wolfchild.'"

Ian smiled. "Wolfchild it is. Now, first we have to gain the girl's trust, bring her into our circle, and turn others against her as often as possible so she has nowhere else to go."

"And what is that supposed to accomplish?" Seer sneered again.

"Why, it should be obvious," The man-turned-boy leered, which looked strange on his nine-year-old face. "We get the Chosen One to trust us, chain her with her weakness, and lead her away from the light of Mahal to the darkness of S'Kotos. If we can't defeat her, then she must join us—or die."

Shadow shivered, but she did not leave. If good or evil were carried through the blood, she had no choice. *With parents like these, who needs enemies*, she thought as they pulled her into the circle and planned Ember's demise.

Chapter One

There was still ash in the sky when it began to rain. Ember watched the fat droplets pound against her window, turning Javak a murky gray as the moon rose over the city of magic. He was still out there somewhere. She could feel him watching her from the darkness, could feel his ever-present spirit, as aware of her as she was of him, now that she knew who he was—now that she knew her father was still alive.

With a sigh, Ember Shandae turned from the window and threw herself back on the bed. Three nights—three sleepless nights she'd spent in this room since the mage council had accepted her into the academy. Three nights of tossing and turning since Laerdish had made his betrayal known—and three nights since Ember had discovered that the white hawk who'd been watching her for so long was actually her father.

Ember rubbed her aching eyes and wiped away the tears she didn't want to shed. She was grateful Paeder had been healed, grateful her mother had a job and purpose that gave her joy once more—grateful that her father wasn't dead. But part of her was furious with the man/hawk. He should have been there. He should have let her know who he was instead of hovering around, watching from a distance. Granted, he'd protected her on several occasions, but he'd done it without ever telling her, without letting her get close. He'd only spoken to her once in all these years. He was her father, for goodness' sake. Even in spirit form, he should have been able to say something.

Ember sat up and surged off the bed once more and paced the small confines of the room, her thoughts and feelings a whirlwind of which she could make no sense. She had to find a way to get some rest. She'd never survive in the academy if she couldn't sleep. "This is ridiculous," she said to no one in particular.

Suddenly feeling claustrophobic and desperate to do anything to relax, Ember grabbed a towel, her weather charm, and a change of clothes and headed out the door. She walked quickly down the hall, her soft boots shuffling across the marble floor of the council house.

She'd been surprised at first when she'd been told to stay in the room Uncle Shad had arranged for her, but it made sense in a way. The people closest to her were nearby to protect her, if necessary—Uncle Shad and DeMunth, Ezeker, Aldarin, and now her mother and Paeder. They'd all taken rooms near hers, though they didn't seem to suffer the same trouble with sleeplessness that Ember did.

Ember left the council house and crossed the water bridge. She walked quickly through town. Only the pitter-patter of raindrops that didn't touch her and the thundering falls escorted her through what had been a bustling market the day before.

Everyone was gone now, with only crumpled paper, mounds of rotting food, and occasional feathers floating across the wet grass to show anyone had been there.

Ember shook her head. Why couldn't people pick up after themselves?

She arrived at the womens' bathing quarters and quickly checked herself in. The bath girl was asleep on a pad inside the door. The girl who had given Ember so much trouble at her trial didn't stir as Ember tiptoed past to write her name in the book and leave a thumbprint.

Within five minutes, she had undressed and slid into the water. The edges were lukewarm and shallow, nowhere near what Ember needed to loosen the kinks that had settled in her shoulders. She waded slowly to the deep end and swam toward the waterfall cascading from the cliff high above. Her toes found the sandy bottom once more as she neared the warm falls. Ember stepped directly into the stream and let the liquid begin its heated massage.

The tension immediately began to fade. The water was almost too hot—pleasurable to the point of pain.

It was perfect.

Ember closed her eyes and sat on a boulder just beneath the waves. Finally, with her muscles beginning to relax, she could address the issues that had kept her sleepless these many nights.

First, her father was not only alive, but had become a messenger of the Guardian Mahal. She didn't know how to feel. She was happy he was alive, disappointed he thought so little of her that he'd never told her he was there, angry that he'd been gone all these years, and elated that he had healed Paeder. She had to admit, she was also a little intimidated, knowing he worked for one of the creators of Rasann. She wanted to get to know him, wanted desperately for him to never have "died," wanted to give him the tongue-lashing of his life and throw herself into his arms and never let go.

She felt like her insides were one giant pot of soup with opposing flavors—pineapple with hot peppers and potatoes and a hand full of dirt for good measure. Whatever it was, it made no sense, and her heart ached with the lack of a solution.

That thought led Ember to the second, and probably more challenging, of her troubles.

She was the first white mage in three thousand years. She didn't know how to use her magic, and there was nobody around to train her. The weight of responsibility was overwhelming. A white mage was supposed to help heal their world, to mend the net of magic that surrounded Rasann. Ember had no idea where to begin, and neither did anyone else. What was she supposed to do? Teach herself? How could she mend a net she couldn't even see?

Ezeker had quizzed her endlessly since her acceptance into the academy, guiding her sight in what ways he could. He seemed to be a wonderful teacher, but Ember didn't see things the same way he did. She understood the concept clearly—she just couldn't put it into practice.

"So there you are," a relieved voice echoed across the waters. Ember jumped, her eyes snapping open as she scanned the room for the figure she knew she'd find on the other end of the voice. She wasn't disappointed.

Feeling guilty for not telling anyone she was leaving, Ember lowered her shoulders beneath the surface and swam slowly toward her mother, enjoying the gradual transition from hot water to warm and finally almost chilled. Marda held up a large towel and stepped forward as Ember stood and climbed from the water. Her mother wrapped the towel around her without a word.

It was strange, being so comfortable with her mother now, since their past relationship had been so challenging. Once the truth was out, Marda had become a different person. She was softer somehow, more full of purpose and compassion. And though she was still strict and kept a close eye on Ember, she'd finally given her daughter some of the freedom she'd craved for so long.

Mother and daughter went to the dressing room, Marda standing guard while Ember dried off and scrambled into her clean clothes, slipping the weather charm around her neck last of all. Ember wasn't going to step foot outside without it until the skies decided to stop spitting rain and mud.

* * *

The next morning, it was still raining, and Ember had been forced to leave the weather charm behind, much to her consternation. No charms or talismans were allowed during practice, and today her new class had moved outside to the fields of Javak—the city that wasn't looking so magical at the moment. She wiped dripping bangs from her face as she straightened and watched her soon-to-be classmates use their magic to clean the garbage left from the mage trials. One couple paired up, the boy levitating the garbage off the ground and the girl incinerating it with a thought. Another girl made the wind blow everything in one direction, where a young boy circled it around him and then

360

shot it outward to the garbage bin. Yet another girl made it disappear entirely.

And then there was Ember. She stabbed downward with a sharpened stick and picked up the trash the old-fashioned way. Things were supposed to be different once she was accepted to the mage school. She was supposed to be able to use her magic just like anyone else. But for some strange reason, her magic wasn't working. Her attempts at conjuring a fireball had summoned nothing but a plume of smoke. She couldn't teleport the garbage, she couldn't make the wind blow it way—she couldn't even change it into something else. All she could do was bend over and pick it up or poke it with a stick.

"Worthless," she muttered aloud. "What good is magic if I can't make it work for me?" She stabbed hard, piercing a sodden mass of paper and embedding the stick into a rock. She pulled on the wood, but it wouldn't budge. She got down on her knees and looked closer. The stick wasn't wedged in a crack, as she'd thought. It was completely embedded in the rock. "How'd I do that?" she wondered aloud, standing and twisting the stick until a sharp snap freed it from the stone . . . minus the bottom three inches.

Frustrated, she threw the stick and yelled, the piece of wood tumbling end over end across the clearing. All the kids in the class stopped to stare for a moment before they went back to picking up their garbage, using their newfound powers.

"Feel any better?" Her stepbrother said from beside her. Ember jumped and turned in one motion.

"Sheesh, don't do that," she growled. She took a deep, shaky breath and let it out in one explosive blast before answering his question. "No. No, I don't feel better. Why can they use their powers when I can't? What's wrong with me?"

"Nothing," Aldarin answered, putting an arm around her. "The whole point of this exercise is to learn how to use and control your powers in a safe environment. Sometimes it takes a little longer."

"At least they had lessons," Ember said, glaring at the group spread across the grass. "All I got was Ezeker telling me to do what feels best. I need a tutor, blast it! How am I supposed to learn this stuff without someone to teach me." Ember snorted. "Do what feels good. Right now, 'doing what feels good' means poking somebody with a stick."

Aldarin laughed. "I don't think that's what he meant."

Ember turned her glare on him. "I know, but it sure would feel good. I don't understand. I can't even change the things I touch any more. What am I doing wrong?"

Aldarin shook his head. "I'm the wrong person to ask, Sis. Only you would go and pick the one kind of magic nobody knows anything about. You'd think that being a white mage, you could use all the colors of magic."

Ember snorted. "Yeah, that's what I thought too. Evidently not. There's got to be a textbook or some magi's journal from the past. Surely they would have kept some kind of record. I'll never get this without some help."

"Wait until we get to the mage academy. The library is endless, and you never know what you might find in there. We can hope."

"Right now, that's all I've got." Ember said. She picked up another stick, pulled out her belt knife, and whittled the end to a sharp point.

It had only been three days since Ember had been unwillingly dragged before the Mage Council, her abilities and very identity thrown into question. She'd finally proven herself by reading the colors of magic for all seventy some-odd members of the Mage Council, and she could still see magic now. She could discern every shade and color of magic in all the people she saw . . . but she couldn't tap into her own power.

She was grateful Aldarin stayed quiet while Ember whittled the stick to a point. Her frustration bubbled and boiled like one of Ezeker's potions, and there was no way to release it except to stab at the garbage. When she had dreamed of being a mage, she'd never imagined how hard it could be.

Her stick whittled to a fine point, Ember went in search of more trash. Most of it had been cleared after four hours of work in the large field, so Ember left Aldarin watching the class and went another direction, anxious to get away from her classmates so she could try some of her own magic in private, where she wouldn't continue to embarrass herself with an audience.

She headed toward the permanent buildings on the west side of town, angling down the alleyways looking for trash that might have been blown about in the storm. Everything was wet. Muddy ash had collected against the buildings and window ledges.

The mage shields suddenly surged to life in a blue wave that made Ember jump, then sigh with relief when the rain stopped pinging off her head. It would dry out soon.

Ember came upon a U-shaped meeting of three buildings where trash had heaped against the walls. She sighed. People were such slobs. She took her stick and canvas bag and moved to the corner, still thinking over her problem.

How could she learn white magic when there were no books, no teachers, and the only person who knew was one of the Guardians who had created the world? What was she supposed to do? Pray for a teacher? She was actually tempted to do just that. She stabbed downward, collecting a soggy mass of paper on the end of her stick, then paused. If she could get her father to talk to her, maybe he could send a message back to Mahal and see if he really *could* help her find a teacher.

Ember heard shuffling footsteps behind her, but paid them no mind. It was most likely another student searching for more garbage just as she had done. It wasn't until the crackle of flames and sizzling heat were almost upon her that she instinctively dove for the mud, a fireball slamming into the stone wall just past where she'd stood. She rolled over and looked up, scrambling to find someplace to hide, but she was cornered. The U-shaped building met on three sides, and the only open space was filled with flittering shadows in the shape of people.

Her heart racing, Ember took her stick in her hands, wishing it were a sword, a polearm, a spear—anything but the wimpy wood she held. A flash of heat sparked across her palms and the weight in

363

her hands suddenly increased, the wood shifting from warm and alive to cold, hard metal in an instant. She didn't even question it, but took the gift for what it was and rushed forward, hoping to take the shadow figures by surprise. She raced into their midst, swinging the iron rod like a club and aiming for the empty space between them.

An arrow flew at her from nowhere, Ember never having seen the shooter. The shaft flicked through her hair, just inches from her neck. In an instant, Ember dropped the rod, and with a surge of overwhelming power, instantly became wolf without any of the slow changes she usually experienced. Her body flared with pain, but with the adrenaline pumping through her, she barely registered it. Suddenly, her sight and sense of smell heightened. The shadows still flickered, but they seemed to slow as her perception changed. And when she could not see them, she could certainly smell.

They moved in to surround her. Ember gathered herself and leaped directly at the shadowy man in front of her. It hesitated just long enough for her to bare her teeth and take the man by the throat. Warm blood gushed into her mouth as she bit down, but her usual gag reflex was buried in her wolf instincts. The group of shadows rushed toward her. Ember let go of the man, and he sank to the earth, clutching his throat and gurgling.

In an instant, she leaped over him and raced toward the field and the protection of Aldarin. She ran full tilt, faster than she ever had, when she hit what felt like a brick wall. She yelped as her nose rammed into solid air and her body flipped up. She saw stars for a long moment, then shook her head and growled. The shadows stalked toward her, more slowly now as they realized the danger she could be to them. The man whose throat she'd nearly torn out still lay on the ground, jerking spasmodically. The flickering shadows seemed to race from place to place, a zipping blur that placed them here one moment, there the next, and Ember couldn't focus on them long enough to defend against them.

Her mind raced. She couldn't do this alone, but it appeared they had created a shield to hold her in, and she had no idea how to break through. She didn't know how to fight. She didn't know how to use her magic. She was alone, defenseless, but for her teeth and whatever magic would sporadically work for her. Terror began to build, and she backed slowly against the shield wall, wishing with all her heart that it would let her through. The shadowy people picked up their pace and raced toward her, still in a zig-zagging blur.

She backed farther, the pressure building behind her and seeming to crawl up her body as she stepped rearward, her tail between her legs, her lips pulled back in a snarl, blood from her victim and drool mixing to drop in rivulets to the ground. The closest shadow leaped toward her, and she jumped away, the growl rumbling in her throat.

Suddenly she was not alone. A figure in glowing yellow armor landed at her side, his shining sword cutting toward her attacker, slicing him neatly in half, top and bottom hitting the ground separately. The shadows stopped and held still for a moment. DeMunth didn't give them a chance to attack again. He raced toward the figures as they turned to flee, his feet moving so fast, he seemed to have wings. Ember sat stunned for a brief moment, then raced after him. She couldn't let him fight alone.

But her efforts were in vain, for by the time she reached DeMunth's side, the shadow figures had reached the U shaped building, leaped to the rooftop, then jumped skyward and disappeared. . . .